Animal Stories

Enid Blyton

The Children at Green Meadows

More Adventures at Willow Farm

MULBERRY EDITIONS

This edition published exclusively for Mulberry Editions
by HarperCollins Children's Books 1992

A division of HarperCollins Publishers Ltd,
77–85 Fulham Palace Road, Hammersmith,
London W6 8JB

Printed in England by Clays Ltd, St Ives plc

Contents

The Children at Green Meadows

First published in a single volume in hardback in 1949 by
Lutterworth Press, London.
First published in paperback in 1968 in Armada

The author asserts the moral right to be identified as
the author of the work

Chapter One

THE FAMILY AT GREEN MEADOWS

"Mother! Mother! Where are you?" called Francis. "Do come here a minute. I've found the very first snowdrop out in the garden."

His mother came out of the back door, drying her hands on a cloth. "Oh, Francis – did you have to call me just when I was so busy washing up?"

"Yes, I did, Mother," said the boy. "You're always busy, anyway, so it wouldn't matter when I called you. I wish you weren't so busy. Fancy not even having time to look at a snowdrop! See, there it is!"

His mother looked down and saw the tiny white flower with its pretty drooping head. It grew in a mass of tangled grass, in a corner of the garden. She bent down and shook it gently.

"I know why you do that!" said Francis. "I *knew* you would. It's lucky to ring the bell of the first snowdrop you see in the new year, isn't it?"

His mother laughed. "That's what country folk say, Francis – and goodness knows we could do with a little good luck!"

She looked round the big, rambling garden and slipped her arm through the boy's. "I'm not too busy to walk round to see if anything else is coming up," she said. "It's St Valentine's Day, the day all the birds marry – hark at them singing! Even the starling up on the chimney is doing his best – he never has learnt that he can't sing properly!"

9

Francis was glad to have his mother for a few minutes. He remembered a time when she was always ready to run into the garden, to play, to plant seeds, to weed – when she laughed a lot and looked young and happy. Now things were very different, and it was quite a treat to have his mother to himself for a few minutes.

"There's a crocus peeping up," she said. "And look, over there is actually a violet – in that sheltered corner at the foot of the wall. Let's see if there are any primroses in the dell at the bottom of the garden."

There weren't. It was too early. His mother stood in the dell under the silver birch trees, and fell silent. Francis looked at her. He touched her gently.

"What are you thinking about? Why do you look like that?"

"I was just remembering how this garden looked four years ago," said his mother. "It was beautiful, Francis! You were almost eight then – you must remember it too."

"Yes. The grass was cut, the beds were weeded, there were thousands of flowers," said the boy, looking back through the years. "The house was different too, Mother. We didn't have half the rooms shut up like we do now – and you weren't so busy always – and . . ."

He stopped because he saw tears in his mother's eyes. "Why are we so poor now?" he asked. "Why don't we get a gardener to put the garden right? Why do you do all the work in this big house? Is it because of Daddy?"

"Partly," said his mother. "Daddy was badly hurt in the war, you know, and he can't work any more, so we haven't much to live on. Granny let us have this house when we were first married, Daddy and I – it's hers, you know – and I was glad, because I was brought up here as a little girl. I knew every corner."

"Well – why can't we let Granny have it back, and go and live in a smaller place?" said Francis. Then, looking round the old garden he knew so well, he suddenly changed his mind. "No. No, I didn't mean that. I couldn't bear to leave Green Meadows! It's our home – Granny's home, yours, and mine."

"I feel the same," said his mother, "but things are getting so difficult that I feel we shall *have* to leave soon, Francis – if only we could sell the house! But it is in such a bad state now that nobody wants it – it's too big a house nowadays, you see. And anyway, Granny won't hear of selling it – so I really don't know what we are to do."

She went to the old wall that ran all round the garden, and looked over it. Not far off an enormous building was going up – a great block of flats. Another one, almost finished, was just behind it.

"Not many years ago this was all countryside," she told Francis. "That's why this house was called Green Meadows – when it was first built we could see nothing but green fields all round, stretching right to those hills over there. Now all the fields are going to be a housing estate – look at those blocks of flats!"

"Well – it will mean that more children come to the village," said Francis. "That will be more fun for us. But I suppose we'll be a town then. We've already got more shops, and a brand-new post office."

His mother turned to go in, suddenly remembering the washing up she had to do. She gave Francis a pat on the arm. "Don't you worry about it, now. These are grown-up worries, not yours. I don't know why I told you so much. I'm all muddled somehow. I want to go on living here in Green Meadows, which I love so much – but not in this mess and muddle, not when I have to

11

do so much that I've hardly time for you and the other two children. And . . ."

Francis finished for her. "And anyway Granny won't sell the house, so we've got to make the best of it! I wish I could make the garden nice for you, Mother – but it's so big! I'm a Scout, you know, and I'm willing to help any way I can. And Clare is a Brownie, and Sam's a Cub – you can *always* ask us to do anything!"

"I do!" said his mother. "But I'm not going to put old heads on young shoulders. Go and ask Daddy if he wants anything, Francis. There! I've asked you to do something already!"

She went slowly indoors. Francis watched her. She looked sad and her merry smile hardly ever came now. "I wish I was grown up!" thought Francis. "It takes so *long* to grow up! I can't earn a penny – all I can do is to run errands and clean the shoes and things like that. Any Scout can do that. I want to do something that will really help!"

But he knew he couldn't. Grown-ups had to manage their own affairs. He went to find his father. It wasn't difficult because he lived all day long in a wheelchair and was never far away.

"Do you want anything, Dad?" asked Francis. "How's your back?"

"Same as usual," said his father. "Can't you go and help your mother a bit, Francis? I hate to sit here and see her tearing about hard at work all day long – I feel so useless. Go and help her."

"She sent me to ask you if *you* wanted anything," said Francis, with a good-tempered grin. "When's the doctor coming again, Dad? Isn't the new treatment any good?"

"Not a bit. Nothing ever will be, I'm sure," said his

father. "If only you were older, Francis! Your mother's got too much on her shoulders."

"I've just been thinking exactly the same thing," said Francis. "Mother's been talking to me and telling me a lot this morning. I don't want to leave Green Meadows, Dad, but for Mother's sake I think we should. She'll kill herself! She has so much to do. Won't Granny sell the house, won't she really?"

"No, she won't," said Daddy, shortly. "Now that she has come back to live with us here she seems to love the old place more than ever, tumbledown though it is. Let's not talk about it, or I shall get angry."

Francis heard his mother calling and went off. What a tangle! He couldn't see what in the world was to be done! Granny was a difficult person to get on with – very touchy and thinking far too much about herself. All three of her grandchildren were afraid of her sharp tongue – and yet at times she could be so unexpectedly kind.

There was the sound of running feet on the path outside. The back door burst open and in came Clare and Sam. Clare was nine, big for her age, curly-haired and merry-eyed. Sam was seven, small and solemn, and seldom laughed – but when he did it was always a surprise, because his laugh was loud and very sudden. It made everyone else laugh too.

"We're back, Mother!" called Clare. "We had a jolly good meeting at the Brownies."

"So did we at the Cubs," said Sam. "I'm the smallest there, but I'm not the worst. I'd better not tell you who is the worst."

"He's *bursting* to tell us," said Clare. "Don't be a tell-tale, Sam. Anyway, we know the answer. Mother, can I

13

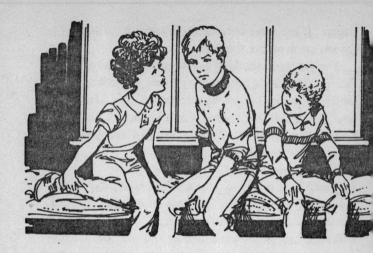

The children often crept in and sat on the window seat

have something to eat? I don't think I can wait till dinnertime. It's ages since breakfast!"

An old lady came into the kitchen. She jingled as she came, for she wore several chains about her – a long gold one that reached to her waist and was fastened to a gold watch tucked into her belt – a silvery one with a locket on it, round her neck – and a chain bracelet on each of her wrists, fastened by tiny padlocks.

"I always know when you are coming, Granny!" said Clare. "You jingle like the coal man's horse!"

"I don't think that's very polite," said Granny. "I'm not in the least like the coal man's horse."

"Clare thinks the coal man's jingling horse is lovely," explained Sam at once. "So do I. I'd like to jingle when I walk about, too. I think . . ."

"That's enough," said Granny. She turned to her daughter, the children's mother. "No wonder you haven't finished yet!" she said. "I saw you wandering

14

about in the garden with Francis, talking away like anything! Why don't you finish everything first – then you might have time for a rest in the afternoon."

Granny took up a duster and a tin of polish and began rubbing the furniture hard. That was exactly like Granny – to scold and then to do what she could to help. The three children ran out of the room. They felt sure that Granny would think of something unpleasant to say if they stayed there!

Francis opened a door on the landing upstairs. The room inside was quite empty, but it had a window seat under the big bow window. "Come on," said Francis. "Let's sit down and eat our biscuits here, and pretend it's our old playroom again!"

It had once been their playroom, but, like so many of the other rooms, its furniture had been sold and the room left empty and unused. The children often crept in there and sat on the window seat.

"It's got such a nice feel about it, this room," said Clare, nibbling her biscuit. "It's a happy room, even though it's got nothing to be happy about now. I expect it keeps remembering all the old dolls and teddy bears and trains that Granny and her brothers played with . . ."

"And that Mummy and *her* brothers and sisters had . . ."

"And the ones we had, too, when we still had this room for our own," said Francis. "You don't remember that very well, Sam. You were too little."

Clare looked out of the window. "Look at that enormous block of flats," she said. "The one that's finished. Someone must have moved into one of the flats, because I can see two children. It seems funny to see those great

15

buildings instead of green fields. Oh, well – I don't expect they'll make much difference to *us*!"

Ah, you wait and see, Clare! You'll be surprised!

There was always plenty for the three children to do at Green Meadows. Out of school hours there were endless jobs to be done. Even Sam helped.

Their mother never nagged them to do their jobs, however tired she was. But Granny did! She was always after them, asking if this had been done and that had been done – and who was supposed to get the wood in for the fire, and why had it been left to the last moment?

Francis and Sam were patient, but Clare was hottempered. Often she came storming to find her mother.

"Mother! Granny says I don't think about you enough! Just because I forgot to wind up the clocks last night! I *do* think about you, and Granny's not to say that!"

"Oh darling – you haven't been rude to Granny, have you?" her mother would say. "Her tongue may be sharp but her heart is kind. It's only because she's worried about me that she says these things. *I* know you think of me – that's all that matters, isn't it? That *I* shall know?"

"Yes, I suppose it is," Clare would say, and smile and give her mother a hug. And then the very next day Granny's tongue would upset her again, and there would be another storm.

"I don't believe Granny loves any of us," Sam said solemnly one evening. "She scolds us all, Daddy and Mother too – but there's only one person she doesn't scold, so she must love him very much."

"Who's that?" said Clare, surprised. "You don't mean Dr Miles, do you? She's fond of him because she thinks he tries to help Daddy."

"No. I mean Mr Black," said Sam. Everyone roared

with laughter. Mr Black was Granny's cat, an enormous fellow with great yellow eyes, a wonderful tail, and fur like thick shiny silk. He was as black as soot. He had been called Blackie when he was a kitten – but he grew up so big and solemn and high-and-mighty that Granny felt she couldn't call him by such an ordinary name as Blackie.

So she called him Majesty because he looked so majestic. He didn't answer to that name at all, of course, because he didn't know it. So then the family called him Mr Black, and that was all right. It sounded enough like "Blackie" to him, and he came when he was called.

He belonged to Granny, and she loved him with all her heart. Blackie adored her too, and always slept in a basket in Granny's room.

He was a very spoilt cat. The three children made a great fuss of him, for they were all fond of animals. Sometimes they talked about Thumper, a beautiful Great Dane who had belonged to Granny some years back. His great paws thumped about the house all day long. As Clare said, you always knew where Thumper was, you couldn't help it, he stamped about so!

"He was so lovely," said Clare, remembering. "He was as big as I was, but he was as gentle as a kitten."

"Kittens aren't always gentle," said Sam, who liked every statement to be quite correct. "When Mr Black was a kitten he bit me."

"Do you remember when Thumper wagged his big tail to greet a visitor one afternoon, and swept all the cakes off the cake-stand on the little table?" said Francis.

Sam thought that was very funny. He gave one of his sudden roars of laughter. "I wish I'd seen that," he said. "What happened to Thumper? I don't remember. And why aren't we allowed to talk about him to Granny?"

17

"Well, it cost an awful lot to feed a big dog like that," said Francis. "Pounds and pounds a year. So one day Granny decided it wasn't fair on the family to keep him any longer."

"Oh," said Sam, looking solemn again. "What did she do with him, then?"

"She sold him," said Francis. "He was a very valuable dog, and she got a lot of money for him. After that she didn't have to feed him, of course, so she saved a lot of money too. Granny loved Thumper. More than she loves Mr Black."

"Did she cry?" asked Sam, looking very serious.

"She cried for two whole days," said Francis. "She couldn't stop. She said we weren't to take any notice of her, she would get over it. You don't remember that, Sam."

"Granny's fond of animals," said Clare. "She's told us about heaps she had when she was a child. She was lucky. All we've got is Mr Black, and he doesn't *really* belong to us."

"No, he's Granny's," said Sam. "I wish we had animals of our own. I'd like a rabbit. And some mice. And plenty of hens. I'd like a monkey too, and perhaps a small bear."

"I'd like dogs," said Francis. "Plenty of them! And puppies and kittens."

"I'd like birds," said Clare. "Pigeons that fly about the garden. There's an old pigeon-house here still lying broken down in one corner, isn't there? I expect Granny kept pigeons there once. She had a horse too, called Clover."

"If we were well-off we could have heaps and heaps of animals," said Sam. "I like them better than toys. They

"He was as gentle as a kitten"

19

are alive, and they can love you. I love toys – but I'm never *really* certain they ever love me back!"

"Sometimes," said Clare, suddenly, looking at Francis out of the corner of her eyes, "*sometimes* I think you must have a dog of your own, Francis!"

"Well, I haven't," said Francis, shortly. To Sam's enormous surprise he went bright red, and turned his face away.

"You've gone red," said Sam. "You're hiding something from us! You always go red when you do that. So do I."

"Lets go out and do something," said Francis, getting up. "I've finished my biscuit."

He went out of the room. They heard him going down the stairs. Sam looked solemnly at Clare. "What did you mean when you said you sometimes thought that Francis had a dog of his own, Clare? He hasn't, has he?"

"No. Not really," said Clare. "But it's funny, Sam – when Francis thinks he's alone and nobody's watching him, he holds out his hands, and says, 'Come on, Paddy – walkie – walk!' Just like that – as if a dog was behind him."

Sam thought about this. "He's pretending a dog," he said. "I know he wants one badly. So do I. When do you see Francis doing this?"

"Oh, often," said Clare. "Sometimes I'm in the garden, behind the hedge – and Francis comes along by himself and talks to his dog then. The other day he threw a ball for him, and said, 'Bring it back, Paddy – that's right! Good dog!' And he bent and patted the air!"

"I'm not going to say anything about this dog to him," said Sam. "If he'd wanted to share him with us he would have told us about him. Does the dog go to bed with him, and sleep on his feet, I wonder?"

"I don't know," said Clare. "You sleep in the same room. You can watch and see."

"I'm always asleep when Francis comes to bed," said Sam. "Always. Even if I try to keep awake I can't. And anyway I'm not going to pry into Francis's secret. And don't you either, Clare! See?"

"You stop telling me what I'm to do or not to do!" said Clare. "A little shrimp like you! I wish I hadn't told you about the pretend dog now. I shan't say anything about it to Francis — unless he teases me about something, and then I'll tease him back — about Paddy!"

"That would be mean of you!" called Sam, as Clare walked out of the room. She slammed the door. Sam didn't mind. He was used to Clare's sudden little flares of temper. She would have forgotten it the next time he saw her, and be as friendly as ever.

He thought about Francis's pretend dogs. Poor old Francis! How he must want a dog of his own to invent one like that! He was like Granny — he really loved animals. He patted every dog he saw and spoke to it. He fed the wild birds in the garden. Every cat came to him as soon as it saw him. The milkman's horse walked right across the road, cart and all, if he heard Francis's voice!

"And when he went to the Zoo and Francis spoke to the monkeys in the cage, they left everything they were doing and came crowding to the wire," Sam remembered. "They put their tiny paws through the wire and tried to take his fingers — though he hadn't any food to give them! They chattered like anything too — I was sure they were telling him they wanted to be friends."

The door opened and Granny looked in. "Sam! What are you doing here all alone?"

"Just thinking," said Sam.

"You think too much," said Granny. "You're too

21

Oh dear – that was Granny's voice!

serious altogether! It's not good for you to sit up here, mooning away by yourself."

"I wasn't mooning," said Sam, getting up. "What *is* mooning, Granny? Is it anything to do with the moon?"

"Oh, don't be *silly*, Sam!" said Granny. "Do go on down and give a hand somewhere."

"Well, here's a hand!" said Sam, and suddenly slipped his into Granny's. "Shall I do something for *you*? Then you won't feel so cross."

Granny looked down at the hand in hers, and gave a sudden laugh. She squeezed Sam's hand. "You're a caution!" she said. "No, please don't ask me what a caution is! It's something quite nice when I call *you* one. Let's go and dig some potatoes, shall we? The potato basket is getting empty."

"I'll dig them. Don't bother," said Sam. "I'll get the spade and the trug now."

He went off to the old stables that belonged to Green Meadows. The horse-stalls were still there, and the harness room led off one end, a place where the family put all their junk. It was always exciting to Sam to look through the junk and rubbish piled in the corners and on the shelves.

He stood in the stables and looked round, pretending that he could hear the stamp-stamp, clop-clop of horses' hooves. Did Francis pretend a horse too that lived in the stables? Over the mangers were little brass plates, green with age, still bearing the names of long ago horses.

"Dapple". That was a pretty name for a horse, Sam thought.

"Clopper". "Benjy". "Captain". They all sounded nice. He must ask Granny about them. Perhaps they were horses she knew back in history, when she was a little girl.

"Sam! I thought you were going to dig potatoes!" Oh dear – that was Granny's voice! Sam picked up the trug and the spade and began to dig vigorously. He liked it. The birds sang madly all round him, and the sun was warm on the back of his neck. He pursed up his lips and tried to whistle, a thing he had never been able to do, much to his shame.

A loud whistle came suddenly from his lips, startling Sam very much. He pursed up his mouth and tried again. Another whistle, as loud as the blackbirds near by, came at once. Sam went red with delight. He could whistle at last!

"It's my lucky day!" thought Sam. "I can suddenly whistle. Now I shan't be the only Cub that can't!"

And whistling loudly and tunelessly, Sam dug up half a row of potatoes at top speed! Who would ever have thought that whistling was such a help to hard work?

Chapter Two

TWO UNEXPECTED FIGHTS!

February slipped into March, and the winds came, the mad March winds that shook the trees in the gardens of Green Meadows and "blew the birds about the sky".

The days had gone by very quietly, and nothing much had happened except that Mr Black had most unexpectedly mixed himself up in a fight with two other cats. This had caused great excitement at Green Meadows.

It had happened at night. Everyone but Sam had been suddenly awakened by a screaming, yowling, squealing noise just under the windows. Everyone had sat up straight in bed, their hearts beating fast. Oh, whatever could it be?

It was two strange cats fighting down in the garden. It sounded exactly as if they were killing one another. Daddy groaned. "If only I could get out of bed and walk to the window I'd empty a jug of water over them!" he said. "Making a row like this in the middle of the night. If it's Mr Black I'll tell him what I think of him in the morning!"

But it wasn't Mr Black. Granny's big black cat had been asleep as usual in his basket in Granny's own room. The yowling had wakened him at once and he sat up, looking twice the size, his tail swelling out till it was as big as Granny's best fur.

Mr Black was furious. What were strange cats doing in his garden? How *dare* they? He leapt from his basket, jumped on to the windowsill, through the open window

24

to a pear tree below – and then leapt straight down on top of the two fighting cats. He must have seemed like a cannonball to them!

Granny was soon at her window, calling in anguish. "Mr Black! Mr Black! stop it, now! Oh, he'll get killed! Oh, I must stop this fight!"

And there was Granny scuttling down the stairs in her dressing gown, ready to tear her beloved Mr Black away from two clawing cats!

But before she or Francis could get there – Francis was close behind her – the cats had moved on over the wall, pursued by an extremely angry Mr Black, who spat and hissed like a furious soda syphon, and used his enormous claws wherever he could. The noise dwindled into the distance, and Granny sat down suddenly on the seat in the porch.

"Oh dear – what a shock I got! Oh, Francis, where are they? What has happened to Mr Black? He'll be torn to pieces!"

"Its all right, Granny. He'll come back, all puffed up with pride, to tell you how he sent away two cat burglars!" said Francis, trying to make his grandmother laugh. She couldn't help giving a little smile. "Help me up the stairs, Francis," she said. "A sudden scare like that makes me feel an old woman!"

Mr Black didn't come back that night, so the next morning Granny was tired out. "I haven't been to sleep all night," she said. "Where can Mr Black be?"

Clare nudged Sam. "Don't you start your whistling again now," she warned him. "Granny will be as cross as two sticks today!"

Sam nudged Clare back, but much harder. "Don't keep on so about my whistling," he said. "It's a very *new* whistle, and I've got to practise it. Granny – I'll go and look for Mr Black for you, shall I?"

But Mr Black came back after dinner, much to everyone's joy. Granny certainly *had* been "as cross as twenty sticks, not two", as Sam said, and Mother was certain that Clare was going to fly into a fury very soon, because Granny nagged her so much!

Mr Black came sauntering across the grass just after the family had finished their dinner. Daddy saw him first. "Here's our Mr Black," he announced from his wheelchair. "Large as life and looking very pleased with himself. The warrior returned home from the wars!"

Granny gave a little squeal and rose from her chair at once. She ran to the window and flung it open.

"Mr Black! Are you all right?"

Mr Black didn't even look at her. He sat down in the middle of the grass, cocked up one of his legs and began to wash himself very thoroughly indeed.

"He's showing off!" said Clare. "I'll fetch him in for you, Granny."

But, exactly as if he had heard what Clare had said, Mr Black stood up and ran to the window. In two seconds he was in Granny's arms, and she was exclaiming over him:

"Mr Black! You've got a bitten ear! And oh dear, look, children – he's got a bare patch on his tail. Oh, *why* did you mix yourself up in a fight, Mr Black? Where's the iodine, children?"

Daddy began to growl, as he always did when Granny made too much fuss over Mr Black. "Fussing over him like that – as if he were a baby! Honestly, it makes me feel sick the way you treat that cat! He can expect a bitten ear and tail if he fights. *He* doesn't mind them, so why should you?"

Granny flashed round at him at once. "You don't love animals. I don't believe you even *like* them!"

"I do," said Daddy. "But I don't believe in gushing over them, that's all. You know I loved Thumper."

There was a silence. Thumper, Granny's long-ago Great Dane, was not supposed to be mentioned by anyone. Granny looked at Daddy.

"Yes," she said. "I know you did. All the same, I still say you don't really ! . . .'

"Yes, Daddy does, yes, Daddy does," began Clare, who always rushed to her father's help if Granny attacked him. Granny attacked everyone at times. "Yes, Daddy does, yes, Daddy does, yes . . ."

"Clare!" said Mummy. "Fetch the iodine, please – at once!"

Mr Black loved all the fuss and bother. He purred as loudly as a sewing machine!

"He's a fraud," said Daddy under his breath to Clare. She nodded. "Yes – but he's a *nice* fraud!" she answered.

Mr Black's adventure was the biggest thing that happened in those few quiet weeks when the crocuses gave place to the early daffodils, and primroses began to come out in the dell. Francis went on with his pretending, and his pretend-dog, Paddy, went with him everywhere. Clare tried to learn knitting from Granny, who thought it was time she was taught – but Granny was too impatient a teacher and Clare was too hot-tempered a pupil, so it didn't come to anything.

Sam's great thrill was his new whistle, which he practised so continually that he nearly drove everyone mad. Sam was upset to think his family didn't share his delight in this great new gift of his, and at last he took to going to the stables, and shutting himself in. There he whistled to his heart's content — trying his hardest to whistle a tune, but never quite succeeding!

And then something quite unusual happened. It happened to Francis one evening when he was going home from a Scouts' meeting. As usual he had his pretend-dog, Paddy, with him. There was no one in the lane he was walking down, so he gave his dog practice in coming to him when he whistled.

He had his Scout whistle with him, and he blew it. Then he signalled with his hand to Paddy, who was supposed to be a hundred or so yards away.

Paddy galloped up at once when the whistle sounded. "Good, Paddy!" said Francis. "Very good! Try again. This time, stop when I put up my hand like this!"

The dog was so real to him that Francis actually thought he could see the dog's tail wagging, and his pink tongue hanging out of his mouth. He could hear the dog panting! Pretends can be very, very real.

"Run off to the same place, Paddy," said Francis. "When I whistle, come running — but stop when I put up my hand. Stop dead! Now!"

He whistled — and then two seconds later put up his hand. "Good!" called Francis. "Good dog! Now come to heel and walk with your nose just touching my ankle."

He could almost feel the dog's nose touching his ankle as he began to walk down the lane again. And then he heard something that made him jump. It was a loud jeering laugh.

"Ha ha! You're crazy, aren't you? Talking to a dog that isn't there!"

Francis looked all round but could see nobody. Then he heard a noise nearby, and a boy slid down a tree, leaping to the ground from the lowest branch.

He was a bit taller than Francis, about thirteen, dirty

and untidy. His hair stood up in a shock, dark brown and curly, and his mouth was curved in a jeering grin.

Francis didn't know what to say. He couldn't possibly explain to anyone about Paddy, the dog he had made up – especially not to a jeering boy like this. So he just said nothing and walked on.

The boy put his fingers to his mouth and gave such a shrill, piercing whistle that Francis jumped. "Paddy, Paddy!" called the boy, trying to imitate Francis's voice. "Good dog, then. Walk to heel! That's right – nose to my ankle!"

Francis was speechless. The boy actually bent down and pretended to pat a dog! Then he began to walk towards Francis, looking down as if the dog were at his heels. "Good!" he said. "Fine!"

"Shut up," said Francis, temper welling up in him suddenly and powerfully.

"Yah!" said the boy. "He's *my* dog now! He won't follow *you* any more! I'm going to take him home to live with my own dog. He wants companionship!"

"I said shut up," said Francis, and he felt his fists clenching themselves tightly.

"You're a Scout. Scouts mustn't fight. Naughty, naughty!" said the aggravating boy. "Why don't you get a *real* dog, instead of a silly pretend one? You're potty!"

Francis said nothing. He was so angry now that he couldn't even speak.

"I've got a beauty!" said the boy. "You should see him, he's a – well, he's a sort of spaniel: but he's real, not like your silly Paddy-dog! Pooh! Here, Paddy, Paddy, let me put a lead on you and take you home to Rex. Come on, boy!"

And the boy bent down and pretended to tie a bit of string to a dog's collar. Francis never really knew what happened then – he just felt his fist hitting the boy's downbent face – biff!

And then something struck Francis on the side of the head – the big boy's clenched fist. The fight was on! Biff! Thud! Biff!

It could only end one way. The other boy was taller and stronger – and in half a minute's time Francis found himself lying flat on the ground, seeing stars all round him! The other boy went off, laughing loudly.

And to make things worse, he was calling Paddy. "Paddy. Come along then! Don't you even bother to lick his wounds! He's not worth it. You come along with me!"

Francis sat up, feeling dazed. The lane seemed to go round and round him, hedges and all. He shut his eyes, feeling suddenly ashamed of himself.

He was a Scout – and yet he had provoked a fight with another boy. He hadn't even the excuse that he had had to defend himself. But – how could he have helped it? The boy had jeered and sneered at his secret – and had actually said he had got Paddy on a lead and was going to take him home!

Francis stood up and went to lean over a nearby gate. He felt in a muddle. He tried to sort it out, but he couldn't. He felt that he had done right, it was the only thing he could do – yet he knew it was wrong too.

He went home, hoping that he didn't look too dreadful. His left eye felt very tender, and his right cheek felt strange. He could see quite a lot of it with his right eye, and usually he couldn't see his cheeks at all!

He slipped in at the garden door, hoping that he could get up to his bedroom unseen. His Granny heard him and called him.

"Is that you, Francis? Come in here a minute, will you?"

"I'll just go upstairs first and wash, Granny," called Francis, and rushed up the stairs before his grandmother could see him. He went into his room and looked into the mirror on the wall.

Gracious! What a sight he looked! What a dreadful sight! His left eye was almost shut now, and a purple bruise was coming up round it. His right cheek was red and swollen. He hurriedly went to the bathroom and began to wash his face in cold water.

His heart suddenly sank – Granny had come upstairs after him, cross because he hadn't come when she called him. "Francis! Why didn't you . . ." she began, and then stopped. "What are you washing your face for? Are you hurt?"

"I'm all right, Granny, thank you," said Francis, desperately. "I'm just coming."

Granny lifted his head and made him look at her. "You're hurt! You've had an accident! What's happened?"

"Nothing. I tell you it's nothing." said Francis. "Just a little swelling."

"You've been fighting!" said Granny, in horror. "Don't deny it! You a Scout too! Oh, to think of it!"

She went downstairs. Francis felt miserable. He held his nose and put his whole head into the basin of water, hoping that that would help his eye and cheek. He felt a tap on his shoulder and took his head out of the water.

It was Clare. "Francis! What's happened? Granny's telling everyone you've been fighting. Are you hurt?"

"No!" said Francis, fiercely. "All this fuss! Anyone would think there had never been a fight before!"

"But *you*, Francis – you're so peaceful," said Clare.

31

"Francis – do tell me what it was all about? I do want to know. It's the first fight our family has ever been in."

Francis dried his face very gingerly indeed, and brushed and combed his hair.

"You look awful," said Clare. "Don't you feel important, Francis, looking like that because of a fight?"

"Why are girls so silly?" exploded Francis, who was longing to be alone and at peace, so that he could think out all that had happened so very suddenly. He pushed Clare aside and went to his room. Clare followed.

"Mother says you are to come straight down," said Clare. "And don't you push me about like that."

"If you don't go away at once I'll *shove* you," said poor Francis. Clare disappeared. Francis glared at himself in the glass, what a sight! Well, it wasn't any good staying up in his room – the whole family would be trailing up the stairs to find him! He might as well go down and face the music.

So down he went. As soon as he opened the door of the sitting room everyone looked up. There were sudden gasps and exclamations.

"Francis dear! Your poor face!"

"What did I tell you? He's been fighting!"

"He wouldn't tell me a thing!" said Clare.

Sam just stared solemnly after his first gasp. How peculiar Francis looked – not like Francis at all.

"How did it happen, dear?" asked his mother, gently. She pulled him to her. Thank goodness – she wasn't going to be too cross! Francis was relieved. What about his father? Would he be angry, like Granny?

It was Granny who scolded him loudly and angrily. Nobody else said a word. At last his father interrupted.

"That's enough," he said. "Leave the boy alone. He's not one to fight without a reason – and most boys get

32

into fights sooner or later. Even Scouts have to fight to defend themselves! Did someone attack you, Francis?"

Francis longed to say "Yes – and I had to defend myself." But it was wrong and cowardly to lie like that, and he wasn't going to begin. He shook his head.

"What happened then?" said his father, in astonishment. "Please don't be so dumb, Francis. We only want to know."

"I – well – I just hit someone, that's all," said Francis. "He er – he said and – and did something I didn't like – and I hit him."

There was silence. "So *you* began the fight?" said his father. "I see. What did the boy say and do that you didn't like? Surely you can tell us that?"

"No, I can't," said Francis, shutting up in his most secret heart his pretence about Paddy the dog. He felt rather peculiar, for he could only see out of one eye now. The left one had gradually swelled up and was shut.

Granny began again. "I do think, I really do think that . . ."

"There is to be no more said unless I say it!" said Daddy, in such a determined voice that everyone was startled. Granny stood up, offended.

"Very well, then – if I can't say what I want to *in my own house*, I'll leave you to it!" And she marched out, stiff and straight as a walking stick.

Mother sighed. "Oh dear – what an upset. Francis, let me put something on that eye."

"Who won the fight?" asked Sam, suddenly.

"I didn't," said Francis.

"I bet the boy was bigger and older than you," said Sam. "Else you'd have beaten him. Knocked him down flat. Biff-thud!"

33

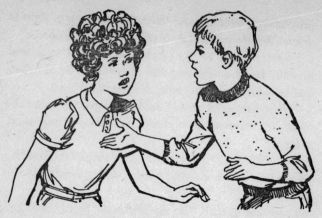

So Francis told her the whole thing

"Be quiet, Sam," said his mother. "Come with me, Francis."

Mother was kind. She put something comforting on his eye, and patted his shoulder, and didn't ask him a single question. Francis squeezed her arm.

"I'd tell you if I could, Mother, but I can't," he said. "Not yet, anyhow."

"That's all right, dear. Everybody has some secret or other – and why not?" said his mother. "You shouldn't start a fight, you know that; but if you did I'm quite prepared to believe that you just had to. So don't fret about it."

But Francis did fret, of course. Suppose the Scout-master got to hear of it? Suppose that boy spread the news around about the dog he had invented, and everyone laughed at him? Suppose, suppose, suppose!

At last he had to tell someone. He told Clare. After all, she already knew about his pretend dog, and she wouldn't laugh if he told her it was something serious – surely she wouldn't?

"Clare – come up into the old playroom," Francis said, two days after the fight. His face looked very peculiar, and he had had a lot of teasing from the boys in his class, but his cheek was not so swollen now, and he could eat without difficulty. Clare nodded.

"All right. I'll just finish laying the table, and I'll come."

She came to join him on the window seat in the playroom. Francis began at one. "It's about the fight. I'm awfully worried Clare, and I've simply got to tell someone. But don't laugh, will you?"

Clare shook her head vigorously. "No, of course not. Tell me."

So Francis told her the whole thing – how the boy up the tree had seen him teaching Paddy, the invented dog, to be obedient, and how he had jeered and laughed; and at last how he had pretended to put Paddy on a lead and take him home with him.

"Oh! What a horrible boy," said Clare. "And you say he'd got a dog of his own too? Fancy wanting to take yours! No wonder you hit him. I would have to, too."

"It all happened so suddenly," said Francis. "What worries me is that I hit him first – and you see, if I tell Daddy or Mother or Granny the whole truth, they would think I was *crazy* to start a fight about a pretend dog. Anyway, I can't tell anyone about Paddy! Except you – and you knew."

"Don't worry about it," said Clare, comfortingly. "What's it matter now? You've still got Paddy, and if I were you I'd teach him to go and *bite* that boy if ever you see him again."

"I can't," said Francis. "I haven't got him any more."

"Where is he then?" cried Clare, astonished.

"Well, you know what pretends are – they sometimes

35

go, all of a sudden," said Francis. "Like when we pretended there was a bear in the old stables and wouldn't go near them. And suddenly the pretend stopped and we knew there wasn't a bear there."

"Yes. But that was because we wanted to go and hunt through that old junk in the harness room," said Clare. "Still – you're right. Pretends do go all of a sudden. Has Paddy really gone? Perhaps that boy is pretending him instead of you? Why don't you get another dog?"

Francis stared at her. "I've tried that," he said. "But one won't come. I mean – it's just pretend and nothing else. Paddy seemed real. Oh Clare, I do wish I had a pet of my own. A horse. Or a dog. Or even pigeons."

"Perhaps if you did *two* good deeds a day instead of one, you'd get what you want," said Clare. "Anyway, I'll put a dog in my prayers each night for you. Do cheer up, Francis. It's awful to see you going about so gloomy. You make Mother worried."

"Well, I do feel better since I've told you," said Francis, looking more cheerful. "Don't tell anyone, will you?"

"As if I should," said Clare, scornfully. "I'm a Brownie, aren't I? Well then, you ought to trust me. Anyway, you know I always keep my word."

She ran downstairs, proud that Francis had told her his worry and no one else. That horrid boy! "I'd like to smack him hard!" thought Clare, fiercely. "And if I ever meet him, I will! But I don't expect I ever shall!"

She did though – the very next day!

Chapter Three

THAT BOY AGAIN

Francis was late home from school the next day because it was his week to fill the ink-wells and keep the shelves tidy.

"I'm always glad when it's a Scout's turn to be the monitor for the week," said his master. "I don't even need to see if the job is done properly. I only wish the whole class were Scouts!"

Francis was pleased. He spent an extra long time doing the job perfectly. Then he went home, half an hour late.

Clare and Sam were watching for him, over the wall. They wanted to tell him that Granny had been in a very good temper all day long, and had bought some special chocolate biscuits for tea.

"Here he comes," said Clare to Sam. "Don't say a word till he gets to the gate. Then we'll yell out 'Chocolate biscuits', and make him jump."

But before they could yell, somebody else yelled first. "Hey! Come here, Paddy! He's not your master any more! Come here, boy! That's right, that's right!"

Francis swung round. The boy he had fought stood just across the road, laughing. He bent down and pretended to pat a dog. He crossed the road, looking down as if the dog was at his heels, and stood just under the wall near Clare and Sam. He didn't see them, he was watching Francis.

"Did you miss your dog?" he yelled. Francis swung in

37

through the gate, slammed it, and went up the path, fuming. Hateful, hateful boy!

The boy laughed jeeringly – and then he suddenly stopped. Someone fell on him, someone pummelled him hard, someone pulled his hair and panted out, "Take that – and that – and that! Oh, you nasty horrid thing!"

The boy shook off the someone and raised his fist to strike. Then he dropped it suddenly.

"Golly!" he said. "It's a girl! What do you think you're doing, you fathead?"

"This," said Clare, and hit out at him fiercely. The boy dodged, the blow missed, and Clare fell over on the ground with a bump.

"I don't fight little girls!" said the boy. "Or little boys either!" he added, as Sam suddenly landed beside him. "What's up, you two? Why are you behaving like this?"

"You give Paddy back," said Clare, standing up and scowling. "My brother loves dogs and he'd give anything to have one of his own. You've got one. You're very very lucky. You be careful *your* dog doesn't come to my brother now you've taken his!"

"Don't be silly," said the boy. "Paddy's only a silly pretend. As for my dog, he'd never, never go to anyone else – and I wouldn't let him, so there."

"Well," said Clare, in a tembling voice, "people that do bad, unkind things always get punished for it. And I wouldn't be a bit surprised if something happens to your dog. But you may be sure if he comes to Francis he'll be well looked after!"

"You're talking nonsense," said the boy, and he laughed. "My dog's mine, I've had him for five years, and I'll never never let him go. We've only just moved here – into one of the flats in that block – and though it's small and hasn't a garden like we used to have, Rex

"Get me a chocolate biscuit. Wooooooof!"

is quite happy, because he's with me. As for the silly pretend-dog, take him – *I* don't want him!"

The boy bent down, pretended to pat a dog, and to undo a lead. "You can go," he said. "I don't want you, Paddy."

He made such a realistic little whine that Clare and Sam jumped. The boy laughed at them. "Goodbye," he said. "And don't you go jumping too many people like that, little girl! I shall pull your hair hard if you jump on me again!"

"You won't," said Sam, fiercely, speaking for the first time.

"I'll pull yours too, tiddler!" said the boy, and went off, still laughing. The two children stared after him. "Horrid, horrid, hateful boy!" said Clare, and stamped her foot.

They ran to their front gate and went in. They went to find Francis and tell him what had happened. He stared in alarm.

"Clare! You *mustn't* do things like that! You're a *girl*! Girls don't behave like that. And you're a Brownie too!"

"I know lots of girls that would behave like that," said Clare defiantly. "And a Brownie has to stick up for the right, hasn't she?"

"She was brave," said Sam, in his slow solemn voice, "Very brave. She wasn't a bit afraid of the big boy."

"And he let Paddy go free, so he's yours again," said Clare, trying to make Francis smile.

He shook his head. "No. I told you the pretend had gone. It was a silly one. I'm too big to invent things now. Let's forget about it."

"Where did your Paddy-dog sleep?" asked Sam, suddenly. "I never heard you talking to him in our bedroom."

"I cleaned out the old dog kennel," said Francis. "He slept there. Come and look. It's got straw inside and all!"

He took them to a corner of the garden, where the old dog kennel stood that Granny's dogs had slept in long ago. It was clean and spotless inside, and had a heap of straw there, flattened down as if a dog had actually slept on it. Outside stood a bowl of water.

"I never noticed the old kennel was cleaned out," said Clare. "Sam – come here! Look Francis he's getting into the kennel! *Sam*!"

Sam crawled right into the kennel, and then turned round and looked out, beaming. "Woof," he said, "woof! I'm hungry. Get me a chocolate biscuit. Woooooof!"

Francis and Clare roared with laughter. Clare pulled Sam out and dusted the straw from his clothes.

"You're an idiot!" said Francis, suddenly looking cheerful. "Now let's forget Paddy and never mention him again. I was silly."

Clare suddenly remembered her news. "Granny has been in a very good temper all day," she said, "and she has got us some chocolate biscuits for tea – heaps of them. We'd better go in, else she'll forget her good temper and take the biscuits away! Come on."

They all went indoors, and Francis explained that he couldn't help being late, because he was room monitor that week. Granny nodded approvingly.

"Then I know you'd do everything well," she said.

"Your eye's looking better today, Francis. Have you seen that boy again, the one who fought you?"

Daddy cleared his throat warningly. "Granny. No more is to be said about that."

Clare kicked Sam under the table, and gave him a little secret smile. A good thing Daddy had said that – or poor Francis would have had to tell about the afternoon happenings over the wall!

Granny didn't like Daddy putting his foot down, and she frowned. Clare looked at her anxiously, hoping that nothing would happen before the chocolate biscuits were all eaten.

Mother changed the subject smoothly, a thing she was very good at. "Has anyone counted the daffodils out in the dell yet?" she said. "I counted twenty-nine yesterday. Remember that as soon as there are more than thirty we can pick some for the house. You'll do that, Clare, won't you?"

"Oh yes," said Clare. She loved picking them and arranging them. Thank goodness Mother had changed the subject! "I'll put some in Granny's room first, then in yours and Daddy's, and then in ours."

"No, get some for the table first," said Granny, pleasantly. "Then we can all share them. Are you ready for a chocolate biscuit, Sam?"

"Oooooh yes. Quite," said Sam.

41

"Quite what?" asked Granny, holding the plate away from him.

"*Quite* ready," said Sam in surprise. "Oh – quite *please*, I mean. Thank you, Granny!"

"Manners, manners, manners," said Granny. "When I was little and forgot my Ps and Qs, my nurse cut out a whole lot of letters – all Ps and Qs – and pinned them on my frock. Each time I remembered she took one off – and each time I forgot she pinned one on."

"Oh! How exciting!" said Clare. "Granny, do do it to me! Please do!"

"It was a punishment," said Granny. "Not a treat. John, why are you laughing?"

She turned to Daddy, who was laughing loudly, a thing he didn't often do. Mother began to laugh too.

"We're only laughing because what you think was a punishment Clare wants for a treat," she said. "But Granny – it's only because Clare has good manners that she wants the Ps and Qs pinned on, she knows quite well that she wouldn't have the paper letters pinned on her for more than five minutes!"

"Did you have them on for hours and hours, Granny?" asked Sam, solemnly staring at her. Then Granny began to laugh too.

"I can't remember," she said. "Now – let's finish up the biscuits, shall we? They're so nice."

After tea Clare went out into the garden to pick the daffodils. They were lovely. "You're dancing!" said Clare. "Do you like the wind, daffodils? Yes, you do, because you're nodding your heads at me!"

She counted them. There were fifty-three. "Twenty-nine yesterday, fifty-three today," she said. "I can pick them all but thirty – how many's that?'

It was a nice big bunch. Clare picked some of the long

green leaves too. She was just turning to go when she heard a voice.

"I say!"

Clare stood still, startled. Where did the voice come from? She looked all round but couldn't see anyone. It came again, more urgently.

"I *say!*"

"Where are you?" said Clare. "I can't see you. Are you in the garden?"

"Yes. Here," said the voice, and from behind a thick tangled mass of bushes stepped the boy. *The* boy – the one who had been in the fight with Francis, and who had been smacked and pummelled by Clare only an hour or so ago.

"What are you doing in our garden?" said Clare, at once. "You're trespassing! Go away. I shall go and tell my mother at once if you don't!"

"No, listen," said the boy. "I'm not trespassing really. I want to speak to your brother – what's his name – Francis, isn't it? It's very urgent."

"What do you want to speak to him about?" demanded Clare. "I don't like you. You're a horrid boy. You go away or I'll yell for my mother."

"No, please don't," said the boy, and he came nearer. "Please fetch your brother. *Please* do."

Clare stared at him. His eyes were red. He was crying! A big boy like that! Whatever was the matter?

"I'll fetch Francis," she said. "Wait here."

Clare flew off to find Francis, the daffodils still in her hands. What was that boy crying about? She had never seen such a big boy cry before. It seemed quite shocking. Even Sam hardly ever cried.

"Francis!" she called. "Francis! Where are you?"

43

"Well, what about your dog?"

"He's up in his room," said Granny. "Don't shout só, Clare. You made me jump."

Clare flew past Granny and past her father in his wheelchair. She ran upstairs to Francis's room. He was there getting ready his Scout uniform for a meeting next day.

Clare ran in and shut the door, panting. "What's up?" said Francis, surprised.

"Francis – you know that boy you fought – the one I jumped on this afternoon, who took Paddy away from you? Well, he's out in the dell and he wants you."

"What for?" said Francis, with a scowl. "Another fight?"

"No. He's crying," said Clare, dropping her voice. Francis looked at her in surprise.

"Crying? What for? I bet he's not. He's too big!"

"He *is*, I tell you. I ordered him out of the garden, but he still kept on begging me to fetch you. I think he must be in trouble of some sort."

"Well, he can't expect *me* to get him out of it," said Francis grimly, getting up. "I don't feel at all friendly towards him. All right – I'll go and see what he wants."

44

"Shall I come too?" asked Clare.

"No. I'll call you if I want to. And warn Sam not to come butting in," said Francis. "I'll take him into the stables and see what he wants."

He went downstairs. Clare followed him, and got a vase from the cupboard to put the daffodils in for the table. She wondered and wondered what the boy had come for. She simply couldn't imagine. She found Sam and told him. He couldn't imagine either.

Francis found the boy behind a bush at the back of the dell. He wasn't crying, but his eyes were still red. He smiled weakly at Francis when he saw him coming.

"What's up?" said Francis. "I call it cheek of you to come here and send my sister for me."

"It isn't really," said the boy. "Something awful's happened – and I thought you might help."

"Come into the stables," said Francis, and led the way. "We'll be alone there. I can't think how I can help you, and I don't feel as if I want to."

The boy went into the stables after Francis, and the door was shut behind them. "Now," said Francis. "Tell me what's the matter."

"It's my dog," said the boy, and swallowed hard. "My dog, Rex." He stopped and couldn't go on.

"Well, what about your dog?" asked Francis. "I don't see what your dog has to do with me. I don't feel *interested* in your dog after your behaviour to me."

"I know. I'm sorry about that now," said the boy. "It was mean of me. But I've been punished for it – because my dog – my very own dog – is going to be taken away from me."

"Not because of our fight!" said Francis, astonished.

"No. No one knows about that," said the boy. "Look, my name's Dan Oldham, and I live in one of the new flats in that big block not far off. And we've just been told that no one is allowed to keep pets in the flats. See?"

"Oh. So you can't keep Rex," said Francis. "That's bad luck!"

"Bad luck! It's worse than bad luck!" said Dan, and his eyes began to swell with tears again. "He's going to be sent away for good, to my Uncle Tom. He doesn't like dogs, so old Rex will be chained up all day long, he'll never have a walk – and – and I expect they'll forget his water and won't give him enough straw, and . . ."

He couldn't say any more. He rubbed his hands over his eyes and turned away. "I'm an idiot, I know," he said. "But I've had him for five years, and he's *mine*. Fancy never seeing him again, or feeling him lick me, or jump up at me to welcome me home! You've never had a dog of your own, so you don't know."

"I can guess, though," said Francis. "How awful, Dan! Won't they really let you keep him?"

"No. My Dad says we'll be turned out of the flat if we keep any pets. We didn't know that before we came. Well, Mum won't be turned out of her nice new flat – she waited for it for years. So Rex has got to go. I only heard this evening, just after I'd left that kid sister and brother of yours." Dan sat down on a box and ran his hands through his mop of hair.

"Why did you come to me?" said Francis after a while.

"To ask you something. To *beg* you really," said Dan. "You love dogs, don't you? I know you do, because of that pretend dog you had. I'm terribly sorry I laughed at you now: this seems a sort of judgement on me for being beastly. Well – I want to know this – could you have my dog here for me? You've got a big garden,

46

there's plenty of room. I'd bring his food for him, and take him for walks . . ."

Francis sat silent. Dan looked at him beseechingly. He put out his hand and touched Francis on the arm.

"You're a Scout. Have you done your good deed for today? This would be the very best good deed you ever did!"

Francis looked at him. "I've done two good deeds today," he said. "But there's no reason why I shouldn't do a third, if . . ."

Dan leapt up in excitement, his eyes shining. "Do you mean you'll have Rex?" he almost shouted.

"Sit down and listen," said Francis. "And don't get too excited, because I can't for the life of me see how we're going to manage a dog here. I don't believe Daddy would allow one. Mother would say he left dirty foot-marks just when she had cleaned the floor . . ."

"But hasn't your mother got someone to help her in this big house?" said Dan wonderingly. "She doesn't do everything herself, does she?"

"*We* help, of course," said Francis. "But we're poor, because my father got hurt in the war and he can't work. And then there's my Granny – now let me see. I don't know about Granny. She simply *loves* animals – but we had to send her dog Thumper away, because he was a Great Dane and ate too much, and it nearly broke her heart. She might not want another dog."

"I see," said Dan. "Well – need we tell anyone? Rex is an *awfully* good dog. He won't bark unless burglars come, and you wouldn't mind that, would you? And I'll feed him and look after him, and everything, if you don't mind me coming into your garden. Honestly, Rex won't be a bit of a nuisance. You'll love him."

"I expect I should," said Francis, a little stir of

excitement coming over him at the thought of a dog in the garden. "If I *do* get to like him, I might want to take him for a few walks myself, Dan."

There was a pause, "Well," said Dan at last, "we could take him for walks together. Er – I want to pay you for keeping Rex for me Francis. I get half-a-crown a week pocketmoney, but Mum pays for Rex's food. If I give you two shillings a week, would that be enough for you? I'll give you the whole half-crown, of course, if it isn't."

"I wouldn't want any pay," said Francis, going red. "I'm a Scout. I do good deeds for nothing. If you were a Scout you'd understand."

"Golly!" said Dan, "there's something in being a Scout if it makes you like that. Francis – are you going to *try* keeping Rex for me? I'll make it up to you somehow, I really will, even if you won't let me pay you in money. Come on."

"I'm going to call Clare and Sam," said Francis. "I'll see what they say." He went out of the stables and shouted for his brother and sister. They came at once, for they had been hanging about hopefully near the stables.

Soon all four were having a great discussion. As soon as Clare and Sam heard of Dan's trouble they were on his side at once. Fights and quarrels were forgotten. Rex was the only thing that mattered.

"Of *course* we'll have Rex," said Clare. "Have you forgotten how you got that old kennel clean, and put straw in it, Francis?"

"No. I hadn't forgotten," said Francis. "It's almost as if it had been got ready for this very thing. It's right out of the way too – nobody ever goes into that part of the garden. We could put some wire round and make a kind of little yard, so that Rex wouldn't stray into the other part and give himself away."

"Yes. We *must* keep this a secret," said Clare. "I don't believe Mother or Daddy or Granny would want Rex – for various reasons. He must be a secret. A secret! What a *lovely* secret! A dog of our own!"

"No." said Dan at once. "He'll still be mine, *all* mine. That's understood."

"But we can share him, can't we?" said Clare. "He sounds such a nice dog, Dan – you won't mind, surely, if we get fond of him?"

"Well – we'll see," said Dan, jealously. "Anyway, I can't stop you doing what you like. You're my only hope. And it's jolly decent of you to help me, considering the mean thing I did to Francis."

"We've forgotten that," said Francis. "We don't ever need to mention it again."

"I'm sorry I hit you so hard now," said Dan. "You must have had an awful eye."

"I said forget it," said Francis impatiently. "Let's talk about when and how we're going to have Rex."

"Could he come on Saturday?" asked Dan. "That's when all dogs have to be out of the flats. I'll bring him then – and his own blanket and bowls. He'll be miserable at first, but if I tell him I'm coming next day and warn him not to whine, he'll be as good as gold."

"Goodness, does he understand everything you say?" said Clare.

"Pretty well," said Dan. "My word, it's a load off my heart, I can tell you. You're jolly decent kids – and if ever I can do something in return I will."

Rex was well and truly discussed. The three children felt as if they knew him very well indeed when they had heard all that Dan had to say about him.

"You know," said Dan, at last, "it's a very queer thing that your sister said to me this afternoon. 'You be careful that your dog doesn't come to my brother!' And I laughed. But sure enough, it's happened."

"Yes, it was funny I said that," said Clare, looking startled. "Very strange."

Dan got up to go. He held out his hand solemnly to Francis. "Many thanks," he said. "I'll never forget this."

"That's all right," said Francis, and shook hands vigorously. Clare held out her hand, and then Sam held out his.

This rather solemn moment was broken suddenly by Granny's voice. "Francis! Clare! Sam! Where in the world are you? Francis!"

"We must go," said Francis. "Stay here till we've gone indoors, then slip out home. See you on Saturday – and good luck, Dan!"

Chapter Four

AN EXCITING SECRET

The three children were so excited at the idea of keeping Dan's dog for him that they could talk of nothing else when they were by themselves.

"Won't it be *lovely*?" said Clare. "I know he'll still be Dan's dog, but he'll really seem like our own."

"I hope it doesn't matter not telling anyone," said Francis. "But I can't see that we are doing anything but help someone in trouble. I wonder what Rex is like – Dan said he was a sort of spaniel."

"I shall like him anyhow," said Sam.

Granny put her head round the door of Clare's bedroom, where they were all sitting talking. "What are you discussing up here so secretly?" she asked. "Clare, your mother is doing the ironing – will you go and help her? A Brownie promises to help in the house, you know."

Clare frowned. She did help in the house. In fact, she was very good in the house, doing plenty of jobs when she would much rather have been reading or playing. "I'm coming, Granny," she said, rather shortly.

"Well, you needn't say it like that," said Granny, who seemed cross. "I oughtn't to have to come and fetch you."

"You could have *called* me," said Clare sulkily as she went out of the room. Oh dear, why did Granny always rub her up the wrong way? Granny was so very kind at heart, she would do anything for any of them – but she was always after them for something, especially Clare! Clare went slowly down the stairs, still frowning – but before she reached the bottom she began thinking about Dan's dog again, and she skipped the last three stairs in delight.

Great plans were being made by the three children. "There's some wire netting in the stables," said Francis. "I *think* there's enough to make a kind of yard for the dog – big enough for him to run up and down in, anyway."

"We shall want some stakes to hold up the wire here and there," said Clare. "Have we any?"

"Yes," said Sam. "I know where." Sam knew where everything was. He knew every corner of the house and garden. When anyone wanted anything they always went to Sam.

"Good. Then you can find the stakes and bring them," said Francis. "Good thing we've got the kennel – such a nice one too. Plenty of room for Rex."

"Yes. And all cleaned out, with straw and everything ready!" said Clare. "I'll give Rex fresh water every day. I shall like to do that."

"No. That's my job," said Francis at once. "Remember, Dan asked *me* to look after Rex. I'm responsible for him."

"Well – I expect *Dan* will want to give him his fresh water," said Clare. "He doesn't really want us to look after Rex, he's jealous that we should – but he's just got to let us because if we don't he'll lose him."

"He can't give him water," said Sam. "The tap is in the scullery, and he'd be seen going there."

"Yes. That's true," said Francis. They fell silent, thinking of all the things they might do for Rex. Sam began to whistle.

"Don't!" said Clare. "Your whistle is dreadful, Sam. Why do you keep *on* whistling?"

"I was only whistling because I feel happy," said Sam, looking hurt. "I was whistling 'Its a hap-hap-happy day.'"

"Well, nobody would know it," said Clare. "It might just as well have been 'God save the Queen.' I wish you hadn't learnt to whistle, Sam. You drive Granny mad."

"All right. I'll try not to," said poor Sam. "But it sort of comes whenever I feel specially happy."

"Whistle, then," said Francis, giving him a friendly punch. "I know that feeling."

"We ought to go and talk to Rex as much as we can," said Clare. "He'll be lonely without Dan."

Everyone agreed heartily. "I shall clean out his kennel," said Sam firmly.

"You will not," said Francis, just as firmly. "That's my job."

"Don't be mean. Take it in turns," said Clare. "As a Brownie, I think that's the right thing to do."

"As a Cub, I agree," said Sam, solemnly. They all laughed.

"This dog is going to be terribly spoilt," said Francis. "Wouldn't it be dreadful if he didn't like us?"

This was an awful thought. Clare changed the subject. "We'll have to hope that none of the grown-ups discover Rex," she said. "It's a pity to have to keep him a secret from them – but it would be so dreadful if Rex was sent away to Dan's horrid uncle."

"I'm going to find the wire netting," said Francis, getting up. "Mother and Granny are out. Only Daddy is in. It's a good moment to go."

"Poor old Daddy. He'd like to join in this, I'm sure, and help to put up the wire," said Clare. "I wish his back would get better. I wish he was like other fathers, and could work and get about and enjoy things. He's so *patient*, sitting there always, watching other people rush about."

"Yes, and each time the doctor thinks of some new treatment, he's as excited as we are about Rex – and then it comes to nothing, and he's back where he was," said Francis.

"When I'm grown up," said Sam, seriously, "I'm going to be a doctor – a very clever one. And the first thing I'm going to do is to cure Daddy."

"You've said that about a hundred times," said Clare. "But I quite believe you. You hardly ever change your mind about anything, like I do. Do come on. Mummy will be back before we've done a thing."

They got the wire netting, and Sam found the stakes in the heap of junk in the harness room. They were just right. Francis got the pliers, and they dragged the wire and the stakes to the distant corner of the big garden. It was right out of sight of the house, and as there was no path anywhere near it, it was a perfect spot to hide a dog. Bushes and trees screened the corner from view.

The kennel stood there, big and clean, straw sticking out of it. Sam rubbed his hands and began to whistle loudly. Clare laughed.

"Happy again?" she said. "Get a move on, Sam. Francis will soon be ready for the stakes. Untie them."

The three children were very busy indeed for about an hour. The wire was unrolled and set up. Francis clipped it to size with the pliers. He forgot what sharp edges cut wire netting has, and got severely scratched on his right hand.

"You're bleeding!" said Sam. "I'll get the iodine," and he tore off on his short legs.

"Don't fuss!" shouted Francis.

"He's not fussing," said Clare. "Cuts like that ought to be cleaned out. If Rex cut his leg you'd clean it and put iodine on it, wouldn't you? Well, you're better than a dog! It won't take a minute."

Sam came walking back. None of them ever ran when they were carrying bottles, it was such a silly thing to do. Granny had taught them that very thoroughly, and had shown them a terrible scar inside her right hand which had been caused by a piece of broken glass.

"I ran with a glass vase," she said. "I fell, and the vase broke and almost cut my hand in half. So don't you be silly, like me!"

Francis's hand was bound up with a bit of rag, and he went on with his work. Sam drove stakes into the wire at intervals, and the netting held up nice and straight. There was just enough to go all round the piece they had chosen for the dog-run.

It looked good when it was finished. There was no gate, but the wire was low enough for them all to jump over, though Sam could only just clear it. It was quite high enough to keep a dog in – unless it was a dog that could jump very well indeed.

Francis pulled all the straw out of the kennel and then put it back again. "You flattened it down terribly, Sam, when you got into the kennel," he said. "A dog likes nice loose straw he can cuddle into."

"He'll flatten it down just as I did," said Sam.

"We can make his bed freshly each day," said Clare. "I wish it was Saturday!"

Saturday came at last – and with it came Dan, leading Rex, his dog. He came in at the back gate, where all three children were waiting for him in excitement.

"Hallo!" said Dan, who looked extremely serious; but

Very busy indeed

then it *was* serious business to hand over a dog in this way. "Rex – shake paws!"

Rex held out his right paw, and shook hands solemnly with Francis, then with Clare, then with Sam. Sam shook it and shook it and shook it. Rex didn't seem to mind.

"That's enough," said Dan. "Don't shake his paw off. Well – what do you think of him?"

The children looked at Rex admiringly. He was

He was certainly a sort of spaniel

certainly a *sort* of spaniel, but not quite. He was a bit too big, and his tail was too long – but he had the beautiful, melting brown eyes of the true spaniel, and the long, drooping, silky ears. He looked up at the children and wagged his tail vigorously.

"He's beautiful!" said Clare, and dropped down on her knees to pet him.

"He's a real dog!" said Francis, and patted the silky coat. "A proper *doggy* kind of dog!"

"I like him very much," said Sam. "Very, very, very much."

Dan looked as if he was about to burst with pride and delight.

"I'm glad," he said gruffly and patted Rex. "He's not bad, and he's as good as gold. Er – I think you're awfully decent kids, all of you. I do really!"

Nobody answered. Rex was taking all their attention.

Pleased at so much fussing he rolled over on his back and pedalled his legs in the air, as if he was riding a bicycle with four pedals!

"Look at him!" said Clare, and tickled him.

Dan began to talk to Francis, telling him all his arrangements. "I told my Mum," he said. "She wasn't very pleased at first – Rex going to strangers. But I begged her so hard that she gave in. She thinks it's jolly decent of you."

"We shall love to have him," said Francis. "What about his food? Will you bring it every day or what?"

"Yes. I'll come and feed him," said Dan. "And I'll come and take him for a walk whenever I can. But you will have to give him fresh water – do you mind?"

"We'd love to," said Francis. "I say – haven't you kept him well? His coat is like silk, and even his ears are brushed."

"Yes, and his feathers too," said Dan proudly.

"Oh, where are his feathers?" said Sam, looking Rex all over in surprise. "I thought he only had fur."

"The shaggy fur at the back of his legs is called 'feathers'," said Dan, with a laugh. "Well, I must go. Goodbye, Rex, old boy. Be good. I'll come and see you this evening!"

The back gate slammed. Dan was gone. Rex stood listening, and gave a little whine. Where was his beloved master?

"It's all right," said Francis, and patted him. But Rex didn't think so. He ran at the wire and found that he couldn't get out. He ran all round, but found no opening. He sat down and whined again.

The children made a fuss of him, afraid that he might bark. But he didn't. He suddenly got up and walked to the kennel, looked at it with interest. He went right inside and sniffed round. The children could hear his sniffs quite well. They sounded quite pleased sniffs.

There was a little thud – and Rex peeped out of the kennel. He had flopped down on the straw, and was now looking out of the entrance, master in his own little house.

"He likes it! He knows it's his," said Sam, in delight. "Look at him!"

They all gazed at Rex, who looked at them out of his trusting brown eyes. Then he suddenly got up, walked out of his kennel and licked first Francis, and then Sam, then Clare. Then he went to his water bowl and drank noisily.

"He ought to have something to eat," said Clare. "He's got nothing he can nibble at if he feels hungry. What about a chocolate biscuit, Francis? I've got one in my room that I saved up."

"No, certainly not," said Francis at once. "Chocolate will make him fat. He's going to be fed properly, like a dog. And I think we ought to let Dan feed him; not even give him snacks ourselves. It wouldn't be fair."

"I would like to buy him a bone to gnaw," said Sam. "I shall ask Dan."

"Oh dear – I suppose we ought to leave Rex and go back to the house," said Clare. "You've got a Scouts' meeting this morning, haven't you Francis? And I've got to help Mummy. Sam, you've got to run the errands."

"I know," said Sam. "But Mother said not till half-past ten. It isn't that yet. You two go. I'll stay with Rex till half-past ten, in case he's lonely."

The other two didn't much like leaving Sam in sole possession of the spaniel. It might be more friendly with him than with them! Still – it would be nice for Rex to have company for a little while. So the two elder ones went off together. They heard Sam beginning to whistle very loudly indeed.

"Sam's happy," said Clare. "Hear him whistling! Isn't Rex *nice*, Francis? Isn't it exciting to have a secret like this?"

They went happily to their jobs, hugging their secret, longing for a minute to spare to rush down to the spaniel.

Mother was wondering where they were. "I've called and called!" she said. "Where were you?"

"In the garden," said Francis. "Sorry, Mother."

"What *were* you doing?" said Granny. "I couldn't find even one of you!"

Francis and Clare didn't know what to answer to that, so they said nothing. They did hope that Granny wouldn't poke and probe into their secret. Mother never did that. But dear old Granny couldn't seem to rest unless she knew everyone's thoughts and doings.

Certainly Granny grew very curious that day as first Clare disappeared when her jobs were done, and then when Sam had done the errands, he disappeared too. When Francis came back from his Scouts' meeting just before dinner, he changed into ordinary things – and then he disappeared as well!

"Where are they?" wondered Granny. "Now they've *all* gone!"

"Let them be," said Daddy. "It's a lovely day. I expect they've got some secret out in the garden – building a little house, or climbing some tree. They've all done their jobs, and done them well. Let them alone, Granny."

"*Well*! Anyone would think I was always after them, to hear you talk!" said Granny. "They're my grandchildren, aren't they? And they're living in my house, aren't they? Can't I wonder where they are?"

"I wish you'd sell the house and let us go into a smaller one!" said Daddy wearily. "All that work for my poor wife — and the children too. We'd have a much easier time in a small house. I know I'm an old crock, not able to earn anything or do anything, and it's dreadful to sit here and watch you all slaving yourselves to death!"

Tears began to run down Granny's cheeks. She went over to Daddy and patted his hand. "Poor boy," she said. "I know it's hard for you — but maybe the doctors will get you right one day, and then you'll be glad we kept this nice house and garden! It was my childhood home, and I lent it to you when you married my daughter, and it would break my heart to sell it and go."

"Yes, I understand," said Daddy. "*You* do more than you should, too — I know that. But I can't bear watching you all doing things and not being able to help at all, except peel apples and potatoes and shell the peas! It makes me crotchety, it makes us all on edge with each other. A family should live in unity and peace and kindliness. Sometimes we don't."

Granny wiped her eyes and made up her mind to go straight out that afternoon and buy sweets for the children, new stockings for their mother, and some cigarettes for their father.

"I'm a bad old woman," she said. "Cross and pernickety and nagging. Aren't I, Mr Black?"

The enormous black cat had come gliding into the room, his yellow eyes shining. He leapt straight up into the little old lady's arms, and purred loudly.

"You and that cat!" said Daddy, smiling. "He's the only person who never aggravates you, Granny!"

Granny squeezed Mr Black a little and he gave a small squeal and struggled to get down. Mother came into the room and looked round. "Where *are* the children?" she said. "Don't say they've disappeared again!"

They disappeared continually for the next week! It was arranged that out of school hours one of them should always be with Rex, if possible. He didn't bark, but he was inclined to whine if he knew the children were in the house. They were terribly afraid that somebody would hear him.

Dan came regularly every day, and took Rex for a long walk. The dog went nearly mad when he heard and saw him coming, but he never once barked. Dan had warned him not to and the intelligent creature understood.

Dan brought him meat each day, and biscuits. He inspected the water bowl to see that completely fresh water had been put into it. It always had. Francis made it one of the first jobs of his day.

One morning Dan saw that the kennel had been shifted round, and was now facing in another direction. "Why have you moved the kennel?" he asked. "It looks funny facing that way."

"Well," said Francis, "we've been having some very cold east winds the last two days, and Rex's kennel was facing east, so the wind blew straight in. And I couldn't help thinking how cold it must be to lie in a draughty east wind each night – so I shifted the kennel round. Now he ought to be nice and snug at night."

"You're a good friend to him," said Dan gratefully. "Doesn't he look well? He's happpy too, isn't he? Though I think he misses me awfully."

"Oh, he does," said Francis. "Everytime anyone

comes in at the back gate, he stands listening, hoping it's you. But he's quite happy. We all love him."

"Could you take him for a walk tomorrow?" said Dan. "I've got to go with my mother and visit my Granny, and I won't be able to come after tea and take him out. But he must have his walk."

Francis's eyes shone. "Oh yes. I'd love to take him. I never thought you'd let me. I say, doesn't it make a difference having a dog? I can't *think* what we did without Rex – always someone to pet and talk to and play with. And, you know, when I did the wrong homework the other day, and got kept in for an hour, I was jolly miserable – and Rex seemed to know, and he made a terrific fuss of me when I went to see him."

"Well, all dogs are like that," said Dan. "They always take your side, you know – rather like mothers do. All right then; I'll come and feed him tomorrow, but you'll take him for his walk. Many thanks!"

It was a real thrill for the children to go out with Rex. Granny was as inquisitive as ever when they said they all wanted to go off together for a walk. She even wanted to come too, and was quite upset when they politely said no, they were going too far for Granny.

They set off when they thought no one at the house was looking. They put Rex on his lead until they got out into the lanes. Then they slipped him off. He raced off madly and for one awful moment the children thought he wasn't coming back. "He won't go to try and find Dan, will he?" asked Clare.

"Rex! Heel!" called Francis. And the well-trained dog came back at once, and walked just behind him, his nose almost touching Francis's heel. It reminded him of Paddy, the dog he had invented only a little while ago. Francis laughed at himself.

"How silly I was! Still, he was better than nothing, even if he was only a shadow dog. Here, Rex – fetch this stick!"

They had a wonderful time with Rex, and they were all tired out when they got back to tea. Rex flopped down in his kennel with an enormous sigh, and put his silky head on his feet, his long ears spread out beside his head.

"I feel like that too, Rex," said Sam, "all floppy. I'm awfully hungry. I hope Granny won't ask us *too* many questions about our walk. I feel I might be silly and say something about Rex."

"You jolly well won't!" said Clare, in horror. "You'll get the biggest kick under the table that you ever got in your life if you do!"

Dan turned up the next day, beaming. "Did he like his walk? He says he did! Look, I've got something for you all. I bought them out of my pocket money. You wouldn't take any payment for looking after Rex, but I've got to do *something*!"

He held out a tin of boiled sweets. "Oh! How *nice* of you!" said Clare. "But – we want to look after Rex for love, not for payment."

"Go on, take them," said Dan. "My Mum said I ought to bring you sweets every week if you won't let me pay you."

"Well – we'll take them this week, thank you very much," said Francis. "But only this once, see? We *want* to look after Rex for nothing. We all like to do it for our good deeds, as well as because we like Rex."

"I never met kids like you before," said Dan. "Doing something for nothing! Most people want all they can get. Well, I'm glad you'll take the sweets this week. They're the best I could get for you. Don't give Rex any, will you? He's got beautiful teeth, and I don't want them spoilt."

"Things are going very well," said Francis, handing the tin of sweets round. "Very well indeed. Granny has given up asking where we disappear to – and I don't think our secret will ever be found out!"

But that was rather a silly thing to say. Because, the very next week, it *was* found out!

Chapter Five

A BIT OF GOOD LUCK

Granny found out about Rex first. It was all because of Mr Black, her cat. He often went bird-catching, and was always most annoyed because as soon as he got within pouncing distance of a bird, it at once flew up into the air, sat on a bough, and sang rude things at him.

Mr Black didn't like that. He wasn't at all good at bird-catching, fortunately, because he was too big and heavy to run fast – and also he was very easily seen. The birds always set up a great clamour when they saw him in the garden.

"Look out, look out! The cat's about!" sang the thrush.

"Beware, beware. The cat is here!" fluted the blackbird.

"Pimm-im-im-im! I see him-im-im-im!" called the bluetit who was nesting in the orchard.

One morning, when the children were at school, Mr Black went bird-hunting again. He saw a fat blackbird, and stalked him warily, keeping behind bushes, never once treading on a twig or a rustling leaf. He was as good as a Red Indian!

The blackbird led him a fine dance, hopping on well ahead. He led him right down to where Rex's yard was. Then he flew up into a tree and called Mr Black such dreadful names that Mr Black couldn't bear it. He leapt right up into the tree as high as he could after the cheeky bird.

The blackbird flew away. Mr Black sat down on the

bough and began to wash himself. He always did that when a bird or mouse had got the better of him. It was just to show the world that *he* didn't care, anyway!

He heard a noise down below and looked to see what made it. What he saw down there made him swell up to twice his size, and the fur on his tail swelled too, so that Mr Black was a truly ferocious sight.

What he saw was Rex, the spaniel, lying down in the sun fast asleep. A dog! A dog in Mr Black's own garden! How dare he!

Mr Black hissed and spat. Rex woke up with a jump. Birdsong and bird calls never distrubed him – but the unusual spitting, hissing noise woke him up at once.

He leapt up and looked round, growling. Mr Black spat again, and Rex looked up. He was amazed to see such an enormous black creature in the tree above his kennel. *Was* it a cat? He had never seen such a big one before.

He growled again. Mr Black hissed. He didn't dare to get down for he didn't realize that Rex was penned in; he was afraid that the dog would catch him as he slid down the tree trunk.

So Mr Black sat up there, hissing and spitting, and Rex got more and more excited, running round his pen, trying to find a way out so that he could jump up against the tree trunk near by.

He forgot that he mustn't bark. He gave a small bark and then a louder one. Then he got so excited that he almost barked the place down, and Mr Black determined to stay up the tree for weeks, if necessary, rather than face this fierce dog.

Granny was alone in the house. Mother had gone to the shops and had taken Daddy in his wheelchair. Granny didn't take any notice of the barks at first. Then as they went on and on, louder and louder, more and more excited, she sat up and frowned.

"Where is that barking dog?" she said. "What a dreadful noise! Who keeps a dog that barks like that? I really must complain. And where is Mr Black? He usually comes rushing in if he hears a dog bark. Mr Black! Mr Black, where are you?"

But as Mr Black was high up in the oak tree over the kennel, he didn't come. Granny called again and again, and all the while she could hear Rex barking madly.

"Oh! I *hope* it's not Mr Black he's barking at!" she thought, suddenly. "I must go and see." So out into the garden she went, in the direction of the barks. And, of course, she came to the dog-run at the bottom of the garden, where Rex was barking his head off! She didn't see Mr Black at first. She was so tremendously aston-ished to see a dog in a little yard, with a kennel, that she had eye for nothing else!

"A dog!" she said. "A dog penned up in the yard here! So *that's* where the children have been disappearing to for the last week or so – they've come down here to the dog. What an *extraordinary* thing! Wherever did they get the dog? And why didn't they tell anybody?"

Rex saw Granny. He stopped barking and looked at her. He ran to the netting and stood against it, his forepaws pressing the wire. He whined. He felt sure this old lady liked animals.

Granny put her hand over the wire and patted his silky head. "What lovely eyes you have!" she said. "Real spaniel eyes, melting and beseeching! What are you doing here?"

"Woof," said Rex, and wagged his tail.

"How do I get into your yard?" wondered Granny.

There was Granny bending over Rex

"There's no gate. I suppose the children just jump over. Well, I can climb over somehow, I suppose."

Then she suddenly saw Mr Black – and heard him too, because he gave a loud wailing yowl that startled Granny very much. "Oh, so *there* you are!" she said, looking up into the tree. "*That's* where you've got to! Stalking birds again, I suppose, and came too near this dog. You can get down – the dog can't get you."

Granny somehow managed to climb over the wire netting, and got into the little yard. Rex flung himself on her as if she were a long-lost friend. He licked her, and fussed round her, and whined. Anybody would have thought he was Granny's dog!

"You're a good dog," she said, patting him. "It's a long time since I had a dog. Well, well, well – I can't get over this! Do you *belong* to the children?"

"Woof," said Rex, and lay on his back to be tickled –

and just as Granny was bending over him, tickling him and making him squirm in delight, the children came home! They did what they always did; ran to see if Rex was all right.

And goodness gracious, there was Granny in the little yard, bending over Rex, and tickling him and talking to him. *Granny!*

They stopped in amazement. Rex heard them and leapt up, running to the wire to welcome them. He loved these children!

"Granny!" said Clare. "Oh, Granny! You've found Rex!"

"Yes," said Granny, looking quite guilty. "He barked at Mr Black – up there in the tree – and I came to see what the matter was. Whose dog is he? Yours?"

"Granny, are you cross about it?" asked Sam, jumping over the wire and going up to her. "It's our secret. We didn't tell *you* because we thought you might not want any dog after your Thumper had had to be sent away. We didn't tell Mother because we thought she wouldn't like a dog racing about and messing the floors with muddy feet. And we didn't tell Daddy because it might worry him."

"I see," said Granny. "I understand all that. But whose dog *is* he? You haven't told me yet. Is he yours?"

Then the whole thing had to come out. Clare and Francis told their secret, standing in the yard with Granny, while Rex and Sam played with one another and listened.

"Granny, *dear* Granny, please keep our secret," begged Clare, earnestly, when she had finished her story. "You can see how important it is to Dan, can't you? He loves Rex like you loved Thumper."

"But Mother might not mind at all," began Granny,

and then, as she saw the look on the children's faces, she nodded her head. "All right. Don't look like that. I know that it's only to save your mother worry and bother that you want your secret kept. I won't be a spoilsport! I'll keep it!"

She was almost swept off her feet by three grateful children and Rex, who thrilled with the sudden excitement of his friends, flung himself on Granny with the rest. Granny began to laugh.

"Oh, set me free! You're choking me! I do promise you this – that as long as Rex is happy here and doesn't make a noise, I'll keep your secret. But Mother may quite well come down to this bit of the garden some time, you know, and find out for herself!"

"She never comes down here," said Sam. "She doesn't like this part. She says it's so untidy."

Granny was really just as thrilled as the children about Rex. She went to visit him when they were at school. She bought him a very big bone, which he at once buried in the depths of his kennel, in case Mr Black should see it. She made such a fuss of him that it was just as well he was a good well-trained dog, or he would have been quite spoilt!

Dan wasn't very pleased that Granny knew, nor was he very pleased when he heard that she was giving him bones! "*I* want to feed him," he said. "His straw will get full of bones! And who's been brushing him? I do that, you know."

"Well, we all do it, actually," said Clare. "He's so nice to brush and he does love it so. Granny bought him a brush yesterday – a nice scratchy one that he loves."

"You should hear Sam when he brushes him," said Francis, with a sudden giggle. "He whistles *all* the time

71

just as if he were grooming a horse! On and on and on, without any tune at all."

"I don't," said Sam. "I have a tune. You're mean about my whistling."

"Do you suppose Rex is safe, now your Granny knows?" said Dan. "Grown-ups do sometimes give things away, you know – to one another, I mean."

"Oh yes, he's safe enough. Mother will never guess!" said Clare. "I tell you she never comes down here, and Granny has *promised* not to tell – and she always keeps her word, always."

Mother did wonder why Granny kept disappearing, though. She had got used to the children disappearing and thought nothing of it now – but she kept missing Granny! Whenever she went to ask her something Granny wasn't there. She wasn't anywhere in the house!

"Dear me – she must have got very fond of the garden all of a sudden," thought Mother. But she didn't go down to see what the old lady was doing. Mother never interfered with anyone, and she was glad that Granny seemed so happy these days.

In fact, it is quite possible that she would never, never have found out about Rex if something rather extraordinary hadn't happened one morning. Mother was in the kitchen making a pudding when there came a knock on the back door.

"If that's the laundry, just bring it in," called Mother. "My hands are all floury."

The door opened – but it wasn't the laundry. It was a small, pleasant-faced woman who Mother didn't know.

"Excuse me," she said. "I'm Dan's mother, and I've come to say thank you very much for letting your children look after his dog for him."

Well! Mother stared at her in amazement. "What *do*

you mean?" she said. "A dog? *I've* never heard of one! I think you must have made a mistake!"

The woman at the door looked as surprised as Mother. "But – this *is* Green Meadows, isn't it?" she said. "And you *are* Mrs Marshall, aren't you – mother of Francis, Clare, and Sam?"

"Yes," said Mother, even more surpirsed. "But how do you know about us? And what is this about a dog? There isn't one here! I ought to know!"

"Oh," said the woman. "Well, I'm Mrs Oldham, mother of Dan, who owns the dog. He told me all about your three. He once had a fight with your Francis, I think – and then somehow they made friends over the dog, and when my Dan was told he couldn't have his dog in our flat, he was upset; and he came to ask your Francis if he'd look after him in your big garden."

"And did Francis say he would?" asked Mother, more and more astonished. "I've not heard a word about this. But dear me – perhaps that's why the children keep disappearing. They go to look after the dog. But why didn't they tell me? It's not like them to do something behind my back."

"Well, Mrs Marshall – I'll tell you what my son said about keeping the dog down the garden," said Mrs Oldham, and she came right into the kitchen. "He said that your three didn't want you to be *worried* with a dog in the house, running about dirtying the floors – he said you'd nobody to help you to clean or cook, and the children didn't want to give you any more trouble; and a dog *is* a trouble and a nuisance sometimes. So they put him at the bottom of the garden. But Dan never told me you didn't know."

Mother took all this in, still full of astonishment. "Let's go down the garden and see if we can find this dog," she said. So, floury hands and all, she led the way down the garden, followed by Mrs Oldham.

And there, in the little yard, was Rex – and dear me, with him was Granny, brushing him vigorously with the new brush she had bought. Rex was loving it.

"Granny!" said Mother, amazed. "So *you* knew about the dog! And you kept it from me too. I really don't know *what* to say!"

Rex nearly went mad when he saw Dan's mother. He thought she had come to fetch him back home to the flat, and he tried his hardest to jump over the wire netting. Mrs Oldham leaned over and patted him. "You do look well!" she said. "All silky and shiny. My, you've found some good friends!"

The three women began to talk, and soon Mother knew everything. "A dog in the garden and I never knew," she said. "Those children!"

"Don't be cross with them" begged Mrs Oldham. "They did it out of the kindness of their hearts, to help my Dan. And do you know, they won't let him pay them a penny for looking after the dog and giving him the kennel and all! Not a penny. Dan says they won't even let him give them sweets now."

"No, I don't expect they will," said Mother. "They've been taught not to want payment for any kindness they do."

"Well, now, look here," said Mrs Oldham, a sudden firmness coming into her voice. "Two can think that way! You won't take anything for doing a kindness; well, I won't accept a kindness without doing one in return. Fair's fair, isn't it?"

Mother laughed. "Yes, that's fair enough. I understand that. I like to return a kindness too."

"Good," said Mrs Oldham. "Now will you let me do

you a kindness, then? Just to make things square between us?"

"What sort of kindness?" asked Mother cautiously.

"I'll tell you," said the little woman, beaming. "I haven't got enough to do in my little flat – so I go out and work in other people's houses now and again. For money, of course, because that's work. And I'd like to come to you for a morning a week, and do anything you want me to do – for *nothing*, because that would be a pleasure, and I'd feel I was returning your kindness."

"Oh no!" said Mother. But Granny interrupted.

"Oh yes!" she said, feeling a great liking for this pleasant-faced little woman. "Oh *yes*! What a wonderful thing it would be for you to have one whole morning a week free – you're working all day long every day of the week. Yes, Mrs Oldham, we accept with pleasure, it's a very kind thought of yours."

And before Mother could say another word, the two of them had fixed it up together. Mrs Oldham would come every Wednesday – and yes, she would do the whole of the kitchen – and dear me, of course she could do a bit of cooking – and she could go over all the rooms too! That was nothing!

They all went back to the house, feeling pleasantly excited. Rex whined dolefully when he saw them go – but very soon the children were home and he greeted them joyfully, trying to tell them of all the visitors he had had that afternoon.

They ran up to the house for dinner. Mother was just finishing her preparations because she had got very behind. She looked up smiling.

"Hallo, dears! Would you like to take this bone down to Rex?"

The three children stared, completely taken aback.

What had Mother said? She laughed. "All right – I know your secret! Mrs Oldham came this morning, and I soon found out everything. It was sweet of you not to want to worry me, but Rex won't bother me a bit. You can let him come into the house whenever you want to. He's a very nice dog."

Well, what a tremendous surprise! Sam flung himself on his mother. "Oh Mother, I do love you! You always say the right things. Can I go and get Rex now, this very minute, at once?"

"Yes, now, this very minute, at once, if not sooner!" said Mother, and everyone laughed to see Sam's feet twinkling fast down the garden path.

Rex was a great success in the house. He made friends with Daddy, at once, and soon learnt not to lean too heavily against his legs. Granny loved having him about, and Mother didn't seem to mind at all, not even when his feet *were* muddy!

Sam tried to teach Rex to wipe his feet, and spent ages lifting up one foot after another, wiping each one carefully on the mat. But Rex just wouldn't learn!

Clare was pleased to hear that Mrs Oldham was coming in a whole morning each week to help. She knew better than the boys, what that meant to her mother. And Mrs Oldham proved to be the greatest help possible. She simply didn't mind *what* she did, and often she came popping in to say she was going to town to the shops, could she fetch anything for Mother?

The only person who couldn't bear Rex coming into the house was Mr Black. He was very dignified about it, but he liked to give Rex a good slap if he came too near – and he hated to see Granny making a fuss of the spaniel.

"Mr Black's sulking again!" Clare would say. "Look,

Granny, he's turned his back on you. Mr Black, turn round."

But Mr Black wouldn't. He sat there haughtily, his back to everyone, and wouldn't turn round at all until somebody said "Dinner". Then he looked round quickly.

Dan came to tea the next week, very clean and well-brushed and neat. "You do look tidy," said Sam. "I've never seen you like this before."

"Well – my Mum's always going on at me because I don't look like you do," said Dan. "She thinks the world of your family. She thinks your mother's tops!"

To say that anyone was "tops" was the highest compliment Dan could pay. The children were pleased. *They* knew that their mother was "tops", but it was nice to hear someone else say so.

Dan enjoyed coming to tea very much, but he was disappointed when Francis had to leave immediately afterwards to go to a Scout meeting. He gazed at him enviously.

"You do look fine, all rigged up like that, badges and all. Can I try on your hat?"

He tried it on and looked at himself in the glass. He gave it back to Francis. "I wish I was coming too," he said.

"Well, why don't you?" said Francis, surprisingly. "Why don't you become a Scout? We want a few more in my patrol. We could do with someone like you."

"Golly!" said Dan. "Do you know, I never thought of being a Scout myself! I'll come along. They won't mind at the meeting, will they, if I come?"

So off he went with Francis. They took Rex with them, and he was delighted. He was always wildly pleased to see Dan, and never really considered himself to be

A kitten came to join the family

anyone else's dog, though the three children did their best to make him belong to them as well.

He loved having the free run of Green Meadows. Two or three times he had run off and disappeared, but he always came back sooner or later. He just ran off to Dan's flat when he felt homesick – but when Dan or Mrs Oldham sent him back again, he went quite obediently.

"He's really got *two* homes," said Sam to Dan, and Dan agreed.

One day Dan brought a girl about his age to see Francis and Clare. "This is Rita," he said. "She's come to live in the flat next door. She's got a kitten – and, of course, we mustn't have even kittens in our flats. Could you have her kitten till she gets a home for it? Her mother will pay for its food and milk."

"But what will Mr Black say?" said Clare. "He might go for it."

"I was wondering if you could keep it in the stables," said Dan. "You told me that once upon a time, when your Granny's father kept horses there, there were so many stable cats she couldn't keep count of them – so it must be a good place for a cat."

Francis laughed. He called his mother. "Mother! Here's another refugee wanting a home – a kitten. Can we keep it in the stables?"

Rita had said nothing at all. She was pale and thin, with eyes much too large for her small face. Mother looked at her, thinking that she wanted a lot of fresh air and sunshine!

"If we have your kitten, will you come two or three times a day and feed it and pet it?" she said. "And take it for little walks round the garden with you?"

"I'd love to," said Rita, almost in a whisper. "It's – it's the first pet I've ever had."

"Well – we'll have it here till you can find a home for it," said Mother. "We all love animals here, you know."

"Thank you very much," said Rita. "I'll bring it tomorrow."

So a kitten came to join the family at Green Meadows. Rex gave it a great welcome, and it loved him, after its first fright at seeing such a big dog. But Mr Black didn't make friends so easily. Mother said it would be just as well not to bring the kitten into the house at all, until it had grown bigger, in case Mr Black flew at it.

So it lived quite happily in the stables, and was named Dapple, after the name on one of the brass plates there. It was a good name for it, for it was dappled all over – brown and black and white.

"We're getting quite a menagerie!" said Clare, pleased. "I wonder what will come next."

Chapter Six

FLASH THE PONY

The kitten grew quickly. It escaped from the stables one day and went to the house, mewing for milk. Rita hadn't arrived yet with its food, and it was hungry.

It crept in at the kitchen door. Nobody was there. It saw a fire glowing in the grate and it padded over to it. It lay down on the rug.

At that very moment Mr Black stalked into the room. *His* place was also on the rug. He stopped and stared at the little bundle of fur lying there quite still. He sniffed delicately – dear me, it smelt like cat!

He put out a paw and touched the little ball of fur. The kitten awoke and leapt up. It saw Mr Black, and thought the big cat wanted to play. So he darted all round him, playfully, patting his waving tail, and making little rushes at him.

Mr Black was most astonished at all this. It was a long, long time since he had seen a kitten, and he wasn't quite sure what this little bit of quicksilver was. He put out a big paw and tried to pat it – but the kitten was away at once. Mr Black followed. Memories of his own mad kittenhood stirred in him, and he wanted to play with this funny little thing.

Granny had the surprise of her life when she came in and found Mr Black trying to squeeze his huge body under the armchair to get at the kitten, which kept putting out a paw and smacking him on his nose.

"Well, Mr Black! You've not played like this since

you were a kitten yourself!" said Granny, in delight. "Who would have thought you would make friends with that little rascal of a kitten?"

After that, of course, there really wasn't any need to keep the kitten shut up in the stables. It became one of the family too. Rita came faithfully each day with fish and milk, and sometimes she brought a little ball or a bit of ribbon. She took Dapple out into the sunshine to play, and the sunshine did her as much good as it did the kitten!

Daddy loved the kitten. He said it made him feel better just to watch it. It chased its own tail endlessly, it went mad regularly every evening after tea, tearing round and round the room at top speed, tail in air, and it dribbled a ball along the floor twenty times a day.

"It would make a very good footballer!" said Daddy. "I never saw anyone dribble a ball so well."

One night something happened. Francis woke up to see a curious light in the sky. What could it be? He jumped out of bed to find out. He looked through the window and saw that there was a fire somewhere.

"I must dress," he thought. "I'm a Scout, and I ought to go and see if I can help. I can at least fill pails of water till the fire brigade comes."

He was soon out of doors. He didn't wake anyone else. It would only worry Mother and Granny to see the fire, and Daddy couldn't possibly go and help. Rex whined to go with him, but Francis shut his ears to Rex for once, as he passed near the kennel.

The fire was at the back of the greengrocer's shop. People were milling about there in a crowd, shouting, and trying to help. The fire engine hadn't arrived.

"The sheds that the greengrocer uses for his stores and for his delivery boys' bicycles are on fire," said a man. "Goodness knows how it happened, this fire. The greengrocer was taken to hospital today, and his wife's spending the night there with him, he's so bad."

"Nobody's in the shop part at all then?" said a woman. "Well, we must try and save it from burning down – it's bad enough that old Miller's sheds should be burnt down, and him in hospital too!"

A man went by dragging a garden hose. Francis ran to help him. Pails of water were being passed up by a chain of helpers, and the sizzling of water on flames was very loud. A horrible smell of smoke was blown over Francis, and he choked.

He ran out of the smoke, coughing. And then he heard a noise that went right through his heart.

It was the sound of a horse, whinnying in terror! A horse! Where was it? Not in the sheds, surely?

Francis ran to the chain of helpers. "I heard a horse whinnying. Is there one anywhere? Quick, tell me?"

"Why, that would be little Flash the pony," said the man. "We forgot all about him. I reckon old Miller kept him in one of these sheds. Poor little thing!"

Francis flew off at once, his heart beating fast. He heard the whinnying again, and ran in the direction it came from. It seemed to come from the last shed of all, where hungry flames were just licking the roof, reaching out from a shed near by.

Francis went to the shed. Yes, the pony must be inside. He heard the frantic sound of hooves as the animal ran round and round the shed, banging into the sides. It whinnied in panic.

The boy had his Scout's pole with him. When he found that the pony's door was locked, he began to rain blows on the old wooden door with his pole. Some of the strips of wood broke, and Francis tore them out. The flames came nearer, and the boy panted as he struck the door again and again.

A man came up to help. He was big and strong, and he soon broke the door down. Francis pushed himself inside while the man went on making the hole bigger. He found the pony very quickly, because the frightened creature ran right into him, almost knocking him over.

Francis caught its mane and held on tightly. He called soothingly to the little thing. "It's all right, I've got you safe. Come out with me."

Somehow, he never quite knew how, he got the pony out of the broken-down doorway. He held on tightly to its mane, for the little creature was frantic, and it was only its fear of leaving this boy that stopped it from bolting.

Francis led the pony right away from the fire, and made it stand still. It was trembling from head to foot. Francis couldn't see what it was like in the dark, he only knew that it was small and had a long thick mane.

He stroked and patted the velvety nose, and spoke in his low, calm voice, saying all sorts of nonsense – but nonsense or not, the pony seemed to understand, and quietened down. It suddenly thrust its head against the boy's shoulder and left it there. Francis was too thrilled for words. It was just as if the little horse had said, "All right. You're my friend. I'll trust you and do what you say!"

The man who had helped to break down the door came to find Francis. "Hallo, Scout!" he said. "You did a jolly good deed in rescuing that terrified little creature. Is he all right now?"

"I think so," said Francis. "What is to happen to him?"

"Goodness knows!" said the man. "All the sheds are

gone now – even the one the pony was in. We've saved the shop and the rooms over it, though. Bad luck for poor old Miller."

"Yes. Awfully bad luck," said Francis. "But what about the pony, sir? I'm afraid he'll bolt if I leave him."

"Where can he go, now?" wondered the man. "He ought to be stabled for the night – but it's so late."

A brilliant idea suddenly flashed into Francis's mind. The old stables at Green Meadows! Of course, of course, of course! He could take this little pony there!

"I think I know what to do," he told the man. "I come from Green Meadows – that big old house, you know, not far from the new block of flats. Well, we've got some old stables there. I could take him there for the night."

"Good idea! Splendid!" said the man. "That will be one good thing done. I'll tell the police you're doing that – they've been asking about the pony. They can come and see you about him tomorrow morning."

So by the light of a rather small moon, Francis led the little pony back to Green Meadows. It went with him willingly. It liked this boy and trusted him. Its little hooves clip-clopped along the road, and in at the back gate, and up to the stables.

"In you go, Flash," said Francis. "That's right. What a good little thing you are! Now, just stand there while I tie you to the post. Can't have you wandering about, you know. I'll get you some straw to lie on. And would you like some water to drink?"

Flash would! Flash was very thirsty indeed, and drank a lot of water from the pail Francis brought. The boy couldn't think what to give him to eat, but he remembered the apples up in the stable loft – getting rather flabby and uneatable now, for it was April. Still, Flash didn't seem to mind at all. He munched four apples with

The pony was happy and at peace

pleasure, and gave little "hrrrrrumphs" of thanks. He wasn't really hungry – but the apples were an unexpected treat in the middle of the night.

It was cold in the stables, because the doors were always left open. Francis fetched an old rug and threw it over the pony. "There!" he said. "You can stand up and sleep or lie down and sleep just as you like. I don't know enough about horses to know which you do! Goodnight, Flash – sleep well, and don't feel afraid any more!"

He shut the stable doors and went creeping back to the house. Nobody had awakened, nobody at all! Francis was just taking off his clothes when he heard a loud whinny from the distant stables.

It was Flash. He didn't like being alone. He had remembered the flames and the noise and the heat. He felt lonely and strange in these stables. He wanted that boy.

"Well! I can't have him whinnying all night and waking everyone up," thought Francis. "I'd better spend the night in the stables. But I'll want a good supply of rugs – and my old eiderdown."

He had taken off his uniform. He pulled on some

shorts, two jerseys, and put his long thick dressing gown over the top. He pulled his eiderdown off his bed and then got two rugs from the hall cupboard. Surely he would be warm enough now!

Rex heard him creeping down the path and began to bark from his kennel. Goodness! Now *he* would wake everyone up! Francis stole down to the dog.

"Be quiet, you silly! It's only me. Do you want to come with me? All right – but don't frighten Flash!"

He lifted the dog over the wire netting and Rex padded happily at his heels. What an adventure! Where was Francis going with all those rugs?

They came to the stables. Flash was lying down in the straw, wide awake. He gave a little whinny when he heard Francis and smelt him.

Francis made himself a pile of straw beside Flash and burrowed into it, on top of a rug. He wrapped himself up in the eiderdown, and pulled the second rug on top of him. Rex flopped down on his legs, and made a nice warm spot there. Flash made another on his left side! In fact, Flash was so very warm that Francis soon threw off the rug.

The pony was happy and at peace. That boy was here with him. He was safe. There was a dog too, but if he was the boy's friend, well, that was all right.

They all three slept peacefully through the rest of the night. The sun came up, and they still slept. Mother got up early as she always did, and soon Sam awoke too. He sat up and yawned.

Then he noticed that Francis's bed was empty. His dressing gown was gone. His eiderdown too! Whatever had happened in the night? He rushed to his mother.

"Mother! Where's Francis? He's gone! His bed is

empty!" And then, dear me, what a search began! "Francis! Francis! Where are you!"

Granny was dressing, and she heard the cries. She slipped on a dressing gown and joined the hunt. Daddy was still in bed, for he didn't get up till after breakfast, when Mother had time to help him to dress. He lay and listened, feeling worried.

What a search there was for Francis! Mother began to feel more and more upset. It wasn't like Francis to slip off like this – in his dressing gown too! And why were his pyjamas still on his bed – crumpled, showing that he must have slept in them?

"He may be with Rex," suddenly said Clare. "He might have heard him barking in the night and gone to see him. I'll run down to the kennel and look."

So down she went – but in half a minute she was back. "Mother, Rex isn't there either! What *can* have happened?"

Sam went to the kitchen door and called loudly. "Rex! Rex!"

Rex was lying against the sleeping Francis in the stables. The door was shut, and the stables were a little distance away, but Rex's sharp ears heard Sam's shout. He got up quietly and ran to the stable door. It was old and did not shut properly. Rex pawed at it and it opened a little. He squeezed through and ran to the house.

"Mother! Here's Rex!" called Sam. "Rex, where is Francis? Tell us!"

"Woof!" said Rex, and turned round and trotted off, looking round as if to say, "Come on! Follow me! I'll take you to him."

"He knows!" said Clare. "Mother, let's follow him."

"Oh dear – I do hope he isn't lying hurt anywhere!"

said Mother anxiously, hurrying after Rex, followed by Granny. Clare and Sam ran in front, excited.

"He's taking us to the stables!" said Sam. "We never thought of going there to look!"

They came to the stables. Rex pushed at the door and it swung open. He went in, his tail wagging. Everyone followed. What a sight they saw!

There was Francis, curled up in his eiderdown fast asleep on the straw beside a small chestnut pony! Flash looked round as if to say, "I'm sorry – but I can't get up because I don't want to wake this boy!"

"Francis!" shouted Sam in amazement, and Francis woke up with a jump! How comfortable he was! How warm! He thought he was in bed. He opened his eyes and stretched.

"Francis dear!" said Mother's voice, anxiously. Francis sat up at once. He looked round in astonishment. Where was he? And then, as Flash the pony struggled to get to his feet, he remembered everything! The fire! The burning shed, the pony, bringing him here – yes, of course. Goodness, whatever time was it?

"Shall I be late for school?" he said, and tried to get up. But the eiderdown was round him and he rolled over. Sam gave a squeal of laughter and ran to help.

"Francis, *do* tell us the meaning of this," said Granny, her voice sharp with bewilderment. "You out here – with a pony! Where did he come from?"

"Oh dear – I meant to get up early and get back to the house and tell you all," said Francis, standing up at last in his crumpled dressing gown. "Mother, it's all right. I'll tell you everything."

"Come indoors then," said Mother. "Good gracious! Whatever will you do next? Hiding dogs – and now a pony! Come indoors, dear."

They all went up into Daddy's bedroom, because he was almost beside himself wanting to know what was happening, but he couldn't get out of bed without help. Rex trotted in too, and behind him came Dapple the kitten. Mr Black was already there, lying majestically on Daddy's bed.

"Daddy! Francis has got a pony in the stables!" cried Sam. "A pony!"

Francis began to tell his story. Everyone listened breathlessly – what a tale! Sam's eyes grew wide when he heard about the fire. Mother swelled with pride when she heard how her Francis had gone out to help, and had actually broken down a shed door to get out little Flash.

"Well!" said Daddy, when the exciting tale was finished at last. "I'm proud of you, Francis. I know you're a Scout, and its your duty to do what you can, where you can, whenever you can – but it takes a *brave* Scout to do what you did! Well Done."

Francis glowed with pleasure. Daddy himself was brave, very brave. He had won many medals, and one of them was for great bravery. Now he had called Francis brave. Sam gave him a slap on the back.

"Good old Francis!" he said.

"But what are you going to do with the pony?" said Granny.

"The police will be coming about it," said Francis. "They'll know what to do. Oh dear – I wish it was Saturday! Mother, it's getting awfully late, isn't it? Goodness, look at the time! We'll be late for school!"

"Now don't get into a state," said Granny. "I'll brush Rex and give him fresh water, and I'll see to the kitten, and I'll slip along and see to the pony too. Well – it's good to see a pony in the old stables once more."

"You know all about horses, don't you, Granny?" said Sam. "You know better than Francis does. Have *you* ever slept beside a horse all night?"

"Once. When I was as small as you," said Granny. "I'll tell you about that another time. You don't get me telling you stories now, just as we've all got to rush and hurry."

Francis only just had time after breakfast to go and give the pony a pat and a stroke, and whisper a few words in his ear. He would have to run all the way to school as it was. But who cared? He had had an adventure – and now there was a pony in the stables. How Francis hoped he would be there when he got back!

"I'll get that pony out into the orchard," said Granny after breakfast. "It's a beautiful day, and he can crop the grass there."

She looked excited and happy. She didn't say one cross word to Daddy. And, dear me, she didn't even stop to help Mother wash up! Mother was most amused.

"The old lady's happy," said Daddy smiling. "How she must have missed all the animals she used to be surrounded with – her dogs, cats, horses, pigeons! Now she only has Mr Black, and the wild birds she feeds – and a borrowed kitten and dog!"

"She's a real animal-lover," said Mother. "She always has been. She taught me to be too, though since I've been so busy I haven't more than a minute a day to think of birds and animals!"

"No. You think of your family all the time, and you have to give up all the things you used to love to do," said Daddy, reaching out for Mother's hand as she passed. "You don't read any more, you don't go walking in the woods and hills – you don't have any time to spend on yourself!"

"But I'm happy!" said Mother, giving Daddy a kiss at the back of his neck. He always liked that. "I've got you and the children and Granny — and we're a *proper* family, aren't we? All for one and one for all!"

She ran out into the kitchen to go on with her work. Daddy took up the paper but he didn't read it. If only, only, only he could get right again! When would Dr Miles come and see him — was it tomorrow? Perhaps he had heard of some new treatment; perhaps one day he would get out of this wheelchair and walk about and teach the boys cricket, and take Clare for walks, and see that Mother didn't do so much! Perhaps! Always perhaps!

Granny bustled in, all her chains jingling merrily. "That's a fine little pony!' she said. "Pretty too. He reminds me of one I had when I was Clare's age. The gallops I had on him! I've given him a grooming and now I've turned him out into the orchard. He's as happy as a sandboy!"

Daddy looked out of the window. "My word — it seems strange to see a pony grazing there!" he said. "What a dear little fellow! He must have been scared last night, when the fire broke out."

"Yes. He's got a hurt leg." said Granny. "He must have hurt it when he galloped round the shed in fright. I've dealt with it as best I can. It's nothing much. Now I must go and help in the kitchen. Dear dear — my poor daughter will think I have deserted her!"

Daddy stared after Granny. She seemed quite different! He looked at the little pony grazing happily under the trees, with Rex running there too, pleased at having a new four-legged companion.

The kitten jumped up on to Daddy's lap and he stroked it. It patted his hand with a soft paw, curled up

What was he going to say?

into a ball with its tail wrapped round it, and fell asleep. Mr Black watched from a nearby chair, and then calmly jumped down, walked to Daddy, and climbed slowly up on him. Mr Black was always careful of Daddy's legs! He settled himself down on top of Dapple, who squeezed himself out, half-suffocated. Daddy laughed. What a pair!

The police didn't come that morning. In fact, they didn't come at all. But just as the family had finished their midday meal, a young man came wandering up the path to find the back door.

"Oh dear – I'm afraid he's come to take Flash away," said Clare, mournfully. "I feel it in my bones. Oh, it was so nice rushing home from school and finding Flash in the orchard. I wish we could have a ride on him before he goes. He's just the size for us!"

"He whinnied like anything when I went to him," said

Francis. "He rubbed his head against me. Granny, you were very very lucky to have a pony of your own when you were small."

"Yes, I was," said Granny. "I'd have liked my grandchildren to have had ponies too. But things change so. I had too much – they have too little."

"We haven't," said Sam, sturdily. "I like my home. I like everyone here. I don't want anything changed."

"Yes, you do. You said you wanted to sleep in *my* bed, because yours was lumpy," said Francis. "You wanted to change over!"

"I don't mean things like that," said Sam. "I mean . . ."

But what Sam meant nobody heard, because it was at that very moment that the young man walked up to the kitchen door. He rapped loudly with his knuckles.

Everyone but Daddy rushed into the kitchen, certain that the young man had come for Flash. Well, Flash wasn't going without a lot of goodbyes said to him.

"Good afternoon," said the young man. "Er – I've come about my uncle's pony. I heard you had him here. Can I have a word with you, please, Mrs Marshall?"

"Come in," said Mother, and he stepped in. The three children looked at him. What was he going to say?

The young man was very polite. He took off his cap as soon as he got indoors, and didn't sit down till he was asked to. He twisted his cap round and round in his big hands and looked very worried.

"I'm so sorry to know that your uncle's sheds were all burnt down last night," said Mother, kindly. "I hear that your uncle was taken to hospital yesterday, very ill. What bad luck to happen all at once!"

"Yes, it is, ma'am," said the young man. "I'm very worried. My uncle's too ill for me to tell him about all this – there's no one to take on his business, because his wife, my aunt, is too upset to leave him. So I've got to decide everything myself."

"Can we help you?" said Daddy. "What's your biggest worry?"

"Well, you see, I and my brother run a greengrocer's business in the next town," said the young man. "My name's Miller, like my uncle's – Sid Miller – and it was my uncle who set us up in business. He was good to us, sir, very good. And now I've got to make up my mind whether to sell his business or close it down, in case he doesn't get better – or whether to hope for the best and come over here myself and run it, hoping he *will* get better and be strong enough to run it himself. My brother could run our own business by himself for a bit."

"I see," said Daddy. "It's a big decision for you to make. But I should certainly take on your uncle's business for the time being, if your brother can manage on his own. It would be a terrible blow to your uncle to come out of hospital and find his business sold! What does your aunt say?"

"She says I'm to do what I think best," said Sid. "But she's so upset about everything, sir, that I can't really get a word of sense out of her, poor thing."

"What do you want to do about the pony?" said Granny, and her chains jingled as she leaned forward.

"That's what I came about, of course," said Sid. "Not to worry you with my troubles! I just told you those to explain things a bit. Now, suppose I do what Mr Marshall here says – leave my brother to run our business, and come over here to run my uncle's – I can't use the pony."

"Why not?" asked Daddy.

"For two reasons," said Sid, earnestly. "One is that

94

"I said no and that's the end of it!"

the delivery cart is burnt; and the other is that I'm used to taking things out in a delivery van. Uncle was a bit old-fashioned – he didn't hold with delivery vans; so he took out the pony and wagon, and went round selling vegetables and fruit, and delivering them too. Of course, he had his delivery boys on bicycles, as well."

"I see," said Daddy. "Well, go on."

"Well, sir – if I'm not using the pony I ought to sell him," said Sid. "He would fetch in a bit of money to help pay for things; my uncle wasn't insured for the sheds. But the thing is – old Uncle Fred was so *fond* of that pony I believe it would break his heart if he found him gone when he got out of hospital."

There was a silence. Then Daddy spoke again. "We can't buy him, if that's what you're after," he said. "We've no money ourselves."

"No, sir. I wasn't going to ask you that," said Sid.

"I'm fond of my uncle, and I'd like to keep the little old pony for him, if he comes back. But where can I keep him? They charge a lot up at the Riding Stables. What I came to ask was this – and please don't take offence, sir – I've heard you're all fond of animals – and – well, couldyoulookaftertheponyhereforme?"

The last nine words came out in such a rush, and in such a desperate voice, that nobody understood them. Sid repeated them. "Could you look after the pony for me here? I'd pay you what you ask, because I know you wouldn't charge like a horse stables would, sir."

Sid's request was so very unexpected that it took everyone by surprise. Then Francis leapt up with a shout:

"He wants us to have Flash! *He wants us to have Flash!* Yes, we will, we will, we will!"

Clare's face glowed. Sam looked solemn and thrilled at the same time, and began to whistle softly.

But Daddy damped it all down. "No," he said firmly. "No. A horse needs quite a lot of looking after. The children are at school all day, and it would fall to my wife to see to the pony. She has too much to do already."

"Daddy!" cried all three children in dismay. But Daddy was quite firm.

"I said no. And I mean no. I'd like to help Sid, but I'm not adding to your mother's burdens. It's no use you children telling me you can do everything. You can't. I said no, and that's the end of it!"

Clare burst into tears. Sam stamped out of the room, not whistling any more. And then something most unexpected happened. Granny began to speak.

"I agree with every word you've said, John," she said to Daddy. "I won't have any more put on to my daughter, and as you say the children will be busy at school. But – we *will* have the pony, because *I* will look after him! I know all about horses, I was brought up here with that stable full of them. *I* will be responsible for Flash, and he shall live in *my* stable, and eat *my* grass in *my* orchard. I say yes. And I *mean* yes!"

The old lady jingled all her chains, and sat up straight, looking so fierce that Daddy burst into laughter. He laughed and laughed. Clare flew to the door and shouted after Sam.

"Sam, Sam! It's all right. Come back at once." And Sam came in quickly, looking round hopefully at everyone. Whatever was Daddy laughing at?

"All right, all right," said Daddy at last. "I'm defeated. I forgot you knew so much about horses, Granny – and as you say, the stables are yours, the orchard, and even the grass in it! And if you'll look after the pony, well, I have nothing more to say. I am quite sure that both you and the pony will be happy!"

Granny beamed round. She had got her way and she always loved that. She turned graciously to Sid. "That's settled then," she said. "We keep the pony. You can supply his corn and let us have hay or straw, I suppose?"

"Oh yes – yes! Anything!" said the relieved Sid. "And please let the kids ride him – he's used to that. I and my brother rode him twelve years ago, when *we* were kids. He's about fourteen now, and he's gentle and hard-working. I'd have hated to get rid of old Flash."

Sam began to whistle loudly, and not even Granny stopped him. Sid got up to go, twisting his cap round and round so quickly that it quite fascinated Clare. He cleared his throat as if he were going to make a little speech. Daddy stopped him.

"You don't need to thank us – we're glad to help you.

And remember this, Sid – hard work never hurt anyone. So go to it, and do your best!"

"Thank you, sir. I'm not afraid of hard work. Not a bit," said Sid. "You've been very nice to me. Er – what shall I pay you for your kindness, sir? Would you prefer money, or shall I bring you fresh vegetables free, each week?"

"Nothing of the sort, young man," said Granny, sitting up very straight again. "I'm doing this because I love horses, and it's good to help a young man who's doing a bit of kindness himself – and you're doing your best for your uncle! Don't you dare to mention payment again! My grass is free, and so is my orchard!"

Sid went very red at this outburst, and looked bewildered. Mother stood up and took him to the door, smiling.

"My mother sounds fiercer than she is," she said. "But she's kindness itself."

"Thank you, ma'am," said Sid. "I'll repay you some day – in spite of what the old lady says, God bless her!"

Sid walked off happily, looking round him at the untidy, neglected garden as he went down the path. Gracious – they must be poor to have a lovely place like this in such an untidy state! Couldn't they even afford a jobbing gardener? Sid saw Flash grazing happily in the orchard, and went to him.

"You're in clover, old fellow!" he said. "Enjoy your holiday! That's what it will be for you, till we get things fixed up. And you deserve it, you're such a hard-working little chap!"

Flash knew Sid and he put his head on the young man's shoulder. It was a little way he had. He didn't quite understand what was happening – but he certainly was enjoying himself!

There was enormous excitement as soon as Sid had gone. Sam flung himself on Granny and almost knocked her off her chair. "You're good, good, good!" he said. "I always knew you were, but now I think you're even gooder!"

Clare sat with her eyes shining. A pony in the orchard every day. *Almost* their own. One they could ride!

Francis rubbed his hands in delight. The stables! He would clean out one of the stalls and make it beautiful for Flash. He would look in the harness room and see if there was an old saddle there – and a bridle. Granny would show him how to put them on Flash. He would polish the leather till it shone!

Granny got up, jingling loudly. She felt very proud of herself. "Well, that's that," she said. "Sam, stop hugging me so hard round the waist, you're squeezing my dinner! And remember, please, *I've* undertaken to look after the pony. You children can just play with him when you've time, and ride him – but I'll do all the work for him. I don't mind you helping at weekends."

"I'm going to help all day long," said Sam, solemnly. "All – day – long!"

"You're not," said Mother. "You're going to school. Don't be silly."

"I'm not going to school," said Sam, and he gave a sudden squeal of laughter. "It's holidays next week – four weeks! Ha ha, Mother – you forgot!"

"Golly – so it is," said Clare. "Oh, Granny – we *can* help then! Holidays, holidays, holidays – they're coming at *exactly* the right time!"

"Look at the clock!" said Mother, suddenly. "Off to school, all of you. Wait, wait! Brush your hair, please, and . . ."

But the children didn't wait to listen. They knew all

that by heart. "Brush your hair, wash your hands, tidy yourself, please!" sang Clare, light-heartedly. And in two minutes' time they all three rushed helter-skelter down the path. How happy they were!

Chapter Seven

EASTER HOLIDAYS

Flash was a great success. Granny loved him with all her heart, and spent a lot of time with him. She still helped Mother as much as ever, but she gave up her afternoon rest so that she would have plenty of time for any jobs for the pony.

At first Mother was cross when she found that the old lady was no longer resting in the afternoon – but Daddy stopped her scolding Granny.

"Don't prevent the old lady from going out and seeing to the pony," said Daddy. "All this fresh air and exercise and being happy with Flash is doing her a world of good. She isn't nearly so crotchety now that she has something else to think of beside the house and the family!"

"You're right, as usual," said Mother. "*You* like going down in your wheelchair to the orchard too, and being with Flash and Rex, don't you? You and Granny are a pair! It's a lovely place now, down there under the pear blossom, with daffodils all round your feet."

"And the cuckoo playing hide-and-seek and calling cuckoo all the time!" said Daddy. "I wish you'd more time to get down there with us, dear – it's so lovely now. Leave the jobs and spend some time out in the sun!"

"I can't," said Mother. "One day, perhaps. The children will be home all day for the holidays soon, and you know what a lot more work that means – though I love doing it for them."

When the holidays came the three children were as happy as the day was long. They persuaded Mother to let them have their meals in the garden, and Francis carried all the trays out himself. It certainly was lovely out there in the April sunshine – and, as Daddy said, it was one way of getting Mother out-of-doors!

Granny was very, very busy at the beginning of those holidays. She and the children turned out everything in the harness room, and a saddle was found to fit Flash, and a bridle too. The stirrup straps were broken and had to be mended. They cleaned and polished all the leather till Clare could almost see her face in the saddle.

They cleaned out one of the stalls in the stable, and put hay in the manger, though Flash much preferred the fresh grass in the orchard. It was long and lush and brilliant green. The children couldn't wait for the saddle and bridle to be ready. They rode him bareback!

He was a solid little pony, good-tempered and cheerful, though a bit on the fat side. When Sam rode him his short legs stuck out comically over Flash's fat flanks, and he found it very difficult to keep on. He rolled off plenty of times, but as Sam was as plump as the pony, he didn't mind in the least.

"I fall on the place where I'm fattest," he told Granny. "So it doesn't hurt, it just takes my breath away. Why don't *you* have a ride, Granny? You're little. You wouldn't be too heavy."

"If you think that an old lady like me is going to gallop bareback under the pear trees, you're mistaken," said Granny. "Go on with you! I never know whether you mean things or not."

"Oh, I *do*," said Sam surprised. "I thought you *would* like to ride Flash just for once. Perhaps you ride him when we're not looking?"

"Sam! Don't be absurd," said Granny, and gave him a tap on his arm. "Go and get some clean straw for me, please. Sid brought a whole lot up yesterday."

Sid was quite a friend, almost at once. He brought up straw and hay and oats and carrots for Flash. He made friends with all the children and with Rex and Dapple the kitten.

"You've got a lovely place here," he said one evening, looking round. "But it's so neglected. It gets on my nerves when I look round and see all those weeds and tangled grass and the mess everywhere."

"We haven't time to garden as well as everything else," said Francis. "We just keep a bit in front of the house weeded and planted for Mother, and that's all. We've had to let the rest go. Mother tried to do it, but Daddy made her stop, she got so tired."

Sid sat silent for a moment and then spoke, rather awkwardly. "Er – I've got a bit of time this evening," he said. "I suppose you wouldn't let me mess about in the garden a bit? I love gardening, I was going to *be* a gardener, but my uncle wanted me to set up in the greengrocery business."

"Do what you like," said Francis. "There are tools in the stables. Hey, Dan – show Sid where the tools are, will you?"

Dan was up at Green Meadows almost every evening, partly to be with Rex and partly because he enjoyed playing – and working – with Francis and the other two. He copied Francis in everything, and admired him very much. He was determined to be a Scout. He had been very much impressed at the Scout meetings he had attended. The things they did! Gracious! – it was a real boy's job that – being a Scout.

He did good deeds in secret, pretending that he was a

Scout already. So he was always ready to give a hand to anyone, especially the Marshall family. He went off at once with Sid and showed him the tools.

"Why don't you come and help me do a spot of work down in that garden?" said Sid, suddenly. "You're a big strong lad – I reckon you and I together could make part of the garden very nice for Mrs Marshall."

"All right," said Dan, surprised. "But – are you going to come another time then?"

"Yes. I've been worrying about how to pay back for the old lady's kindness about Flash," said Sid. "And it suddenly came to me this evening. 'Silly donkey!' I said to myself, 'look at this garden staring you in the face! Get down to it, Sid,' I said, 'That's the way to pay back the Marshalls' kindness!'"

Dan agreed. "I'll help too," he said. "You see, they won't let me pay money or buy them sweets, so my Mum comes each Wednesday and helps in the house – for nothing, of course. But I don't do anything, so I'll do this. It would be a good deed, wouldn't it?"

"You a Scout then?" said Sid. "No? Well, you don't need to be a Scout to do good deeds. Come on. You take the spade, I'll take the fork, the barrow, and the trowel."

Mother was extremely astonished when she came down the garden to get some mint for mint sauce. There was Sid digging hard in a piece of ground full of overgrown rose trees – and there was Dan busy grubbing up weeds, and trying to find the edges of the bed!

"What in the world are you doing?" said Mother, astonished.

Sam was there, waiting to wheel the barrow to the rubbish heap when it was full. "They're paying back," he said. "Don't tell them to stop, Mother. They're not paying *you* back – they're paying Granny. She came up and said they could. Aren't you, Sid and Dan?"

Sid looked sheepish, and stood up straight, his face red and hot with hard work. He was enjoying himself.

"I like this kind of thing, ma'am," he said. "I wanted to be a gardener once. I'd like to get a bit of this garden nice for you all. It's a shame to let it go like this."

Mother was touched. "That's good of you," she said, and went indoors smiling, to tell the news to Daddy. She took the mint with her, sniffing its clean strong smell.

"Good for Sid!" said Daddy. "He's not afraid of work, that young man. He'll go far. It's the lazy ones who stay put and never get anywhere. I like Sid."

Francis was very happy. He had Rex, he had the mad, bad little kitten, and now he had Flash. There was only one thing that worried him – and it worried Granny too.

It was Flash's hurt leg. The wound on it had seemed to heal all right – but now it had broken out again and Flash had begun to limp. Granny had done all she could, but she was afraid the leg was poisoned. She and Francis discussed the matter together.

"There's a vet at Langham Down, six miles away," said Granny. "But Flash couldn't walk all that way to him with his hurt leg, and we couldn't afford to ask the vet to come here and see to him. He might have to do quite a lot to Flash's leg."

"I've saved up nearly five shillings," said Francis.

"It would be more than five *pounds*, I'm afraid," said Granny. "Perhaps ten if Flash has to have treatment. We can't ask Sid for the money – he's running his uncle's business at a loss, as it is, till he gets used to it. He's only a young fellow, and hasn't any money saved up that he can draw on. This is a thing we must settle ourselves, Francis."

"The leg looks a *bit* better tonight," said Francis, looking at the sore place. Granny didn't think so. What *could* they do? Money, money, money – she had been spending too much lately, and she had hardly any left till her next quarter's cheque came along.

It was Rita who solved the whole problem. She came to be with Dapple, and to bring him a new rubber ball to play with. She saw Granny and ran up to her with Dapple.

"Isn't the kitten growing?" she said. "Doesn't he look well?"

"He does – and you're looking a lot better yourself!" said Granny. "Playing up here in the open air is better for you than being mewed up in a flat with no garden to give you space to play in the sunshine! Look here a minute – we are worried about Flash's leg. It seems bad, doesn't it?"

Rita looked. She knew nothing about horses except that Flash was lovely to ride, but even she could see that the leg was bad, and that poor little Flash was in pain.

"Why don't you take him to the Animal Van?" she said, rubbing Flash's long velvety nose gently. She loved him as much as the others did. "It's in Packhorse Dene today, but it will be gone tomorrow. It's on its way to Langham Down."

"Whatever's the Animal Van?" said Francis in astonishment. "I've never heard of it!"

"Well, I don't know much about it," said Rita, playing with the kitten. "I only heard someone telling my mother that she once had a sick cat, and took it to the Animal Van and the Animal Doctor inside cured it. So I thought he might cure Flash's leg."

"What *can* she mean?" wondered Granny, as Rita

darted after the kitten, which had scampered under a bush.

"I'll ask Sid. Maybe he knows. Sid! Come here a minute. Do you know anything about an Animal Van with an Animal Doctor inside – or is it just a makeup of Rita's?"

"The Animal Van? Oh, yes – that's one of the motor-caravans belonging to the P.D.S.A.," said Sid. "I once took my dog there."

"P.D.S.A.! And what does *that* stand for?" said Granny.

"People's Dispensary for Sick Animals," said Sid, promptly. "It's a society that is run for sick animals. They have vans out all over the country – Caravan Dispensaries is their right name, but the kids call them Animal Vans. Anyone can take a sick or hurt animal to the Van Doctor, and get it seen to."

"Van Doctor! I've never heard of anyone called that before!" said Granny.

"Oh well – the right name is Technical Officer – T.O.s they are called for short," said Sid. "But most Technical Officers are known as Animal Doctors by the children. It's quite a thrill when the Animal Van comes along with the Animal Doctor inside, ready to help."

"Do they charge much?" asked Granny.

"They don't charge a penny!" said Sid. "Not a penny! The help is for the people who can't afford to pay fees, you see. It's all run and paid for by animal lovers who can't bear animals to be sick or hurt and not have help. So the Animal Doctors never charge anything. Honest! Of course – if you like to give what you can afford, they're jolly pleased. There's always a collecting box there, just in case! Why do you want to know about it?"

"Well, look at Flash's leg," said Granny. "I thought it

was better – but it's broken out again. Could we take him to the Animal Van, do you think – or Caravan Dispensary as you said it was called?"

"My word – it's bad, isn't it?" said Sid, alarmed. "The van's at Packhorse Dene this evening: it may be gone after that. Can't we take old Flash now, straight away, before he gets too bad to walk? Poor old fellow, he's in pain."

"We'll take him," said Granny, in her most determined voice. "He can walk that far, though I'd really rather he didn't. But if we wait and send a message to the Caravan Dispensary, it might just have left. Come along, Flash, dear old boy."

So, attended by Granny, Sid, Dan, Rita, and the three Marshall children, Flash set off slowly. It was quite a procession that moved off down the lane towards Packhorse Dene. In her anxiety to get to the van before it was too late, Granny quite forgot to send word in to Mother. So Mother was extremely astonished when she came out into the garden, to find it completely deserted. No Granny, no Sid, no children, no pony, dog, or kitten. How very extraordinary!

Flash limped along slowly. He was such a good, patient little thing that Clare felt as if she would burst into tears.

"I wish I could carry him!" she said. "He must wonder why we're taking him for a walk just when his leg is hurting him most. I don't think we ought to!"

"It's all right, darling," said Granny. "It isn't very far. He knows we're all sorry for him."

Rex ran ahead, delighted at this unexpected walk on a lovely April evening. Celandines shone in the ditches and white violets made the evening air smell sweet. It

"I wish I could carry him!"

was a beautiful walk to Packhorse Dene – if only Flash had been able to walk properly too!

They came into the quaint little village. The van was still there. The Animal Doctor's sister ran the little inn at the corner nearby, and he had been given permission to see his sister and spend the night there. The van was open – and anyone could bring sick animals or birds to be examined.

The news had gone round that the caravan was spending the night at the village. "The Dispensary is here with its T.O.!" said the grown-ups. "That Animal Van is here with the Animal Doctor!" said the children. So when Flash and his companions walked into the village street, they saw quite a little crowd of people waiting near a big cream caravan with the letters P.D.S.A. in blue lettering along the sides.

A small man with a firm, kindly face was standing at

the doorway, handing a cat to a small girl. He twinkled at her through his glasses.

"Here you are. Here's your Tibs. Nothing much wrong. I've dosed her and she'll be quite all right in a day or two."

"Oh, thank you!" said the small girl, and clutched Tibs eagerly. "Thank you! Oh, Tibs, do you feel better?"

She went off happily. The Animal Doctor looked round at the waiting people. "Who's next? You with the dog?"

A boy got up with a small dog in his arms. The dog lay still and seemed in pain.

"I've brought my dog, sir," said the boy. "He got into a fight. His neck's badly bitten. Oh, sir, he won't die, will he? He's such a *good* dog!"

"Dear me, no! I'll soon see to him," said the doctor, glancing at the wound. "Come along into the van with me. He'll feel better with you there. You can help me. We'll clean out the wound, and I'll give you ointment to put on it. It's a good thing it's at the back of his neck. He can't lick himself there!"

The boy went into the van and the door closed. Everyone hoped and hoped that the dog would be all right. In a surprisingly short time the door opened again, and out came the boy with his dog, beaming all over his face.

"I held him while the doctor did his neck," he announced proudly. "Wags was as good as gold. You'll soon be all right now, won't you, old boy? I've got your ointment in my pocket, and I'm going to carry you all the way home!"

There was another cat to be seen too, with a swollen face, and a canary in a cage, that had hurt its wing. There was even a mouse with a broken tail!

The child with the cat went into the van to hold her pet while the doctor examined it. She came out very quickly, with the cat still in her arms, looking very sleepy.

"He pulled one of Fluffy's teeth out," said the little girl. "It was very, very bad. Now Fluffy's face will be all right. It won't be swollen tomorrow, he says. He just put her to sleep for a minute, and pulled it out then. Fluff never even knew. He's *clever*."

Soon it was Flash's turn. "I'll see him where he stands," said the little Animal Doctor. "Ah – it's his leg, I see. How did it happen?"

Francis told him. The doctor looked at him. "Aren't you the boy that rescued a pony from a burning shed?" he said. "I heard about that. My sister at the inn there told me. Well done!"

He turned to the pony, and rubbed his nose and spoke to him gently before he even examined the leg. Flash pricked up his ears. He liked this man's voice very much. He suddenly put his head on the doctor's shoulder – and then Francis knew that it wouldn't matter what the man did to him, Flash would bear it!

"I'd better take him into my sister's stable, over there at the inn," said the little doctor. "I can see to his leg more easily there, in private. I'll just fetch a few things that I shall need from the van."

Flash was taken across to the inn stable. "I think I'll have him alone, without anyone with him," said the man. He shut the door and left everyone outside. Nobody spoke a word. There was complete silence except for a sudden little whinny from Flash, inside the stable.

Clare was in tears. Poor Flash! She put up a sudden little prayer in the way she often did when she was anxious or worried. "Dear God, please help Flash, please

111

help him, he's so sweet, and you can see how bad his leg is."

Sam saw Clare's lips moving and he knew what she was doing. He shut his eyes tight and said urgently, "Please God, look after little Flash, do look after him."

He opened his eyes – and at the same moment the stable door opened too, and out came Flash with the Doctor, rather bewildered but not at all upset.

"Here he is," said the little man, smiling. "Good thing you brought him when you did! The leg was very nasty. But the wound is quite clean now, and I've bandaged his leg well."

Sid, Francis and Granny all surged forward to take Flash. He still limped, but he seemed quite cheerful.

"Thank you very much," said Granny. "I must pay you."

"We never charge anything," said the little doctor. "Not a penny."

Francis had seen a collecting box on the table inside the van. "I've got five shillings here," he said. "It was lucky I saved it up. I shall put it all into your box!"

Granny put in something too – and then Sid put in half-a-crown; it was all he could spare.

"I've got a penny," said Clare, and that went into the collecting box too! The Animal Doctor looked very pleased.

"I've got nothing," said Sam, mournfully. "What can I do?"

"Well, why don't you belong to the Busy Bees?" said the little doctor. "They are children who love animals and care for them and help us in our work. Here – take this form, it tells you all about it. Next time I see you, young man, I hope I shall find you wearing our little yellow badge with the bee on it!"

Sam was delighted. He took the piece of paper, folded it up carefully and put it into his pocket. A Busy Bee! It sounded good. Sam liked to be busy, and he liked bees — nice, humming, buzzing things that made him honey for his tea. Yes, certainly Sam would be a Busy Bee and help this kind man to carry on with his work for animals like Flash and Dapple and Rex!

"Can I have one of those papers too, please," said Rita, shyly. "I've got a kitten, look, and I'm an animal lover too. What do Busy Bees do?"

"Ah, you just join and see!" said the man. "There are plenty of things, and all of them are interesting. Here, take half a dozen forms, your friends may like to see them."

Rita proudly took the little bundle of papers. She was thrilled to think she had been bold enough to speak out like that, and get the papers. She hugged Dapple and went off, crimson with pleasure.

"Anyone else?" said the little doctor, looking round. There was only one more person who had arrived just after the children, on a bicycle. It was a man with a puppy. He had it in his bicycle basket, a tiny creature that whined feebly.

"Have you got time to see this pup?" asked the man. "There's something the matter with his leg. It's broken, I think. If you want to shut up for the night I'll bring him in tomorrow, to Langham Down. I can cycle in."

"Good gracious no! Of course I'll see to him now," said the doctor. "Let's have a look at him."

The man took the puppy from the basket. One leg hung limp and useless. "Gently, now, gently," said the Animal Doctor. "Don't handle him too roughly. Is he yours?"

"No. He belongs to my little girl," said the man. He

113

was a rough-looking fellow, with a dirty white scarf round his neck, and hair much too long. "I've no patience with animals – but she loves this pup, and she's crying her eyes out about him."

"How did it happen?" said the doctor, stroking the tiny creature gently.

"Well – he got under my feet, and I sent him flying," said the man. "Always getting in my way, he is. But then I've no patience with animals in the house."

"So you kicked him and broke his leg," said the little man, coldly. "I see. Well, let us hope that *you* never get into anyone's way, and have your leg broken! Come into the van. I want you to watch what I do – then perhaps you won't kick at him again."

The van door shut. Clare turned to Granny, tears in her eyes. "I hate that man, I hate him, I hate him, I hate him! I'd like to steal that little puppy and take it to Green Meadows. Horrible, horrible man!"

Sam was white. It had never even occurred to him that anyone could be cruel to animals. He looked very solemn and slipped his arm through Granny's.

"I'm going to be a Busy Bee." he said. "Granny, you'll explain about it to me, won't you? I want to get busy immediately, at once, forever!"

"You shall, you shall," said Granny "Now cheer up – look at Flash, he seems better already! Off we go home; and dear oh dear, good gracious me, not one of us remembered to send word in to Mother and Daddy that we were going off to Packhorse Dene with Flash!"

It was late when they got back. Sid left them and went to the shop, and Rita and Dan slipped off too. Mother, looking out of the gate, suddenly saw her three coming along with Granny and Flash. Rex ran by Francis, and Clare carried Dapple. Where in the world had they been?

"Mother, we've been to the Animal Van!" cried Sam, running to her. "The S.A.D.P., you know. No, I mean the P.A.S.D. No, I don't mean that either. Clare, what *do* I mean?"

"You mean the P.D.S.A., silly," said Clare, and out came the whole story to Mother, all about Flash's leg, and the Animal Doctor, and the animals there, and how he had bandaged Flash's leg – dear me, Mother could hardly believe it!

"Now really, you *must* come in to supper," she said. "You are a whole hour late! But I don't mind now I know what you've been up to. Naughty Granny, not to send word to me! Granny, you're as bad as the children!"

"Yes, I know," said Granny, looking quite ashamed of herself. "I can't think what came over me to forget to tell you. Still, all's well that ends well – and our Flash is soon going to be much better!"

Chapter Eight

GRANNY'S SECRET

Early next morning Francis went out to see Flash. He came back at a run. "Granny! Mother! Flash isn't limping nearly so much this morning! Isn't that good!"

"Splendid," said Mother.

"He's wandering round the orchard quite happily – and once he forgot to limp!" said Francis. "Mother, do you know what I'm going to be when I'm grown up?"

"Let me see now – is it a lorry driver, a cowboy or an express train driver?" said Mother. "I've forgotten!"

"No. I've grown out of those ideas," said Francis. "I'm going to be an Animal Doctor and have a caravan of my own, and go round the country helping people with sick animals. Mother, don't you think that's a good idea?"

"Anything that helps others is a grand idea," said Mother. "Now, do you mind cleaning the shoes, Francis? You'll not be in time for breakfast if you don't get on with your jobs!"

"Oh dear – life is so exciting these days that there's hardly time to fit in all I've got to do!" said Francis, rushing to get the boot-cleaning box. "But I like lots of things to be going on, don't you, Mother?"

Mother didn't answer. What she would *really* have liked was a nice bit of peace, with nothing to do and nothing going on at all – for a week, at any rate! She went on cooking the breakfast. Thank goodness it was Wednesday, and kind little Mrs Oldham was coming.

116

"We shall soon be able to ride Flash again," said Clare, at breakfast. "Granny says his leg will heal quickly now it's been properly seen to. Mother, I've got an idea."

"Really? How unusual!" said Francis, at once, and got a glare from his sister.

"Be quiet, Francis, I'm not talking to *you*," she said. "Mother, listen. Mother, you're not *listening*!"

"Yes, I am," said Mother. "What's your idea?"

"Well – my idea is this," said Clare. "And Sam thinks it too. We both think Flash would like to pay back for having his leg mended – so Mother, when he's better, could we let him give other children rides for a penny a time?"

"They'd pay a penny," said Sam. "They said so. They keep asking for rides, but as he's Sid's pony, we didn't like to say yes."

"Well, I think you must ask Sid," said Mother. "I'm sure he won't mind – but ask him first. I think it's a very good idea indeed, so long as you don't let anyone too heavy ride him, and don't overdo it. Flash would quite enjoy it."

"Oh, Mother! I'm glad you think it's a good idea," said Clare, beaming. "Shall we charge a penny from our gate to the end of the lane and back?"

"Yes," said Mother, smiling. "That would be worth a penny. But don't let anyone ride Flash who might pull at his mouth too hard, or kick his sides to make him go fast."

"Of course not!" said Sam. "If anyone does that I'll push him off the pony – crash thud!"

"I shan't let George ride him," said Clare. "He took Rex's bone away and made him growl."

117

Flash felt very important trotting up and down

"And not Janet, either," said Francis, joining in. "She's . . ."

"You're telling tales!" said Sam. "You are, you are! And you won't let *me*!"

"Be quiet, Sam," said Francis. "Butting in like that! I was *not* going to tell tales."

"Who's going to take Daddy more toast?" said Mother, changing the subject. "You, Sam. Carry the rack upstairs carefully, and don't drop the toast on every step!"

"I only did that last year, when I was young," said Sam, solemnly. "I don't drop things now. Shall I tell Daddy about the penny rides?"

"Oh yes – he loves to hear the news," said Mother, and Sam trotted off. His mind was full of Flash and penny rides and full money-boxes, and Busy Bees; really, how exciting everything was!

The Easter holidays really were very thrilling indeed. For one thing, Flash's leg healed rapidly, and in two days' time he was not limping any more – in fact, he took a little gallop round the orchard, using his legs!

Granny untied the bandage. "Look there!" she said. "Healed beautifully! Dear old Flash, you're all right now. I'll just rub some of this stuff on, that the Animal Doctor gave me, and put a bandage on for another day or two."

When Flash's leg was perfectly all right, the Penny Rides began. The news went like lightning round the village, and the nearby housing estate, where the blocks of flats now had a great many people in them.

Children flocked to Green Meadows with their pennies, their eyes shining. A ride on a pony! Hardly any of them had ridden anything before, except a horse or other animal on a roundabout. They loved Flash with his big brown eyes and thick mane.

Flash felt very important trotting up and down the lane with a different child on his back each time, and Francis, Clare or Sam running beside him. Sam was sure that the pony knew it was part of his "paying-back," and was angry with Dan when he laughed at the idea.

"Well, anyway, he's the kind of pony that would *like* to pay back, isn't he?" said Sam, quite fiercely. "You just dare to say he isn't, Dan!"

"Oh, I *wouldn't* dare!" said Dan, with a grin, "I'd be afraid you would knock me down and pummel me all over, Sam! I'd have a black eye and a swollen cheek and . . ."

That made Sam laugh. He liked Dan. Dan was a Scout now, and very proud of it. He had been enrolled at the last meeting, and had made his Scout promises very solemnly indeed. At home he had the promises framed like a picture, and they were opposite his bed, so that he could see them every morning.

Sam was very interested in Dan's good deeds. "Do

you really do one every day?" he said. "What do you do. What did you do today? Do tell me. Francis, never, never will! What did you do today, Dan?"

But Dan wouldn't tell either. He just grinned and gave Sam a friendly poke in the ribs. Sam amused him. He was always so solemn, so much in earnest, so very interested in everyone and everything. Dan thought it must be fun to have brothers and sisters. He had none. Still, he had Rex, and that was something.

The penny rides were not the only exciting thing that happened those holidays. As more people came to the flats and learnt that pets were not allowed, but that they could be cared for at Green Meadows, quite a number came to ask Mother if Francis could look after a rabbit, or a guinea pig, or a puppy.

"You see, we thought we'd be allowed to keep a cage on our little balcony," said one flat-dweller. "That's not really keeping it *in* the flat, is it? But no – were not even allowed to do that. And my little boy does love his rabbit. I daren't give it away. Could you possibly find a place for it somewhere? Ronnie would come here each day and see to it himself."

So the rabbit came, a big white one called Fluffy. The hutch came too – but it was so terribly small that Sid made a nice new one, big and roomy, with a daytime room, and a sleeping room.

"You oughtn't to house a rabbit in such a small hutch," Francis said to Ronnie. "It's unkind. And look, don't give him his food so wet. Goodness, fancy keeping an animal and not even knowing how to feed him properly. Now look here: unless you feed him and look after him the proper way – the way I tell you – I won't have him here."

"All right," said Ronnie, meekly. He was a bit older

than Sam, very spoilt and cheeky. But he was so anxious about his rabbit that he didn't dare to behave badly at Green Meadows. He caught sight of Francis's new badge. All three children, and Dan and Rita too, had joined the Busy Bees, and now wore the little yellow badges with the bee on. The pennies that Flash collected went into an empty honey pot, ready to send off to Busy Bees headquarters – Flash was "paying-back"!

"We're bees, and we're collecting honey in the honey pot," said Sam to Ronnie, when Ronnie paid a penny for a ride and put the penny into the jar. Ronnie hadn't known what Sam meant, but now he saw Francis's yellow bee-badge, and he asked him about it.

"What's that?" he said.

Francis explained. "*You* ought to belong," he told Ronnie. "For two reasons. You love your rabbit, so you're an animal lover, but you don't look after him properly, so you ought to learn how to. You soon know a lot about animals if you're a Busy Bee."

And a week later Ronnie proudly displayed the little yellow badge too! "We're quite a hive!" said Mother. "Let's have a hive of Busy Bees here and call it Green Meadows Hive. We can have meetings and tea-parties, and collect all kinds of honey between us – pennies to send up to headquarters! And tinfoil and stamps – all kinds of things!"

Not only Ronnie's rabbit came. A guinea pig came next, a dear little fellow with no tail at all. He belonged to a boy called Harry, and Francis never had any need to take him to task for not seeing to Gilbert the guinea pig properly. In fact, Harry was so anxious about him that he used to visit him quite late at night, and make Rex bark frantically when he heard someone stealing quietly up the garden path!

A puppy came, a mad little creature, who made friends with Dapple at once. He was put in Rex's old pen, for Rex now had the free run of the whole place, of course.

The puppy was quite untrained, and Pam and Sue, the twins who owned him, had no idea of training him at all.

"Look here," said Francis, who was now quite an important person, dealing with so many animals and children, "look here, Pam and Sue – do you want your dog run over? Because he will be, unless you train him to walk to heel in the road. You must be mad, playing ball with him when you take him into the lane! Sid told me he nearly ran him over when he was out in the delivery van, and passed you this morning."

"Well, how *do* we train a dog?" said Sue. "I mean – Pongo is so mad that I don't see how he *can* be trained."

Francis called to Dan. "Hey, Dan? Done your good deed for today? Well, here's one for you. Give these kids a lesson on how to train a dog – they're hopeless!"

So Dan took *them* in hand and the puppy too. Really, Green Meadows was a very busy place those holidays!

And then one day a man called at Green Meadows. Mother wasn't about, so he saw Granny. He was shabbily dressed, but neat and clean. He took off his cap when he spoke to Granny.

"Excuse me," he said. "I come from one of the new little houses beyond the blocks of flats. I keep pigeons – fantails, ma'am, very pretty they are. And now I've been told that the rules of the blocks of flats about keeping pets is to apply to us people in the little houses too. And I heard that you took in creatures here, ma'am. I wondered if you took birds?"

Granny looked round cautiously. She wasn't at all

122

sure that Mother would welcome pigeons. She had already said that there were enough creatures at Green Meadows.

But oh – there was the old pigeon house – it could easily be mended; and Green Meadows would once more have its fantail pigeons flying round, and their cooing would echo round the old house as it had done years ago!

Granny nodded. "All right, I'll take them. Come up this evening and I'll show you where we have an old pigeon house. You can mend it, and we'll use that – but listen! Don't say a word to anyone! I'll meet you at the back gate about six o'clock!"

That evening, after tea, Granny tried cautiously to find out where everyone would be at six o'clock. She was now feeling very guilty about the pigeons. She knew that her love for animals and birds was rather running away with her common sense. Goodness, Green Meadows was becoming quite a menagerie! And oh dear, it was dreadful of her not to tell Mother!

"Not to tell my own daughter! What's come over me?" thought Granny. "I'm a bad old woman! Still – I'll see what happens. I *know* everyone will love the pigeons – the pretty, pretty things!"

It appeared that there was a Scout meeting at half-past five, and that Clare and Sam were going to a party. How very fortunate! She would be able to see the pigeon-man in safety. Granny disappeared that afternoon and went to have a look at the fallen-down wooden house, with its six little doorways at the top for pigeons to go in and out. Yes, a strong man could easily mend that. But it would need two people to erect it.

"I'll ask Sid," thought Granny. Sid was a great standby. He not only worked a lot in the garden, which was beginning to look much tidier, but he was always ready to do any odd jobs too. In fact, he rather regarded himself as one of the family now, and thought the world of Mother.

The coast was quite clear at six o'clock and Granny slipped down to the back gate. Pam and Sue had taken their puppy for his daily lessons, and Ronnie had fed his rabbit, cleaned the cage, and gone. Nobody was about at all.

The pigeon-man was waiting at the gate. He lifted his cap to Granny. She took him to the stables, feeling that that was a safe place to talk.

"What's your name?" she asked.

"Joe Silver," he said. "I'm an odd-jobman, and I go out by the day, gardening, or mending fences – well, I do anything really. And I keep pigeons; always have done, since I was so high! Some folks are mad on dogs or cats or horses. I'm mad on pigeons."

"I used to be too," said Granny. "They came and fed out of my hand – they sat on my shoulders and head. They . . ."

"That's right! Mine do the same with me!" said Joe Silver. "Well, ma'am, these I've got are all my own breeding – I had them from eggs. They're white fantails. I never thought I wouldn't be allowed to keep them when I got that little house down on the estate. But they're strict there – they say pigeons spoil the roofs or something – and I was to kill all mine."

"Wicked!" said Granny. "I'm glad you came to me. Now listen, Joe, I'll take you down to where there's my old pigeon house. It fell down in a gale of wind one night, and there it's been ever since."

They went down to the corner where the old pigeon house lay. Joe was most impressed. "It's a beauty!" he

124

said. "A real good one. I've only got a poor little house – made it myself. I don't reckon you'd have liked it in *your* garden, for the pigeons. I can easily mend this one. My word, my pigeons will think themselves grand to be in a house like this."

"What are they called?" asked Granny, as Joe began to examine the wooden house on its long pole.

"Snowdrop, Snowball, Snow-White, and Snowflake," began Joe, "and there's Coo-Roo and Fanny – short for fantail," he added, in case Granny didn't know!

"Lovely names," said Granny. "Well – I must leave you now. Do you know Sid Miller? He'll be along soon, and you can ask him to give you a hand. He'll tell you where everything is."

"Er – what about paying you, ma'am?" asked Joe. "I can't ask favours if I don't pay for them."

"I shan't want paying, thank you," said Granny. "If you mend the old pigeon house, put it up, and lend me your pigeons, that's enough! And, by the way – I'd like you to keep it to yourself that I'm having the pigeons. I'm – er – well, I'm going to surprise the family, you see!"

She walked off, jingling. Joe looked after her respectfully. His pigeons would be safe here! He'd bring their corn himself. Nobody else must feed them, or they'd forget him, and wouldn't come like a white cloud on to his shoulders and head.

He went to find Sid, who was hard at work clearing yet another bed. The rosebeds were now beautifully tidy, and all the roses had been pruned. Other flower-beds were finished too, and Sid had been debating whether he might bring up a few nice plants from the shop and put them in when nobody was looking. The shop sold plants as well as fruit and vegetables, and it was just the time of year to put things in.

"A few delphiniums would be nice at the back," thought Sid. "And some columbines there – and I could put a whole mass of forget-me-nots in that corner, where Mrs Marshall could see them from the kitchen window. I've got some beauties at the shop now."

He was surprised to see Joe Silver. "Hallo," he said. "What are *you* doing here?"

Joe told him. Sid listened with great interest, and then told him about Flash the pony.

"The only thing that bothers me is how to pay the old lady," said Joe. "What do you pay them for keeping Flash here?"

"This!" said Sid, waving his fork round him. "I come and garden – I'm tidying it up. See those beds? Well, they were in a forest of weeds. Now look at them. Can't you do something like that in return? They won't take money. It's not a bit of good asking them. They're like that."

"Don't often meet people like that these days," said Joe. "Most people take, take, take all the time, and don't give anything. Right. I'll first of all mend the pigeon house, and then I'll get you to give me a hand and put it up. Then I'll have a look round and mend up the walls a bit, and the stable doors; and I could paint up the front of the house if they'd let me."

It was quite extraordinary, but not one of the Marshall family except Granny knew that the pigeon house was being mended. Joe finished the job in two evenings and then he and Sid put it up. It looked fine!

"I'll bring the pigeons along tomorrow," said Joe. "I'll have to wire them into the house for a week, so that they

126

get used to this for their new home, else they'll all fly back to me. Give me a hand with them, will you, Sid?"

It was Sam who discovered that the pigeon house was up – and that there were six white pigeons wired into it! The wire netting enclosed the top of the house like a cage. The pigeons could get out on the ledge round the house and go in and out of their holes, but they couldn't fly away.

Sam stared in utter amazement. Then he tore indoors. "Mother! Mother! There are pigeons in the pigeon house – and it's up again! But Mother, somebody's been cruel. They're all wired in, they can't fly into the air!"

Mother rushed out, followed by Francis and Clare. Well, well – Sam was right. The pigeon house was up, and pigeons strutted about on the ledge!

"Rookity-coo," said one, in his pretty cooing voice. "Rookity-coo-coo-coo!"

"Oh Mother!" cried Clare in delight. "Where did they come from? Oh, aren't they lovely! Look, they spread their tails out just like a fan."

"Oh, *now* I know why they're called fantails," said Sam, pleased. "But who put them there? Mother, it's cruel to wire them in, isn't it?"

"No, dear – not if they've just been put there," said his mother. "They have to get used to their new home, you see. The wire stops them from flying away. Now – I have a sort of feeling that Granny's behind all this! She's been looking rather *peculiar* these last few days – a kind of guilty look. I believe it's a surprise for us."

They went to tackle Granny. "Those lovely pigeons!" said Mother. "What do you know about them, Granny? Oh, the pretty things! How glorious they will look flying about Green Meadows! Where *did* they come from?"

A great load rolled off Granny's mind. Mother was

pleased. She *liked* pigeons – oh, what a relief! Granny beamed.

"Well," she said, "I suppose it *is* a kind of surprise. But actually I kept it a secret because I thought you mightn't want pigeons, but I hoped that when you once saw them flying about, clapping their white wings in the air, you would love them! I'm a bad old woman. I thought you might not say yes at first – but I wanted them so badly that *I* said yes, without telling you!"

"Granny's naughty! Granny, you look as if you know you're naughty!" said Sam in delight. "Are you?"

"Yes, I am," said Granny. "Now stop it, Sam – you are hugging me like a bear. Goodness me, what I'll do when you're a bit bigger I don't know! There won't be anything of me left. Well – you like the pigeons then?"

There wasn't any doubt of that – and they liked them even more when Joe at last took away the wire and they flew into the air, rookity-cooing and clapping their white wings in glee. Then down they came like great snow-flakes, and settled on the grass, fluffing out their feathers, and holding their pretty heads proudly.

They were soon ready to perch on anyone's head and shoulders, and Sam was delighted when one day he had the whole six on him! Mother grew used to having one or two on the kitchen windowsill, watching her at work. She loved their cooing.

Daddy liked them too. He sat out in the sun in his wheelchair, and the pigeons flew down to him, settling on his shoulders and knees. Really, they were a great success.

Joe was a great success too! He was a born handyman and liked nothing better than to mend this and strengthen that, and paint here and creosote there. Mother let him. She saw that he was happy and hard-working, and intensely grateful to the family for taking his beloved pigeons. He promised that the first three pigeon eggs to hatch should belong to the three children.

The holidays came to an end. Francis wandered round the garden with his mother. It was the beginning of May, and the lilac bushes were out, scenting the air. Francis looked round.

"You know, Mother," he said, "Green Meadows is looking very different from how it was when we walked round in February, and saw the first snowdrop! See how tidy and trim it is! All the beds are cleared — and Sid's cut the grass twice with the old mower that Joe mended."

"Yes," said his mother. "It's *quite* different. Joe's done such a lot, and Sid's a real wonder. He ought to have been a gardener, no doubt about that. He's got green fingers — everything grows for him!"

"It's only you, Mother, that things are still hard for," said Francis, struck by his mother's pale face. "Are you doing too much? You're not ill, are you?"

"No, darling," said Mother. "Just tired. Dear old Granny is so happy with the animals and one thing and another that she can't help me so much — and holidays always mean more work — and Daddy doesn't seem to get any better. I just feel a bit tired and worried, that's all. Oh, for a nice little house, a *tiny* little house — and yet I couldn't bear to leave this lovely garden!"

"You rang the first snowdrop for luck — but it hasn't brought *you* much luck, Mother," said Francis. "Look — I found a four-leaved clover today — that's one of the luckiest things there is. It's for you. Now just see if things don't get better for you!"

He pressed the little four-leaved clover into her hand. She laughed. "I'll put it under my pillow tonight," she said. "Then we'll see what luck it brings."

Chapter Nine

A NEW PET – AND A SHOCK!

One day, two weeks after the children had gone back to school, a young man came to see Mother. He was dressed in chauffeur's uniform and looked very smart. He saluted Mother and asked if he could see Francis.

"He hasn't come back from school yet," she said. "What do you want him for? You can leave a message for him if you like."

"Well, it's like this," said the young man. "I live near the new housing estate – not far from Joe Silver, madam – and I've got a dog."

Mother knew what was coming then, of course! She smiled. "Go on," she said.

"Well – I wondered if you'd let your boy have the dog here," said the young man.

"Aren't you allowed to keep him, then?" said Mother.

"Oh yes – but the neighbours don't like him," said the young man. "He's big, you see, and he sometimes wants to play with the children. If he's a bit rough, he almost knocks them down, he's so big. So I've had to keep him chained up, and he howls the place down. My neighbour's been to the police about him and . . ."

"Did you keep him chained up all the time?" said Mother. "Not on a short chain, surely?"

"Yes. I had to, madam," said the young man. "I tell you, the neighbours were downright nasty about him. His name's Duke. He's an Alsatian, and a beauty."

"And what is your name? And where do you work?" asked Mother. "You're a chauffeur, aren't you?"

"Yes, madam. My name's Harrison, Bill Harrison – and I'm chauffeur to Sir Giles Heston-Baker," said the young man. "Actually I live in the lodge by the gates of Harrow Manor, where Sir Giles lives; but the housing estate stretches right up to there. I think the people are jealous because they are not allowed to keep dogs or chickens on the estate, and I can keep both, though I'm almost on the edge of it."

"I see," said Mother. "Well – bring the dog along this evening and I'll let my son see him. You'll have to provide his food, of course. A big dog like that must eat a lot."

"Yes, madam," said Harrison. "I'd like to pay something too, but Joe Silver tells me you won't take payment. Is that right?"

"Quite right," said Mother. "Well – you'll be along this evening, then?"

Bill arrived that evening with Duke. He was on a short lead, and was a big powerful dog, very handsome indeed. He pulled vigorously at the lead, and Bill had hard work to keep him at his side.

"Oh! What a beautiful dog!" said Clare, and went to pat him. To her enormous surprise, he growled. She stepped back in alarm.

"It's all right," said Bill. "He just doesn't know you, that's all. He has to be introduced. Duke – friends, Duke, friends. All friends!" And Bill patted the three children on the back. Duke watched, his tongue hanging out, his eyes wary. Then he suddenly wagged his big tail.

"There! Now he knows you and he'll always be your friend," said Bill. "Shake, Duke!"

Duke offered a paw, just as Rex had done, and the

Duke growled but Flash went on sniffing

children shook it, though Clare was a little scared. No dog had ever growled at her before.

"He's laughing," said Sam. "Look!" And, indeed it did look exactly as if Duke were laughing, for his mouth was wide open, and he showed his teeth as if he were smiling. His tail waved to and fro.

"Will he get on all right with the other animals?" asked Francis, anxiously. "He's so big he could almost eat them up!"

"Well – not at first. He'll have to get used to them," said Bill. "Have you got a yard anywhere? He'll have to be chained up, or he'll run away. And he can jump like anything – over the highest wall! He can go halfway up a tree too."

"Goodness!" said Clare, looking at Duke with much respect. "Is he valuable?"

"Very," said Bill. "Actually I'm looking after him for my master, Sir Giles Heston-Baker, who's away for a bit. I've had him with me so much I almost feel he's mine – but he's not really."

Dan came up the path and Duke growled and snarled. Dan backed away in alarm.

"Tell Duke it's Dan, quickly," said Clare. "I don't like him when he looks like that."

So Dan was introduced and shook paws, and was relieved to see Duke's tail waving in a most friendly manner.

"You see," said Bill, "the kids on the housing estate don't like Duke, and they tease him. They shout at him and throw stones at him, and he nearly goes mad, because he's on a chain and can't get free."

"Throw stones at him! No wonder he won't be friendly at first when he sees children!" said Francis, indignantly. "It isn't his fault if he's not friendly. I expect he thinks *we* might throw stones at him. We wouldn't, Duke. You can trust us."

Duke's tail waved again, and once more he opened his mouth, hung out his tongue and looked as if he were laughing.

"Except for Rex, he's the handsomest dog I've ever seen," said Dan. "But I say – have we got to keep him on a chain?"

"We can have a run-wire," said Francis. "We'll make him a nice big run down in the orchard where Flash is. We'll string a wire from one tree to another, and fasten his chain to that, so that he can run about a lot, as much as he likes, but the wire will keep him from running away, or attacking anyone he doesn't know."

"That's a good idea," said Bill. "I hadn't heard of a run-wire. He's always been on his short chain – this one, see – and I tell you, he sometimes nearly went mad, especially when I had to leave him and take the car and go off for the day somewhere."

"It's enough to make a dog really vicious," said Francis. "You shouldn't have done that. All right, we'll

133

As for Sam, he rolled on the grass with Duke

have him. Let's go down to the orchard straight away, and find a good place for him."

Duke was soon running up and down on a run-wire in the orchard. Bill went off and came back with a huge supply of meat for him, and promised to come each day to take him for a long walk. Flash the pony was most interested in this big, energetic dog, running up and down the wire. He wandered up and bent down his head to sniff at him. Duke growled; but Flash went on sniffing, and then gave a little whinny.

Duke's tail began to wag slowly. He put out his tongue and licked Flash's nose. Clare was watching nearby and she laughed. "They're freinds!" she said. "Flash, *you* weren't afraid of his growl, were you? He's been badly treated, Flash, so you must be kind to him."

Duke settled in. He didn't howl, and the only person he barked at was the dustman. "That's because he sees the dustman come in with empty hands, and go out with the dustbin – and he thinks he's robbing us!" said Mother. "We can't cure him of that!"

One evening Rita came to see her kitten, which had now grown much bigger, and had a lovely coat. She found Dapple playing in the orchard near Duke, who was lying down with Flash the pony beside him. The two were great friends. Duke had Rex's old kennel, because Rex now slept in the house, promoted to a fine basket, bought for him by Dan. Clare said that if only Flash could get into Duke's kennel, the two of them, dog and pony, would sleep there side by side!

Rita caught up her kitten and hurried away, holding it tightly. Francis saw her. "Whatever's the matter?" he said.

"*Please* don't let Dapple go near Duke," begged Rita. "I met Joan and Dick today, who live near where Bill Harrison lives, and they told me that Duke chases cats and kittens, and once he nearly bit a kitten's tail off."

"I don't believe it," said Francis. "He was always kept on a chain. Bill said so."

"But he used to escape sometimes," said Rita. "He used to break his chain. He attacked cats and dogs – and he bit a little girl one day, and another time he bit a boy. Dick said he goes quite mad sometimes, when he breaks his chain. Nobody's safe then."

Francis laughed. He was fond of Duke, and could handle him well now. Even Clare had forgotten her first little scare. As for Sam, he rolled over and over on the grass with Duke, who pounced on him, pretended to worry him and reduced Sam to squeals of laughter. He even liked Duke better than Rex!

But the twins, Pam and Sue, came with the same story two days later. "You be careful of Duke," said Pam. "The milkman told our mother that he's fierce, and they warned us not to go too near him. He's already bitten two or three people."

135

"I don't believe it," said Francis. "A dog is only allowed one bite."

"Well, you be careful," said Sue. "The milkman said that sometimes he goes quite crazy, breaks his chain and tears off to see if he can find his *real* master, Sir Giles. And it's then he turns and bites anyone in his way. You be careful."

Francis said nothing of this to the others. He thought it might upset them, and Clare might even believe it and be frightened of Duke. He wondered how it was that the stories got about? Surely there wasn't really any truth in them? Duke *couldn't* behave like that!

But one day something unpleasant happened. The three children had gone for a picnic with their mother and Granny. Daddy was left in his wheelchair in the garden. All the animals were either shut up in their cages, or safe in the orchard. The pigeons sat on their pigeon house in the bright sun, and cooed to one another, kissing with their beaks.

Four children came by. They heard the pigeons cooing and looked over the wall. They saw the orchard, with Flash the pony pulling peacefully at the grass under the trees. They saw Duke!

He had heard them coming and he was sitting up watchfully, his pointed ears pricked.

"Coo, look! That's Duke, isn't it! You know, the big Alsatian Bill Harrison used to have, chained up in his yard!" said a boy.

"Is he chained?" said a girl, cautiously. "He's fierce, you know. I've seen him snarl like anything."

"Yes. He's chained," said another boy. "Listen – he's growling. Yah! You can't get at us! Brrrrrr! Yoo-hoo!"

Duke got up angrily and growled again. The boy picked up a stone and sent it whizzing at him. It struck

136

the dog on his back and made him jump. He growled again, then snarled, showing all his gleaming white teeth. The girls were scared and ran away, but the two boys stayed there, grinning.

"Yoo-hoo! Silly dog! Ugly dog! Brrrrrr!"

They threw more stones, and Duke ran up and down his run-wire, trying his hardest to get free. He barked and barked. Daddy heard him, and, using his hands on the wheels of his chair, he turned them and ran the chair slowly down to the orchard. Whatever was the matter with Duke?

He was just in time to see a boy hurl a large stone at the dog. It hit him on the head. Duke went completely crazy, racing up and down the run-wire, tugging at his chain, almost choking himself. The boys saw Mr Marshall and fled.

And a very good thing they did, because there was a sudden *snap*. The wire broke, and Duke found himself free. His chain was still on him, trailing beside him – but he was free!

He leapt straight over the wall and disappeared, barking wildly.

Mr Marshall didn't know what to do. He couldn't get out of his chair because he couldn't walk by himself. He could only wait for the others to come home. He couldn't even send for Bill, because Bill was away for the day. Sir Giles his master was coming home, and Bill had taken the car to fetch him.

The children, their mother, and Granny came home sunburnt and tired, after a lovely picnic. Rex danced along beside them. He was never tired! Sam was whistling loudly.

As soon as they got to the gate they heard their father

calling them. "There's Daddy shouting – quick – run and see if anything's the matter," said Mother.

The children ran – and were surprised to see their father's chair in the orchard. He had stayed there, hoping that Duke would come back. But he hadn't.

He told them what had happened. Clare wept bitterly, and the corners of Sam's mouth went right down.

"Poor Duke," wept tender-hearted Clare. "Those hateful, hateful children! Where's he gone, Daddy?"

Daddy didn't know. "He'll come back," he said. "Don't worry."

But Francis worried very much. He remembered those tales he had heard. Duke had now been tormented again – and he might quite well go crazy and bite somebody. Then that would be the end of him. He was very quiet as he ate his supper with the others.

Clare kept crying, till Granny got quite cross. "What good do tears do?" she said. "You make us all miserable, Clare. Do stop now."

"She's tired," said Mother. "We all are after our long walk and lovely picnic. Off to bed now – Granny and I will wash up."

"I've just got to go out and see that all the animals are all right," said Francis. He went out into the evening. It was still light. He walked down to the orchard, and Flash came towards him. He put his big head on the boy's shoulder and stood quite still while Francis talked to him and fondled him.

"What's happened to Duke?" asked Francis. "I wish you could tell me. I'm so worried, Flash. You see, if he gets crazy with anger, he might bite somebody, and then we would never see him again."

Flash whinnied; he couldn't tell the boy anything. He

had been scared and upset himself when the stones had been thrown and he had galloped away frightened when he heard Duke barking and tearing up and down.

Francis left the pony in the sweet-smelling orchard and went slowly up to bed. Sid had come as usual to do what he called his "spot of gardening", and Mother had asked him to call at the police station and see if there was any news about Duke, and to leave a message at Bill's cottage, at the gates of Harrow Manor. There didn't seem anything else to do except to wait and see if Duke came back.

Francis couldn't sleep that night. He lay tossing and turning, worrying about Duke. Had he bitten someone? Would he be taken to the police station if so? Would they ever see him again? It wasn't Duke's fault. Those hateful boys! They ought to be whipped. So his thoughts went, on and on.

He heard his mother come up, and he got out of bed and went to the door. "Mother! Are you going to bed?"

"Yes, it's late, dear," said his mother. "You ought to be asleep. You're not worrying about Duke, are you?"

"Yes. Have you heard any news of him?" asked Francis.

"A little. Sid came up to say that Duke had been seen tearing down the road towards Bill's cottage. But he isn't there. It's in darkness, and Bill isn't back. He won't be home till late, Sid says."

"Oh," said Francis. "Perhaps he's somewhere there waiting for Bill. Mother – has he bitten anyone? I did hear that he bit people when he was furious."

"I didn't hear," said Mother. "But it's enough to make a dog bite when he's tormented as he was. Daddy says quite a large stone struck him on the head."

"I know. I keep thinking he may have a horrid cut

139

there," said Francis. "Well – goodnight, Mother, and thank you for the lovely picnic. It *was* nice to have you out for the whole afternoon like that."

"Goodnight, dear," said Mother and kissed him. "Sleep well! Maybe Duke will be back in the orchard in the morning."

Francis got into bed. He waited till his mother had put her light out. He heard the click, and then he got up and dressed himself. He was going to Bill's cottage to find Duke! Perhaps he was hiding somewhere near there. Francis was sure he would come if he called him.

He slipped down the stairs and out of the garden door. It was bright moonlight, and he could see everything almost as clearly as in the daytime. He sped down the garden and into the lane.

It was only about ten minutes' walk to Bill's. Francis ran most of the way until he saw the big burly form of Mr Streetly, the village policeman. He hid in the hedge at once. Mr Streetly would be sure to send him straight back home – and he must find Duke, he must!

He crept out of the hedge when the policeman had gone by. He was soon at the gates of Harrow Manor. He came to Bill's cottage, on the right-hand side of the gates. It was in darkness. Bill wasn't back yet then.

"Duke!" called Francis, softly. "Duke, old boy! Where are you? It's me, Francis. I've come to find you Duke! Duke! Duke!"

But no Duke came, and not a sound stirred anywhere. Not even the trees moved, for there was not a breath of wind. Francis went through the open gates of Harrow Manor and walked a little way up the drive.

"Duke!" he called, and whistled the little familiar whistle that the dog had grown to know and obey. "Duke!"

There was no sign of the dog. Francis went on walking up the drive in the clear moonlight. "Duke! Duke! Come here, old boy! Poor old boy!"

And then at last he heard a sound. What was it? He called again. "Duke."

The sound came again – a growl! Francis stopped dead and listened. "Duke!"

"Grrrrr!" Yes, it *was* a growl – but surely, surely Duke wouldn't growl at a boy who loved him. The growl seemed to come from a small summerhouse not far off. Francis went cautiously towards it. It was not far from the drive itself. He called again. "Duke, old boy!"

No answer. Francis walked quietly over the little stretch of grass to the summerhouse. The moon shone right into it. Francis stood at the doorway and looked in.

Duke was there! He crouched right at the back, his eyes gleaming in the moonlight, his upper lip curled back and his teeth showing white. He snarled at Francis.

The boy stood still, shocked. He had never seen Duke look like that before. The dog looked cruel, wicked, vicious – and this was the same Duke he had fondled that morning, and who had licked him and loved him!

"Duke!" said Francis, helplessly. "Come here, old boy. Don't look like that!"

Duke crept a step forward, crouching low to the ground as if he were going to leap like a cat. He snarled again, and Francis stepped back in panic.

"He means to bite me!" he thought. "He's going to pounce – and I'm all alone here! He must have bitten others, after all, when he was just like this."

He was too afraid to stay. He backed away slowly, followed by growls. But Duke didn't rush out of the door as Francis had half-expected. The boy reached the drive and found tears running down his face. He brushed them away. He never, never cried – never! He was a Scout, and he thought himself brave. But after all he wasn't. But oh, Duke! What was to happen to him?

He heard a sudden noise and stopped. It was the sound of a car racing up the drive. It must be Bill bringing his master back! Bill would know what to do, Bill would go in and get Duke out! Francis stood in the middle of the drive as the car came up, waving frantically.

The car stopped suddenly and Bill leapt out. "What's up? Francis, what's the matter?"

"It's Duke. Some children tormented him today and he broke the wire and ran off, half-crazy. He's in the summerhouse, growling, and I'm afraid of him," said Francis, with a gulp. "He looks so awful – not a bit like himself. Oh, Bill, come and get him. I'm sure he's hurt."

"What's all this?" said a voice from the back of the car. Bill ran to the back window and spoke to Sir Giles, his master. He told him quickly what Francis had said. Sir Giles got out of the car at once.

"Duke in the summerhouse! Half-crazy! I can't believe it! He was always the gentlest, best-tempered of dogs! What's been happening to him since I've been away? We'll go and get the poor fellow. He'll be beside himself with joy to see me!"

But Duke wasn't. He didn't seem to be pleased to see either Bill or Sir Giles. In fact, he growled so ferociously at them both that the two men stepped very hurriedly indeed from the doorway.

"Duke!" said Sir Giles and Bill, at the same time. But Duke would not come, and still lay and snarled.

"Look here – the dog's dangerous," said Sir Giles. "He'll have to be shot before he does somebody damage.

142

What a pity! Such a beautiful, sweet-tempered dog too! What's changed him into that snarling brute?"

"Shot!" said Francis in utmost horror. "What do you mean, sir? Shoot old Duke? It isn't his fault. He was teased and tormented till he went half-crazy. He'll be all right tomorrow. I'll stay here all night, somewhere in the bushes near by. You *can't* shoot him!"

"My dear boy, don't upset yourself," said Sir Giles. "What's he to do with you, anyway? And what are you doing here at this time of night? Good gracious me, what a peculiar affair this is! You go home, my lad – this dog has got to be shot."

"But sir – he's hurt. I know he is," said Francis. "And when dogs are hurt they get frightened and snarl and growl, even at their friends. I don't believe he'd really bite either you or Bill – and, after all, he belongs to you. Couldn't you – couldn't you *possibly* go in and pat him or something?"

"I wouldn't dream of it," said Sir Giles. "I'd be scared stiff. No, he must be shot, and as soon as possible. He's dangerous."

Francis said no more. He was so upset and troubled that he hardly knew what he was doing. He went softly back to the summerhouse. Sir Giles called him sharply. "Come here, you little idiot."

Duke was in there, crouching as before. Why was he in such a strange position? The boy's keen eyes searched the dog's body. Then he gave a cry.

"Oh, poor old Duke! You've got your chain twisted all round your hind legs! It's cutting into them. Let me free you, Duke, poor old Duke!"

And the boy went right into the little house and knelt down by the growling dog. "Dear Duke, poor Duke – let me see the chain. Don't be afraid, it's me, and you know

I love you. Poor old Duke, never mind, old boy, I'll put you right. *You* wouldn't bite me, Duke, would you – you're just frightened and in pain. There – move over a bit. Poor old Duke!"

Sir Giles and Bill were staring in amazement into the summerhouse. Francis had made Duke move over a little and was trying to disentangle the chain from the dog's hind legs. It had got wound round and round them, binding them together and cutting into them.

Duke gave a little whine, and then put out his tongue and licked Francis. The boy's heart turned over with happiness. "*I* won't let you be shot," he said. "Don't you worry, Duke! I'll stay with you all night – don't you be afraid!"

Chapter Ten

WELL DONE, FRANCIS!

Once the cruel chain was unwound from his bleeding legs, Duke tried to get up. He just managed to stand and then fell down again. "Sir, he's hurt," called Francis, his voice trembling. "He's all right now – he's licking me. He was only frightened; he didn't know why his back legs were locked together."

Sir Giles went cautiously into the summerhouse. Duke whined in pleasure and tried to get up, but fell down again. He licked his master lovingly. When Bill came in he licked him too.

"There you are, you see," said Francis, overjoyed. "He's not dangerous. He's just a poor hurt dog. You won't shoot him, will you?"

"You're really a most extraordinary boy," said Sir Giles, with wonder in his voice. "And just about the bravest I've ever seen. That dog might have flown at you and bitten you badly. Poor old Duke! You'll never have a better friend than this boy here tonight!"

"You won't shoot him, will you?" said Francis again. "You haven't said you won't."

"I certainly won't," said Sir Giles, who was now kneeling down beside Duke, examining his legs. "These wounds want seeing to – there's one very bad one on this left leg."

"Oh, what a pity the Animal Van isn't near," said Francis. "The Animal Doctor – the vet there, you know,

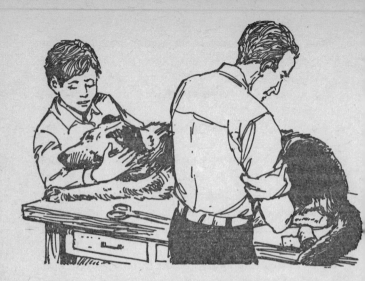

Sir Giles rolled up his sleeves and set to work

sir – would turn out of bed to see to him. I know he
would."

"You needn't worry," said Sir Giles, "I'm a surgeon –
and if I can see to the wounds of humans, I can certainly
see to the wounds of a dog. Bill, can you carry him
indoors?"

Bill could and did, and Duke allowed him to pick him
up, heavy as he was, and take him up the drive. Sir Giles
unlocked the front door and went in. A startled butler
appeared, quite speechless at the sight of Bill carrying
the Alsatian, Sir Giles behind, and a small boy following.

"You'd better go home, son," said Sir Giles, kindly.
"I'll come and see you tomorrow and we'll have a talk
about this. I'm going to tell your father all about it. I
wish I had a son like you!"

"Please don't send me home, sir," said Francis. "Let
me stay here and be with Duke."

"You are a most persistent young man," said Sir Giles, with a laugh. "All right. Bill, take the car and go and tell this boy's people he's all right and will be home in the morning. Or wait a bit – have you a telephone in your house, my boy?"

"No, sir," said Francis, happy again. Now he could stay with Duke and get him absolutely right again – no more snarling, no more growling, no more threats of shooting!

Bill went off. The butler was given a few orders from Sir Giles. A wooden trestle table was put up quickly and Duke was lifted gently on to it. Sir Giles took off his coat, rolled up his sleeves, and set to work.

Duke was as good as gold. Francis was told to talk to him and stroke and pat him while the surgeon cleaned up the wounds and bandaged deftly. There was a wound on his head too, where the stone had struck him. "Nothing much," said Sir Giles, "but enough to make a dog very angry. There, my boy – he's finished. Do you really want to stay with him tonight?"

"You said I could," said Francis. "Will Duke be able to walk all right after this? His legs were rather bad, sir, weren't they?"

"Oh, he'll be all right," said Sir Giles. "Look – he's trying to stand on them now. Up you get, Duke – that's right. See, he's even walking a few steps, though it must hurt him!"

Duke and Francis went to sleep together. The butler put a pile of rugs in a corner of a small study for Duke and made up a couch for Francis to sleep on. But as soon as the door closed Francis was off the couch and cuddled down by Duke. The dog licked his face and whined. In half a minute both dog and boy were asleep.

Francis was awakened in the morning by Duke licking

his face all over. He sat up, rubbing his eyes. "Goodness, Duke! I shan't need to wash my face at all if you go on like that! How are your legs? Do you feel better?"

Duke felt fine. His legs felt stiff, but he was in no pain. He walked a few steps. His right hind leg wasn't too bad, so he lifted his left one and carried it off the ground running round the room on three legs.

Francis was delighted. "You'll be all right, Duke! Isn't Sir Giles clever. How did you get that chain all round them – it must have swung round as you ran and tied itself tightly so that it lamed you. Never mind. Your master is back, and you're all right!"

There was a knock at the study door, and the butler came in. "Good morning, Master Francis," he said. "I've been sent by Sir Giles to see if you're all right – and would you like a bath, sir? You were so tired last night that we didn't bother to worry you about washing or undressing or anything."

"Well – I *am* rather dirty," said Francis, looking down at himself. His knees were black! His hair was on end and his face was extremely dirty. "I suppose it's crawling about in that summerhouse."

"A very dusty place," said the butler. Francis felt rather scared of him. He was so very stiff and correct! Then, quite suddenly, he unbent.

"Bill Harrison says you went into that summerhouse when Duke was raving mad!" he said. "He says he and Sir Giles wouldn't go near him – and Sir Giles was just going to have him shot. Is that right?"

"Well – he wasn't raving mad, nothing like it," said Francis. "He was just terrified because he'd got his legs all wound up with his chain – and he'd lamed himself trying to run like that with the chain biting into him. He's all right now – look at him!"

"You're a caution, that's what you are," said the butler. "I wouldn't go near a snarling dog for anything in the world. Come along, and get into that bath. You can't have breakfast with Sir Giles, looking as dirty as that."

"Goodness – am I to have breakfast with him?" said Francis, startled. "I'd better hurry up and have a bath then. What a pity my clothes are so dirty too."

When he was taken into a most magnificent bathroom, he looked at himself in a long mirror there. "Gracious, I look like a beggar boy! Whatever would Granny say?"

He hopped into a steaming bath, and soaped himself well, even washing his hair. An enormous thick snowy-white towel hung ready for him on a warm rail. It covered him from head to foot when he got out of the bath, and trailed on the floor.

There was a knock on the door. "Master Francis, breakfast is ready when you are. I'll wait in the hall and take you in. I'll brush and shake your clothes if you'll hand them out."

Francis opened the door and handed them out. He dried himself well and smoothed his hair down. Soon the door opened and his clothes were handed back. They looked quite different now, though they were still rather dirty.

He went down into the great hall, feeling clean and very hungry. Duke was waiting there for him, and the butler too. They were taken in state to a pleasant morning room, where Sir Giles was already seated at breakfast.

"Good morning!" he said. "I hope you slept well and feel hungry for your breakfast. There are sausages, bacon, or eggs – or all three together!"

Francis had a wonderful breakfast with Sir Giles.

Duke sat close beside him, putting his head on the boy's knee at times. Sir Giles asked Francis quite a lot of questions, and the boy talked away frankly about his family.

"There's Granny – she adores animals! Our house, Green Meadows, belongs to her, but she won't sell it even though it's much too big, and we're too poor to use even half the rooms. It's got a lovely garden, very very big – and stables, which we just use as a junk place! Then there's Daddy – well, Daddy isn't very lucky. He has to live in a wheelchair, and . . ."

"What's the matter with him?" asked Sir Giles.

"I don't really know," said Francis. "He was hurt in the last war, in the back – I don't remember that of course – and he had lots of treatment, but nothing seems to do any good. His legs don't seem any use. That's why he has to be in a wheelchair. But he's very cheerful, sir. And he's got lots of medals – one very special one for great bravery."

"Well, I should like to tell him that he's got a son who also deserves a medal for great bravery," said Sir Giles. "So I'll run you down in the car, and we'll have a word with him together. I sent a message to your mother last night to say you were safe here with me. She was very astonished, of course."

"What about Duke?" asked Francis. "Don't let Bill have him, sir – the children tease him so, and he's chained up in Bill's small garden. I had a long run-wire for him in our orchard."

"Would you like him to go back with you?" asked Sir Giles. "I would take it as a very great kindness if you would have him. I shall be out a lot, and Bill, who as you know is my chauffeur, will be with me. I don't want the dog left alone."

"I'd love to have him!" said Francis, eagerly. "And I could see to his legs, sir, if you'd show me how to. I'm going to be a vet, an animal doctor, when I grow up. I'd like to run one of those big Animal Vans – you know, the ones belonging to the P.D.S.A."

"Are all your family like you?" asked Sir Giles, amused.

"Well – we're all animal-lovers, if that's what you mean, sir," said Francis, puzzled. "Or do you mean are they all like me to look at?"

"No. I didn't mean that," said Sir Giles. "I only thought that if all your family were like you, they must be a very nice family. Now, you work that out, while I go and get my coat and hat. We'll go down to Green Meadows straight away. Take Duke to the car. Let him walk if he wants to."

Soon they were all on the way to Green Meadows, driven by Bill, who was very glad to see that Duke seemed so much better. They came to the gate and Francis jumped out of the car and held open the door for Sir Giles before Bill could. Francis thought the surgeon was a wonderful man. While he had been waiting for him with Duke, Bill had told him that Sir Giles was one of the cleverest surgeons in the whole country.

It was Saturday, so everyone was at home. Dan and Rita, Pam and Sue were there too, looking after their pets, and so were Ronnie and Harry.

Granny was the first to welcome Sir Giles, for she was in the orchard nearby with Flash the pony. Sir Giles raised his hat as Francis introduced them.

"This is my Granny," he said.

"Good morning," said Sir Giles. "You seem to keep a kind of Animals' Home here!"

151

"I only wish it was!" said Granny smiling. "But we've only a few creatures really! Well, Francis? Another adventure – what a boy you are to be sure!"

They all went into the house. Mother and Daddy were in the sitting room, and Daddy was just being helped into the wheelchair.

"Good morning, Mr Marshall," said Sir Giles "I've come to have a few words with you – about your son."

But it wasn't a *few* words they had that morning; it was a long long talk – a talk that had the most surprising and unexpected results!

After the talk was over, and Sir Giles had gone. Mother and Granny turned to each other in excitement. Francis saw tears in his mother's eyes.

"He said he could do something to John's back!" said Mother.

"He said he might walk again, in a few months' time!" said Granny, sniffing, and trying to find her hanky.

"He only said might, you know," said Daddy, who looked as excited as Mother and Granny. "We've had so many disappointments over various treatments. This might be another."

"Oh, but Sir Giles is such a *clever* surgeon," said Francis. "He's the best in the kingdom. Bill told me so."

He sat near his father, with Duke beside him. He felt very happy. He kept remembering the things that Sir Giles had said to his father about him. "Very great courage. A half-crazed dog, that even I and Bill were afraid of. Boy to be proud of. Like father, like son – and the son deserves a medal too! Wish he was *my* son. Congratulate you on having a boy like that."

Mother had cried with pride to hear about it all. Daddy had sat and listened with shining eyes. Granny couldn't keep still, she was so excited, and she had

152

jingled all the time. Yes, Francis was very happy – and to crown it all, Sir Giles had offered to examine Daddy's back, and had said he was almost certain he could do something to make the pain go, and *perhaps* Daddy might hobble about with two sticks.

When Sir Giles had gone, Francis rushed out to the others, and told them the news. Everyone was pleased, and Clare and Sam were full of joy. Dear old Daddy – he did deserve to have a little luck. It wasn't fair that great bravery should be rewarded by great pain and crippled legs.

Of course, they all listened open-mouthed to the tale of the night before. Duke listened open-mouthed too, his tongue hanging out, looking just as if he were smiling. He sat as close to Francis as he could possibly get. He couldn't seem grateful enough to him.

Francis put his arms round the big dog's neck. "You didn't bite, did you?" he said. "I love you, dear old Duke, and I wish you were mine! I'd like you!"

Duke licked him, and the others watched enviously. It was quite clear that Duke regarded himself as belonging to Francis, and to no one else.

Sam suddenly stared at Rita. "You've gone awfully red," he said. "Why have you?"

"Well," said Rita, "it wasn't true what I told you about Duke. He *hadn't* bitten anyone! It was just a tale made up by the children he had barked at – a sort of excuse for them to throw stones at him. I thought they were telling the truth, but they weren't. I'm sorry about that, Francis."

Francis felt angry. He turned to the twins, Pam and Sue. "*You* said the same thing!" he said.

"Yes. The milkman told us," said Sue. "But he's

153

always full of tales, and our mother says half of them aren't true. So I expect that wasn't, either."

"So Duke never *has* bitten anyone!" said Francis. He stroked the dog's head, as he lay down close beside the boy. "And you never will, will you – unless it's somebody wicked who is doing wrong. Oh, I'm glad I went into the summerhouse and saved you last night, Duke. It would have been dreadful to have you shot when you had never bitten anyone, and didn't even bite *me!*"

Sir Giles wasted no time about having a look at Daddy's back. He sent his car for him the very next day, and took him up to his hospital in London. When Daddy came back he was half cheerful, half sad.

"He says there's hope, but I must go to a hospital rather far away, one that specializes in my kind of back," said Daddy. "And oh dear – I shan't be back for some months. It's a very long job."

"Oh, what a pity!" said Mother. "We shall miss you so dreadfully!"

"Shall we be able to see you?" asked Granny. Daddy shook his head.

"No. It's too far away and the fare there and back would cost a terrible lot of money. We must just do without each other, all of us, and hope for the best," he said. "It will be worth it if it makes me just a bit better! If I could even *dress* myself, it would be something. All these jobs are such a strain on Mother, when she has so much else to do."

"They're not a strain," said Mother. "You know I love doing them. Oh dear – when do you go?"

"In two days' time," said Daddy. "Bill is going to take me all the way there in the big car. It's unbelievably kind of Sir Giles."

"*Really* great people are always unbelievably kind," said Granny.

"How are we ever going to pay him?" said Mother, looking worried.

"Francis has arranged that," said Granny, and Francis and everyone else looked at her in amazement.

"I haven't Granny," said Francis. "I haven't arranged anything! I've only got three pence in the world!"

"You *have* arranged it, all the same," said Granny, smiling at him. "Sir Giles told me that he's so grateful to you for saving Duke from being shot, and for being willing to look after him and keep him happy, that he's arranged to look after Daddy for you in return!"

"He never told me!" said Francis, amazed.

"I expect he thought you knew," said Granny. "He said 'One good turn deserves another', and this is *his* good turn, you see."

Daddy went off in the big car two days later, lying comfortably on the back seat, waving till he was out of sight. Everyone felt rather mournful when he had gone. It seemed funny to see the wheelchair with no one sitting patiently in it.

Mother wrote to him every other day. Granny wrote whenever she felt like it, which was quite often. The children wrote each Sunday, just before they went off to Sunday School. And all the animals wrote one day, under Sam's direction!

Daddy got the letter and laughed. On the first page was the imprint of four different-sized paws, and at the bottom Sam had printed:

"Wags from Duke, Rex, Pongo the puppy, and a purr from Mr Black (a loud one)."

On the next page was the imprint of a rabbit's paw, a

"What's the matter? Tell me"

smaller paw belonging to the guinea pig, and a little paw belonging to Dapple. At the bottom Sam had put:

"A woffle of his nose from Fluffy the rabbit. A wag of Gilbert the guinea pig's tail. (He would wag it if he had one.) And a mew from Dapple."

On the third page was pinned a long hair, and there were also prints of pigeon feet!

"A hair from Flash's tail (I couldn't get him to put his hoof on the paper). And coos from the pigeons. Do you like the way they have all signed their names, Daddy! I dipped their feet in mud, and pressed them on the paper."

Daddy laughed when he got that, and put it away carefully to keep. Dear old Sam! Was he still whistling tunelessly? Was Granny still jingling as she walked briskly about? Did Mother look tired and pale, or was she better? Was Clare still flying into hot little tempers and flying out of them again just as quickly? And what about his courageous son, Francis?

Daddy thought of his family over and over again, just as they thought of him. It was a good thing he couldn't see Mother, though! She had gone very thin, and her eyes looked too big for her face, just as Rita's used to do.

Francis was very worried about her. He saved her all the work he could; but no matter how much he saved her, there was always more to do, in that big old tumble-down house, whose doors wanted mending, walls painting, floors repairing, and a hundred and one other things!

Joe had done a lot to it, and had made it look gay and pretty – but he couldn't do the big jobs, and there was no money to get anyone else to do them. The garden looked lovely now, for Sid, Dan, and even Bill were working hard in it each evening they could spare. Dan was a fine helper too, and his mother felt pleased, and was very proud when she saw him going off to Scouts' meetings with Francis.

One evening Francis tackled Granny about his mother. "Granny," he said, "is Mother ill? She walks about so slowly, and she looks so sad."

"She's not well, that's certain," said Granny. "*I'm* worried about her too, but she won't see the doctor – she's afraid he'll pack her off for a holiday, or send her to bed."

"Granny, can't you sell Green Meadows, and we'll go somewhere smaller?" said Francis, desperately.

"I don't want to leave it," said Granny, and she put on her old, obstinate look. "Good days will come again, and then we'll be glad of a lovely place like this."

"Good days won't come if Mother gets ill – and how do we know Daddy will come back better, Granny? Oh dear, I wish I was grown up! I'd know better what to do. Granny, let's go and live in the stables! They're not so big as the house!"

"Don't be silly, Francis," said Granny. "*Please* don't be silly. It isn't like you to have wild ideas like that. It's more like Clare."

"Well, it *was* Clare's idea!" said Francis. "She thought it could be made into a lovely little house, and so it could – and you'd still have the lovely garden, or part of it, at any rate."

"You are *both* silly," said Granny. "Where do you suppose the money is coming from to make the stables into a proper little house?"

"I don't know," said Francis, helplessly. Granny went out of the room, jingling furiously. She was always cross and snappy when she was worried, and she was worried now about Mother, and all the work there was, and what would happen if Mother fell ill – and oh dear, how was John *really* getting on in that faraway hospital?

Francis went to find Duke. He was in the orchard with Flash and Rex. All three ran up to Francis at once, and both dogs leapt up at him. Francis sat down on the grass.

The dogs at once sensed that he was miserable and vied with one another to comfort him. Duke put his head on Francis's shoulder and Rex laid his on the boy's knee. Flash stood above them all, swishing his tail from side to side to keep the summer flies away.

Rex gave a little whine as if to say, "What's the matter? Tell me."

"There's nothing much to tell," said Francis, stroking the silky head. "Daddy's away, so I'm the man of the family now – but I simply don't know what to do! Mother's ill, I know she is. If something doesn't happen

158

soon, I'll have to ask Sir Giles to lend me the car so that I can go and see Daddy about things – but I don't want to worry him. But nothing nice *will* happen! Things will just go from bad to worse."

And then, at that very moment, something *did* happen. A car drove slowly by, and suddenly stopped. A window was lowered, and a woman's face looked out.

"This is the place!" she said. "I'm sure it is. Yes, look – Green Meadows. The old lady must live here. Let's go and see!"

Chapter Eleven

"IT'S A HAP-HAP-HAPPY DAY!"

Francis got up and went to the front gate to see who the visitors were. Two women got out of the car, about his mother's age. They were beautifully dressed. One carried a little dog, and they left a beautiful poodle behind in the car.

"Good evening," said Francis, politely. "Did you you want to see anyone here?"

"This must be one of the grandchildren!" said the first woman. "Yes – we have come to see if Mrs Linton is at home. She must be your grandmother, I think,"

"Mrs Linton? Yes, she is my granny," said Francis. "Will you come in? I'm Francis, her eldest grandson. Granny is indoors. Who shall I say wants to see her?"

"Tell her it's Ellen Surrey and a friend," said the visitor and followed Francis up the path.

Francis put them in the sitting room and went to find Granny. His mother was lying down with a headache.

"Granny!" he called. "Someone to see you. She says her name is Ellen Surrey, and there's a friend with her."

"Ellen! Ellen Surrey!" cried Granny. "Oh, what a surprise! She is the daughter of my greatest friend – I've often told you of the little girl whose parents were abroad, and who lived here with my family nearly all her childhood. She loved animals as much as I did. Well, well – to think Ellen is here!"

Granny hurried into the sitting room, and there were exclamations and kisses. Granny called to Francis: "Dar-

"What a wonderful idea!"

ling, get some iced lemonade and some of those little biscuits, will you?"

Francis put the ice into a jug, then the right amount of lemonade and added water. He set out the biscuits on a pretty plate. He was used to doing all kinds of household jobs, and he was as good as Clare at most of them!

"Oooh," said Sam, appearing, as he always did, when there was any sign of something to eat. "Who's that for?"

"Not for you," said Francis. "Visitors. Get out of my way, Sam, do – and go and see where Dapple is. I've not seen him for ages."

Sam disappeared. Francis took the biscuits and lemonade into the sitting room. The two visitors and Granny were talking at top speed.

"So this is your eldest grandson," said Miss Surrey. "And is he as fond of animals as you are, Aunt Lilian?"

It seemed queer to Francis to hear his Granny called Aunt Lilian, but Ellen Surrey had always called her that when she had lived with the family as a little girl. She had known Mother very well indeed too.

"All the children are fond of animals," said Granny. "It runs in our family! Your mother was very *very* fond of them — she loved them all. I missed her very much when she went out to South Africa, and I was shocked to hear she had died there not so long ago."

"Well, you won't be surprised to hear that she left all her money to animals, then," said Ellen Surrey. "She knew I had plenty of my own, and in her will she said that she wanted me to buy some place where animals could be kept in peace and happiness: sick animals — injured ones — horses that were too old to work — lost creatures. Well, you knew my mother; she had a place in her heart for any creature in trouble."

"Yes, I know," said Granny. "She was a wonderful woman. It's just like her to want her love for all creatures to continue even when she is dead. Where is this place you have bought? I'd like to come and see it. I'd like to see the animals you have there too. If I were a younger woman I'd have wanted to help!"

"Oh, we haven't bought any place yet," said Ellen Surrey. "We've only just got the money, you see. Patricia Hemming, my friend here, is helping me with everything, and she thought it would be nice to have a Home for Animals somewhere in this part of the country. And while we were driving back after seeing over lots of houses today, I suddenly remembered the old place here — Green Meadows — that I loved so much as a child. And I thought I'd come and see if you were still here!"

"And I *am* still here!" said Granny. "But the place isn't kept up as it was; half the rooms are shut, even the old playroom!"

"But it looks so gay and pretty – and the garden is very well-kept," said Ellen. "Isn't it, Patricia?"

They talked and talked and at last they went. Francis had slipped out of the room halfway through the visit, but Granny called him to see the visitors to the gate. He went with them politely and saw them into the car. Ellen Surrey took the wheel, and Patricia Hemming, her friend, leaned out to say goodbye to Francis.

"Goodbye!" she said. "You know, your Granny's house is the *only* one we've seen today that would do for a Home for Animals! It's exactly right, garden and all – but it *would* be just the one we can't have, of course!"

And with a last wave, the two visitors sped away. Sped away before Francis could call them back! Yes, call them back and say, "Please ask Granny to sell her house! We want a smaller one! *We* know it's a good place to keep animals – we've tried it!"

The boy watched the car speed away. He went into the orchard and sat down beside Duke to think. He was filled with a peculiar excitement. Did Ellen Surrey and her friend *really* think Green Meadows was just what they wanted? Would Granny sell it if she thought that her friends would have it, and that many creatures would find peace and happiness there, in the house and garden? There was still a small, unbuilt-on field at the back that could be hired for old horses or ponies. Excitement rose still higher in him. He could see it all! The house could also lodge students who wanted training with animals – Miss Surrey had spoken about them too.

Francis got up and walked straight back to the house,

Rex and Duke beside him. Dapple dropped down on to his shoulder from a tree branch, a little habit he had. "That's right," said Francis. "Come and back me up!"

Granny was still in the sitting room, putting it tidy. She looked pleased and excited, for she did not often have visitors.

"Granny," said Francis, in a suddenly grown-up voice, "I'm the man of the family now, aren't I? Well, I want you to sit down and listen to me, please. I've got something important to say."

"Good gracious!" said Granny, startled, and sat down at once, jingling loudly. "Whatever is it?"

"Granny, listen. I think Green Meadows is *exactly* the place that Miss Surrey wants for the Home for Animals," said Francis. "Her friend said so. I am sure they would give you a good price for it, especially as Miss Surrey loved it so much when she was a child."

"Good *gracious*!" said Granny, again.

Francis went on firmly. "It's a waste of this nice house to have half the rooms shut up, and let the whole place fall to pieces. It's a good thing Sid and Joe and Bill have done so much to make it tidy and neat – for I'm sure Miss Surrey wouldn't want to buy it if she could have seen it a few months ago! So Granny, I want you to tell her that if she *really* wants Green Meadows, she can have it!"

"But Francis dear – where would *we* live?" said Granny. "I don't think I could bear to go away from here. I know I'm a selfish old woman, but . . ."

"You wouldn't need to go away, Granny," said Francis, still in his grown-up voice. "With the money you got for the house and part of the garden, you could easily have the stables made into a darling little house – just the right size for Mother! There are big lofts above the stables, for bedrooms – it could be made beautiful!"

"I never heard of such a thing!" said Granny, really surprised. "Anyone would think you were grown-up, talking to me like this."

"Well – *someone's* got to do something," said Francis desperately, suddenly speaking like a little boy again. "Because of Mother! Granny, you know you'd love this dear old house to be a home for the creatures you love – and the garden too. Old worn-out horses and donkeys, sick or injured animals, ones who are cast off, unwanted. It's almost a Home for Animals now – we've so many creatures ourselves."

Granny sat lost in thought. "I could help with all the animals the Home kept," he said, her face lighting up. "And if we *could* have the stables made into a little house, why, we'd be next door to Green Meadows! And we'd keep the bit of garden we love most – the dell, and the flowerbeds, and the bit where the pigeons are."

"Yes. And we'd have any amount of creatures to play about with," said Francis, delighted to see that Granny was swinging round to his idea. "And better than anything – Mother wouldn't have so much to see to in a small house, and nor would you."

"Fancy you thinking all this out!" said Granny, suddenly looking astonished again. "Anyone would think you were grown-up."

"Daddy said I was to look after Mother," said Francis. "And this is a very good way."

"I'll talk it over with Mother this very night," said Granny, looking excited. "Oh dear – look at the time. Do get Clare in and tell her to help you with the supper. I must see how Mother's headache is."

When Mother came to supper, with Granny behind

her, the headache was quite gone. She looked very cheerful indeed. She went straight up to Francis and kissed him.

"Clever boy!" she said. "What a wonderful idea! Have you told the others?"

Francis hadn't, because he was afraid perhaps his mother would say no to his idea. So they all spent a most excited, and very pleasant, supper talking about future plans. Sam began to whistle loudly.

"*Not* at supper time, Sam," said Granny, and Sam stopped, only to begin again almost immediately, and this time nobody stopped him. He was very happy and so were they.

The next thing was to ask Miss Surrey if she really would like to have Green Meadows. They had to find out her address, which she hadn't left with them, and then Granny wrote a letter. She wrote it and rewrote it, and spent two whole days over it, nearly driving the family mad!

"Granny! Miss Surrey will buy a house somewhere else if you don't hurry!" said Francis. And that gave Granny such a shock that she finished her letter in a great hurry, and sent Francis out to post it.

Then came a long wait for an answer. Clare rushed to the door every time the postman came, but no answer arrived. Granny fidgeted about the house, jingling anxiously. Now that she had made up her mind to sell Green Meadows, she couldn't wait!

And then at last a telegraph boy cycled up to the front gate with a telegram. Mother took it and opened it with a trembling hand. She read it out aloud.

"Sorry for delay in answering, but have been away. Delighted to buy Green Meadows. Even more delighted to hear you will be our neighbours. Ellen Surrey."

Well, what a shout went up! Flash heard it down in the orchard. Duke and Rex heard it and came tearing up to the house. The pigeons heard it and rose into the air in a cloud, clapping their snow-white wings.

"Hurrah! Now we've turned the corner – and things should be all right!" cried Francis. "What fun we're going to have in the next six months!"

Once Granny had made up her mind to sell Green Meadows, she lost no time in pushing things on as quickly as possible. She got a builder to come in and look at the stables, she told Mother to make up her mind exactly how much of the garden she wanted, and she wrote to Daddy to tell him the news.

"I'm delighted!" Daddy wrote back. "The stables can be converted into a dear little house – they're lovely now, with the old red-brick walls, and red-tiled roof with moss all over it. I'm happy thinking about it, and knowing that you and Mother will be able to have plenty of time there to do all the things you haven't been able to do for so long."

Daddy's news was rather changeable. One week he sounded very cheerful and much better, and said that he really thought things were going well. The next week he said that he was on his back again, and the treatment had been stopped. Apparently once the right treatment had been found, then things would go well. How he wished he could be at home to share in all the excitement there!

Granny arranged that the builder should get to work at once on the stables, and she and Mother pored over plans that showed all the changes there were to be – windows pulled out and others put in, partitions to be put up for bedrooms in the loft, a kitchen made here, and a larder there.

"I shall like having a bedroom in the loft," said Clare. "I shall imagine horses down below, stamping and swishing their tails."

"I'm going to have a bedroom of my own," said Sam, pleased. "The tiniest you ever saw. I shan't be sleeping with you any more, Francis."

"Good thing," said Francis. "You won't wake me up with your whistling every morning. Mother, can't you teach Sam how to whistle a tune? I've tried, but I only make him worse."

"It'll come," said Mother. "Don't keep worrying Sam about it. Once upon a time *you* couldn't whistle a tune either! Look at this plan – we've decided to keep *this* bit of garden. We can manage it quite well by ourselves. The rest will go with Green Meadows, but, of course, it will still seem like ours because Ellen Surrey says we may go there whenever we like."

"And see all the animals," said Sam. "I'm going to visit all the old, old horses and donkeys each day. Mother, did you hear that Flash was going back to the shop?"

"Yes. Not yet, though," said Mother. "Sid's uncle is well again, and some of the sheds are rebuilt, because he was insured, after all. He's buying a new little cart for Flash, and so our little pony will once more trot round the village with it!"

"He's had a lovely holiday," said Clare. "What's Sid going to do, Mother? Go back to his brother? We *shall* miss him!"

"No. He told me last night that his brother is managing well by himself, and so Sid isn't going back. You won't guess what job he's got!" said Mother.

"What?" asked the children.

"He's asked Ellen Surrey if she will take him on as

gardener!" said Mother. "He has got so fond of Green Meadows, and enjoyed doing the garden so much. He can't bear to give it up to another gardener!"

"Oh! Then we'll see Sid every day!" said Clare, delighted. "I was afraid that if a strange gardener came he wouldn't like us running in and out of our old garden – but Sid won't mind a bit!"

The workmen came and began to work on the stables. Joe was with them, because Mother had asked the builder to give him a job. Joe was pleased. "First you do me a good turn and let me keep my pigeons here," he said. "Then I do you a good turn back, and mend up things a bit for you. And now you've done me a good turn again! Well, it's my turn now to do something, ma'am – and I'm going to work on these stables for you as well as I can!"

The job went very well indeed. The weather was good, and the men were good too. It was arranged that the family should go away for two months' holiday when school broke up in July, and that would allow the men to get on with the repairs to Green Meadows while it was empty. When the family came back, the stables would be ready for them to live in – a quaint little house with a pretty garden of its own, and pigeons flying about everywhere. There were twelve of them now, for they had laid eggs and hatched out babies that summer.

Each of the children owned one. Francis had one called Bobbo, Clare's was called Clapper because he clapped his wings so loudly, and Sam called his White-wings. They all came flying when they were called.

School broke up. Holidays came – and Granny went off with the children to a little house by the sea, leaving Mother and Mrs Oldham to strip Green Meadows of carpets and curtains, and to put the furniture into store till the stables were ready.

"Mother won't work too hard, will she?" said Francis, anxiously, to Granny, after they had said goodbye to her.

"No. Mrs Oldham will see to that," said Granny. "Now that I have sold Green Meadows and got the money, I can do lots of things I couldn't before. Go for this long holiday, for instance – and pay Mrs Oldham to come and help Mother every day."

"I hope Rex and Dapple and the rest will be all right," said Clare. "I don't like leaving them. I'm glad Flash has gone back happily to his master. I saw him yesterday, trotting along pulling his new little vegetable cart – and oh, Granny, he saw me, and he came right over to me, cart and all!"

Mother joined them down by the sea in two weeks' time, and they all had a wonderful time. They were as brown as berries, even Mother. They tried to persuade Granny to swim, but she wouldn't.

"You can wear your chains too, if you think you'll miss their jingling," said Sam, and got a tap on his hand!

They went back in September. Mother had gone ahead to see the furniture moved in, and curtains put up. Mrs Oldham was there to greet her, and Rex too.

Dan had proved a great standby. He had taken on the care of the pigeons, the rabbit, the guinea pig, Dapple, and Mr Black while the Green Meadows family had been away. Pongo the puppy had gone on a holiday with the family who owned him. It was a lovely thing for Dan to do, actually, because he had plenty of time to spare in the holidays and was up at Green Meadows all day long – while his mother cleaned up the rooms in the stables as they were finished.

The day came for the children and Granny to go back. They were in a great state of excitement – and when they saw the dear little house awaiting them, they were even more excited! It looked lovely, clean and gay and welcoming. And there was Mother on the doorstep, smiling all over her face!

"Let's explore, let's explore!" cried Clare, and they went all over the house at once, exclaiming in delight.

"There's a lot to be done yet," said Mother. "Sam's bedroom isn't finished, nor are two of the rooms downstairs, and there's some more painting to be done. But at any rate it was ready enough to move into!"

"If only Daddy could see it!" said Clare. "When's he coming home, Mummy! He's been away *too* long!"

"Sir Giles is coming to see me about him tomorrow," said Mother. "I'll tell you what he says."

The surgeon came in next day with Duke, who had been staying with his old master. He fell upon Francis with joy. The boy hugged him. The dog was very dear to him because of that dreadful night in the early summer.

"I've come for two things," said Sir Giles. "One is to say that your husband will be home by Christmas, Mrs Marshall. At last we have got to the root of the matter and now I hope we can make headway."

"Will he walk?" asked Mother, almost in a whisper.

"He'll hobble – I can't say more than that," said Sir Giles. "But he'll have no more pain, and he can certainly take some sort of job – brainwork, I mean. Wait and see; I'm quite hopeful now. And anyway he'll be home for Christmas."

"What's the second thing you've come about?" said Mother.

"It's about Duke," said Sir Giles. "I have to go away

again, this time to America. I don't want to leave him in Bill's care again. I want to give him to Francis – for his own dog. I know he loves him, and there's no doubt that Duke loves him back with all his heart. He's really more Francis's dog than mine. Will you have him, Francis?"

Would he have Duke! Francis couldn't believe his ears. He went bright scarlet, and couldn't say a word. But Duke said plenty!

"Woof! Woof-woof! Woof!" And he leapt on Francis and licked him on all the bare places he could find!

"Oh, sir!" said Francis, at last. "Yes, I'll have him. I always wanted a dog like Duke. Thank you very very much. Can you really spare him?"

"Only to you," said Sir Giles, with a smile. "I'll come and see him sometimes when I'm back again. May I leave him here now, Mrs Marshall?"

So Duke came to live with them, and was the happiest dog in the kingdom. For the first few days Francis went about with his arm round Duke's neck, the dog trotting beside him. He simply couldn't believe that Duke was really his!

The days flew by. Christmas came nearer and nearer. Daddy wrote cheerful letters, and said he was out of his chair and hobbling with two sticks to visit other patients in the ward. The next letter said he had hobbled too much and was in bed again. The next one said he was up once more. Would he be all right for Christmas?

"He's coming!" said Mother, one day, looking up from a letter. "He's coming next week – two days before Christmas! Bill is to fetch him in Sir Giles's car, by Sir Giles's own orders. How good he is!"

"What else does Daddy say?" asked Sam.

"He says he has a big surprise for us all," said Mother. "Bless him, I expect he's been working hard at making

172

some wonderful present for us. They have a fine work-shop at that hospital, you know, to help patients to pass the time. Fancy – next week! And at the end of *this* week the workmen will be out and we'll have the house to ourselves."

"That four-leaved clover was lucky after all," said Francis. "I began to think it was a fraud!"

Mother got ready for Christmas in the new little house. It hadn't a name yet, for nobody could think of a nice enough one. The Christmas tree arrived and stood in the hall, gaily decorated. The children put up paper chains and picked red-berried holly from the Green Meadows garden, with Sid's help. Mysterious parcels were hidden in every corner.

The day came for Daddy's arrival home. It was the first thought everyone had when they awoke that morn-ing. "Daddy's coming!"

What time would the car arrive? Nobody knew exactly. But at three o'clock, which was the earliest it *could* come, all the children were at the gate. Their front gate was now the one that used to be the back gate. It was mended, and painted white. Daddy had been told to come to that gate, though Bill himself knew that quite well, of course. Bill said he would help Daddy to hobble up to the house, and would even carry him, if necessary.

Three o'clock. Half-past three. Four o'clock. Oh dear! Would Daddy never come? Quarter-past four! Mother called from the door.

"Come up to the house for a minute, dears, and take a bun each, in case Daddy is very late. You had your dinner so early."

They all ran up – but just as they were taking their buns, they heard the sound of a car stopping outside.

"Daddy's come! Daddy's come!" squealed Clare, and dropped her bun to run to the gate.

Yes, there was the big car. As they got to the gate, the car door swung open, and a man leapt out. He walked briskly to the gate, smiling all over his face.

"Daddy!" screamed Clare. "Daddy! You're walking!" She ran to him and he swung her up in his arms. Then Sam came running, wide-eyed and wondering, and last of all Francis. Sam looked at his father's legs. Yes, they were walking. And Daddy hadn't even got *one* stick! Sam threw his arms round his father's waist and buried his head in his coat. To have a father that *walked* – what a truly wonderful thing!

Mother heard the excitement and came running, bright-eyed and breathless. When she saw Daddy walking, with the three children clinging to him, she stopped, amazed.

"John! Oh, *John!*" she said and ran to him in joy. "Was *this* your surprise? Oh, I never thought of that! Welcome home to us all – we've missed you so much!"

Granny jingled down the path with Mr Black behind, and met them halfway. Her eyes were full of happy tears. At last, at last, Daddy was well.

"Yes. I'm absolutely all right!" he said, smiling round. "Stand away from me. See me jump! See me run! And on New Year's Eve Mother and I are going to a dance – do you hear that, Mother? No, don't say you haven't a frock. I'm going to buy you the most beautiful one in the world!"

Half-laughing, half-crying, the little family went into the house. What a homecoming! How different Daddy was! Sam had never seen him like this before, and he stared at him as if he was something out of another world.

They all sat down to an enormous tea at last. "There's one thing you've left me to do, I see," said Daddy. "You haven't given this dear little house a name!"

"We couldn't think of one," said Mother. "Oh dear – to think of all that's happened this year, John. I was so miserable at the beginning. Do you remember, Francis, you and I went out into the garden in February. You made me come – and I told you all my troubles."

"I remember," said Francis. "And you stooped and rang the bell of the very first snowdrop – oh, Mother, you did, and said it was lucky. And it was, it was!"

"Then," said Daddy, at once, "I here and now name this little house Snowdrop Cottage – and may it bring us as much good luck as the ringing of the first snowdrop bell this year!"

"Oh *yes* – Snowdrop Cottage – it's a lovely name!" said Clare. "We'll get Joe to paint it on the gate as soon as ever he can. Snowdrop Cottage!"

Sam listened happily, his solemn face still turned towards this new and astonishing father. He pursed up his mouth and began to whistle. He whistled very loudly indeed, because he was so very happy.

Everybody turned and looked at him. "Sam!" said Clare, in wonder. "You're whistling a *tune!* A real *tune!*"

Sam stopped, delighted. "What is it, then?" he asked, red in the face.

"The best one you *could* whistle!" said Clare. "It's a Hap-Hap Happy Day!"

More Adventures on
Willow Farm

First publishedby Country Life Ltd.
This edition was first published in paperback in 1970 in Armada
as *Adventures on Willow Farm*

Copyright © Enid Blyton

Chapter One

Christmas Holidays at the Farm

Four children sat looking out of a farmhouse window at the whirling snow. It was January, and a cold spell had set in. Today the snow had come, and the sky was leaden and heavy.

Rory was the biggest of the children. He was fourteen, tall and well made, and even stronger than he looked. A year's hard work on his father's farm was making him a fine youth. Then came Sheila, a year younger, who managed the hens and ducks so well that she had made quite a large sum of money out of them since the Easter before.

Benjy pressed his nose hard against the leaded panes of the old farmhouse windows. He loved the snow. "I wonder where Scamper is," he said.

Scamper was his pet squirrel, always to be found on his shoulder when they were together. But Scamper had been missing for a day or two.

"He's curled himself up somewhere asleep, I expect," said Penny, the youngest. "Squirrels are supposed to sleep away the winter, aren't they? I'm sure you won't see him again till this cold spell has gone, Benjy."

Penny was eight, three years younger than Benjy, so she was the baby of the family. She didn't like this at all, and was always wishing she was bigger.

"Do you think Mark will come, if it keeps snowing like this?" she asked.

Mark was a friend of theirs. He took lessons with them at the vicarage away over the fields, and the children's mother had said he might come to stay for a few days. He had never been to Willow Farm and the children were longing to show him everything.

"Won't he be surprised to see our donkeys?" said Benjy. "My word, mine did gallop fast this morning!"

Each of the children had a donkey, a Christmas present from their father. They had worked well on the farm, and deserved a reward—and when the four donkeys arrived on Christmas morning there had been wild excitement. The children were looking forward to riding on them when school began again. The fields had been too muddy to walk across, and they had had to go a long way round by the roads. Now they would be able to gallop there on their donkeys!

"I'm longing to show Mark over our farm," said Rory. "I hope this snow doesn't last too long."

"Everywhere is beginning to look rather strange," said Sheila. "Snow is rather magic—it changes everything almost at once. I hope my hens are all right. I wonder what they think of the snow."

Sheila felt sure her hens would not lay many eggs in the snowy weather. She made up her mind to give them a little extra hot mash morning and night to keep them warm. She slipped out into the kitchen to talk to Fanny about it. Fanny was the cook's niece and helped Sheila willingly with the poultry.

The snow went on falling. Soon all the farm-buildings were outlined in soft white. When their father came in to tea he shook the snow from his broad shoulders and took off his boots at the door.

"Well!" he said, "we can't do much this weather, except tend the beasts and see they have plenty to eat and drink. Aren't you going to help milk the cows, Benjy?"

"Gracious, yes!" said Benjy, who was still dreaming at the window. He rushed to get his old mack and sou'-wester, and pulled on his rubber boots. Then he disappeared into the flurrying snow and made his way to the sweet-smelling cow-sheds.

Only Rory and Penny, the eldest and the youngest, were left at the window. Rory put his arm round Penny. "Have you seen Skippetty lately?" he asked.

Skippetty was the pet lamb that Penny had had the spring and summer before. The little girl had been very fond of him, and he had followed her all over the place. But now he had grown into a sheep, and had gone to live in the fields with the others. Penny shook her head sadly.

"I don't know Skippetty when I see him!" she said. "He's just exactly like all the others. I wish he didn't have to grow up. I miss him very much. Wasn't it fun when he used to trot at my heels everywhere?"

"Well, you'll have another pet lamb this spring, so don't worry," said Rory. "Won't it be lovely when the winter is over and the sun is warm again—and all the fields are green, and there are young things everywhere?"

"Yes," said Penny happily. "Oh, Rory, don't you love Willow Farm? Aren't you glad it's ours? Wasn't it lucky that it did so well last year?"

Her father came into the room and heard what she said. He laughed. "Beginner's luck!" he said. "You look out this year—maybe we shan't have such an easy time!"

183

Harriet the cook came bustling in. Fanny was out collecting the eggs with Sheila, and Harriet had come to lay the tea. She put down a dish of golden butter, and a dish of home-made cheese. Then came scones and cakes and a home-cured ham. A big jug of cream appeared, and a dish of stewed apple. Penny's eyes gleamed. This was the sort of high-tea she liked.

"Everything grown on our own farm," she said. "Doesn't it look good? Are you hungry, Daddy?"

"Famished!" said her father. "Where's your mother? Ah, there she is."

Mother had been in the ice-cold dairy and she was frozen! "My goodness, I'm cold!" she said. "Our dairy is wonderfully cool in the hot summer months—but I wish it was wonderfully hot in the cold winter months! I've been helping Harriet to wrap up the butter for sale. Daddy, we've done very well out of our butter-sales, you know. I feel I'd like to try my hand at something else now, as well."

"Well, for instance?" said Daddy, pulling his chair up to the table. "We have hens, ducks, cows, sheep, pigs, dogs, and goodness knows what else! There doesn't seem much else to have."

"Well, we haven't got bees," said Mother, beginning to pour out the tea. "I'd like to keep bees. I love their friendly humming—and I love their sweet yellow honey too!"

"Oooh—bees would be fun," said Penny. "Oh, Mother—let's keep them this year. And we haven't got a goat. Couldn't we keep one? And what about some white pigeons? And we could have . . ."

"We could have a bull!" said Rory. "Fancy, we haven't

184

got a bull, Daddy. Aren't you going to get one?"

"One thing at a time," said his father, cutting the ham. "After all, we haven't had our farm a year yet. I dare say we'll have everything before the second year is out! Now, where are Sheila and Benjy?"

The two soon appeared, rosy of cheek. Benjy was pleased with his milking. He always got a wonderful froth in his pail, the sign of a good milker. He was tremendously hungry.

Sheila had good news about the hens too. "Four more eggs today than we had yesterday," she announced. "Mother, the hens don't like the snow at all. They all huddle in the house together, and stare out as if they simply can't imagine what's happening."

"Silly creatures, hens," said Rory. "Give me ducks any day! Pass the scones, Sheila."

All the children discussed the farm happenings with their parents. They knew all the animals and birds, they knew each field and what had been grown in each, they even knew what the sowing and manuring had cost, and what profits had been made. Each child was a keen little farmer, and not one of them was afraid of hard work. Benjy was the dreamy one, but he could work hard enough when he wanted to.

"Mark's coming tomorrow," said Rory to his mother. "He'd better sleep with me, hadn't he, Mother? He's never been to stay on a farm before. He lives in an ordinary house with an ordinary garden—and they don't even grow easy things like lettuces and beans. They buy everything."

"Won't he like the things *we* grow?" said Penny. "You know—this cheese—and that butter—and this jam—and that ham?"

"He'll like the live things better," said Rory. "I bet he'll like a ride on old Darling. Listen—she's coming into the yard now."

Everyone heard the slow clip-clop of Darling's great hooves, biting through the snow on to the yard below. Everyone pictured the big, patient brown horse with her lovely brown eyes and sweeping eyelashes. They all loved Darling.

"One thing I like about farm-life," said Benjy, cutting himself a big slab of Harriet's cream-cheese, "is that there are so many things to love. You know, all the animals seem friends. I'd hate to live in London now, as we used to do—no great horses to rub down and talk to—no cows to milk—no lambs to watch—no hens to hear clucking—no tiny chicks and ducklings to laugh at. Golly, wouldn't I miss all our farmyard friends."

"I wonder what Tammylan is doing this snowy weather," said Penny. Tammylan, the wild man, was their firm friend. He lived in a cave in the hillside, and looked after himself. All the animals of the countryside came to him, and he knew each one. The children loved visiting him, for he always had something fresh to tell them, and something new to show them.

"We shan't be able to go and see him if the snow gets thick," said Sheila. "And I did want to tell him how we love our four donkeys."

Tammylan had got the donkeys for their father to give them. He had arrived on Christmas Day, leading the four fat little creatures, and had stayed for the day and then gone back to his cave.

"Won't you be lonely tonight?" Penny had asked him.

But Tammylan had shaken his head.

"I've no doubt some of my animal-friends will come and sit with me this Christmas night," he had said, and the children had pictured him sitting in his cave, lighted by a flickering candle, with perhaps a hare at his feet, a rabbit near by, and one or two birds perched up on the shelf behind his head! No animal was ever afraid of Tammylan.

Darkness came, and the children's mother lighted the big lamp. The children felt lazy and comfortable. There were no lessons to do because it was holiday-time. There was no farm-work to do because it was dark outside and snowy. They could do what they liked.

"Let's have a game of cards," said Penny.

"No—let's read," said Benjy.

"I'd like to sew a bit," said Sheila.

"Well—I vote we have the wireless on," said Rory. He turned it on. There was a short silence as the set warmed up a bit. And then a voice boomed out into the room.

"This evening we are going to devote half an hour to 'Work on the Farm'."

"Oh, no, we're not!" laughed Daddy, and he switched the wireless off. "This evening we're all going to play Snap! Now then—where are the cards?"

And play Snap they did, even Mother. It was good for them to forget the farm and its work for one short evening!

Chapter Two

The Visitor

Mark arrived the next day. Rory went to meet him at the bus-stop, a mile or two away. The snow was now thick, but would soon melt, for the wind had changed. Then everywhere would be terribly muddy.

"Will you lend me Bray?" asked Rory of Benjy. "I thought I'd ride on Neddy to meet Mark, and if you'd lend me your donkey, I could take it along for Mark to ride back on."

"Yes, you can have him," said Benjy. So Rory went off on Neddy, his own donkey, and Bray trotted willingly beside him. They came to the bus-stop and waited patiently for Mark. The bus came in sight after a while, and Mark jumped down carrying a small bag. He was astonished to see Rory on a grey donkey.

"Hallo, Rory," he said. "I didn't know you had donkeys. You never told me."

"Well, we didn't have them till Christmas Day," said Rory. "Did you have a good Christmas? We did! We each got a donkey for our own. This is Neddy, the one I'm riding on. And this is Bray. He belongs to Benjy. You can ride him home."

"Well, I've never really ridden a donkey before, except once at the seaside," said Mark, who was smaller and fatter than Rory. "I fell off then. Is Benjy's donkey well behaved?"

Rory laughed. "Of course! Don't be silly, Mark!

Gracious, wait till you've been on the farm a few days. You'll have ridden all the horses, and all our donkeys, too. And Buttercup the cow if you like. She doesn't mind."

Mark had no wish to ride horses or cows. He looked doubtfully at Bray, and then tried to mount him. Bray stood quite still. Soon Mark was on his back, holding tightly to the reins.

"Give me your bag," said Rory, trying not to laugh at Mark. "That's right. Now off we go."

But Bray did not seem to want to move. He stood there, his ears back, flicking his tail a little. Mark yelled after Rory, who was cantering off.

"Hie! This donkey's stuck. He won't move!"

Rory cantered back. He gave Bray a push in the back with Mark's bag. "Get up!" he said. "You know the way home! Get up, then!"

Bray moved so suddenly that Mark nearly fell off. The donkey cantered quickly down the road, and Rory cantered after him. Soon Mark got used to the bumpity motion of the little donkey, and quite enjoyed the ride. Once he had got over his fear of falling off, he felt rather grand riding on the little donkey.

"We'll soon see the farm," said Rory. "It's a jolly good one. It's a mixed farm, you know."

Mark didn't know. He wondered what a mixed farm was. "Why is it mixed?" he said.

"Well—a mixed farm is one that keeps animals and hens and things, and grows things in the fields too," explained Rory. "It's the most paying sort of farm. You see, if you have a bad year with the sheep, well, you probably have a good year with the wheat. Or if you

189

have a bad year with the potatoes, you may make it up
by doing well with the poultry. We love a mixed farm,
because there's always such a lot of different things to
do."

"It does sound fun," said Mark, wishing his donkey
didn't bump him quite so much. "I shall love to see
everything. I say—is that Willow Farm?"

It was. They had rounded a corner, and the farmhouse now lay before them. It was built of warm red
bricks. Its thatched roof was now covered with white
snow. Tall chimneys stood up from the roof. Leaded
windows with green shutters were set in the walls, and
Rory pointed out which belonged to his bedroom.

"You're to sleep with me," he said. "I've a lovely

view from my room. I can see five different streams from it. All the streams have willow trees growing beside them—they are what give the farm its name."

Mark gazed at the farmhouse and at all the old farm-buildings around—the barns and sheds, the hen-houses and other outbuildings, now white with snow. It seemed a big place to him.

"Come on," said Rory. "We'll put our donkeys into their shed, and go and see the others."

Soon the five children were gathered together in Rory's bedroom, hearing Mark's news and telling him theirs. Then they took him to see the farm and all its animals.

"Come and see the horses first," said Rory. "Benjy and I look after them. We groom them just as well as the men could, Daddy says."

Mark was taken to the stables and gazed rather nervously at three enormous shire-horses there.

"This is Darling, the best of the lot," said Benjy, rubbing a big brown horse. "And that's Captain. He's immensely strong. Stronger than any horse Daddy's ever known. And that's Blossom."

Then Mark had to see the cows. He liked these even less than the horses because they had horns!

"See this one?" said Benjy, pointing to a soft-eyed red and white cow. "We'll hope she'll have a calf this spring. We want her to have a she-calf that we can keep and rear ourselves. If she has a bull-calf we'll have to sell it. Jonquil, you'll have a little she-calf, won't you?"

"We may be going to have a big fierce bull of our own this year," said Penny, twinkling at Mark. She guessed he wouldn't like the sound of bulls at all! He didn't. He looked round nervously as if he half expected to see a bull coming towards him, snorting fiercely!

"Well—I hope I shan't be here when the bull arrives," he said. "I say—what a horrid smell! What is it?"

"It's only Jim cleaning out the pig-sties," said Sheila. "Come and see our old sow. She had ever so many piglets in the summer—but they've all grown now. We hope she'll have some more soon. You've no idea how sweet they are!"

"*Sweet?*" said Mark in amazement. "Surely pigs aren't sweet? I should have thought that was the last thing they were."

"*Piglets* are sweet," said Penny. "They really are."

"Well, your old sow is simply hideous," said Mark. The five children stared at the enormous creature. The four farm children had thought she was very ugly indeed when they first saw her—but now that they were used to her and knew her so well, they thought she was nice. They felt quite cross with Mark for calling her hideous.

She grunted as she rooted round in the big sty. Mark wrinkled up his nose as he smelt the horrid smell again. "Let's come and see something else," he said. So they all moved off over the snowy ground to the hen-houses. Mark saw the hens sitting side by side on the perches. They did not like walking about in the snowy run.

"I manage the hens, with Fanny, our little maid," said Sheila proudly. "I made a lot of money through selling the eggs last year. I put some hens on ducks' eggs as well as on hens' eggs, and Fanny and I brought off heaps and heaps of chicks and ducklings."

"Cluck-luck-luck," said a hen.

"Yes, you did bring us luck," said Sheila, laughing.

"Luck-luck-luck-luck!"

In the fields were big folds in which Davey the shepherd had put the sheep. He did not want them to roam too far in the snowy hills in case they got lost. Penny stood on the fence and called loudly.

"Skippetty, Skippetty, Skippetty!"

"She's calling the pet lamb she had last year," explained Rory. "Oh, Mark, do you remember when it followed her to school, like Mary's lamb in the rhyme? Wasn't that funny?"

Mark did remember. He looked to see if a little lamb was coming. But no lamb came. Instead, Davey the shepherd let a fat sheep out of the fold. It came trotting across the snowy grass to Penny.

"Penny! This isn't your lamb, is it?" cried Mark, in surprise. "Gracious! It's a big heavy sheep now."

"I know," said Penny regretfully. "When I remember that dear little frisky, long-leggitty creature that drank out of a baby's milk-bottle, I can hardly believe this sheep was once that lamb. I think it's very sad."

"Yes, it is," said Mark. Skippetty put his nose through the fence and nuzzled against Penny's legs. To him Penny was still the dear little girl who had been his companion all through the spring and summer before. She hadn't changed as he had.

"I wish I could show you my tame squirrel," said Benjy. "He's been missing the last few days. We think he may be sleeping the cold spell away."

"Oh, I've seen Scamper, you know," said Mark, remembering the times when Benjy had brought him to school on his shoulder. "Whistle to him as you used to do. Maybe he'll come. Even if he's asleep somewhere surely he will hear your whistle and wake!"

"Well, I've whistled lots of times," said Benjy. "But I'll whistle again if you like."

So the boy stood in the farmyard and whistled. He had a very special whistle for Scamper the squirrel, low and piercing, and very musical. Tammylan the wild man had taught him the whistle. The five children stood still and waited.

Benjy whistled again—and then, over the snow, his tail spread out behind him, scampered the tame squirrel. He had been sleeping in a hole in a nearby willow tree—but not very soundly. Squirrels rarely sleep all the winter through. They wake up at intervals to find their hidden stores of food, and have a feed. Scamper had heard Benjy's whistle in his dreams, and had awakened.

Then down the tree he had come with a flying leap, and made his way to the farmyard, bounding along as light as a feather.

"Oh, here he is!" yelled Benjy in delight. The squirrel sprang to his shoulder with a little chattering noise and nibbled the bottom of Benjy's right ear. He adored the boy. Mark gazed at him in envy. How he wished he had a pet wild creature who would go to him like that. "Would he come to me?" he asked.

"Yes," said Benjy, and patted Mark's shoulder. The squirrel leapt to it, brushed against Mark's hair, and sprang back to Benjy's shoulder again.

"Lovely!" said Mark. "I wish he was mine."

A bell rang down at the farmhouse. "That's Harriet ringing to tell us dinner's ready," said Rory. "Come on. I'm jolly hungry."

"So am I," said Mark. "I could eat as much as that

old sow there!"

"Well, I hope you won't make such a noise when you're eating, as *she* does!" said Benjy. "Listen to her! We've never been able to teach her table-manners—have we, Penny?"

Chapter Three

An Exciting Time

It was thrilling for Mark to wake up in Rory's bedroom the next morning and hear all the farmyard sounds, though they were somewhat muffled by the snow. He heard the sound of the horses, the far-off mooing of the cows, and the clucking of the hens. The ducks quacked sadly because their pond was frozen.

"I wish I lived on the farm always," thought Mark. He looked across to Rory's bed. The boy was awake and sitting up. He looked at his watch. "Time to get up," he said.

"What, so early!" said Mark, in dismay. "It's quite dark."

"Ah, you have to be up and about early on a farm," said Rory, leaping out of bed. "Jim and Bill have been up ages already—and as for Davey the shepherd, I guess he's been awake for hours!"

Mark dressed with Rory and they went down to join the others, who were already at the breakfast-table. Rory's father had had his breakfast and gone out. The children sat and ate and chattered.

"What would Mark like to do today?" said Sheila politely, looking at Rory. "It's too cold for a picnic. One day we'll take him to see Tammylan, the wild man. But not today."

"Oh, I don't want you to plan anything special for me at all," said Mark hastily. "I don't want to be treated as a visitor. I really don't. Just let me do the things you all do. That would be much more fun for me."

"All right," said Rory. "I dare say you are right. I remember when we all went from London to stay for a while at our uncle's farm, the year before last, we simply loved doing the ordinary little things—feeding the hens and things like that. You shall do just the same as we do. Sheila, you take him with you after breakfast."

"He can help me to scrape all the perches," said Sheila. "And he can wash the eggs too."

"I want to do that," said Penny. "Since the calves that I looked after have grown up, there isn't much for me to do."

"Davey the shepherd will let you have another lamb soon," said Mother. "Then you can hand-feed it and look after it as you looked after Skippetty last year. You will soon be busy."

"And you can come and milk a cow this afternoon, Mark," promised Benjy. "We'll see if you are a good milker or not."

Mark wasn't sure he wanted to milk a cow. He thought all animals with horns looked dangerous. But he didn't like to seem a coward, so he nodded his head.

"Have you finished your breakfast?" asked Sheila. "Have another bit of toast? You've only had four. We've all had about six."

"No thanks," said Mark, whose appetite was not quite so enormous as that of the other children. "Are you going to do the hens now, Sheila? Shall I get ready?"

"Have you brought some old things?" asked Sheila. "Good. Well, put on an old coat and your rubber boots and a scarf. I'll go and get ready too."

It wasn't long before both children were carrying a pailful of hot mash that Harriet the cook had given them. The snow was now melting and the yard was in a fearful state of slush. The children slithered about in it.

"Oh, isn't this awful?" said Sheila. "Snow is lovely when it's white and clean—but when it goes into slush it's simply horrid. MARK—be careful, you silly!"

At Sheila's shout Mark looked where he was going. He had turned his head to watch Jim the farm-hand, taking a cart full of mangels out of the yard—and he walked straight into an enormous slushy puddle near the pig-sty. He tried to leap aside, and the pail of mash caught his legs and sent him over. In a trice he was in the puddle and the pail of mash emptied over his legs.

"MARK! What a mess you're in!" cried Sheila in dismay. Mark scrambled up and looked down at himself. His coat was soaked with horrid-smelling dampness, and his rubber boots were full of hot hen-mash. He was almost ready to cry!

"Don't worry," said Sheila. "Your coat will dry."

"I'm not bothering about that," said Mark. "I'm bothering about the waste of that hot mash. Just look at it, all over the place."

"You go in and ask Mother to lend you some old clothes of Rory's," said Sheila comfortingly. "I'll get a spade out of the shed and just get most of the spilt mash back into the pail. It will be dirty, but I don't expect the hens will mind very much."

Mark disappeared into the house. Sheila shovelled up most of the spilt mash. She took it to the hen-houses and the hens came down from their houses into the slushy rain, clucking hungrily.

"I'll let you out into the farmyard to scratch about there as you usually do," said Sheila, who had always talked to her hens as if they were children. "Your yard is nothing but mud—but so is everywhere else. Now then, greedy—take your head out of the bucket!"

Sheila put the mash into the big bowls, and then broke the ice on the water-bowls. There had been a frost in the night, and the ice had not yet melted. She went to get a can to put in fresh water. The hens clucked round it.

"I know that your water must always be clean and fresh," said Sheila to her hens. "Look—there's the cock calling to you. He's found something for you!"

The cock was a beautiful bird, with an enormous drooping tail of purple-green feathers, and a fine comb. He had a very loud voice, and always awoke all his hens in the morning when it was time to get up. Now he had found a grain of corn or some other titbit on the ground and he was telling the hens to come and get it.

Mark arrived again, wearing an old brown coat of Rory's, and somebody else's boots. "Look at the cock," said Sheila. "He's a perfect gentleman, Mark—he never eats a titbit himself—he always calls his hens to have it."

"Cock-a-doodle-doo!" said the cock to Mark.

"He's saying 'Good morning, how do you do?'" said Sheila, with a laugh. She always amused the others because whenever her hens or ducks clucked or quacked, she always made it seem as if they were really saying something. Penny honestly thought that they said the things Sheila made up, and she felt that they were really very clever.

"Come and scrape the perches for me," said Sheila. "The hens haven't very good manners, you know, and they make their perches in an awful mess."

Mark had the job of scraping the perches clean. He wasn't sure that he liked it much, but he was a sensible boy and knew that there were dirty jobs to do as well as nice ones. You can't pick your jobs on a farm. You have to be ready to do everything!

Sheila looked to see if there was enough grit in the little box she kept for that purpose. She told Mark what it was for. "It's to help the hens digest their food properly," she told him. "And that broken oyster-shell over there is to help them to make good shells for their eggs. Take this basket of eggs indoors into the kitchen, Mark. You can begin to wash them for me. Some of them are awfully dirty."

Poor Mark broke one of the eggs as he washed it! It just slipped out of his fingers. He was upset about it, but Sheila said, "Never mind! We brought in twenty-three eggs, and that's very good for a day like this."

Mark soon began to enjoy the life on the farm very much. The days slipped by, and he was sad when Saturday came and he packed to go home. Then, quite unexpectedly, his mother telephoned to ask if he could be kept there a little longer as his grandmother was ill, and she wanted to go and look after her.

"Oh!" said Mark, in delight, "oh, do you think I *can* stay? If I can, I promise I'll do my best to help on the farm. I'll even clean out the pig-sties!"

Everyone laughed at that, for they knew how Mark hated the smell. "Of course you can stay," said Mother, who liked the quiet, but rather awkward little boy. "You are really quite useful, especially since you have learnt how to milk."

It was a very funny thing, but Mark had been most successful at milking the cows. He had been terrified at first, and had gone quite pale when he had sat down on a milking-stool, and had watched whilst Benjy showed him how to squeeze the big teats and make the milk squirt down into the great clean pails.

He couldn't get a drop of milk at first—and then suddenly it had come, and Mark had jumped when he heard the milk go splash-splash into the pail. The boy's hands were strong, and he just seemed to have the right knack for milking. Jim the farmhand had praised him, and Mark had felt proud.

"Milking is quite hard work," he said to Penny. "And what a lot you get! Isn't it creamy too? No wonder you are able to make a lot of butter."

All the children worked during the holidays, and they disliked the slush and wet very much. Rain had come after the snow, and everywhere was squelchy, so that it was no pleasure to go round the farm and do anything. The farm-hands were splashed with mud from head to foot, and the old shire-horses had to be cleaned well every day, for they too were covered with mud.

"I shall be quite glad when it's time to go to school again," said Rory, coming in one day with his coat soaked, and his hair dripping. "Farming really isn't much fun in this weather. I've been cleaning out our donkey-stable. Mark's been helping me. He kept holding his nose till he found the smell wasn't bad after all. Daddy says the manure will be marvellous for the kitchen-garden, where Mother grows her lettuces and things."

"Nothing's wasted on a farm, is it?" said Mark. "Jim told me yesterday that he takes all the wood-ash for that field called Long Bottom. He says it's just what the soil wants there. And Bill is piling the soot from the chimneys into sacks in that shed behind the donkeys. He says you will use that somewhere on the farm too."

Mark was learning a great deal, and liked airing what he had learnt. He had ridden all the donkeys now, and all the horses too—though that wasn't very difficult, for the shire-horses had backs like sofas! He wouldn't ride on Buttercup the cow. The children themselves were not supposed to, but actually Buttercup didn't mind at all. She was a placid old lady, and loved having children round her.

The Christmas holidays only had a day or two more to go. The children began to look out their pencil-boxes and pile together their books. All of them went to the vicarage for lessons, but later on, perhaps in the autumn, the two boys were going to boarding-school again. They hated to think of this, and never talked about it.

Mark was to go home after the first day at school. The others were sorry, for it had been fun to show him all round Willow Farm. Mark was sad too. He knew all the animals there by now, and it was such a nice friendly feeling to go out and talk to a horse or a cow, or to Rascal, the shepherd's clever dog.

"If only holidays lasted for always!" he sighed. But alas, they never do!

Chapter Four

The New Horses

"You know, I *must* get a couple of strong horses for light work," said the farmer, one morning at breakfast, as the children were hurrying to get off to school. Rory had gone out to get the donkeys, so he was not there. "It's silly to use our big shire-horses for light cart-work. We really could do with a couple of smaller horses."

"Oooh, how lovely!" said Penny, who always welcomed any addition to the farm's livestock. "Oh, Daddy, do let me go with you."

"I shall go on Wednesday afternoon," said her father. "It's market-day then. You'll be at school, little Penny."

"I shan't, I shan't!" squeaked Penny. "It's a half-holiday this week. I shall come with you. I do love market-day. Will you use one of the new horses for the milk-round, Daddy?"

"Yes, I shall," said her father. The children were all very interested in the sale of their milk. Some of it was cooled, and put into big churns to be sent away to the large towns—and some of it was delivered to people near by who were willing to buy the good creamy milk of the farm.

Sometimes their father grumbled and sighed because he had so many papers to fill in about his cows and their milk. He had inspectors to examine his cow-sheds, and other men to examine and test his cows to make sure they were healthy.

"You see," he explained to the children. "I want my milk to be as perfect as it can be, free from any bad germs that might make people ill. Well, you can only get milk like that if you buy the right cows who come of a good stock, and are healthy and strong, and good milkers. Our cows are fine, but our cow-sheds could be made much better."

"How could they, Daddy?" asked Benjy, in surprise. He always liked the old, rather dark cow-sheds. They smelt of cow, and it was cosy in there, milking on a winter's day, whilst the cows munched away happily.

"I'd like to take them down and put up clean, airy sheds," said his father. "I'd like cow-sheds where you could eat your dinner off the floor, it would be so clean! Well—maybe if I get a good price for the potatoes I've got stored, I can think about the cow-sheds. And you can help me then, Benjy, and Rory! We'll think out some lovely sheds, and get books to see what kind are the best."

"Oooh yes," said Benjy. "We'd have more cows then, wouldn't we, Daddy? Sixteen isn't very many, really, though it seemed a lot at first. Daddy, I wish you'd let me and Rory do the milk-round on Saturdays once or twice. It would be such fun."

"Oh no—Jim has time enough for that," said his father. "But if he's ever too busy, as he may be when the spring comes again, I'll let you try. You had better go with him once or twice to see what he does."

"Can we all go to the market with you to buy our new horses?" asked Sheila eagerly.

"Yes, if you like," said their father. "Now, off to school, or you'll be late. Look—there are your donkeys at the door, waiting for you."

"Sheila! Benjy! Penny!" shouted Rory impatiently from outside. "Aren't you ever coming?"

The children tore out to their donkeys. "Hallo, Canter!" said Sheila, giving him a lump of sugar. "Did you sleep well?"

"Frrrrumph!" said the donkey, nuzzling against Sheila's shoulder.

"He said yes, he had an awfully good night," said Sheila to the others.

Penny turned to her donkey too. "Did you sleep well, darling Hee-Haw?" she asked.

"Frrrrumph!" said her donkey too, and tried to nibble at her sleeve.

"Oh, Hee-Haw didn't have a good night at all," said Penny solemnly, turning to the others. "He says a mouse ran over his back all night long."

The others laughed. "Now don't *you* begin making up things like Sheila!" said Rory. "Do come on, Sheila. What's the matter? Is your saddle loose?"

"A bit," said Sheila, tightening it. "Rory, Daddy's going to the market on Wednesday to buy two new light horses—not cart-horses—and we can go with him!"

"Good!" said Rory, galloping off in front. "I love the market. Get up, Neddy, get up—you're not as fast as you usually are, this morning!"

The children were glad when they galloped home after morning school on Wednesday. A half-holiday was always nice—but going to the market made it even nicer. They ate a hurried lunch, and then went out to get their donkeys again. Their father set off in his car and told them where to meet him.

The donkeys were ready for a run, and a run they

205

had, for it was quite a long way to the town where the market was held. The little fat grey creatures were glad to be tethered to a post when the children arrived at the market. Rory went round them to make sure they were safely tethered, for it would not be easy to trace a lost donkey in a big crowded market.

They soon found their father, who was talking to a man about the horses he needed. He went to the part of the market where patient horses were standing ready for sale. The boys went with him and the girls went to look at some fat geese cackling nearby. There were no geese at Willow Farm, and Sheila longed to have some to add to her hens and ducks.

"They only eat things like grass, you know," said Sheila. "They are awfully cheap to keep."

"They're very hissy, aren't they?" said Penny, who wasn't quite sure about the big birds. "Hissy and cackly."

"You are a baby, Penny!" laughed Sheila. "You always say that when you see geese. Why shouldn't they hiss and cackle? It's their way of talking."

"What are they saying?" asked Penny, looking at the big birds.

"They're saying, 'Ss-ss-sss-it's funny Penny's frightened of us-ss-ss-sss!'" said Sheila solemnly.

Meanwhile the boys were looking at horses with their father and his farmer friend. Horses of all colours and sizes were paraded up and down in front of them. Benjy liked a little brown one with gentle eyes. She had good legs and he was sure she was just the right horse for the milk-round.

"She'd be good for the milk-round, Daddy," he said. "I'm sure she'd soon learn what houses to stop at without being told!"

"Oh, it's for a milk-round you want her, is it?" said the man.

"Among other things," answered the farmer.

"You can't do better than have that little brown horse then," said the man. "She's been used to a milk-round already. She's strong and healthy, and as gentle as a lamb."

So little Darky was chosen, and Benjy was delighted. He mounted her at once and she put her head round and looked at him inquiringly out of her large brown eyes, as if to say, "Hallo! I'm yours now, am I?"

The other horse chosen was an ugly fellow, but healthy and good-tempered. He was brown and white in patches, and had long legs and bony hind-quarters. He moved in an ungainly manner, but it was plain that he had great strength.

"He's a good stayer," said the man who owned him. "He'll work till he drops. He's done more work on my farm than any other horse, and that's saying something. I wish I hadn't to let him go—but I need cart-horses, not light horses."

So Patchy was bought too, at a fair price, and the man promised to take them both back to the farm that evening. Rory paused to look at a magnificently-built horse in a near-by stall. The horse looked at him and then rolled his eyes so that the whites showed.

"Daddy, this is the finest-looking horse in the market," said Rory. "I wonder why he isn't sold!"

"He's bad-tempered," said his father. "Look how he rolls his eyes at you. Keep out of the way of his hind feet! Nobody wants a bad-tempered horse, because so often he is stupid, though he may be strong and healthy. I'd rather work a horse like Patchy, ugly though he is, than this magnificent creature."

The children wandered round the market before they went back to their donkeys. It was such an exciting place, and so noisy at times that they had to shout to one another to make themselves heard!

Sheep baaed loudly and continuously. Cows mooed and bellowed. A great strong bull, safely roped to his stall, stamped impatiently. The children watched him from a safe distance.

"I do wish we had a bull," said Rory. "I'm sure a farm isn't a proper farm without a bull."

"I'll get one in the spring," said his father. "He can live in the orchard. My word, look at those beautiful goats!"

In a pen by themselves were three beautiful milk white goats. Penny immediately longed for one.

"I don't think a farm is a farm unless it has goats, too," she announced. "Daddy, do buy me a goat when I have a birthday."

"I'll buy you a baby-goat, a kid, when it's your birthday," said her father. "Yes, I promise I will. Now, don't go quite mad, Penny. You may be sorry you've got a goat when it grows up. They can be a great nuisance."

Penny flung her arms round her father's waist and hugged him. The thought of the kid filled her with joy for the rest of the day. She tried to think out all kinds of names for it, and the others became impatient when she recited them.

"Penny, do wait till you get the kid," said Sheila. "What *is* the good of thinking of a name like Blackie when the kid maybe as white as snow? Don't be silly."

When they had seen everything in the market and had looked at the big sows there and wondered if their own sow at home was as big, the children made their way back to their donkeys.

"Well, it's been a lovely afternoon," said Penny. "Goodness, it's cold now. Gee-up, Hee-Haw. Gallop along and bump me and get me warm!"

Whilst the children were having tea, there came the noise of hooves and a knock at the back-door.

"The new horses!" squealed Penny and rushed out to see. "I'm going to give them each a carrot to let them know they've come to a nice farm. Harriet, can I take two carrots? Oh, thank you. Here you are, Patchy; here you are, Darky. Crunch them up. Welcome to Willow Farm!"

"Well, Missy, if that's the sort of welcome you give horses, they'll work well for you!" said the man who had brought them. Jim appeared at that moment and took the horses off to their stable. They both looked round at Penny as they went, and said, "Hrrrrumph!"

"They told me they were *awfully* pleased to come here," Penny told the others. "They really did!"

Chapter Five

Darling in Trouble

The two new horses settled down well. They put their noses to the muzzles of the big plough horses and seemed to talk to one another.

"I suppose that's their way of shaking hands," said Penny, watching them. "I do like the way animals nose one another. I wish we could do that too."

"Our noses aren't big enough," said Benjy. "Besides, we'd always be catching colds from one another if we did that."

"Animals don't," said Penny. "I don't think I've ever seen an animal with a cold, now I come to think of it."

"Well, I have," said Benjy. "I've seen dogs and cats with colds—and I've seen Rascal when he had a tummy-ache too."

"It's a good thing horses don't get the tummy-ache," said Penny. "They've such big tummies, haven't they?"

Her father overheard what she said and laughed. "Oh, horses do get ill," he said. "It's tiresome when they do, though—they're such big creatures, and kick about so. Thank goodness none of mine have ever been ill."

It was a funny thing that the farmer said that, because that very night Darling, the biggest horse, was taken ill in her stable.

It was Benjy who found out that Darling was ill. He had rubbed her down with Rory when the three plough horses came in from the field, and had watched them eat their meal.

"Isn't Darling hungry?" he said to Rory. "She always gobbles, but tonight she is eating twice as fast as the others. Darling, don't gobble!"

Darling twitched back a big brown ear, but went on gobbling. She really was very hungry indeed, for she had been working hard in the wet fields all day. The boys gave each horse a slap behind and a kind word and went out. They had rubbed down the two new horses too. Patchy and Darky liked the children very much, especially little Penny, who was always talking to them and bringing them titbits.

As usual the family went to bed early, even the grown-ups being in bed and asleep by ten o'clock. Nobody heard the noise from the stables—except Benjy. He suddenly awoke, hearing some unusual sound.

He lay for a little while in his small bedroom, wondering what had awakened him. Then the sound came again—a sound he had never in his life heard before! He couldn't imagine what it was like.

"What *is* it?" thought the boy, sitting up in alarm. "It's somebody—or something—groaning—but who can it be? It's such a funny deep groan."

Then he heard another noise—the sound of hooves against wood, and he leapt out of bed.

"I must see what it is," he thought. He put on a thick coat, took his torch, found his shoes, and slipped out down the stairs. He undid the big front door and ran into the wet yard. The noise of groans was now much more clearly heard. The boy ran to the stables and opened the door. He switched on his torch and saw a sight that shocked him.

The great plough horse, Darling, was lying on the floor of the stable, groaning terribly, and gasping as if for breath. She moved her hooves as she groaned and these struck the wooden partition between her stall and the next. The other horses were standing quietly in their own stalls, puzzled by the sounds that came from Darling.

"Oh, Darling, whatever's the matter?" cried Benjy. The big horse took no notice of the boy, but lay with her hooves twitching curiously. Benjy sensed at once that the horse was really ill. He tore out of the stable and went to wake his father.

In two minutes the farmer was in the stable, bending over Darling. "She's got colic," he said.

"What's colic?" asked Benjy.

"Just what I said my horses had never had!" said the farmer, with a groan. "Tummy-ache! And Penny was right when she said it must be dreadful for horses to have that. It is! Very dreadful."

"Will Darling die?" asked Benjy, in a whisper. It really seemed to him as if the horse was dying under his eyes.

"She will if we don't save her," said his father. "Go and get Jim and Bill. Quick now. We've got to get Darling on her feet. She'll die if she lies there. We've GOT to get her up. I can't do it by myself."

Very frightened, Benjy sped to the cottages where the two farm-hands lived. It wasn't long before they were in the stable with the farmer.

"We must get Darling on to her feet," said the farmer. "Come on, Jim, you get to her head. Bill, slap her on the rump—hard. Go on, hard! I'll help Jim. Come on now, old girl—up you get!"

But Darling didn't get up. Instead she began to groan and pant again, and the awful noises made poor Benjy feel quite sick. The three men heaved and hauled, and the great horse made no attempt to help them at all. She felt too ill to stand and she just wasn't *going* to stand. The men gave up after a while and stood exhausted by the horse, panting almost as loudly as the great animal.

"Go and telephone the vet, Benjy," said his father, wiping the perspiration off his forehead. "Tell him Darling has colic and ask him to come as quickly as possible. Good heavens, this horse is worth forty guineas—we can't afford to lose her!"

"Oh, Daddy, who cares about the forty guineas!" cried Benjy, almost in tears. "If she was only worth a penny, we'd have to save her because we love her!"

"Of course, silly boy," said his father. "Now go quickly and tell the vet to come. Jim—Bill—let's try again to get Darling up."

"She's that heavy and obstinate," grunted Jim. He was a tiny fellow, with immensely broad shoulders and long strong arms. He began to try again to get Darling up, helped by the others. The horse seemed to realise what the men were doing this time, and herself tried to rise. She fell back again with a thud and put her great patient head to the ground, groaning deeply.

"Poor creature," said Bill. "She's in a bad way, sure enough."

"I hope the vet comes quickly," said the farmer, leaning exhausted against the stall. "Ah—here's Benjy back again. What did the vet say, lad?"

"Oh, Daddy, he's out to a farm twenty miles the other

214

way," said Benjy, his eyes full of tears. "So I rang up the other man who came here once—but he's ill in bed and can't possibly come. He said we were to keep the horse on her feet and walk her up and down, up and down till we got someone to come and give her what he called a 'drench'."

"Get her on her feet!" growled Jim, looking at the poor horse lying flat down, her hooves twitching. "That's easier said than done. Come on—we must try again. She's getting worse."

Bill had an idea that pulling her up with ropes would be a good plan, so the three men between them tried that next—and with a terrifying groan Darling was at last got to her feet. She stood there, swaying as if she was going to fall down the next moment.

"Get her out of the stable and walk her round a bit," gasped the farmer. "We mustn't let her get down again. Open the door wide, Benjy."

Benjy opened it, and the great plough horse staggered out, swaying, her head hanging down in a pathetic manner.

"Daddy, what's made her like this?" asked Benjy. "It's awful."

"She eats too fast," said his father. "It doesn't sound anything much, I know, to say she has eaten too fast— but a horse can die of the colic brought on by that. And Darling's pretty bad. Hold up there, my pretty—hold up. Jim, go to the other side. She's swaying over."

It was a terrible business to keep the great horse on her feet. Whenever it seemed as if Darling was going to fall over again, or appeared to want to lie down because she really wasn't going to stand or walk about any more, the farmer shouted loud words of command at her, and the well-trained horse tried to obey them. Jim and Bill slapped her smartly too, and the poor old horse somehow managed to keep on her feet and stagger round the farmyard, making a great noise with her feet. The sounds awoke everyone in the house, and one by one, Harriet, Fanny, Mother, and the other children came out to see whatever was the matter.

"Go back to bed," ordered the farmer. "You can none of you do anything. You go too, Benjy."

"I can't, Daddy, I can't," said Benjy. "I love Darling so much. I can't go back to bed till I know she won't die. I can't."

"When is that vet coming?" said Jim, who by now was getting very tired. "You left a message for him, didn't you, Benjy?"

"Of course," said Benjy. "But goodness knows when he'd be back and get my message."

"Horse'll be dead by that time!" said Bill gloomily. "Whoa there, my lady. Oh—down she goes again!"

With a terrific thud the horse half fell and half lay down. She lay there in the mud of the yard, her hooves kicking feebly by the light of the big lantern.

"And now we've got to get her up again," groaned the farmer. "Benjy, is that you still there? I told you to go to bed. Go on now—you can't do anything to help, and it's only making you miserable to watch us."

"Please, Daddy," began Benjy. But his father cut him short angrily, for he was tired and worried.

"Do as you're told—and at once!"

Benjy fled away into the darkness, very unhappy. He went up to his bedroom, thinking of the great horse that he and Rory loved to brush and comb each day. He remembered her soft brown eyes and long eyelashes. She was the dearest horse in the world—and she might not get better if the vet didn't come quickly and cure her.

No sooner had Benjy got into bed, as cold as ice, than a thought came to him that made him sit up and shiver with excitement. Why, oh why hadn't he thought of it before? He would go and fetch Tammylan, the wild man. Tammylan knew how to handle all animals—he knew how to cure them—he knew everything about them. Tammylan, oh, Tammylan, you must come and help old Darling!

Benjy put on a coat again, and his rubber boots. He wound a scarf round his head and neck, for the night really was very cold. He took his torch and slipped down the stairs for the second time that night. Then out into the yard and away up the lane as fast as he could!

"I hope I don't lose the way in the dark," thought the boy desperately. "Everything looks so different when it's night-time."

Tammylan's cave was about two miles away, Benjy ran panting up to the top of Willow Hill, and then across Christmas Common, which looked strange and queer in the starlight. If only Tammylan was in his cave! If only he would come! Then Darling would be saved and wouldn't die. Oh, Tammylan, do be in your cave, do be in your cave!

Chapter Six

Tammylan Comes

It was difficult to find exactly where the wild man's cave was at night. It was always well hidden in the hillside, for Tammylan did not like his dwelling-place to be easily seen. He liked to live alone in peace with his friends, the wild animals and birds. Benjy flashed his torch over the dead heather and lank grass growing on the hillside, trying to find the entrance to the cave.

"There it is!" said the boy thankfully, at last, and he made his way to it, calling as he went. "Tammylan! Oh, Tammylan! Are you there?"

There was no answer. Tammylan must be asleep. Benjy didn't dare to think he might not be there. He stumbled into the dark cave and flashed his torch around. There was the wild man's rough couch of dead bracken and heather, with a gay, knitted blanket thrown over it. Sheila and Penny had made that for him. And there was the little carved stool that the two boys had made for him—and Tammylan's small collection of dishes and tin plates.

But no Tammylan. The couch was empty. The cave had nobody there except a small mouse who sat up inquiringly and looked at Benjy with brown eyes.

"If only you could tell me where Tammylan is!" said Benjy desperately to the mouse. "What bad luck to find him away just this one night!"

He went out of the cave and stood in the starlight.

He called loudly and despairingly.

"Tammylan! Tammy-lan! TAMMYLAN!"

He listened, but there was no answer anywhere. "This is like a bad dream," thought the boy. "A dream where something horrid happens, and everything goes wrong, and you can't put it right, no matter what you do. I wonder if I *am* dreaming!"

But he wasn't. The stars twinkled down. An owl called somewhere. Sheep baaed on the hillside far away. Benjy felt very much alone and very sad.

"I must go home," he thought. "I can't stay here all night waiting for the wild man. I'll just give one long whistle first—the way he taught me—and then go."

He pursed up his lips, took in a deep breath, and gave the piercing, musical whistle that Tammylan had taught him, the same whistle he used when he wanted to call Scamper, his squirrel. And oh, how wonderful—an answering whistle came back through the night—Tammylan's whistle!

Benjy almost wept for joy. He whistled again, trying to put as much urgency into it as possible, and once more the answering call came back, fluting through the starlit night.

Then Benjy had a shock. Something ran up his body and jumped to his shoulder, chattering softly. For a moment the boy stiffened in fright—and then he cried out in joy and relief. "Scamper! Where were you? You've been missing again, and now you've come back. You heard my whistle, didn't you—but I was really whistling for Tammylan, not for you. And Tammylan's coming! He's coming!"

The squirrel chattered softly against Benjy's ear and

his warmth was very comforting to the boy. He felt happy all of a sudden. He called loudly.

"Tammylan! Is that you?"

And a voice answered from a distance. "I'm coming, Benjy, I'm coming!"

In two minutes the wild man was standing beside the boy, his arm round his shoulders, questioning him anxiously.

"What's the matter? Why have you come to me at this hour of the night?"

"Oh, Tammylan, it's poor Darling," said Benjy, and he poured out the whole story. Tammylan listened without a word to the end.

"If the vet doesn't come till the morning Darling will certainly die," he said. "I'll come with you and bring her some medicine of my own making."

"The vet said she wanted a 'drench', Tammylan," said Benjy. "What did he mean? Did he mean a bath?"

"No—medicine to put her tummy right," said Tammylan, and he disappeared into his cave. "I've got what she needs—not quite what the vet would give her, perhaps— but it will set her right in no time!"

He took down a tin, whose lid was very tightly screwed on. He opened it and took down another tin. He shook some powder from one tin into the other, and then swiftly made up some concoction that smelt rather strong. "Now come along," he said to Benjy. "Every minute may count. Hurry!"

They hurried. It was much easier to go with Tammylan than to go alone. It seemed hardly any time before the lights of Willow Farm showed below them, as they went over the top of Willow Hill.

"I can see the light of the big lantern in the yard," panted Benjy. "That means that Darling is still there. I wonder if they got her on her feet again. Oh, Tammylan—I hope we're not too late."

"I can hear her groaning," said Tammylan, who had ears as sharp as a hare's. They hurried down to the farm and went into the yard where the three men were still struggling to keep Darling walking about. They had managed to get her on her feet once more.

"Who's that?" called the farmer sharply, as he saw the two figures by the light of the lantern. "Is it the vet?"

"No. It's Tammylan," said the wild man, and he stepped up to the gasping, groaning horse. "She's bad, isn't she? I've got something to give her. You can't wait till the vet comes. You must trust me to give her what she needs."

Bill and Jim looked at Tammylan rather suspiciously. But the farmer knew him well and heaved a sigh of relief. "Well, I don't know that you'll be able to do anything, Tammylan—she's pretty well exhausted now."

The horse was so enormous that the wild man could not give her the "drench" from where he stood on the ground. The men had to lead the horse to a near-by cart and Tammylan mounted the wagon and waited for the horse's head to be swung round to him.

Darling did not want anything more done to her—but Tammylan's voice reached her half-fainting mind. She pricked her ears feebly and turned towards the wild man. All animals heeded his voice, wild or tame. In a trice Tammylan had given her the medicine, helped by Jim, Bill, and the farmer, who held on valiantly to the struggling horse. She swallowed with a great deal of

221

noise, and jerked her head hard.

"Now keep her walking," said Tammylan. "Here—let me take her for a while. You must all be tired out. I'll see she doesn't lie down again."

Harriet came out with a can of hot tea. The three tired men turned to her eagerly. Tammylan took the horse by the bridle and firmly walked her round the yard, talking to her in his low voice.

"Could I have some tea too, Daddy?" said a small voice, and Benjy came out of the shadows.

"So *you* fetched Tammylan, did you?" said his father, pouring out some tea for the small boy. "Well, it was a good idea—a very good idea indeed. Here you are— drink this up. My word, it took three of us to keep that horse on her feet this last hour or two—and there's Tammylan handling her all by himself. He's a marvel, no doubt about that."

Benjy sat contentedly by his father, sipping his hot tea. He listened to the men talking, and felt very grown-up. To be out here in the yard, long past midnight, having tea with three men was marvellous—and he felt happy now that Tammylan was there. Tammylan could put things right—he could put—things—

Benjy's head fell forward and he was asleep. He was awakened by a laugh. Then he heard a curious sound. "It's rather like the band tuning up before it plays," thought the boy drowsily. "I wonder if the band is going to play." Then he sat up straight, wide awake. "But there isn't a band, of course. How silly I am. Well, what's that noise then?"

He said these last words out loud and his father laughed again.

"The medicine is working inside old Darling," he said.

"That's her innards making music," said Jim, with a chuckle. "She'll be all right now, so she will."

It was simply amazing to hear the strange musical noises that came from inside the enormous horse as Tammylan walked her firmly round the yard. Darling groaned once or twice more, but not so deeply as before.

"She'll be all right now," said the farmer. "And this time you really *must* go to bed, Benjy. That's definite. If you don't, I'll give you some of the medicine that Tammylan's brought for Darling!"

Benjy stood up, laughing. He felt very contented and happy. Darling was safe. She wouldn't die. He had saved her by getting Tammylan. He ran across to the wild man and put his hand in his. Scamper was on Tammylan's shoulder, and leapt to Benjy with a little cry of delight.

"I'm going to bed," he said. "Oh, Tammylan, I'm so glad you came. Thank you ever so much."

"I'm glad I could help," said the wild man, still firmly walking Darling about, whilst strange noises gurgled and sang inside her. "You go off now, Benjy—and don't you dare to get up early tomorrow morning. You can't have had any sleep tonight."

Benjy went back to bed again. He was so tired that he didn't think of taking off his old coat and scarf, though he managed to remove his boots. He fell asleep half dressed, intending to be down bright and early for breakfast, to tell all the others what had happened in the night.

But he didn't waken in time—and nobody dreamt of disturbing the tired boy. Mother told Harriet to keep his breakfast hot till he awoke.

Benjy didn't wake up until ten o'clock! It was the clock downstairs striking that roused him. He stretched himself lazily and rubbed his eyes. The early sunshine came into his room, lighting up everything, and he sat up, puzzled.

Usually it was dark, these winter mornings, when he woke up. Why was the sun in the room? He looked at his watch. Golly! Ten o'clock! Then, in a flood, he remembered the happenings of the night before. He threw off the old coat and was out of bed in a twinkling, and downstairs, in his pyjamas.

"Mother! Mother! Where are you? Is Darling all right? MOTHER! Where are you?"

And then he caught sight of something that pleased and relieved him enormously. It was Darling herself, looking rather sad and sorry, but walking quite steadily out of the farmyard gate with Jim the herdsman.

"She's all right again!" shouted Benjy, overjoyed. "Darling! How do you feel?"

Benjy actually went out into the cold farmyard in his pyjamas and bare feet, yelling to the horse. Darling turned her big patient head.

And then an astonished voice called to him from the house. "Benjy! What in the world do you think you are doing out there in nothing but pyjamas and bare feet! You must be mad. Come in at once! BENJY!"

It was his mother—and by the tone in her voice Benjy knew she must be obeyed at once. He was in the house in a moment, grinning all over his face. "I couldn't help it, Mother. I just had to speak to Darling. Oh, isn't it marvellous that she's better?"

"Wonderful," said his mother. "Everyone is as pleased

as can be. Now dress quickly and see if you can eat the enormous breakfast that Harriet is keeping hot for you."

Benjy could—and did—and when the others came home from school, what a story he had to tell them of the night before! It was just as good as a chapter out of a book.

Chapter Seven

Penny is Busy Again

February was a lovely month that year and the four
children enjoyed riding to school and back on their
donkeys, doing their jobs on the farm, petting all the
animals, and sometimes going joyfully off to find their
friend, Tammylan.

Tammylan knew every bird and creature of the
countryside, so it was marvellous to be with him. He
had taught all the children to move and talk quietly
when they went along the lanes, through the woods and
over the hills.

"If you can learn to move as quietly as the animals do,
you'll see far more and make friends with them much
more easily," he told them.

Tammylan nearly always had some animal or bird
living with him in his cave. Sometimes they came to
him when they were hurt, and he healed them when
he could. Benjy remembered a robin with a broken leg
and a hare whose hind legs were so badly damaged that
he could no longer run.

The hare had never forgotten Tammylan's kindness
and came to see the wild man almost every day. Sometimes when the children were sitting with him in his
cave, they would look up to see the hare sitting at the
entrance, looking inquiringly inside, his large eyes wide
open, and his big ears standing straight up. At a word
from Tammylan he would come inside and the children

would sit as still as mice watching him. He would go to Benjy sometimes, but not to any other of the children.

"Well, Penny," said Tammylan one day when the little girl had come to see him with Benjy, "how are Davey's lambs getting along? Are you helping him with them?"

"Oh, Tammylan, isn't it bad luck for me—not one of the mother-sheep has had three lambs this year," said Penny. "You know, Davey the shepherd *promised* I could have another lamb for my own as soon as a sheep had three, instead of one or two. He says three is too much for a mother to manage properly. But not a single sheep has had more than two lambs. I do feel upset. I haven't any pet of my own at all now—and nothing to look after."

"You could help Sheila with her hens and ducks," said the wild man.

"No," said Penny. "She has Fanny to help her. I just stand and watch, and I don't like that. I like to *do* something!"

Penny soon had her wish granted. When the two of them went back home, they found a great disturbance going on. Something had happened!

"What is it?" shouted Benjy, as he saw Jim running up to the hillside where the sheep were grazing. "Has anything happened?"

"Sheep got caught in the barbed wire up yonder!" yelled back Jim. "Sort of hanged itself, I reckon. We're trying to save it."

Benjy and Penny ran to join the men who were doing their best to disentangle the sheep from the twisted strands of barbed wire. It had evidently tried to jump the ditch to join its two little lambs on the far side, and had

227

got caught in the wire. It had struggled and struggled, and had got the wire all round its neck. It was baaing piteously.

Its two little lambs stood near by, bleating in fright. Rascal was there, preventing them from jumping into the ditch. The men worked hard with wire-clippers, cutting the wire here and there to help the sheep. One strand sprang back and cut a long, deep scratch down Jim's arm. The red blood flowed at once—but Jim did not seem even to notice it.

"Oh, poor Jim!" said Penny, in distress. She never could bear to see anyone hurt. But Jim gave her a cheerful grin.

"Never felt it!" he said. "Don't you worry!"

At last the poor sheep was free from the cruel wire. She tried to run a few steps over the grass, but fell down. Rascal ran to her and gently nosed her towards the waiting shepherd. Her two lambs ran up to her, bleating, for they wanted her milk—but she butted them away angrily. She was too frightened and hurt to want her lambs just then.

"I reckon she won't want to feed her lambs again," said Jim, and Davey the shepherd nodded gloomily.

"That's so," he said. "She'll not have any milk for them after this scare. I'll have to try and put them to another ewe."

Then he felt a warm little hand in his and turned to see Penny's bright eyes looking up at him pleadingly.

"Davey!" she said. "Davey! Why can't *I* have them? You promised me a lamb to feed and I haven't had one. Can't I have these two? They are so miserable—listen how they bleat. They are saying, 'We want Penny to look after us!

We want Penny!'"

Davey laughed. He patted Penny on the head. "Now, now, Tuppenny!" he said, "don't get all excited till we see what the old ewe is going to do. Maybe she'll want her lambs after all. But if she doesn't—why, then, you shall have them!"

"Oh, thank you!" cried Penny, skipping about like a lamb herself. "I'm sure I shall have them. What shall I call them? Let me see—Frisky—Frolicky—Wriggly—"

Benjy laughed just as Davey had done. "Oh, Penny, you and your names! Come and tell Mother. We'll have to hunt out a couple of feeding-bottles if you are going to have the lambs."

Penny went off with him happily, and Mother found two feeding-bottles just in case they were needed in a hurry. Lambs needed many feeds when they were small, and it would not do to let the two little lambs go too long without milk.

Penny had her way. The mother-sheep would not even try to feed her little lambs again, and Davey brought them down to Penny that afternoon. Rascal ran round them when the shepherd set them down outside the kitchen door. He had carried them under his arms from the hillside, little, sad, bleating creatures, their whole world changed because their mother butted them away from her. Poor thing, she had had a terrible shock, and it would take her a week or two to get over it.

"It's a good thing Rascal found her when he did, and came to fetch me," said Davey to Penny's mother, who had come out to see the lambs. "She would have died if we hadn't cut her free, and we can't afford to lose a good ewe like that. Now, little Tuppenny—you'll be happy to

have lambs again, won't you?"

Davey always called Penny Tuppenny, because he said a penny was too cheap for her. The little girl was fond of the big shepherd with his wise blue eyes and weather-beaten face. He knew so much about his sheep—but he always said that his dogs knew even more!

Harriet filled the feeding-bottles with milk and gave them to Penny. The little girl put on the teats firmly. "They're exactly as if they were to feed a baby, not a lamb," said Fanny, whose mother had a new baby at home, often fed by Fanny from its bottle. "But, my word—those lambs suck the milk more quickly than a baby does!"

The lambs were terribly hungry, poor little things. Penny went to them, and offered the smaller one the first bottle. She squeezed the teat a little so that milk came into it and the smell reached the lamb's nose. It turned towards the little girl, and it was not long before it was sucking noisily! The other one came nosing round at once, and soon Penny had the joy of feeding both the tiny creatures, a bottle in each hand.

"You won't be able to feed both at once in a few days' time!" said Benjy, watching. "They will come rushing as soon as they see you, Penny—and you'll have to feed them one at a time, and keep the other lamb off as best you can!"

What Benjy said was true. The lambs soon grew to know Penny, and even if she had no feeding-bottles full of milk with her, they would come rushing up to her eagerly, almost knocking her over. They even put their front-legs up against her waist almost as if they thought they were puppies!

Penny loved them. "You are just every bit as sweet as the lamb I had last year," she told the two little creatures. "He was called Skippetty—and he *was* skippetty too! He skipped about all over the place. I shall call you Jumpity and Hoppitty, because you jump and hop all round me. Jumpity, you're the one with the black nose. Hoppitty, you're the one without."

Soon the lambs followed Penny everywhere, and she was very happy. "If only my birthday would hurry up and I could have the little kid that Daddy promised me!" she thought. "Then I would have three dear little creatures of my very own. I wish lambs didn't grow into sheep and kids into goats. It does seem such a pity."

Penny's birthday came at the beginning of March, and she was very excited. "I'm going to be nine," she told everyone. "Then next year I shall be ten, and be in double figures. But I shall never catch up Benjy or the others."

"Of course not," said Mother. "Now I wonder what I can give you for your birthday?"

When Penny's birthday came at last, she had a lovely day. Mother gave her a new mirror for her bedroom, with flowers all round it. It looked beautiful on her chest-of-drawers. Benjy gave her a pencil-box with two lambs on it that he said were exactly like Hoppitty and Jumpity. Sheila gave her a work-box made of shells and Rory gave her a fat little walking-stick. This pleased her very much, for she had always wanted a proper stick of her own.

Harriet made her a wonderful birthday cake with nine candles on it, and pink roses all round. It had "A happy birthday to Penny" on it, written in pink icing in Harriet's best icing-handwriting.

Tammylan came to tea and brought Penny a very curious stone. It shone a dull blue, and in the middle of it was a twisted line in yellow, almost exactly like the letter P.

"P for Penny," said Tammylan solemnly. "I found it at the back of my cave, in that little spring there that wells up. Perhaps the hare brought it for you. Anyway, it's very strange and unusual, but it *must* be meant for you, because it has P on it."

Penny was thrilled. She felt quite certain that the stone was magic, and she slipped it into her pocket at once, keeping her hand on it till it grew warm. "It's a magic stone," she told everyone. "Very magic. If I want anything very badly I shall hold it in my hand till it gets warm, and then I shall wish—and my wish might come true!"

The present that Penny liked best of all was from her father. He kept his promise to her—and brought her a little kid! It was snow-white with a black mark in the middle of its back. It bleated in a little high voice, and Penny loved it the moment she saw it.

"Oh!" she squealed in delight. "Daddy, what a darling little kid! It can run about with my two lambs, can't it? Oh, I do love it. Thank you, Daddy, ever so much. Oh, what shall I call it?"

"Squealer," said Rory.

"Sniffy," said Sheila.

"Sooty," said Benjy, with a laugh, fondling the kid's snow-white head. Penny looked at the others with scorn.

"You're all silly," she said. "I shall think of dozens of names much, much better than any you could think of!"

Penny did. She went round the house and farm-yard saying strings of names, trying to find one that would suit the little kid. The two lambs ran beside the little white creature, butting it gently with their noses. It was funny to see them.

"Snowy, Snowball, Snowdrop, Snow-white," chanted Penny, as she went. "No—somehow none of these names suit you, little kid. Oh, come away from those hens! They don't like you a bit!"

A hen turned on the kid and pecked him. The little thing bleated and jumped straight on to the top of a bin. The lid was half balanced on it and slipped off. The kid disappeared inside the bin, and Penny had to rescue him from the corn inside.

"Really!" she said, "whatever will you do next?"

The next thing he did was to run under Blossom,

one of the cart-horses, and give her such a start that she reared up. The kid leapt out from under her and fell into the duck-pond.

"There's only one name for that kid of yours, Penny," said Fanny, with a laugh. She had come out to feed the hens. "Call him Dopey. He's quite mad, and always will be. You can tell it from his eyes. He'll be a darling—but quite, quite mad—just like the dear little dwarf Dopey in the story of Snow-white."

"Yes—Dopey is a nice name," said Penny. "You shall be called Dopey, little kid. Now I've got Hoppitty, Jumpity, and Dopey. I *am* lucky! I really am!"

Penny had a wonderful time with her three pets. She fed them herself, and, as Fanny had said, little Dopey was quite, quite mad. He was maddest of all when he tried to eat things he shouldn't—from muddy shoes left out in the yard, to barbed wire round the gaps in the hedges! There was just no stopping him.

"You'll get a dreadful tummy-ache, just like Darling did once," Penny warned him. But somehow he never did!

Chapter Eight

The Coming of the Bull

The children's father sold his store of potatoes at top prices. They were wonderful potatoes, quite untouched by the frost, and he had had a marvellous crop. He was very pleased indeed.

"I've made quite a heap of money," he told the children. "Now—what would be the best thing to do with it?"

That was the nice part about their father—he always told the children what was happening, and they listened and learnt a tremendous lot about profits and prices, as well as about the animals and crops themselves. As they all meant to be farmers or farmers' wives when they grew up, they took the greatest interest in what was told them.

"Daddy—what about a bull?" said Rory at once. "We ought to have a bull. Let's buy a good one."

"And what about new cow-sheds?" asked Benjy. "I like our old ones—but since you said you'd like to have new ones, Daddy, I've been reading up about them. And ours really *are* old-fashioned. It would be lovely to have proper ones. Do you know, Daddy, that in some cow-sheds the cows can actually turn on their own water-tap in their drinking bowls so as to get perfectly fresh water when they want it? And, Daddy, we must have curved mangers, so that they don't get corners full of dust like ours. And . . ."

"Half a minute, half a minute!" laughed his father.

"My word, I've only just got to mention a thing and you've got it all at your finger-ends at once. Cow-sheds cost an awful lot of money—we'd better wait a while for those—but a bull I *could* get. Yes—I think we'll go off to market and get a bull this very week!"

This was a great thrill. The children talked of nothing else but bulls, and when Mark came to spend the day with them, they talked to him about it too.

Mark was not at all thrilled. He had hardly got over his dislike of the horns on cows, and to him a bull was creature that ran at you and tossed you whenever you came by! He secretly hoped that there would be no bull at the market to buy. He felt that he would not enjoy coming to Willow Farm nearly so much if it had a bull.

The children were going to market with their father to get the bull that very day—so Mark went with them. They all set off on their donkeys, but Mark went with the farmer in his car, feeling rather grand—though really he would have preferred the fun of riding on a donkey.

There were three bulls at the market that day. One was a youngster, big and strong, dark brown all over. The other two were older, enormous creatures that bellowed loudly enough to set all the sheep baaing, hens clucking, ducks quacking, and cows mooing. It was astonishing to hear them.

The price of the young bull was low. The children's father liked the look of him, and thought that he would live for many years as master of the herd of quiet cows. Perhaps he would be the father of many good milking-cows. Benjy was the only one of them who didn't like the bull, and he couldn't say why. Sometimes, like Tammylan, the boy sensed something and didn't know why. He just felt that the bull wasn't going to be a success.

"Well, I can't afford to pay the price of either of the other two," said his father. "It's a pity Tammylan isn't here. He might be able to tell me if this bull is really a good bargain. Everyone seems to think he is—so I'll risk it and buy him."

So the bull was bought. Penny couldn't name him, for he already had a name that he knew. He was called Stamper—a good name for him because he stamped a great deal in his narrow pen, and roared to be let out.

"I should think his second name is Roarer," said Penny, looking at him. "Look at the ring through his nose. Mark, do you know what he wears that for?"

"So that he can be led by it, of course!" said Mark, who already knew this from Benjy. "A bull can't do anything much if someone puts a stick through his ring—it hurts him too much if he tries to be silly and run away—or chase anyone. I say—I hope your bull doesn't chase any of *you*."

"Of course not," said Rory. "It's only bulls in story-books that do that. You'll see our bull will soon settle down—and I expect Penny will try to take him lumps of sugar, just like she does Darling. I believe she would give sugar to the ducks if they'd have it!"

The bull was brought to Willow Farm that evening by the man who had reared him from a calf. He was a little man with a most enormous voice and hands as big as hams. His face was as red-brown as an autumn apple, and his eyes were so blue that you simply had to look at them in astonishment. He spoke to the bull in his enormous voice, and bade him behave himself in his new home.

"Now don't you disgrace me," boomed the little man fiercely, and he gave the bull a smack on its big head. "You behave yourself. No monkey-tricks! No nonsense—or I'll be after you, so I will."

The bull backed a little away from the fierce little man, and blinked at him. The man gave the ring in the bull's nose a little pull by way of farewell.

"I hope the next I hear of you is that you are the proud father of many beautiful calves!" he said. "Well—good-bye, Stamper. I'm right sorry to part with you!"

He was paid his price and went away, calling back to the bull as he went.

"Now see you behave yourself, Stamper—I'll be after you if you don't!"

The children thought all this was very funny indeed. Jim took the bull to the little paddock where he was to live. He led him in and shut the stout gate. The bull gave a mild roar, and stamped round a bit. Penny sat on the gate watching him.

"You come down from there, Missy," said Jim. "That bull feels strange tonight, in a new home. He might tip you off."

"Oh, do come down, Penny," begged Mark, who was still with the children. "You'd just hate to be tossed."

Penny didn't get down. She really didn't feel afraid of the bull, and she felt sure he liked her. But he didn't. He didn't like anything that night. He hadn't liked the strange market. He hadn't liked walking to Willow Farm. And now he didn't like that little girl on his gate.

"Wooooooorrrrrr!" he roared suddenly and stamped loudly. He lowered his head and looked under his eyelids at Penny. Then he made a rush for the gate, his horns

238

lowered ready to toss.

Rory just managed to pull Penny down in time. The bull crashed into the gate and got such a shock that he stood still, glaring round him.

"Penny, you really are a little idiot!" said Rory, angry and frightened. "Daddy will forbid us all to go near the bull if you behave in this silly, foolish way. You might have been gored by his horns."

Penny looked a bit white. She had got so used to farm life and to all the creatures, big and little, welcoming her, that it was a shock to her to find that the bull had been about to hurt her.

"I won't be silly again, Rory," she said quickly. "Don't tell Daddy. I promise not to sit on the bull's gate again."

"He looked quite mad when he rushed at you," said Benjy. "Really, I don't like him a bit. I hope he soon settles down and gets used to us. Some bulls get quite tame."

Stamper did settle down after a few days. He seemed to like his paddock, and curiously enough he always welcomed Hoppitty, Jumpity, and Dopey when they squeezed through a little hole and came to visit him. He would trot up to them and make a curious noise in his throat to welcome them. They would all three frisk round him madly, and he would pretend to chase them, his great powerful head lowered. But he never did them any harm at all, and Penny soon stopped being afraid that he would toss them over the gate.

The only time he ever got annoyed with the two lambs and little kid was then they came into his paddock one day when he was lying down, and Dopey actually began to nibble his tail. Dopey, of course, would eat anything he came across, but he should have thought twice before he tried to eat the tail of a bull. Stamper leapt up with a bellow and chased the three swiftly round the paddock. They squeezed out in fright and didn't go near Stamper for two days. But when they did go he had quite forgotten his annoyance and gave them a great welcome.

Everyone grew used to Stamper. Nobody bothered about his roaring. He seemed to like the cows, and was just about as good and sensible a bull as could be. He grazed peacefully in the orchard, on the watch for the two lambs and the kid, and he no longer minded if any of the children climbed up on the gate.

"He isn't the tiniest *bit* fierce," said Penny. "Honestly, Benjy, I believe I could teach him to nibble a carrot or a lump of sugar."

"Well, don't you try," said Benjy, who still did not trust Stamper, though he felt rather silly about this, and could not imagine why he did not like the bull. Usually Benjy liked every animal, and because they felt that, they trusted him and came to him. But Stamper would never come to Benjy.

"He was a good bargain," said the farmer, when he passed Stamper's paddock. "We did well to choose him. He's settling down fine."

But he spoke too soon. when the warmer days came, Stamper became very restless. He roared a great deal and galloped savagely round his paddock. The men soon began to dislike to go in there.

"He's going mad!" said Jim. "Look at the whites of his eyes showing. He's going mad! We'll have to look out!"

Chapter Nine

A Nasty Accident

That springtime there came some very heavy gales. The children awoke in the mornings and saw the trees outside bending their heads in the wind, and at night they heard the howling of the gale round the old farmhouse.

At first they all liked the wind and the sound it made. "It's a bit like the sea, really," said Rory.

"It's exciting, I think," said Penny. "I like to run out in the wind and feel it pulling my hair back almost as if it had fingers!"

But after the wind had howled without stopping for three or four days, everyone became very tired of it. "It gets inside my head," complained Sheila.

"I shall go mad if someone doesn't keep the dairy door shut, to stop it banging," said Mother.

"Look at my ankle," said Rory, pulling down his stocking. "The lid blew off the corn-bin this morning and it simply *raced* across the yard, and met me just round a corner. Look at the bruise I got!"

"Scamper's tired of the wind too," said Benjy, putting up his hand to stroke his squirrel, who was nestling on his shoulder. "It blew him over sideways yesterday when he went across that windswept bit of ground up by the orchard."

The wind grew wilder that night. It seemed to grow a voice of its own. It bellowed down the big chimneys and shook and rattled every door and window in the house.

Nobody could sleep. They lay in their beds and listened to the howling of the gale. The farmer was worried. He wondered if the roof of the cow-shed was safe. He wondered if any trees would fall.

And then, in the middle of the night, there came a curious sound. It was like a very large creaking at first, mixed with a kind of sighing. Then there came an extra large creak, and a long-drawn-out crash. Then silence.

Everyone sat up in bed. "What's that?" asked Penny in fright.

"Don't know," said Sheila. She pattered across to Rory's room. He was awake too. "Rory, did you hear that? What was it?"

"A tree falling," said Rory. He and Sheila went to the window and looked out into the dark, wind-blown night. But they could see nothing at all. They couldn't imagine which tree it was. It must have been a big one, that was certain.

In the morning Jim came knocking early at the farm-house door. The farmer opened it. He was having his early morning cup of tea.

"There's a tree down, sir," said Jim. "It's the big elm over beyond the cow-sheds. It's caught itself in the next tree, so the sheds are safe. But I reckon we'd better do something about it soon, in case it slips and knocks in the shed roof. It's a mercy it didn't hit the sheds. It would have given the cows a nasty shock, if it had."

The farmer hurried to see the damage. It looked a queer sight. A big elm, rotten at the roots, had not been able to stand against the gale. It had not been broken in half, but had simply been uprooted and had fallen. Instead of falling on to the cow-sheds, which were near, it had crashed into another elm, which had just saved it from breaking down the sheds with its topmost branches.

"We'd better get Bill here, and he and I must get to work to lop up the old tree before it does any more damage," said Jim. "I can climb up into the second elm there, and saw the topmost branches of the fallen tree out of it. Then Bill and I can tackle the rest of the tree between us. It will mean a waste of time, and we're busy enough in the fields just now—but anyway, there'll be plenty of logs this winter."

The children all went to look at the half-fallen tree, on their way to school. They danced their donkeys round and round it, exclaiming at the sight.

"It might have smashed in the sheds!"

"It might have killed half the cows!"

"No wonder it made a noise. It's a simply enormous tree, the biggest on the farm I should think!"

The farmer came up, rubbing his cheek as he always did when he was troubled. "If that other tree hadn't been there, things might have been serious," he said. "As it is, we'll lose a few days' work, have some extra trouble—but plenty of good wood for the winter fires!"

The children hurried home that day to see how Bill and Jim had got on with the fallen tree. Both men were up in the tree next to it, sawing away hard. They had already managed to saw off many of the topmost branches, and these lay on the ground. Scamper ran along them inquisitively.

The children stood and watched. The fallen tree had broken many of the branches of the tree next to it. It seemed to Rory as if that tree had been pushed a little sideways!

He stood looking at it. Yes—it really did seem as if it was leaning over a little. He was sure it had been quite straight up before.

"Don't you think the fallen tree has pushed its neighbour over a bit?" he said to Benjy. Benjy looked too. Then he looked again.

"Rory," he said, "I think it's moving now, this very minute! I think it's going to fall!"

The children stared, their eyes wide. Surely it wasn't moving. But then it gave a slight creak.

Rory yelled to the men in the tree. "Your tree's going to fall! The other one's pushing it over. Get out, quick!"

"It won't fall," said Bill, still busy sawing. "It would have fallen before, if it was going to."

There came another creak. Rory jumped violently. He was very anxious. "Bill! Jim! You *must* come down! I know your tree is going to fall, I know it is!"

Scamper took a look up at the tree and then fled away, his tail streaming out behind him. He smelt danger.

Bill stopped sawing. Another creak came, and he scratched his head. He didn't for one moment think there was any danger, but he reckoned he'd better go down and see what was worrying Rory. There might be danger for the children.

So down he swung, slipping easily from bough to bough, landing with a jump on to the ground. "Now," he said, with a grin, "let's see what all the fuss is about."

There came such a creak that it sounded almost like a groan—and before everyone's eyes the tree that Bill had just left slipped a good bit sideways. Half its roots came out of the ground. Bill gave a terrified yell.

"Jim! Come on down! The tree's going to fall. Get

out of the way, children. Run! RUN! Quick!"

The four children ran. Rory caught hold of Penny's hand and pulled her along fast. She almost fell over. Behind them came enormous creaks and groans as the tree heaved itself out of the ground.

"Oh, is Jim all right, is Jim all right?" cried Penny. She was very fond of Jim, who was never too busy to talk to her. "Is he out of the tree?"

The children stopped and turned, when they were well away from the tree. It was a strange sight they saw. The fallen elm's weight had been too much for its neighbour and now the second tree was falling too. Over it went, as the children watched in terror. It fell slowly, so slowly—and caught in its big branches was poor Jim, who had had no time to save himself!

Everyone watched in fear, trying to see where Jim was. He gave a shout as the tree fell. It reached the ground with a terrific crash and then settled itself there as if it meant to go to sleep. Its neighbour lay on top of it, and their branches were tangled and mixed so that one could not be told from the other. The trees seemed enormous as they lay there on the ground. They just missed the cow-sheds, though some of the lighter branches struck the roof, doing no damage.

"Jim! Where are you, Jim?" cried Bill, and he ran at once to the trees. The children's father and mother came running up too, for they had heard the crash. Harriet came and Fanny, and even Davey the shepherd hurried down from the hillside.

There was no answering cry from Jim. There was no movement of someone scrambling out of the tree. The farmer waved the children back, as they ran up to the trees.

All the grown-ups began to scramble over the spreading, fallen branches, trying to get into the middle of the tree, where Jim had been. The farmer shouted to Sheila.

"Sheila! Better go and ring up the doctor and tell him to come at once. We'll need him when we get Jim."

Sheila sped off, and Penny went with her, crying from fright and anxiety. It had all happened so suddenly. She could hardly believe it!

The farmer soon found Jim. He was lying in the middle of the tree, his eyes closed, and a great bleeding bruise on his head.

"Careful now," said the farmer, as he and the others gently lifted poor Jim out. "Careful! He may have a leg or arm broken."

Jim was laid on the ground, and the children's mother examined him anxiously. "He doesn't seem to have any limbs broken," she said. "I think it's just his head. He must have been knocked unconscious when the tree fell. Get some water, Harriet, and I'll see how bad this bruise is."

The doctor was in when Sheila telephoned, and as soon as he heard what was the matter he jumped into his car and came round at once. He was soon bending over Jim, feeling his body here and there.

"Will he be all right?" asked the farmer.

"There's not much wrong," said the doctor cheerfully. "He got a knock on the head from the trunk or a branch. He's got concussion, and he'll have to be kept quiet for a bit, but he'll be as right as rain in a week or ten days!"

Everyone was glad to know that Jim was not seriously hurt. Davey and Bill carried him back to his cottage and his wife put him to bed. He had not opened his eyes.

"He may not come to for a while," said the doctor. "Let him be. He's a strong fellow and it won't be long before he's himself again."

"I wish I hadn't let him go up into that tree," said the farmer that evening. "Elms are dangerous trees. They go rotten at the roots, and then, in a storm, they suddenly get top-heavy and fall. I might have guessed that that second elm was rotten too."

"I shall go and see Jim every day and take him one of my books to read," said Penny. "It will be quite a holiday for him, won't it, Daddy?"

"Yes," said her father. "But unluckily this has come at one of our busiest times of year, when I need Jim out in the fields all day long. And there's the milk-round too. I can't see how I can possibly spare Bill for that. He's not good at things like that, either. He'll probably get into a frightful muddle, and charge all the bills wrong."

"Daddy! Oh, Daddy! Can't Rory and I do the milk-round whilst Jim is ill?" cried Benjy eagerly. "Darky's so good, Jim says she already knows half the houses she has to stop at."

"You can't do the milk-round," said the farmer, half laughing. "There's more in it than simply taking bottles of milk and standing them on doorsteps! You have to keep the milk-book very carefully too, and enter up everything in it."

"Well, Rory is awfully good at that sort of thing," said Benjy earnestly. "He's the best at maths in our little school. I could give out the milk and drive, and Rory could do the money part."

"I don't see why they shouldn't try," said Mother

suddenly. "It would save you a good deal if they could do that, wouldn't it? You wouldn't need to take Bill from his field-work then. Let them try just once. If they don't do it properly, *I'll* do it!"

"No, you won't, Mother!" cried Rory. "Benjy and I will manage beautifully. We shall have to be late for school each day, that's all."

"All right—you can try," said their father, with a laugh. "Begin tomorrow. You'll have to harness Darky into the cart, get the milk and everything. Bill can give you a hand tomorrow, and then we'll see how you get on!"

Chapter Ten

The Two New Milkmen

The boys were really excited about their milk-round. They felt very grown up. They fetched Jim's books and had a look at them. In the books were entered the names and addresses of every customer, the amount of milk they took each day, and what was paid. There were some "standing orders"—that meant that the same amount of milk was to be left each day. Those would be easy to do.

"I know what we'll do tonight," said Benjy. "I'll copy out the names and addresses on a big sheet of paper, and we'll pin it in the cart, so that we don't have to keep on and on looking up the books. Jim knows everyone by heart, because he does the round so often, but we don't. We shall waste an awful lot of time if we keep having to look up the names."

So that was done, and a big sheet was soon ready for the next day. Then Rory made out a list of the "standing orders" so that those could be dealt with easily in the same way. It was fun. They felt important.

"We'd better begin at this street," said Rory, pointing to an address on the list.

"No," said Benjy. "We'll begin here, look. We don't want to overlap the streets at all. We want to deliver the milk and go the shortest distance to do it."

But it wasn't any good planning *that!* Darky had her own ideas about which was the best way to go! She took charge of the milk round, as the boys soon found out.

They were up early the next morning. They went out to the sheds, where Bill, Harriet, and Fanny were already milking the cows. It was cooled, and put into the waiting bottles which had been cleaned and sterilised the day before.

"Well, roundsmen?" said Harriet, a twinkle in her eye. "Ready for your work?"

"We're going straightaway, as soon as the milk's in the bottles," said Rory.

"Not going to stop for anything?" said Fanny.

"No," said Rory.

"Dear me, what a pity!" said Harriet. "Jim always stopped for a cup of cocoa and a slice of cake before he set off."

"Oh, well—we could stop for *that*," said Rory, with a laugh. So, when the bottles were all ready and the boys were setting them carefully in the racks in their milk-cart, Fanny was sent off to the kitchen for the cocoa and the cake. The two roundsmen ate and drank quickly, for they were anxious to be off.

"We shan't be so quick as Jim was, at first," said Rory. "He knew everyone to go to and we don't. But we shall soon learn. Now—let's get Darky. You fetch her, Benjy."

Benjy went off to get the little horse. Darky looked at him out of her gentle eyes, rather astonished to see Benjy, instead of Jim. But, like all the horses, she loved Benjy, and whinnied softly as he took her out to the cart. He harnessed her and then rubbed her soft nose.

"Now, Darky! *We're* the milkmen today! So you go, and show us the right houses to call at!"

The milk was sold to four or five villages around. Darky set off at a canter, dragging the little milk-cart easily behind her. Benjy drove, his lean brown hands holding the leather reins loosely.

"Let's go to Tittleton first," said Rory, looking up from the list he was studying.

"Right," said Benjy, and when he came to the road that forked to Tittleton, he pulled on the rein to make Darky go the right way.

Darky took no notice at all! She just tossed her brown head, and took the other way, cantering steadily along!

"Darky!" yelled Benjy, pulling at the rein. "You're going the wrong way!"

The little horse stopped. She looked round inquiringly, gazed at the milk-bottles, said "Hrrrumph" softly and set off down the road again, taking her own way!

Benjy began to laugh. He let her go the way she wanted. "Rory, isn't she funny?" he said. "Did you see how she stopped and looked round at the milk-bottles? Then she thought to herself, 'Well, there the bottles are, as usual, so I must be right. Off I go!' And off she went!"

"Better let her go the way she wants to," said Rory, with a grin. "We'll see where she takes us to. She's a clever little thing."

She was! She cantered smartly into the nearest village and came to a stop outside a house called "Green Gates".

"Quite right, Darky," said Rory, laughing. "Green Gates. Standing order, two pints of milk. Here you are, Benjy. Leave it on the door-step."

Benjy jumped down, took the quart of milk, sped in with it, dumped it down on the step and ran out again. Almost before he was in the cart, Darky was cantering down the quiet street, coming to a stop before a row of little houses.

A woman came out with a jug. She was surprised to see two boys instead of Jim. "Pint, please," she said, "and here's the money."

"Are you Mrs. Jones?" asked Rory, and he put a tick against the woman's name and wrote down the money she had given him. Benjy gave her the milk. Darky took a few steps on, and stopped again, at No. 10.

"Standing order, one pint," said Rory, and Benjy hopped out again. Whilst he was out, Darky moved on again, missing out three houses and stopping at the fourth. It was No. 18.

"Golly, isn't Darky clever?" said Rory, looking at the list. "You're right, Darky. No. 18 is the next customer!"

The little horse knew the milk-round just as well as Jim did. She knew where to stop, and Benjy felt certain that if she could speak she would tell him whether to leave a pint of milk, or two or three! She turned her head each time to watch the boys take the bottles.

"Just as if she was watching to see if we were taking the right amount!" said Rory.

Then off to the next village they went at a canter. Darky was just as good there. Once the boys could not see where a house called "Top Wood" was. Darky stood outside a gate, but when the boys went through it, they could see no house.

Darky whinnied to them as if she wanted to tell them something. They came back to the gate. Darky suddenly left the roadway and walked up to the gate with the cart. She went through it and then went a little way up a small dark path the boys had not noticed.

"Oh. That must be the way, not the other path, I suppose," said Benjy. And he was right. The first path, the wrong one, led to a workshop belonging to the little house, which was built among trees and hard to see. It was reached by the little path that Darky had shown the boys.

The milk-round was easy with Darky to help them so much. The horse really seemed to think. She seemed to know that the boys were new at the job and wanted help. It was difficult sometimes when a house had only a name, not a number, to know exactly where it was. But Darky always knew.

"Oh dear—where's Cherry Trees?" sighed Benjy. "It's got no number, and not even a street. It must be one of those houses standing by itself."

"Cherry Trees, Darky!" called Rory. And, as if she quite understood, Darky trotted over to a house, and there on the gate was the right name—Cherry Trees! It did make things easy.

"We shall know much better tomorrow," said Rory, marking down the money he had been given at Cherry Trees. "It is really rather fun, isn't it, Benjy? Now we know the history of our milk from the time it leaves the cow to the time it reaches the people who make it into custards and puddings!"

They were tired when the round was finished. Darky cantered home at a smart pace, and the boys waved to their father when they met him in the road beyond the farm.

"How did you get on?" he called.

"Fine!" cried Rory. "Darky knows everything. *She* did the milk-round, not us! How's Jim, do you know?"

"He's much better," said their father. "I've been in to see him. He's come out of that faint he was in. He says he's got an awful headache, but that will pass. Nobody is to see him till tomorrow, except me. Then tomorrow you can go and tell him how you got on with the milk-round!"

The boys gave their mother the lists of money they had taken, and told her about Darky. She gave them a good breakfast and then told them to get their donkeys and hurry off to school. "You'll be tired at the end of the morning!" she said. "You'll be wanting *me* to do the milk-round tomorrow."

"We shan't!" said Benjy stoutly. Mother was right when she said they would be tired. They were. But it made no difference to their feelings about the milk-round. They were going to do it just as long as Jim was ill. And they were going to do it properly too.

So they were up early again the next morning, seeing about the milk, harnessing Darky to the cart, and setting off in the early morning sunshine. But it rained during the milk-round and they were wet through. That wasn't so pleasant. The wind was cold, and the boys were chilled when they got back for breakfast, very hungry and wet.

"Change your wet things," said Mother. "Yes, at once, before you have breakfast, please. I don't want to have you in bed as well as Jim! We'd have to get Penny and Scamper to do the milk-round then."

It was pouring with rain the next day too when the boys set off. The milk-round did not seem quite so jolly. The boys said very little as they set off in the cart.

"This is beastly, isn't it?" said Benjy, pulling his collar up to stop the rain falling down his neck. "I don't feel at all excited about the milk-round today!"

"Nor do I," said Rory honestly. "But we've got to stick it, and stick it without grumbling, Benjy. We took it on and we've got to keep it going all right."

"Of course!" said Benjy. "Get on, Darky! We'll be as quick as we can today."

For a whole week the two boys did the milk-round between them. They soon knew almost as well as Darky did what customers to serve and what houses to stop at. The little horse worked in very well with the boys, and enjoyed their company.

Jim got rapidly better. The great lump on his head went down, and healed beautifully. Penny kept her word and took one of her books for him to read each day. Sheila and the others laughed at her.

"Fancy taking Jim books like yours!" they said. "He doesn't want to read books about dolls and toys and things, Penny!"

But Jim thanked Penny solemnly, and said he enjoyed the books immensely, and certainly when the children went in to see him he always had one of the books open on his bed.

"It's real kind of you to do the milk-round for me and save Bill the trouble," Jim said to the two boys. "It means he can get on in the fields, and there's a mighty lot to do there now!"

"Oh, we like doing it!" said Rory. "And as a matter of fact, Darky does most of it! We never bother to guide her to the customers—she always knows them and goes there by herself. She's wonderful!"

"Yes, she was a good bargain," said Jim. "I'll be glad to handle the little thing again tomorrow. I miss my milk-round! I lie here thinking of all the things I ought to be doing, and it worries me."

"Did you say you were going to do the round

tomorrow?" asked Rory. He couldn't help feeling a little bit glad! "Are you sure you'll be well enough?"

"Doctor says so," said Jim. "And I'm just spoiling to be at my work again. But I don't want to rob you of any pleasure—if you want to go on with my milk-round, you just say so, and I'll speak the word to your father. But I reckon he wouldn't want you to be missing an hour's school each morning, as you've had to do!"

But Rory and Benjy did not ask Jim to speak to their father! They were glad to have had the chance of doing the round, and had enjoyed the change—but they were quite ready to give it up now Jim was better!

"Thanks, boys," said their father that day. "You've helped a lot. It hasn't been pleasant, I know, when the rain poured down on your open cart—but you've stuck it well, and I'm proud of you! I shall know who to turn to another time!"

The boys glowed with pride. They went to give Darky some lumps of sugar. "You did most of it!" said Benjy, patting the big brown head. "Thanks, Darky! You're a very good sort!"

"Hrrrrumph!" said Darky, and crunched up the sugar lumps in delight.

Chapter Eleven

What Can Be Done With Stamper?

Jim went to complain about the bull to the farmer. "You should come and see him today," he told him. "He's just as mad as can be. There's no doing anything with him. None of us dares to go into the orchard—only those three little things of Miss Penny's go in and out still—and I'm afraid for them too."

"Well, you'd better wire up the gap they squeeze through," said the farmer. "I'll go and see Stamper for myself."

The children's father was not afraid of any animal at all. He went to the bull's paddock and had a look at him. Stamper was lying down quietly in the far corner. He did not even turn his head to look at the farmer. Wandering beside him were Hoppitty, Jumpity, and Dopey, butting one another and playing touch-you-last in the funny way they had.

The farmer felt certain that Jim was exaggerating. Stamper looked as peaceful as any old cow.

"I'll go in and speak to him," the farmer thought. "I don't believe he'll even get up!"

So he sprang over the gate and went into the paddock—but as he approached the bull, Stamper rose slowly to his feet. He turned to face the farmer and showed the whites of his eyes in a curious fashion. Then he gave a bellow, lowered his head, and rushed straight at the startled man. The farmer only just had

time to dodge. The bull's horns ripped a little bit out of the edge of his coat. The farmer knew then that he was in grave danger. He glanced at the gate—if only he were nearer!

Jim was passing by and he caught sight of the farmer in the paddock with the roaring bull. He ran at once to the gate.

"He's mad, sir, he's mad!" he yelled. "Yes, he's roaring mad. You come on out, sir, or he'll toss you!"

The bull saw Jim and turned to bellow at him. The farmer edged round nearer to the gate. The bull turned again at once and pounded over the grass. He would most certainly have gored the farmer and tossed him, if something had not happened.

Little Dopey, the kid, thinking that the bull was having a kind of game, ran between his legs with an excited bleat. The bull stumbled and almost fell. That one moment gave the farmer a chance to get to the gate. He was over it and safe on the other side even as the bull was tearing up to the gate, landing against it with a crash.

The farmer fell off the gate and rolled on the ground. Jim helped him up. "He hasn't hurt you, sir, has he?" he asked anxiously. "What did I tell you? He's mad! He's just gone right off his head. He'll be no use to us at all. Nobody will dare to tend him now."

"Oh, look!" said the farmer, and Jim turned to look at the bull. Poor little Dopey hadn't known that the bull was in a raging temper and he had run around him once more, bleating playfully. Stamper, furiously bellowing, lowered his huge head, got the little kid on his horns and tossed him high over the hedge.

The two men saw the snow-white kid sailing through the air, bleating in the greatest surprise. He landed in a big blackberry bush, and scrambled out as best he could.

"He's not been gored," said Jim, looking at the frightened little creature. "He's scared out of his wits—not that he's got many! But he's not hurt. Those little things are like cats—they always fall on their feet. I wish the lambs would come out. They'll get tossed next."

The lambs heard Dopey's frightened bleating and decided that it was time to escape from the paddock before they too were sent flying through the air. So they squeezed out and joined Dopey, who, with many high bleats, told them exactly what he thought of bulls.

The two men stood and looked at the mad bull.

Stamper was now rushing round the paddock, tossing any old bough or log that was in his way. What was to be done with him?

"Hallo, Daddy!" came a voice behind him. "What's happened to Stamper? He's in a fine old rage, isn't he?"

The farmer turned and saw Benjy, with Tammylan beside him. The wild man was looking intently at the bull, a troubled expression on his face.

"Why, Tammylan!" cried Benjy's father, delighted to see the wild man. "Can you do anything with our new bull? He seems to have gone completely mad."

"You'll never do anything with him," said Tammylan. "He's a bad bargain."

"Well, I'll have to get rid of him then," said the farmer. "Can't keep him here with all these children about. And anyway, the men wouldn't handle him. He'll be no use. But who *can* handle him? And what can I do with him?"

"Where did you buy him? Who sold him to you?" asked Tammylan. The farmer told him.

"Well, there is only one man who will be able to handle that bull and make him come to heel," said Tammylan. "And that's the man who brought him up from a calf. The bull will still remember him and how he had to obey him—and maybe he'll go off with him like a lamb. You know, great fully-grown lions can be handled perfectly easily by a trainer who has had them as cubs. They remember the words of command and the smacks they had as cubs, and even when they are fully grown they still remember and have a respect for that man."

"Well—I'd better telephone to Farley then," said the

260

farmer. "That's the man who sold him to me. Maybe he can tell me who had the bull as a calf, and I could get him along here. But goodness knows if I can ever sell the bull now."

The farmer went indoors to telephone. He was feeling rather miserable to think he had wasted so much money on a bull who was no good.

"Still, that's the way of farming," he thought to himself, as he looked up the number he wanted to ring. "You have to take the good with the bad!"

Mr. Farley was in. He listened to the tale of the mad bull, and was sorry to hear it. "Well, sir," he said, "I'm right sorry he was a bad bargain. But I'll tell you what I'll do for you. I'll take him back again—and give you half the price you paid for him. I can manage him all right and maybe he'll behave with me. He's of good stock, and I'll find some use for him."

"Did you handle him as a calf?" asked the farmer.

"I did so!" answered Mr. Farley. "Ah, he'll remember me all right, the rascal. Many's the slap I've given him for cheeking me! Well—will you take half-price for him, sir?"

"I'll be glad to," said the farmer, pleased to think that he need not lose all the money he had paid. "Thanks, Mr. Farley. When shall we see you?"

"I'll be along after tea," said Mr. Farley. "I'll come on my bike, and maybe one of your lads can bring it back for me later. I'll walk the bull home."

The farmer was amazed. Walk the bull home! Walk mad, roaring, furious Stamper along the road, home! Why, surely no one could do that? Wouldn't it be too dangerous to allow Mr. Farley to take the bull out? He

261

would surely be tossed high into the air.

Mr. Farley arrived on his bike after tea, his blue eyes twinkling in his red-brown face. He shouted as soon as he arrived, and his enormous voice boomed round the farmyard.

"Where's that bull?"

Everyone came hurrying out to him. Penny thought he must be the bravest man in the world. She had heard how poor Dopey had been tossed over the hedge, and had made such a fuss of the little kid that he would now hardly leave her side.

"The bull's in the paddock over there," said the farmer. Everyone went up to the paddock. Stamper was lying down but he got up and bellowed as soon as he saw the little company coming.

"You children are to stand right away," ordered their father. "Rory, take Penny's hand, and don't let her go."

"No, don't, Rory," said Penny, trying to pull her hand away. "I'm nine now. Don't hold my hand."

But Rory did. He had an idea that if Dopey or the lambs went too near the bull, Penny would go after them to rescue them—and he wasn't going to have her leave his side. So Penny had to be content to leave her small hand inside Rory's big one.

Mr. Farley swung himself lightly over the gate. Stamper stared in surprise at this daring fellow. He bellowed loudly.

Mr. Farley had a voice that bellowed too! He yelled at the bull.

"STAMPER! You wicked fellow! How dare you behave like this? I'm ashamed of you, downright ashamed of you! Don't you remember how I clouted you when you weren't as high as my shoulder? Now just you listen to me—and don't you roar at me, either!"

The bull had run a few steps towards Mr. Farley, his head lowered as if to toss him. But at the sound of the man's voice, something stirred in his memory. Yes—that was the voice of the man he had known when he was a little bull-calf. He had respected that man. He had had to do as he was told with that man. He had been slapped and smacked if he hadn't obeyed. Stamper paused, remembering.

"You be careful, sir," called Jim, who felt perfectly certain that Mr. Farley was as mad as the bull. To go into that paddock without even a pitchfork in his hands—well, well, a man was mad to do that!

Mr. Farley took not the slightest notice. He actually went right up to the bull! Stamper couldn't make it out at all. He stood looking at Mr. Farley, his eyes rolling.

"Yes, you roll your eyes at me!" roared Mr. Farley, shaking his fist at the enormous creature. "That won't do you any good. You come along with me. I'm going to take you back home again. Ashamed of you, I am!"

The bull made as if he would butt Mr. Farley. But the man did not budge. Instead, he caught the bull's horns in his enormous hands and shook hard. It was a tussle between the man and the bull, with Mr. Farley doing the bellowing!

"Look at that now, look at that!" cried Jim, beside himself with admiration and delight. "I never saw such a sight before! Go it, Mr. Farley, sir, go it!"

Everyone was thrilled, but Mr. Farley took not the slightest notice. All his attention was on his bull. He had no fear at all, and to him the big bull was simply the obstinate little bull-calf he had trained from babyhood. And, to the bull, Mr. Farley was the man who had seen to him, fed him, scolded him, fussed him and punished him.

"Now, don't you dare to struggle with me, Stamper!" cried Mr. Farley, and he gave the bull a resounding slap on his tough head. The bull hardly felt it, but it made him remember that he had feared slaps when he was small. He shook his head slightly and stopped rolling his eyes.

Mr. Farley slipped a stick through the ring in the bull's nose. He gave him another slap for luck, and then spoke to him firmly.

"Now we're going to walk back home. And ashamed I am to be taking you, you great unruly creature! If you so much as bellow at me I'll give you a smack you'll remember to your dying day! Do you hear me?"

The bull heard. He looked meekly at Mr. Farley. The man walked him to the gate, and everyone scattered at once. Rory dragged Penny into the barn and shut the door. She was very much annoyed.

"You can look out of the window, Penny," said Rory. So she did, and saw the amazing sight of Mr. Farley and the bull walking through the farmyard together; Mr. Farley holding the big bull firmly by the ring in his nose, talking to him at the top of his enormous voice.

Even when they got to the lane everyone could still hear Mr. Farley. "A great bull like you behaving like that! What do you think you're up to? Bringing you home in disgrace like this! Sure, it's downright ashamed of you I am!"

The noise of the big voice died away. The children, their father and the farm-hands rejoined one another.

They were all smiling. They simply couldn't help it.

"As good as a play!" said the farmer. "Well, we were lucky to get rid of a mad bull so easily. Thank goodness, Tammylan gave me the tip to get the man who'd reared Stamper from a calf! Well—that was a bit of bad luck, choosing a bull like that. Never mind—we'll know better another time."

Everyone was glad that Stamper was gone. Nobody missed him except Dopey and the lambs. They wandered in and out of the bull's paddock quite unhappy, seeking their lost friend.

"Dopey's very forgiving," said Penny. "If Stamper was still there, he'd go and play with him."

"That's because he's stupid," said Benjy, with a laugh, and ran off before Penny could catch him and pummel him with her small fists!

Chapter Twelve

Rory Wants a Dog

"You know," said Rory, one day, "we've none of us ever had a dog of our own. Isn't that strange? To think how fond we all are of animals—and yet we've never had a dog! I know Davey's got three—but they're not really ours, though they come to the farmyard often enough."

"Well, let's ask Daddy if we can have a dog," said Penny eagerly. "A nice little puppy-dog called—called—let me see—called . . ."

"Oh, Penny, let's get the dog before you find a name for it," said Rory. So they asked their father at breakfast-time the next day. But he shook his head.

"Three dogs are enough," he said. "We don't need any more. Anyway, we've enough cats to make up for any amount of dogs!"

That was true. There were dozens of cats about—or so it seemed! At first Penny had been sure she knew them all, but now she felt she didn't. Kittens appeared in the stables and in the barns, and she loved them and tried to pet them. But they were wild little things, and spat and scratched. Harriet had a cat of her own who lived sedately in the kitchen. He was called Mr. By-Himself, because he wouldn't mix with the stable cats.

"But, Daddy, a dog is worth a dozen cats," said Rory. "I'd so love a dog of my own."

"Well, we'll see," said Daddy. "If I hear of a good

puppy, I'll perhaps get it for you."

But Daddy didn't seem to hear of one—and it was Benjy who produced a dog after all for Rory! He was going down the lane one day, whistling softly to himself, Scamper on his shoulder, when he thought he heard a little whine from somewhere. Benjy stopped. Scamper leapt down from his shoulder and went to hunt around in the ditch. He found something there and leapt back to Benjy's shoulder, making tiny barking noises in his ear, as if to say, "Come and see, come and see!"

Benjy went to the ditch and parted the nettles there. Lying among them was a dog, his brown eyes looking beseechingly up at the boy.

"What's the matter?" said Benjy. "Are you hurt?"

The dog whined. Benjy stamped down the nettles that stung his hands and legs, and tried to lift up the dog. It was a mongrel dog rather like a rough-haired terrier.

"You've been run over!" said Benjy pityingly. "Poor creature! I'll carry you home."

Benjy knew that it was dangerous to touch hurt animals, for they will turn on anyone, even their owner. But animals always loved the boy, and he was never afraid of them. The dog allowed him to carry it in his arms, and he went down the lane with it, Scamper on his shoulder, peering down at the hurt animal in his bright, inquisitive way.

Benjy took the dog to Rory. "Rory! Look at this poor hurt dog! Wouldn't you like to have it for your own? I'm sure Daddy wouldn't say no."

"But it must already belong to someone!" said Rory. "Oh, Benjy—it's bleeding. I'll get a bowl of water and a rag."

Rory bathed the dog, which allowed him to do everything, though once or twice it bared its teeth when Rory accidentally hurt it. Rory liked the dog immensely. It licked his hands, and the boy's heart warmed to it. Benjy liked the dog too, but he wanted Rory to have it. He knew how much his brother longed for a pet of his own. After all, he had Scamper.

Their mother and father were out. The two boys made the dog as comfortable as they could, and gave it water to drink. Penny, Sheila, and Fanny came to look at it, and they all thought it was a darling.

"Its eyes look at you so gratefully, Rory," said Penny. "It keeps on and on looking at you. I'm sure it loves you."

Rory was sure it did too. When he went to bed that night he put the hurt dog in a basket in his bedroom. His father and mother had still not come back, and he felt that he really must have the dog near him. He hoped his mother wouldn't mind.

Next day he showed the dog to his mother. "Oh, Rory," she said, "it's badly hurt, poor creature. I don't think it will live! I wonder who it belongs to?"

Nobody knew who the dog belonged to. It hadn't a collar on, and the police said that no dog had been reported to them as lost. Rory looked after it all the next day which was Saturday, and tried to make it eat. But it wouldn't.

"Do you think we'd better ask Tammylan to make it better?" said Rory at last. He could no longer bear the pain in the poor dog's eyes.

"I'll fetch him," said Benjy. Off he sped, and came to Tammylan's cave in about half an hour. He poured out the tale of the dog, and Tammylan nodded his head and said yes, he would come with him.

But when the two of them arrived at the farm-house, they found Rory almost in tears, big boy though he was. The dog was in his arms, breathing heavily. Its eyes were looking glazed and its paws were limp.

"It's dying," said Rory, in a trembling voice. "I can't bear it, Tammylan. I did everything I could. I do like it so much, and it looked at me so gratefully."

"Don't fret so, Rory," said Tammylan, putting a gentle hand on the dog's head. "This dog would never be any use to itself or to others if it lived. Its back is hurt too badly. But it has had a long life and a healthy one. It is an old dog. It would have died in a year or two, anyhow. It must be happy to die in the arms of someone who loves it."

The dog gave a heavy sigh and then stopped breathing. "Poor thing," said Tammylan. "It is at rest now—no more pain. You could not wish it to live if it could no longer run or hunt, Rory. Give it a good burial, and put up a little post of wood with its name on."

"I don't know its name," said Rory. "We'll have to put 'Here lies a poor dog without a name'."

Everyone was sad because the dog had died. "I shan't ever want a dog again," said Rory sadly. "Not ever. It's spoilt me for having a dog. I only had that dog for a day or two, but it seemed as if I'd loved it for years."

About a week after that Tammylan came again to the farm. "Where's Rory?" he asked Sheila, who was busy with her hens.

"Oh, hallo, Tammylan," said Sheila, looking out of the hen-house at the wild man. "Rory's in the barn. He's gone all mopey this week, poor Rory—since the dog died, you know."

Tammylan went swiftly to the barn. He peeped inside. Rory was getting seeds out of a bin. He had lost his usual cheerful expression. He was a boy who, when he felt things, felt them very deeply.

Tammylan went up to Rory. "I've brought you a present, Rory," he said. "Hold out your arms."

And into Rory's arms he put a fat, round, wriggling little puppy! Rory looked down at it in surprise. His arms tightened over the tiny creature in pleasure.

"Oh, Tammylan—but I don't want a dog now," he said. "I don't really. I couldn't love it. This is sweet, but I just don't want it."

"Well—if you feel like that, of course, you don't need to have it," said Tammylan, at once. "But would you mind looking after it for me, just for a day or two, Rory? Then I can take it back to the man who let me have it."

"Yes—of course I'll mind it for a day or two," said Rory. "What sort of dog will it grow into?"

"A collie like Rascal," said Tammylan. "A clever sheepdog. He'll be a fine fellow."

Tammylan left the puppy with Rory. Rory ran to show it to the others. Penny squeaked over it in delight, and the puppy frisked round Dopey and the lambs in a most comical way.

"Oh, where did you get it from?" cried Penny. "Oh, Rory, it's the darlingest puppy I ever saw. What shall we call it? Don't you think Dumpy would be a good name. It *is* such a dumpling."

"Well—Tammylan brought it to give to me for my own," said Rory, "but I said I didn't want another dog—I'd just mind this one for a day or two for him. So we'd better not name it. Anyway Dumpy's a silly name for a dog that's going to grow into a collie! Fancy calling a collie *Dumpy!*"

Rory took the puppy to bed with him that night. It was supposed to sleep in a small cat-basket on the floor—but although it began the night there, the puppy ended it by curling up on Rory's toes, a warm delicious little weight. It awoke Rory by licking him on the nose.

It was such a playful little thing. It capered about, and gambolled like a lamb. It had the most ridiculous little bark in the world. It found one of Rory's slippers under the bed and dragged it out in delight. Then it grew tired, curled itself up inside the slipper and went to sleep.

"I'll look after it for you today, if you like," said Penny. But Rory didn't want anyone else to do that. He took the puppy with him wherever he went. Davey the shepherd saw it and he approved of it.

"That's a fine pup of yours," he said. "I can tell he'll be clever. He's got a look of my Rascal about him. You are lucky to have him, Rory."

"Well," said Rory, "I'm not keeping him, you know. I'm just minding him for Tammylan for a day or two."

The puppy slept on Rory's toes again that night and once or twice when the boy awoke he stretched out his hand to the pup and patted him. A sleepy pink tongue licked him. There was no doubt about it—the puppy was fine company—and how he adored Rory!

"Rory, if you're not going to keep the puppy, couldn't *I* have him instead?" begged Penny. "I do love him so. And he would be company for Dopey, Hoppitty, and Jumpity. Do let me have him for my own."

"No," said Rory, picking up the pup and fondling him. "He wouldn't love you. He only loves me. He would follow me about all over the place, and then you wouldn't like that."

The next day Tammylan came to fetch the puppy. He found him capering about Rory's heels as the boy groomed Darling. Rory was talking to him.

"That's right—you bite my heels off! Yes, now go and nibble Darling's great hoof! *She* won't hurt you! Oh, you monkey, you've pulled my shoe-lace undone again!"

"Hallo, Rory," said Tammylan. "Thanks so much for looking after the little pup for me. I hope he wasn't any bother."

Rory looked round at Tammylan. He went rather red. "No bother at all," he said. "He's—he's perfect!"

"Yes, he is," agreed the wild man, looking down at the fat little puppy who was now careering round Tammylan's feet. "Well—come on, little fellow! Back you go again!"

Tammylan picked up the puppy. "Want to say goodbye to him, Rory?" he asked.

"No," said the boy, in a funny sort of voice, and went on brushing Darling, his back to Tammylan.

"Right," said the wild man, and went out of the stable, talking to the pup, who was struggling wildly to get out of his arms and go to Rory. "Now, now, you rascal—you'll have to forget Rory and come with me. You must have a new little master who will love you very much."

Suddenly Rory threw down his brush and ran after Tammylan. "Tammylan! Don't take him! *I* love him. He's mine, you know he's mine. He wants *me* for his master. Give him to me!"

"Well, well, now, how you do change your mind!" said the wild man, giving the puppy back to the boy at once. "Of course you shall have him—didn't I bring him for you? Didn't I choose the best pup out of the litter especially for you? Of course you can have him!"

Rory took the puppy and squeezed him till the little creature yelped. "I was silly," he said. "I want him awfully. I feel he's just *meant* to be my dog. Oh, Tammylan, I simply couldn't bear it when you said he must forget me and have a new master. I don't want him to forget me."

"He never will," said Tammylan gently. "He knows he is your dog and no one else's. You must feed him and train him and love him, and he will be your constant companion and friend till you grow to be a man, and have a farm of your own."

"Yes," said Rory. "He'll be a true friend to me, I know. And I shall be a true friend to him. Oh, Tammylan— don't you think that would be a wonderful name for him—True? It would be quite good to call, True! True! True! It sounds all right, doesn't it?"

"Quite all right," said Tammylan, smiling. "Well—as you won't let me have the pup back, I'll go. Oh, I'll just go and see Penny and her three pets first. Has the kid been eating anything else it shouldn't?"

"Gracious, yes," said Rory, looking very happy again now. "I should just think so! It ate Daddy's newspaper yesterday, and we *couldn't* think where it had gone till we saw a bit sticking out of the corner of Dopey's mouth. And it ate my rubber too—my best one. I was cross about that. I just dropped it on the floor, and before I could pick it up, Dopey had eaten it. What it will be like when it's a goat I can't think. It will be a walking dust-bin!"

Tammylan went across to Penny who was playing with Dopey, Jumpity, and Hoppitty. She had just fed her lambs from the bottles, and Dopey had tried his best to push them away and take the milk himself. She looked up as Tammylan came to her.

"Oh, Tammylan—have you come to fetch that darling little puppy?" she cried.

"Well—Rory won't let me take it," said Tammylan, with a smile. Penny gave such a squeal that Dopey jumped two feet in the air with fright and the lambs darted under a near-by cart.

"Oh, Tammylan, is Rory going to keep it? Oh, I shall think of a name for it. Rory, let's call the puppy Tubby—or Roundy—or . . ."

"He's already got a name," said Rory. "I've called him True."

"Oh—I like that," said Penny. "Let's go and tell Mother. There she is!"

Mother was pleased about the puppy. She patted the little thing and smiled at Rory.

"Wasn't it a good thing Tammylan asked me to take care of him for a day or two!" said Rory.

Mother laughed. "Oh—I expect he knew that if he left the pup with you for even a short while, you wouldn't be able to part with it!" she said. "Tammylan did that on purpose!"

"*Well!*" said Rory, with a delighted chuckle. "I'll pull old Tammylan's nose for that. Just see if I don't!"

Chapter Thirteen

A Little About Dopey and True

Everyone was pleased about the puppy, True. The farmer said he would grow into a fine collie, who would be useful with the sheep.

"But, Daddy, I want him for my companion, not to be with Davey all the time," said Rory, in dismay.

"Well, my boy, you plan to have a farm of your own when you are grown up," said his father, "and maybe you'll keep sheep, just as I do, and will want a good sheep-dog. You could let Davey train True for you whilst he's young, and sometimes help Rascal and the others. Then you will find him of great use to you on your farm, as well as a companion."

"Oh yes—I hadn't thought of that," said Rory, pleased at the idea of True guarding his sheep for him one day in the future. "Do you hear that, True? You're going to get good training. *Two* trainings. One from me to make you into a good farm-dog and companion—and one from Davey and Rascal to make you into a good sheep-dog. Aren't you lucky?"

"Wuff!" answered True, capering round Rory's feet as if he was quite as mad as Dopey the kid. He was so small and fat that it seemed impossible he would ever grow up into a long, graceful collie. Penny wished he would stay a puppy. It always seemed to her such a pity that young animals grew up in a few months. It took children years to grow up. Animals were quite different.

True was a great success. Even Harriet, who would not put up with any creatures in her kitchen except her cat, Mr. By-Himself, liked True running in and out. Mr. By-Himself didn't like it at all, however, and made such alarming noises when the puppy dashed into the kitchen that True set back his ears in fright.

Dopey loved True. Rory said that Dopey had a very bad influence on the puppy. "The pup is quite mad enough as it is without having Dopey for a friend," he said. "Honestly, Penny, I've never seen any creature quite so silly as Dopey."

Dopey certainly was completely mad. When he was tired of playing with the two lambs, he would caper off by himself, making ridiculous little leaps into the air. He would go into the kitchen and eat the cushion in Harriet's chair. Then when she shooed him out he would go into the dairy and see if he could find a pan of cream to lick. He was able to leap up on to any table with the greatest ease.

Once he even went upstairs into Rory's room and ate all the homework which Rory had put on the low window-shelf.

Rory was very angry about this and darted angrily at Dopey, after he had tried to rescue half a page of French verbs from the kid's mouth. The kid bleated in fright and Penny came running upstairs in fright, wondering what was the matter. She saw that Rory was about to cuff her pet and flew into a temper with him.

"Rory! You cruel boy! How *can* you hit a little creature like Dopey? Oh, I do think you're mean."

"Look here, Penny—I spent a whole hour over my French today," said Rory, exasperated. "And that kid of yours has eaten all the pages I wrote. He deserves a smack. You must stop him doing this kind of thing. Little wretch!"

"You're horrid," said Penny, with tears in her eyes. "As if he could help it! He doesn't know what he's doing. He's only a baby."

"Penny! He'll go round eating the house down if you don't train him," said Rory. "Go away. You're both silly."

Penny went downstairs, crying. Rory felt rather ashamed of himself after a time. But he still thought Dopey should be punished. He looked round for the puppy-dog, True. But True was not there.

He went downstairs to look for him. His mother was in the dairy, wrapping up the butter with Sheila.

"Rory! Why have you made Penny cry?" said his mother. "It's not like you to be unkind."

"Mother, I *wasn't* unkind," said Rory. "It's that tiresome kid of hers. It will keep doing things it shouldn't, so I smacked it. That's all. Penny should make it behave better."

Suddenly there came a wail from the sitting-room, and Rory's mother looked up in dismay. "Rory! That's Penny. She sounds as if she's hurt herself. Go and see."

Rory and Sheila rushed into the sitting-room at once. Penny's wails were so dreadful that both of them thought she must have burnt herself or something. The little girl was holding up her knitting. The needles were out and all the stitches were coming loose. True, the puppy, was sitting near by, a strand of wool sticking out of his mouth.

Penny looked at him, wailing. She stamped her foot at him. "You horrid puppy! I don't like you any more!

You've spoilt all my lovely knitting. Come here!"

Before Rory could stop her she had got hold of True and given him a hearty smack. The puppy fled away, howling, his tail between his legs.

"Penny! How dare you smack True!" cried Rory.

"Well, he's spoilt my knitting. He's a bad dog, and you ought to train him better!" sobbed Penny.

Mother had appeared at the door, her hands greasy from the butter. She immediately burst into laughter and the three children stared at her in amazement.

"Mother! What's the joke?" asked Rory, rather indignantly. "*I* don't think it's funny that True should be smacked when he really didn't mean to do harm."

"And *I* don't think it's funny that my knitting should all be spoilt. It was a scarf for you, Mother," wept Penny.

"My dear, stupid darlings, I'm not laughing at either of those things," said Mother, with a chuckle. "I'm laughing at *you*. First Dopey spoils your homework, Rory, and you smack him and make Penny angry. Then True spoils Penny's knitting, and *she* smacks him, and makes *you* angry. You're quits, aren't you? You have both got naughty little creatures to train, and you must both make allowances for them. Stop crying, Penny. I can easily pick up your stitches for you. And Rory need not do his homework again. I'll write a note to explain things."

Rory and Penny looked rather ashamed of themselves. "Thank you, Mother," said Penny, and ran out of the room with a red face.

"You're right, Mother—we deserve to be laughed at," said Rory. "It's very funny. I see that now."

"Well, what annoyed each of you was that you

punished the animal belonging to the other," said Mother. "You felt just as I would do if I saw another woman smacking *my* children. Make an arrangement between you that if your pets do wrong, no one shall punish them but yourselves. Then things will be quite all right."

"Mother, you're so sensible," said Rory, and gave her a hug. "I love True and I did hate to see Penny smacking him, though I knew I would have punished him myself if I'd discovered what he was doing. And I expect Penny felt the same when I whacked Dopey. I'll go and find Penny."

"Mother, you're the wisest person in the world!" said Sheila, as they went back to the dairy. She looked out of the window and saw Rory running after Penny. The little girl had her kid in her arms. Rory had True in his.

"Sorry, Penny," said Rory, putting his arm round his little sister and squeezing her. "Mother says we'd better each punish our own pets, and I think she's right. So if True annoys you, tell me and *I'll* smack him. And if Dopey gets into trouble with me, I'll tell you and *you* shall punish him. See?"

"Yes, Rory," said Penny, smiling at her big brother through her half-dried tears. "I do love True, you know that. Do you think he'll hate me for slapping him?"

True licked Penny's nose. Dopey nibbled Rory's sleeve. Both children laughed.

"They've made it up with us," said Penny happily. "They don't like quarrelling with us any more than we like it!"

So after that it was an understood thing that pets should only be punished by their owners. True soon learnt what things were considered bad and what things were good and became a very adorable little puppy, answering eagerly to his name, or to Rory's loud whistle. He lay curled up on Rory's bed at night, and the boy loved him with all his heart. The puppy adored Rory and was always on the lookout for him when he came home from school. Harriet said she was sure he could tell the time from the big kitchen-clock!

"That puppy-dog comes into the kitchen regular as clockwork at just a quarter-to-one," she said. "And why does he come here? Because he knows my clock is the only one in this house that's kept exactly right! He's a cunning fellow, he is!"

Benjy loved the puppy very much, but he was careful not to pet him a great deal. All animals preferred Benjy to any other children, and sometimes True begged to be allowed to go with Benjy when he was going for a walk. But Benjy knew that Rory wanted him all for his very own, and he would shake his head.

"No, True!" he would say. "I'm taking Scamper. You wait till Rory can take you. Go and find him!"

Dopey the kid never learnt the difference between right and wrong, no matter how hard Penny tried to teach him. She tried scolding him, reasoning with him, slapping him. He simply did not remember a single thing he was told, and he did the maddest, most stupid things that could be imagined.

"You'll be quite mad when you're a grown-up goat, Dopey, I'm afraid," Penny would say sadly to him. And she was right. Little Dopey grew from a silly, mad little kid into a silly, mad big goat, and though everyone loved him and laughed at him, he did get into more trouble than all the other animals in the farm put together. He just couldn't help it. His appetite was his biggest trouble. He ate everything and anything, from small nails to big posts.

"One day he'll start eating his own tail and he won't be able to stop himself till he's eaten up to his head," said Benjy solemnly. "Then that will be the end of poor old Dopey!"

Chapter Fourteen

Mark Makes a Lot of Trouble

Mark loved coming to Willow Farm to spend the day and all the children liked him, because, although he knew very little really about farm-life, he was so willing to learn that it was a pleasure to teach him.

He came about once a fortnight, and then he nearly stopped coming because Harriet scolded him for letting the big sow out of the pig-sty. Mark hadn't meant to. He stood on the gate and jiggled it, and it suddenly swung open. It was a nice feeling to stand on it whilst it swung back, and Mark began to swing on the gate, to and fro, to and fro.

In the middle of this, the sow, astonished at the sight of the gate opening and shutting so regularly, had the idea that it would be good fun to walk out. So she walked out, her great, fat, round body hardly able to squeeze out between the posts!

"Hie, hie! Don't do that!" shouted Mark, in a panic, and he tried to shut the gate hurriedly. But the sow took no notice of that. She just went on walking, and her great body forced the gate wide open.

It was quite impossible for Mark to make her go back, and he was really rather afraid of her. He ran round her in circles, begging her to return to her sty. She walked on with her nose in the air, taking not the slightest notice of the anxious boy.

Mark felt most uncomfortable about it. What should

he do? Go and tell someone? No—he'd wait till some-body came by. After all, the sow couldn't come to any harm, just taking a walk round the farm.

The sow certainly did not come to any harm—but Harriet's washing did! The sow walked straight into the end-post of the washing-line, and broke it clean in half with her great weight. Down went the clean washing into the dirt.

Out came Harriet and scolded the sow roundly, picking up her washing as she talked. Then she turned on Mark.

"What did you let that sow out for? You know she mustn't stir from her sty unless Jim takes her. You're a bad boy to make trouble like that, and I've a good mind to tell the farmer. You take that sow back at once."

"She won't come," said poor Mark.

"Ho! Won't she!" said Harriet, and picked up a stick. The sow got a thwack on her back and she turned round promptly, made for her sty and got herself inside in half a minute! Mark shut the gate tight.

"Now, don't you do a thing like that again," scolded Harriet. Mark was very red. He hated being scolded and did not take it in good part as the farm-children did. He almost made up his mind not to come again. But when the children asked him to join them in a picnic the next Sunday to go and visit Tammylan, he felt he really must go. He wouldn't need to see Harriet!

So at twelve o'clock he was at the farm, ready to set off. Penny popped her head out of the window and called to him.

"We're not quite ready, Mark. Would you mind doing something for me? Would you go to the field where the horses are, and see if the lambs are there? Harriet's going to feed them for me today."

"Right," said Mark, and set off to the field. He knew it well. It was a pleasant field, almost a water-meadow, with streams running on three sides, where the horses loved to go and water. He opened the gate, and looked into the field.

"There they are—and Dopey too," said Mark. He called them in the same high voice that Penny always used to call her pets. "Come along, come along, come along!"

The three little creatures heard his voice and tore at top speed towards him. They shot out of the gate, capering and gambolling, and Dopey did his best to butt him with his hard little head.

"You rascal!" said Mark, and tried to catch Dopey.

But the kid leapt away from him, his tail wriggling and jumped right over Hoppitty. They rushed off to the kitchen, where they could hear Harriet clinking a pail.

Mark followed, laughing. He didn't know that he had forgotten to shut the gate. He had always been told very solemnly and earnestly that every gate must always be shut, and the lesson with the sow should have taught him the importance of this on a farm. But Mark was not so responsible as the other children and he didn't even think of the open gate, once he had left the field.

Nobody knew that the gate had been left open. It was Sunday, and except for the ordinary everyday work of the farm, such as milking the cows, and feeding the animals and poultry, nothing else was done. The horses had a rest too, and how they enjoyed the quietness and peace of a day in the fields!

The children set off for their picnic, chattering to one another at the tops of their voices. True went with them, and Scamper. Penny badly wanted to take Dopey, but nobody would let her.

"He'll eat all our lunch," said Rory.

"He'd be under our feet the whole way," said Sheila.

"He'd do something silly and mad," said Benjy. So Dopey was left behind with the lambs, bleating in anger, and trying to eat the padlock on the gate that shut him into the orchard.

Tammylan was in his cave waiting for them all. Mark loved the wild man. He was so kind and wise, he could tell such marvellous tales of animals and birds, he made the children laugh so much, and often he had some wild animal to show them.

Today he took them to a sun-warmed, wind-sheltered copse, where primroses were flowering by the thousand. They shone pale and beautiful in their rosettes of green, crinkled leaves, and on the tiny breeze came their faint, sweet scent.

The children sat down among the primroses and undid their lunch packets. Scamper darted up a near-by tree and leapt from branch to branch. Mark picked a primrose leaf and looked at it.

"I wonder why primrose leaves are always so crinkled," he said.

"So that the rain may trickle down the crinkles and fall to the outside of the plant, not down into the centre where the flower-buds are," said Tammylan.

Mark looked with a new interest at the curious wrinkled leaves. That was the best of Tammylan. He always knew the reasons for everything, and that made the whole out-of-door world so interesting. He knew why sparrows hopped and pigeons walked. He knew why cats could draw back their claws and dogs couldn't. He could tell the children anything, and hardly ever did he put them off with the usual "I don't know" they got from other grown-ups.

"Have you any animal to show us today, Tammylan?" asked Penny. Tammylan nodded.

"You wait a moment and you'll see him," he said. The children ate their lunch and waited. In a little while they heard a scrabbling noise in the hedge near by and saw a big prickly brown hedgehog hurrying towards them, his bright little eyes hunting for the wild man.

"Here he is," said Tammylan, and reached out his hand to the hedgehog. The prickly creature touched it with his nose, then ran all round the wild man, as if to make sure there was every bit of him there!

"Tammylan! Do you remember once you gave me a baby hedgehog for a pet?" said Penny eagerly. "It went away into the countryside when it grew big. Do you possibly think this could be my hedgehog grown up?"

"It might be, little Penny!" said Tammylan, with a laugh. "Call it and see!"

"Prickles, Prickles!" called Penny, in excitement. To her intense delight the hedgehog, which had curled itself up by the wild man, uncurled itself and looked at Penny inquiringly. She felt perfectly certain that it was her old hedgehog.

"Oh, Prickles, I do hope it's really you," said the little girl. "Do you remember how I squirted milk into your mouth with a fountain-pen filler?"

The hedgehog curled itself up again and made no reply. After a moment it gave a tiny little snore.

"I do love the way hedgehogs snore," said Penny. "I do really think it's the funniest sound."

It was fun to be with Tammylan. The rabbits always came out of their holes and sat around when Tammylan was with them. Birds came much nearer. A bog moorhen came stalking by, and said "Krek, krek," politely to the wild man.

"Don't they jerk their heads funnily to and fro?" said Benjy, watching the bird slip into a near-by stream and swim away, its head bobbing like clockwork. "Oh, Tammylan, what a lot of things people miss if they don't know the countryside well!"

"Yes," said the wild man dreamily. "They miss the

sound of the wind in the grasses—the way a cloud sails over a hill—the sight of bright brown eyes peering from the hedgerow—the call of an otter at night—the faint scent of the first wild rose . . ."

The children listened. They liked to hear the wild man talking like this. "It isn't poetry, but it's awfully like it," thought Benjy to himself.

It was just at this moment that Mark remembered, with a terrible shock, that he hadn't shut the gate of the horses' field! What made him think of it he couldn't imagine, but he did. The thought slid into his mind. "I didn't shut that gate when I fetched the lambs! I know I didn't."

He sat bolt upright, his face scarlet. Tammylan looked at him in surprise.

"What's the matter?" he asked.

"I've just remembered something perfectly awful," said Mark, in rather a loud voice. Everyone stared at him. "I—I didn't shut the gate of the horses' field when I went to get Dopey and the lambs," said Mark. "Do you suppose the horses are all right?"

"You *are* an idiot, Mark," said Rory, sitting up too. "How many times have you got to be told to shut gates before you remember it? All the horses may have got out and be wandering goodness knows where!"

"Wouldn't someone see the gate was open and shut it?" said Mark hopefully.

"No. It's Sunday," said Benjy. "Look here—we'd better get back and see if the horses are all right. We can't have them wandering half over the country. Daddy wants them for work tomorrow."

The picnic was broken up at once. The wild man was

288

sorry, but he said of course the children must go back and see. "And you had better *all* go," he said, "because if the horses have wandered away, you'll want everyone giving a hand in the search. Come again another day."

The children set off home. They said no more to Mark about the open gate and did not grumble at him—but he felt most uncomfortable because by his silly carelessness he had spoilt a lovely picnic.

Their father and mother saw them trooping down over Willow Hill above the farm, and were most astonished.

"You've finished your picnic early!" cried their mother. "Why are you home already? It isn't nearly tea-time."

"I left the gate of the horses' field open," said Mark. "We've come to see if the horses are still there all right. I'm most terribly sorry."

The children ran to the big field where the horses lived. They saw Darling near by. Then Rory saw Captain and Blossom drinking from the stream. Good—the three cart-horses were safe.

But where were Patchy and Darky, the two new horses? The children slipped into the field, and shut the gate behind them.

They looked carefully round the big field—but there was no doubt about it, the two horses had gone.

"The shire-horses would be too sensible to wander off, even if they saw the gate open," said Rory. "Oh dear—where can the other two have got to?"

They went to tell their father. He looked grave. "I'd better get the car out and see if I can see them anywhere down the lanes," he said. "You children scout about a

289

bit and see if you can find out if anyone has seen stray horses."

Then began such a hunt. The five children separated and searched all over the farm to find the missing horses. It was a serious thing to lose horses, because, although they were certain to be found again some time or other, some days might pass before they were traced—and that meant so many hours' work on a farm left undone for lack of the horses to do it. Loss of labour was loss of money on a farm.

Mark hunted harder than anyone, for he felt guilty and was ready to search till he dropped, if only he could find the missing horses in the end. Suddenly he gave a loud shout and pointed to something on the ground. The others came up, one at a time, panting, to see what he had found.

"Look—hoof-marks! That's the way they went," said Mark excitedly, pointing away from the farm, up Willow Hill. "We must follow these prints until we find the horses. Come on!"

Chapter Fifteen

Where Can the Horses Have Gone?

The children ran to tell their parents that they had found hoof-marks and were going to track them. "We'll bring back Patchy and Darky, *you'll* see!" said Benjy. "Even if we have to follow them for miles."

"You may quite well have to," said the farmer. "I can't come with you, because I've got a man coming to see me about a new bull. I'll go hunting in the car after that."

"Penny's not to go," said the children's mother firmly. "I'm not going to let her rush for miles. She's too little."

"*Mother!* I'm *not* little any more!" cried Penny indignantly. "It isn't fair. When you want me to do anything you tell me I'm a great big girl, big enough to do what you want. And when you don't want me to do anything, you say I'm too little. Which am I, little or big?"

"Both!" said her mother, with a laugh. "A dear little girl who does what she's told—and a great big girl who never makes a fuss about it!"

Everyone laughed—even Penny. "Mother's too clever for you, Penny," said Rory. "Stay behind and look after True for me, will you, there's a dear. I can't take him with me."

The idea of looking after True was so nice that Penny at once gave up the pleasure of going to hunt for lost horses. She held out her arms eagerly for the fat little

291

pup. He snuggled up to her and she took him indoors to play with.

The others set off up the hill after the hoof-marks. They could see them easily. They followed them right to the top of the hill and then down to the east.

Rory stood on the top of the hill, shaded his eyes and looked down into the next valley, and over the common that lay to the east.

"I can't see a sign of the horses," he said. "Not a sign."

"Well, come on, we've got the hoof-marks to guide us," said Benjy, and the four set off down the hill.

They followed the marks for two or three miles. It was tiring. The prints went on and on, often very difficult to see. Sometimes the children lost them for a while and then found them again after a ten minutes' hunt to the right and left.

"Bother these horses!" said Rory. "Why couldn't they have stayed somewhere near instead of taking a ten-mile walk!"

"Surely we'll come up to them soon," said Mark.

They went on. After another hour they came to the common—and here, alas, the hoof-marks disappeared entirely. Not a sign of them was to be seen. The children stared hopelessly over the wide expanse of common.

"It's no good hunting over the common," said Benjy. "We might hunt all day and night and never see the horses. We'd better go back."

"I'm so hungry," said Rory. "It's long past tea-time. Come on."

The four children were disappointed, hungry, and miserable, especially Mark. He didn't say a single word all the way home. Sheila was sorry for him and walked beside him. She guessed how he was feeling.

When they got back Penny rushed out to meet them. "Have you got the horses? Where were they?"

Rory shook his head. "The hoof-marks led to the common, Penny—and there we had to stop and turn back—because there were no more marks to follow. We couldn't hunt the common. It's too big."

"Poor children," said Mother, coming out too. "Go and wash. I've a lovely Sunday tea for you. Hurry now."

They couldn't hurry, even for a lovely tea, hungry though they were! But they felt much better after eating slices of ham, new-boiled eggs, hot scones and butter and one of Harriet's currant cakes. True darted under the table, pulling at everyone's laces. There was no stopping him doing that! He seemed to think that shoe-laces were tied up merely for him to pull undone.

After a while the farmer came in and sat down to a late tea too. He had been scouring the countryside in his car, looking far and wide for the horses. He had notified the police of their loss and was hoping that at any moment he might hear where they were.

But nothing was heard of the horses that evening and Mark felt so dreadful that he was near to bursting into tears.

"It looks as if we'll have to let one of the cart-horses do the milk-round tomorrow morning," said the farmer. "That's a nuisance, because I wanted him in the fields. Such a waste of time!"

"I'm very sorry, sir, for leaving the gate open," said Mark, stammering over his words and feeling rather frightened of the worried farmer.

"I bet you won't do it again," said Rory.

"Leaving a gate open is a very small thing," said the farmer, "but unfortunately small things have a way of leading to bigger things. An open gate—wandering cattle or horses—maybe damage done by them to be paid for—loss of hours of their labour—loss of our time looking for them. It all means a pretty big bill when you add it up. But we all make mistakes, Mark—and providing we learn our lessons and don't make the same mistakes twice, we shan't do so badly. Don't worry too much about it. You can't afford to be careless on a farm. Those horses will turn up sooner or later, so cheer up!"

Mark went home, not at all cheerful. The others went to bed, tired out. Rory was asleep almost before True had settled down on his feet.

In the morning there was still no sign of the missing horses, and Darling had to be harnessed to the milk-cart for the milk-round. Jim grumbled at this because he wanted her for heavy field-work. Blossom was put to the farm-wagon to take root-crops to the field where the sheep were grazing. This was usually work that one of the light horses did. The children went off to school.

Fanny and Harriet were just as upset about the missing horses as everyone else. "I wish I could find those horses," Fanny said, a dozen times that morning.

And then, when she went into the yard to fetch a broom, she heard a faint sound that made her turn her head.

"That's a horse's whinny, sure as I'm standing here!" said the girl, and she listened again. She heard the noise once more, borne on the wind. It seemed to come from the next farm, whose fields adjoined Willow Farm. She rushed in to Harriet.

"Aunt Harriet! I believe those horses are in Marlow's Field!" she cried. "I heard them whinnying, and Farmer Marlow hasn't any horses in his field, has he?"

"Not that I know of," said Harriet. "Well—you better go and look, that's all. You can sweep out the kitchen when you come back."

Fanny sped off to the next farm. She went across one of the Willow Farm fields, splashed through a stream for a short cut, and then made her way into the field belonging to Farmer Marlow. He only had a small farm, and went in for crops, not livestock.

The girl looked about the big field she had come into—and, to her enormous delight, she saw Patchy and Darky standing at the far end! To think they had been there all the time, within five minutes' walk, and not miles and miles away!

The girl called to them. "Patchy! Come here! Darky, come along. Come along!"

The horses cantered over to her. They knew her for one of the people belonging to Willow Farm. She took hold of their manes and pulled them gently.

"Bad creatures! You've had everyone worrying about you and hunting for you for hours! Now you come along with me, and don't you wander away again, even if your gate *is* left open!"

The horses came along willingly enough. They had wandered out of the open gate and had made their way slowly to Farmer Marlow's deserted field. No one had noticed them there at all. They had not had the sense to find their way back again, but had stayed there together all the night, waiting for someone to find them.

Fanny proudly marched them back to the farm-house.

To think of everyone hunting away for them—and she, Fanny, had found them! Her aunt, the cook, heard the clip-clop of hoofs in the farmyard outside, and came out.

"Good girl!" she said. "Well, well—I'm right glad they're back again. They look a bit ashamed of themselves, don't they? You give a call to Jim and tell him you've got them. Then come back and sweep out the kitchen."

Fanny went off with the horses and shouted to Jim. He was amazed when he turned round and saw Fanny with the horses.

"Where did they come from?" he asked, staring.

"Oh, I got them from Farmer Marlow's field," said Fanny, feeling quite a heroine. "They must have been there all the time, and nobody noticed them."

Jim took Patchy and Darky, and soon they were at work, happy to be back again with the others. They whinnied to the big cart-horses and seemed to be telling them all that had happened.

That morning, when he got to school, Mark asked Rory anxiously about the horses, and was very upset when he heard that they had not yet returned. All the children were gloomy, and they did not expect for one moment that Patchy and Darky would ever be found by the time they returned for dinner.

But what a surprise for them! When they got near to Willow Farm, Rory gave a shout.

"I say! There's old Patchy—look! And there's Darky—see, in that wagon with Bill. Hie, Bill! Hie! Where did the horses turn up from after all?"

"You ask Fanny," said Bill, with a grin. "She's the clever one!"

So Fanny had the delight of telling and retelling her little story to four admiring children. They crowded round her, listening. She felt like a heroine.

"Well, to think of us following those hoof-marks all those miles!" said Rory, with a groan. "Miles and miles! What idiots we were!"

"They must have been old marks," said Benjy. "Now, if only Tammylan had been here, he would have told us at once that those marks had been made ages ago, and we'd have known they were no good to follow. I say—won't old Mark be pleased?"

He was! His round, red face was one beam of joy when the children told him, at afternoon school, how the horses had been found.

"They were just four or five minutes' walk away from us all the time we were at the farm, and we never knew it," said Rory.

"I shall never be careless again," said Mark. "That *has* taught me a lesson."

It certainly had. Poor Mark got into such a habit of shutting gates and doors behind him that he couldn't leave them open when he was told to! "I think all this ought to be put into a book, to warn other children," he said solemnly to his mother.

"Maybe one day it will," she answered.

And so it has.

Chapter Sixteen

Willow Farm Grows Larger!

The Easter holidays came and went. The summer term began, and the children galloped their donkeys across the fields to school. It was lovely to canter over the emerald green meadows and to see the trees putting out green fingers everywhere.

Penny liked the beech leaves best. She had discovered that each leaf inside its pointed bud was pleated just like a tiny fan, and she had been amazed and delighted.

"Who pleats them?" she asked Sheila. But Sheila didn't know.

"I suppose they just grow like that," she said.

"Yes, but *some*body must have pleated each leaf into those tiny folds," said Penny, puzzled. "I shall ask Tammylan."

Penny was very busy before and after school hours with Dopey and the lambs. She fed them and played with them and they followed her around as if they were dogs. They had all grown very fast indeed, and looked strong and healthy. Davey was delighted with the two lambs.

"My word, Tuppenny, you made a better mother to my lambs than the ewes do themselves!" he said, with a laugh.

"Davey, is that poor mother-sheep all right that got caught in the wire?" said Penny.

"Quite all right," said Davey. "I believe she would have had her lambs back again in a week's time—but

I hadn't the heart to take them away from you!"

"I wouldn't have let you!" cried Penny. "I just *love* Hoppitty and Jumpity. But I wish they weren't getting so big."

"Oh, it doesn't matter your lambs growing," said Davey, "but it's that kid of yours I'm sorry to see getting big! He'll be the wildest goat we ever had on the farm. He came up here yesterday, and bless me if he didn't find my old hat in my hut and chew it to bits."

"Oh, Davey—I'll give you a new one for your birthday!" cried Penny. "Isn't Dopey bad? I just can't teach him to be any better. He nearly drives Harriet mad. He *will* jump in through the low kitchen window and chase Mr. By-Himself."

"Ho!" said Davey, with a chuckle, "that won't do that sulky old cat any harm. I'll give Dopey a good mark for that!"

"Isn't our flock of sheep getting big?" said Penny as she looked down the hillside at the sheep and the lambs grazing together. "Willow Farm is getting larger and larger, Davey. Sheila and Fanny have heaps of young chicks and ducklings again, so we'll soon have hundreds of hens and ducks! And you know we've got lots of new piglets? They *are* so sweet!"

"Ah, the springtime brings new life everywhere," said Davey. "I reckon we'll soon be having little calves too."

"Oh! Is Daddy going to buy some?" cried Penny, skipping for joy. "Oh, last year we had some dear little calves and I fed them out of the milk-pail. It was lovely to feel them sucking my fingers, Davey."

Mark came to spend the day, and Penny ran to show him all the new creatures that had arrived since he had last been to the farm. He was very interested in the piglets.

"Did you buy them?" he asked. "I do like them."

"No, the sow borned them," said Penny. Mark stared at her. "We didn't buy them. They belong to the old sow."

Mark didn't understand. Penny thought he was very silly. She wondered how to explain to him about kittens and puppies and calves and lambs and piglets.

"Listen, Mark," she said. "You know hens lay eggs, don't you?"

"Yes," said Mark.

"Well, silly, cats lay kittens, and dogs lay puppies, and pigs lay piglets, and cows lay calves, and hens lay eggs with chicks in them, and ducks lay eggs with ducklings in them, and turkeys lay eggs with baby turkeys in, and geese lay eggs with goslings in them, and—and—and—"

"Well, of course!" said Mark, thinking what a silly he had been. "Of course—how lovely! Let's go and ask Jonquil the cow what she thinks her little calf will be like when it's born."

They went to the big field where the cows were kept and looked for Jonquil. She was a red and white cow, with big soft eyes, a great favourite with the children. Cows rarely look for caresses, but Jonquil was different from most cows. If the children came near, she would turn her big head and ask for a pat or stroke on her nose.

"Wherever is Jonquil?" wondered Penny. The two children counted the cows. They had sixteen at Willow Farm—but now they could only count fifteen.

"We'd better look for her," said Penny. "Come on, Mark."

They went round the big field which had many old willow trees here and there—and behind one big hollow tree, its long branches springing high into the air, they found the red and white cow.

She was standing in the tall grass there, looking lovingly down at a little red and white heap on the grass. Penny and Mark ran up to see what it was. Then Penny gave one of her piercing squeals.

"Oh! Oh! It's Jonquil's calf! It's born! Oh, look at the dear, darling little thing! It's *exactly* like Jonquil. Isn't it, Mark? Oh, Jonquil, it's lovely, it's lovely!"

Jonquil gazed at the two children. She was very proud of her little long-legged calf, which had been born only a little while before. She bent her head down and licked it. The calf raised its head and looked at its mother.

"Isn't it sweet?" said Mark. "I do think baby things are lovely. I wish you'd let me help you to feed the calf, Penny."

"Well, you can if you come to see it," promised Penny generously. "I do, do hope it's a girl-calf. Daddy says the boy-calves have to be sold when they are three weeks old. But we are going to keep the girl calves this year because they grow up into cows, which give milk and are valuable."

"Oh," said Mark, who felt that he was learning a great deal that afternoon. "I say—why do you have to feed this calf, Penny? Surely its mother can give it all the milk it wants, because she's a cow!"

"Ah, but Daddy says that when a cow has a calf she has such wonderful rich milk that it's good for children and grown-ups," said Penny, looking very wise. "So we take the calf from its mother after a little while, and feed it on separated milk . . ."

"Whatever's that?" asked Mark.

"It's the milk that's had the cream taken away, Mark," said Penny, feeling quite clever as she related all this to the big boy. "Last year I put a few drops of cod-liver oil into the milk to make up for the cream that wasn't there."

"I do think you know a lot, Penny," said Mark looking admiringly at the little girl. She felt pleased. It was so tiresome always to be the youngest and smallest and to have to ask the others things she wanted know—and here she was, telling a big boy all kinds of things he didn't seem to know at all. It was marvellous. Penny felt quite swollen with importance.

"Let's go and tell Daddy about Jonquil's calf," said Penny. She took Mark's hand and they went to find the farmer. He was two fields away, hard at work.

"Daddy! Jonquil's got a lovely little new-born calf!" shouted Penny. The farmer looked up at once.

"Where is it?" he asked anxiously.

"Come and see," said Penny. "Oh, Daddy, I hope it's a girl-calf, then we can keep it. We had three last year, and they were all girl-calves. I was sorry when you sold them—but we kept them a long time, didn't we?"

The farmer went to see Jonquil's calf. It certainly was a pretty little thing.

"But it's a boy-calf!" he told Penny. "Yes—a little bull-calf. So you must make up your mind to lose it in three or four weeks' time, Penny."

Penny looked ready to cry. She had so badly wanted the calf to be a girl. "Cheer up," said her father. "Daisy is having a calf, too—so maybe she will present you with a girl that you can feed for months! Now—what are you

going to call this one? He's a fine little fellow."

Penny cheered up when she had to think of a name. She turned to Mark. "What shall we call him? Let's think hard."

"Radish, because he's red," said Mark.

"Don't be silly," said Penny. "Nobody's ever heard of a cow called Radish."

"Well, *I've* never heard of a cow called Jonquil before," said Mark.

"That's because you haven't known many cows," said Penny. "You ought to know that most cows are called by the names of flowers."

"Well—let's call the calf Peony, then," said Mark. "That's red too."

"It's the wrong red," said Penny, who didn't really

mean to let Mark choose the name himself. "And besides, this is a boy-calf. Peony sounds like a name for a girl-calf. Let *me* think."

But before she could think of a good name, the other three children came running up, with Fanny behind them, to see the new calf. It was always such a thrill when any new animal arrived—especially one born on the farm itself. Jonquil stood patiently by whilst everyone admired her new-born.

"It's beautiful, Jonquil," said Sheila, giving the tiny calf her fingers to suck. "Simply beautiful. You ought to call your boy-calf Johnnie, after you, Jonquil!"

"Oh, *yes!*" said Penny. "That's lovely. Jonquil, your calf is christened Johnnie."

And Johnnie he was, and Johnnie he remained even after he was sold at the market, three or four weeks later. Penny went with her father when he took him to the market, and she told the buyer that the calf was called Johnnie.

"So please go on calling him that," she said. "He's nice. I've been feeding him out of a pail, and he's really very good."

"I'll look after Johnnie, Missy," said the man, with a smile.

Daisy had her calf not long afterwards, and to Penny's joy it was a girl-calf, so it was allowed to live on at the farm. "I shall have you for months and months," said Penny to the soft-eyed little creature, as she and Mark took turns at feeding it, dipping their fingers into the pail of milk and then letting the calf suck. "Perhaps Daddy might even let you stay with us for always till you grow into a cow. That would be lovely."

It was fun to be on the farm in the late spring and early summer, when the whole place was full of young new things. And how they grew! The little lambs grew big and no longer frisked quite so madly. The calves grew. The chicks turned into young hens and the ducklings into ducks. The piglets grew as fat as butter. In the hedges, new young wild birds were seen, and tiny baby rabbits scampered on the hillside among the sheep.

"It's lovely to see so many things growing up," said Sheila. "They're all growing as fast as the corn in the fields—but it's a pity they stop being funny and get solemn and proper."

There was one little creature that grew too—but he didn't become solemn and proper. No—Dopey remained as funny and as mad as ever. He just simply *couldn't* grow up!

Chapter Seventeen

Good Dog True!

One of the animals that grew the fastest of all was Rory's puppy, True. For a few weeks he was a round ball of a pup, his short legs hardly seeming able to carry his fat little body.

"Now he's sort of got *longer*," said Penny, looking at him one day. "Hasn't he, Rory? He's not so fat. It's a good thing we didn't call him Dumpy."

Everyone looked at True. He was sitting in his basket, his head on one side, his bright eyes looking at Rory. Rory's heart warmed with love towards him. He thought secretly that never since the world began could there have been such a wonderful puppy as True.

True wagged his tail as he saw the boy's eyes on him. He leapt out of the basket and ran to his master. He put his paws up on his knee.

"Yes—he *is* growing," said Benjy. "His nose is getting longer too—not so snubby. I believe he will be awfully like Rascal. I should think he'll be every bit as clever too."

"Oh, much cleverer," said Rory, at once. "Why, he already walks to heel whenever I tell him, and do you know, yesterday I made him sit on my school satchel and guard it, whilst I walked on for a quarter of a mile!"

"And did he guard it?" asked Penny, with great interest. "Didn't he run after you and leave it?"

"Of course not!" said Rory scornfully. "He knows better than that! He just sat on that satchel looking after me as I went off, and he didn't stir from it till I suddenly turned round and whistled to him!"

"How clever of him!" said Sheila.

"He was even cleverer than that," said Rory. "He tried to bring the satchel with him! He pulled and pulled at it with his baby teeth, and in the end, everything spilt out of it, and when it was empty it was light enough for him to drag along to me. You should just have seen him, dragging it along, falling over the strap, trying to get to me. I did laugh."

"Aren't you going to let Davey have a hand in his training soon?" asked Daddy. "Or rather—let Rascal teach him a few things. After all, he's a sheep-dog, you know, and ought to use his fine, quick brain for good work."

"Oh, I know, Daddy," said Rory. "I'm taking him up to Davey tomorrow. It's Saturday, and I can watch him having his first lesson."

"I'll come too," said Penny.

"Well, don't bring Dopey," said Rory. "I don't feel very kindly towards him at the moment. He's eaten my best handkerchief."

"I won't bring him," promised Penny. So the next day, when Rory yelled to Penny that he was going up the hill to find Davey, Penny hurriedly shut Dopey into a shed, and ran to join Rory and True.

Dopey was most annoyed at being shut up. He was mad and silly, but he always had brains enough to try and outwit anyone who wanted to shut him up. He scrambled up on a bin that stood beneath a window. He butted the window with his small, tough head and it opened a little way. He butted it again, bleating at it. It opened wide enough for him to jump out. With a flying leap the kid was out into the yard, startling the hens there enormously. They fled away, clucking.

Dopey ran at them, just for fun. Then he went to say a few rude words to the piglets who lived with their big sow-mother in the sty. Then he looked around for Penny.

The little girl was half-way up the hill with Rory and True. Her clear high voice came floating to Dopey's sharp ears. With bounds, leaps and jumps he was off after her, only pausing to leap at a scared rabbit that shot into its hole in fright.

"Penny! There's Dopey!" said Rory, in disgust. "I asked you to shut him up."

"Well, I *did!*" said Penny, in astonishment. "I put him into the shed. How did he get out?"

Only Dopey knew, and he wasn't going to tell. He frisked round True and tried to bite his tail. Then he butted him with his head. True snapped at him playfully. He liked Dopey and the lambs.

"Catch the kid and shut him up in that little old sheep-hut there," said Rory. But that was easier said than done! Dopey had brains enough to know that Penny meant to shut him up again, and he skipped out of her way whenever she went near him. He could be most exasperating. Penny gave it up at last.

"Oh well, I dare say it won't make any difference if he's here when True gets his first lesson," said Rory at last. "Come on. Hallo, Davey."

"Good morning, young sir! Good morning, Tuppenny!" said the old shepherd, his eyes wrinkling in the sun as he turned to look at them both. "You've brought little

308

True for his lesson, I see."

"Yes," said Rory proudly. "He's as clever as can be, Davey. Where's Rascal?"

"Over there, with Nancy and Tinker," said Davey. He whistled, and the three dogs came running up to him. The shepherd turned to Rory.

"I'll get the dogs to take the sheep down the hill, and then bring them up again," he said. "True must run with Rascal. Tell him."

"True! Rascal!" called Rory. The dogs came up. True was wagging his tail so fast that it could hardly be seen. "Now listen, True. You're to keep with Rascal. See?" said Rory. "Rascal, see that True is by your side!"

Rascal understood perfectly. He had taught Tinker and Nancy, and he knew that this young pup was to be trained too. He liked the look of him!

Davey gave a few sharp orders to the dogs. He used as few words as possible, and pointed with his stick. Each of the grown dogs knew exactly what he meant. They were, for some reason, to take the sheep down the hill, and then to bring them up again. Rascal nosed True gently to make him start off with them.

The three dogs and the puppy set off together. At first True thought it was just a run, and he enjoyed scurrying along. Then he found that the sheep were running too. Ah—that was even more fun. Were they chasing the sheep? That was really rather strange, thought True, because Rory had already taught him not to chase the hens, ducks, or cats.

He made up his mind that they *were* chasing the sheep, and he ran at one, trying to snap at its hind legs. But that was quite the wrong thing to do! Rascal was beside him in a moment, pushing him away, talking to him in dog-language.

"Silly pup! You should never frighten a sheep. We are running them down the hill, that's all, not chasing them. Help to keep them together in a bunch!"

True felt ashamed of himself. His quick mind saw that the dogs were now bunching the sheep together, and taking them somewhere. He must help.

So, when he saw a sheep leaving the flock, he ran to it. He nosed it back again into the flock.

"Good dog True!" shouted Rory proudly. "Did you see that, Davey? Did you see that, Penny? He's learning already!"

The dogs took the sheep down to the bottom of the hill. Rascal looked back at the shepherd to make quite sure that he still wanted them brought back again. Davey waved his stick. Rascal understood. He *was* to take them up again. The dog was a little puzzled, because there did not seem much sense to him in this order, but he was used to obeying.

True was running with him now, trying to do all that Rascal was doing. He ran round the flock to keep them together.

"He's learning to bunch them already!" said Rory.

It was more difficult to get the sheep back up the hill again than it had been to run them down. They did not want to go. They wanted to stay there and graze. The three grown dogs did their best to send them up the hill, but it took time. True grew tired of this new game. He ran off by himself and put his nose in a rabbit hole.

"Hie, True! Hie, hie!" yelled Rory. "Back to your work again at once."

"Rascal! Fetch True!" ordered Davey. The amazingly wise sheep-dog understood. He ran off at once to the puppy and pushed him smartly back to work again. True was not too pleased, for he felt sure he could go down a hole and get a rabbit just then. But he ran round the sheep once more and they began to move slowly back up the hill, trying to stop and nibble the grass every now and again, but driven steadily onwards by the three dogs and the puppy.

Then Dopey chose that moment to try and behave like a sheep-dog too. He began to run round the sheep and to butt them with his hard little head. But the sheep were not standing any nonsense of that sort from a kid! They didn't mind obeying the dogs, whom they sensed to be their guardians and friends—but to be told what to do by a silly little kid! No—that was too much!

With one accord all the near-by sheep turned on Dopey and ran at him. He found himself enclosed in the flock. He could not get out! Squeezed by the fat woolly bodies of the sheep, Dopey was lost and he bleated pitifully.

Rory and Davey laughed till the tears came into their eyes. "It serves him right," said Rory.

"Oh, poor little Dopey!" said Penny, half laughing too. "Let me go and rescue him."

"No, you stay where you are," said Rory. "It will do Dopey good to be squashed by the sheep. He thinks far too much of himself! Look—there he is!"

Dopey had managed to get free from the sheep when the dogs moved them on again, and he came leaping out from the flock, looking really scared. He sprang right over True and Rascal and leapt up the hill to Penny faster than he had ever moved before!

"Little silly!" said Penny, picking him up. He was still small enough to be carried, though he wouldn't be much longer. "Did you think you were a sheep-dog, then?"

The sheep were brought right back to the shepherd and he told the dogs to lie down. They lay down, panting, their watchful eyes turning to their flock every now and again. True lay down with them too, feeling most important.

"He's done some work for the first time in his life, and he's feeling good," said Davey. "Well done, little True. We'll make a fine sheep-dog of you yet, so we will. You'll be as good as my Rascal."

"He'll be better," said Rory.

Davey laughed. "Maybe," he said. "We'll see. I'd trust Rascal to look after my sheep for me if I had to go away for a week! He can count them more quickly than I can, because if one is missing he knows it sooner than I do and is off to find it. What I'd do without my dogs I don't know."

"And I don't know what I'd do without True now," said Rory, picking up the puppy and fondling his ears. "I can't imagine what it was like when I didn't have him. Come on, True—back home we go! You shall have an extra good feed as a reward for working hard at your first lesson!"

So back they went and True certainly did have a good meal. Dopey came to share it with him. The little kid thought he had worked as hard as the puppy, and he didn't see why he shouldn't have a reward too!

Chapter Eighteen

The Coming of the Bees

"Mother, don't you want to keep bees?" asked Sheila, one day, as she helped herself to some golden honey out of the pot. "You said you were going to."

"So I did," said Mother. "Well—I'll talk to the bee-man about them today. I've got to go into the village and I'll really see if we can't get a hive or two and keep bees."

"Oooh!" said Penny. "Lovely! I shall like bees. I think they are such happy things."

"Why happy?" asked Rory in surprise.

"Well, I hum when I'm happy, and bees are always humming, so they must always be very happy," said Penny. Everyone laughed. Penny did have such funny ideas.

Mother went down to the village to talk to the bee-man. When the children came back from school that day she told them that she had arranged for two hives of bees. Everyone was thrilled.

"Will there be enough nectar in the flowers we've got to keep two hives going?" asked Rory. "We haven't really got a great many flowers in our garden, have we, Mother? The farm garden mostly grows salads and things like sage and thyme that Harriet uses for seasoning things."

"Oh, bees love thyme," said Mother. "But we have plenty of other flowers that bees love. They are growing by the thousand—by the million—for the bees to make honey from."

"What flowers?" asked Penny in surprise.

"Well—what about Daddy's clover field?" said Mother. "Haven't you walked by that and seen and heard the bees humming there by the hundred? Clover is full of nectar for them. You know that, Penny darling, because I have often seen you pull a clover flower head, and pick out the little white or pink tubes from the head and suck them to taste the sweet nectar inside!"

"Yes, I have," said Penny, remembering. "It tastes as sweet as this honey!"

"And then there is the heather on the near-by common," said Mother. "When that is in flower, the bees swarm there in their thousands! Heather honey is most delicious. Oh, our bees will be able to fill the combs in their hives with any amount of sweet honey for us!"

"Do they have brushes as well as combs?" asked Penny. Everyone roared with laughter.

"Idiot!" said Rory. "Mother, you wouldn't possibly think Penny was nine, would you?"

"Don't tease her," said Mother, looking at the red-faced girl. "Yes—they do have brushes, funnily enough! You know, they collect pollen from the flowers too, and put it into tiny pockets in their legs. Well, they have brushes on their legs to brush the powder! So they *do* have brushes and combs! But the combs are for holding the honey. I'll show you some empty ones when the hives come."

One evening the bee-man came. The two white-painted hives had already arrived, and were set up in Mother's own piece of garden, just behind the

314

farmhouse. The children were on the look-out for the bee-man. He was a funny little fellow with a wrinkled face like an old, old apple and eyes as black as ripe pear-pips. He had a funny high voice that squeaked.

"Good evening to you, Ma'am," he said to Mother. "Now, where are the hives? Ah, we'll have to move them from there, so we will. I'll tell you where to put them."

"Does it matter where we have them?" asked Mother. "I rather thought I'd like to have them there on the lawn so that I could see them from my window."

"We'll put them over the other side," said the bee-man. "You can still see them from the window then. You see, Ma'am, there's a gap in the hedge just behind where you've put the hives and the wind will blow cold on them when it's in that quarter. Ah, bees don't like a draught. Never did. Over there will be splendid."

So the hives were moved. Then the bee-man dressed himself up in a most peculiar way. He put on a funny broad-brimmed hat, and then put on some puffed white sleeves. Then he pulled a black veil out of his bag, and put that over his head and tucked it in at his waist.

"What's all that for?" asked Rory. "Are you afraid of getting stung?"

"No," said the bee-man. "But I want to be sure that no bee gets up my sleeve, or down my neck, because if one does, it will get squashed and will sting me—not that I mind that overmuch but I don't want to kill any of these bees. A bee will always sting if it's squeezed or squashed!"

Penny was not quite sure if she liked having so many bees close to her. The bee-man had brought them with him, and was going to put them into the hives. Clouds of them flew about, and the children began to move away.

One buzzed round Penny's head and she gave a squeal. Then she turned and ran.

"Now what's the use of running from bees?" said the bee-man scornfully. "Don't you know they can out-fly even the fastest train! You stand your ground, Missy. They won't sting you if you don't interfere with them."

"You've got some on your belt," said Sheila.

The bee-man flicked them away as if they were bits of dust. He didn't mind them at all. Some crawled over his hands and he shook them off.

"Did they sting you?" asked Rory.

"Not they!" said the bee-man. "Look—you've a couple of bees on your arm, my boy. You flick them away as I do!"

So Rory did and the bees flew off into the air.

Mother showed Penny the comb full of holes in which the bees would store their honey. "They will seal each hole up when it is full," she said. "You shall have honey-in-the-comb to eat later on in the season. You will like that."

The bees soon settled into the hives. It was fun to see them each day sailing up into the air, getting their bearings as it were, and then flying straight off to the clover-fields. There was such a coming and going all day long!

"It must be hot in the hives today," said Sheila, one very hot morning. "Mother has put an electric fan into the dairy to make it even cooler. I guess the bees wish they could have an electric fan in their hives too."

"They cool their hives quite well themselves," said Daddy. "If you could look inside the hive you would see that many of the bees have been given the job of

316

standing still and whirring their wings to make a cool draught. They are the electric fans of the hive!"

"Well—that's marvellous!" said Penny, only half believing this. But Daddy spoke the truth, and the inside of the hives was kept cool in this way by the bees themselves on very hot days.

Harriet liked the bees. She could hear their humming from the kitchen window and it was very pleasant. Penny liked sitting on the low kitchen window-sill, listening to the bees outside, whilst she ate a scone hot out of the oven.

"Harriet, did you know that we've got another calf born today?" she said, as she ate. "It belongs to Pimpernel."

"There now!" exclaimed Harriet, pleased. "We shall have some wonderful rich milk from Pimpernel and be able to make the finest butter you ever saw. Be sure you tell the bees about it, Penny dear."

"Tell the bees?" said Penny in great astonishment. "Why should I tell the bees?"

"Oh, don't you know you should tell the bees whenever anything happens in a household?" said Harriet, who was full of country customs. "You should always tell them when there is a death in the household, or any change—and they like to hear of such happenings as a new calf being born. It brings good luck to the household if you tell the bees the news. You go and tell them, Penny."

Penny went first to tell her mother what Harriet had said. Mother laughed.

"Oh, I don't expect the bees mind whether they know our news or not," she said. "It's a very old custom that

317

country people follow, Penny dear. You needn't bother."

"But I'm a country person, and I like to do things like that," said Penny. She felt certain that if she was a bee hard at work all day, she would simply love to hear any bits of news there were. "I shall tell the bees everything, Mother!"

So Penny went solemnly out to tell the bees about Pimpernel's calf. "Bees, I have to tell you something," she announced. "Pimpernel's calf is born, and it's a dear little girl-calf. But I'm sorry to say that Pimpernel isn't very well. Isn't it a pity?"

The bees hummed round her head, and Penny felt sure they were listening. "Please bring us good luck because I've told you the news," finished Penny.

And the funny thing was that Pimpernel was very much better that evening, and Jim couldn't think why!

"It's because I told the bees," said Penny solemnly. "It is, really, Jim. I shall always tell them things in future. They like it."

"You do so, Missy, then," said Jim, who had as great a belief as Harriet in the old country customs. "And you look out for swarms too—maybe one of the hives will swarm in the hot weather."

"Why do bees swarm?" asked Penny.

"Well, you see, each hive has a queen bee," said Jim. "But sometimes in the season there's another queen bee born, and there can't be two in a hive. So some of the bees fly off with the second queen to found a hive of their own. And you have to go after it and take it, or you'll lose half your bees!"

"Bees seem to be just as exciting as everything else," said Penny. "But what I'm really looking forward to is

318

tasting their honey. Won't it be lovely to have our own?"

It *was* lovely. When the time came for the honey to be taken, there were so many pounds of it that Mother was able to put it away in store to use the whole winter through! She sent a large pot to Tammylan, who was very fond of honey. The children gave it to him the next time they visited him. They had brought him a fine lot of things, for besides honey each child had a present.

"I've brought you six of my hens' best brown eggs," said Sheila.

"And I've brought you some of Mother's finest butter," said Rory.

"And there's some home-made currant jelly," said Benjy.

"And I've got you the biggest lettuce I've ever grown in my bit of Mother's garden," said Penny. "It has a wonderful big heart. You feel it, Tammylan."

"As big a heart as you have, Penny!" said Tammylan, with a laugh. "My word, I'm lucky to have four friends like you. By the way, tell your father I've heard of a bullock that wants fattening up. If he'll take it, I'll bring it along tomorrow."

The first thing Penny did when she got home was to go to the bees and tell them about the bullock!

"Bees, there's a bullock coming!" she announced. "There's a bit of news for you!"

And when she went in, the little girl was quite certain that the bees were talking over her news as they flew to get the heather-honey from the common.

"A new bullock is coming, he's coming, yes, he's coming!" she thought she heard the bees humming. And maybe she was right!

Chapter Nineteen

Rory is too Big for his Boots!

That summer was a very dry one. The children revelled in the heat and grew as brown as the old oak-apples on the trees. Haymaking time came and went. The hay was not as good as the year before, because the rain held off whilst the grass was growing. So it was not as lush as it should have been.

"Well, let's hope the rain keeps off when we cut the hay and turn it," said the farmer. It did, and the children had a wonderful time helping with the haymaking. They were allowed a holiday from school, and they made the most of it. True helped too, galloping and scrabbling in the mown hay, sending it flying into the air.

Dopey, of course, joined the haymakers. He was now growing into a goat, and was completely mad. He still seemed to think he was a silly young kid, and played the most ridiculous tricks. He loved to spring out at the sheep and the cows, and leap around and about them so that they stared at him in the greatest amazement.

"I wouldn't mind his being such a clown," said the farmer, "but I do wish he wouldn't eat anything and everything. It was a mistake to give you Dopey for your birthday, Penny."

"Oh *no*, Daddy!" said the little girl. "I know he's silly and mad—but he does love us all."

"H'mm!" said the farmer. "I think I could manage quite well without Dopey's love and affection. I'm always very suspicious when that goat comes along with me."

Penny's lambs were in the field with the other sheep now, because they ate grass. Penny always let them out when she was free from school, and they wandered around after her, baaing in their high voices. They were not allowed in the hayfield. Scamper the squirrel was allowed there, though, and he enjoyed himself very much, bounding about among the haymakers, and frisking up and down on Benjy. Those days were fun, and the children were sorry when the haymaking was over.

"Daddy, will you have enough hay to feed all our cattle this winter?" asked Sheila, when she watched the haystacks being built. "We've more cattle now, you know—and Paul Pry, the bullock, will eat an awful lot."

The bullock had been called Paul Pry by Penny because he always appeared whenever anything was going on. He was rather a pet, very tame and very affectionate for a bullock. He simply adored joining the children when they watched such things as the ducklings going into the water for the first time, or the piglets being set free to run about the yard, squealing for joy.

"Well, we may have enough this year, but we ought to plant another field with hay next year," said the farmer to Sheila. "Willow Farm is growing! There's that field we haven't used yet—the one right away up there—we might burn the bad grass and weeds in it, and then plough it up next season. The field would burn quickly enough this weather."

But soon after that the rain came and it was impossible to burn the rubbishy field. The children thought the idea of burning it was very exciting.

"It's a quick way of getting rid of the rubbishy grass there," said Rory. "I hope Daddy will do it as soon as the hot weather sets in again. Won't it be fun to set light to it?"

Rory was feeling rather big these days. He had done well on the farm that summer, because he was now very strong, and could do almost a man's work. The farmer was proud of him and praised him often. A little too often! Rory was getting "too big for his boots," Jim said.

"Why don't you ask Mother to buy you some new boots, Rory?" said Penny, looking at her brother's feet. "Jim says you are getting too big for your boots—you'll get sore feet, if you're not careful."

"You *are* a little silly, Penny!" said Rory crossly. He went out and banged the door.

"What's the matter with Rory?" asked Penny in astonishment.

"Well, don't you know what 'getting too big for your boots' means?" said Sheila, with a laugh. "It means getting vain or conceited or swollen headed—having too high an opinion of yourself!"

"Oh," said Penny in dismay, "what a silly I am!"

Rory had gone out into the fields. He was hailed by his father. "Rory! I've got to go over to Headley's farm to look at some things they've got to sell. Keep an eye on things for me, will you?"

"Yes, Dad!" called back Rory, feeling all important again. He saw Mark coming along and hoped he had heard what his father had said. Mark had. He looked rather impressed.

"It's a good thing Dad has got me to see to things for him whilst he's away here and there, isn't it?" said Rory to Mark. "Come on. Let's look how the wheat's coming along. We'll be harvesting it soon."

The two boys went through the fields. Mark listened to Rory talking about this crop and that crop. He was not so old as the bigger boy, and he thought Rory was really very clever and grown-up.

They came to the field that had lain waste since the farmer had taken over Willow Farm the year before. It was the one that was going to be burnt.

"This is an awful field, isn't it?" said Mark. "It's not like Willow Farm, somehow."

"We're going to burn it up," said Rory. "It's no good as it is. We must set it on fire, and then the rubbishy grass and weeds will go up in smoke, and we can put the field under the plough. Maybe next year it will be yielding a fine crop of hay, or potatoes, or something like that. Potatoes clean up a field well, you know."

"Do they really?" said Mark, thinking that Rory knew almost as much as the farmer himself. "I say—what fun to burn up a field? It looks about ready to burn now, doesn't it? All dry and tindery."

"It does," agreed Rory. He looked at the big four-acre field. He wished he could burn it then and there. It would be fun!

"You'll have to wait till your father gives orders for that, I suppose," said Mark. "He wouldn't allow you to start a thing like that unless he said so, would he?"

"Well—you heard what he said—I was to keep an eye on things for him," said Rory. "I don't see why I shouldn't burn up this field today. It looks about right for it. Which way is the wind blowing? We mustn't fire it if the wind is blowing in the wrong direction. We don't want those sheds to go up in smoke!"

The boys wetted their hands and held them out to the breeze. It seemed to be blowing away from the sheds, and towards the open country.

"Well—what about it?" said Mark, his eyes gleaming. "Do you really dare to without your father telling you?"

"Of course," said Rory grandly. "I'll go and get some matches. It's easy. You just set light to a patch of grass, and then let the breeze take it over the field. We shall see the grass and everything flaring up, and by the time Daddy comes back, the field will be done."

The two boys went to get some matches. "What do you want them for?" asked Harriet.

"We're going to fire that rubbishy field away up above the horses' field," said Rory.

Harriet thought that the farmer was going to be there too. She handed over some matches. "Well, see you don't burn yourselves," she said. "It's easy enough to light a fire, but not so easy to put it out!"

"Oh, a bit of stamping soon puts out a field fire," said Rory grandly, as if he knew everything about it. He took the matches and he and Mark set off back to the field. Penny joined them, Dopey skipping about behind her.

"Where are you going?" she asked. She jumped in excitement when she heard what they were going to do. "I'll come with you!" she said.

So they all of them came to the field. Rory struck a match, bent down and laid the flame to a few tall dry grasses. In a trice they flared up, and the flame jumped to other grasses nearby. The fire ran as if by magic!

"Look at it, look at it!" cried Penny, jumping about in excitement. "Isn't it grand?"

It might have been grand for a minute or two—but it very soon ceased to be grand and became terrifying! Rory had started something that was impossible to stop!

Chapter Twenty

An Unpleasant Adventure

"Oooh!" said Penny in surprise. "I never thought flames could go so fast!"

Mark and Rory hadn't known that either. It was simply amazing to see the fire spread over the field. The weeds and grass were very dry from a long hot spell, and they crackled up at once. The fire grew a loud voice, and a long mane of smoky hair.

"It's alive!" said Penny, dancing about. "It's a dragon with a mane of smoke. It's eating the field."

Mark was excited too. He didn't dance about like Penny, but he watched the fire with shining eyes. This was much better than an ordinary bonfire.

The breeze blew a little, and the fire crackled more loudly and grew a bigger mane of smoke. Rory looked a little worried. He hadn't guessed that the flames would rush along like this. They tore over the field, leaving a blackened track behind them.

As the fire burned, the sun went in, and a pall of clouds gathered. The children hardly noticed they were so intent on the field-fire. But then Rory saw something queer.

"Look!" he said. "The wind must be changing! The flames are blowing the other way now."

So they were. Instead of blowing straight down the field towards the open country, they were blowing sideways, eating up all the grass towards the east. The

crackling grew louder, the smoke grew thicker.

"Rory! Won't those sheds be burnt!" cried Penny suddenly. "Oh, Rory! Make the fire stop!"

"Stamp it out, quick!" cried Rory, and ran to where the edge of the fire began. But it was quite impossible to stamp it out. Soon the soles of their shoes were so hot that their feet felt as if they were on fire. Rory pushed Penny back. He was afraid the flames would burn her. Dopey, the kid, was the only one who seemed quite unafraid. He danced around the fire-edge, bleating at it.

"Mark! Run and tell Jim what's happened, and you, Penny, go and find Bill," said Rory. They sped off, fear making them run even faster than usual. Mark soon found Jim, who was already staring in puzzled amazement at the stream of smoke coming from the field up the hill. In a few words he told him what had happened.

Penny found Bill and before she had half told him what had happened, he had guessed and was rushing towards the out-building where empty sacks were kept. He yelled for Harriet as he ran.

"Harriet! Come and soak these sacks. The old field is afire. Those sheds will be burnt down!"

Harriet and Fanny came tearing out in surprise. The three of them dragged the sacks down to the duck-pond and soaked them well. Then they ran as fast as they could with the heavy sacks up to the flaming field. Half-way there they met Jim rushing along with Mark. Bill threw them a couple of wet sacks.

Soon they were all in the flaming grass, beating frantically at the fire. Slap, slap, slap! Harriet, Jim, Fanny, Bill, and Rory beat the wet sacks down on the flames, trying their hardest to put them out.

"I've got the fire out in this bit!" gasped Bill. "Look up there, Jim—it's getting too near those sheds. You go there and beat it, and I'll work around behind you. We may save the sheds then."

"The flames are running to that electric pole!" squealed Penny. "Oh, quick; oh, quick!"

Rory and Harriet ran to the pole and tried to beat off the flames. "Go and get some more wet sacks!" panted Harriet to Mark. "Ours are getting dry with the heat. Oh my, oh my, who ever thought of firing this field today! With the grass as dry as it is, who knows where the fire will end!"

"Oh, it won't burn our farmhouse, will it!" cried Penny in fright.

"Come on, help me get some wet sacks," said Mark, and pulled the frightened little girl along with him.

In half an hour's time nobody would have recognised any of the people who were beating out the flames. They were black with the smoke, they smelt terrible, and they were so hot and parched with thirst that they could hardly swallow.

Fanny gave up first. Her arms ached so badly with slapping at the flames that she could no longer lift them. She let her sack fall, and with tears rolling down her blackened cheeks, she staggered out of the smoke and sank down by the gate of the field. "I can't slap any more," she said. "I can't do it any more!"

Harriet gave up next. She stood and looked at the burning field, shaking her head.

"It's no use," she said. "No use at all. The fire's like a mad thing, running this way and that!"

So it was. The wind had got up properly now, and blew in furious gusts that sent the flames careering now here and now there. There was no saving the field or the hedge at the top, which was already a blackened, twisted mass, all its green leaves gone.

Rory, Bill, and Jim were trying to save the sheds from being fired. Already flames licked along one shed. Jim was beating madly at them, his trousers scorched, and his feet so hot that he could hardly walk. The two men and the boy were now so tired that they, like Harriet, could hardly lift up their arms to slap their wet sacks at the flames. But still they went on valiantly, slap, slap, slap. Rory was so horrified at the damage he had caused that he was determined not to stop fighting the fire till he dropped down with tiredness.

"We can't do any more," said Jim at last. "The fire's beaten us, boys."

"No, no, let's go on!" cried poor Rory, whose face was now so black that it was like a negro's. "I can't let Daddy's sheds be burnt."

"You'll have to," said Jim. "And those telegraph poles too. Let's hope the fire won't jump the hedge and get into the next field."

Everyone stood and watched the hungry fire, which crackled along the edge of the first shed, shooting out little red tongues of flames at the other two huts. There was nothing to be done. Nothing could save the sheds and the poles—and maybe the next field too would soon be in flames.

Nothing? Well, only one thing. Water would put out the flames—but where was water to come from? The nearest stream was two fields away, and it wouldn't be any good trying to cart water from it to the fire.

And then Penny gave such a squeal that everyone jumped in fright, thinking that the little girl was being burnt.

"Look, oh LOOK!" yelled Penny, pointing to the sky. "RAIN! RAIN!"

Everyone looked up at the black sky. Heavy drops of rain began to fall, splashing down on the upturned, tired faces, washing patches of white in the black skins. Down and down fell the thunder-rain, while a crash suddenly sounded to the west.

"A storm!" cried Fanny. "That will put the fire out. Oh, what a blessed mercy!"

Trembling with tiredness and relief, the exhausted little company stood there in the pouring rain, watching it put out the hungry flames. Pitter, patter, pitter, patter, down it fell, great drops as round as a penny when they splashed on the burnt ground. Everyone was soaked. Nobody cared at all. It was marvellous, wonderful, unbelievable that the rain should have come at such a moment, when everyone had given up hope!

Penny began to cry. So did Fanny. And suddenly poor Rory burst out into great sobs too. He had been so worried, so anxious—and it had all been his fault!

"Come now," said Harriet, putting her arm comfortingly round Rory. "It's all right. No harm's done. None at all, except that the hedge is burnt over there, and that shed got a bit of a scorching. You come along with me and Fanny, and I'll give you all something to eat and drink. Come along now."

So everyone went along with Harriet in the pouring rain, far too tired to run. Penny went with Rory, her hand in his, so sorry for her big brother that she could not squeeze his hand hard enough. Rory's tears had made a white channel down his blackened cheeks and he looked very queer.

Soon they were all sitting down in the kitchen, whilst Harriet, who had not stopped to clean herself, got them something to eat and drink.

Benjy and Sheila came in to see what was happening and they stared in the utmost amazement at the black company. Mark laughed at their astonished faces. Everyone was feeling much better already, and the adventure was beginning to seem more exciting than unpleasant, now that it had ended better than they had hoped.

"What's happened?" said Benjy at last.

331

"That field atop of the hill there got fired," said Jim. "It's a mystery how it did."

"I fired it," said Rory, his face red beneath its black.

"Well—you *were* a wonderful great ninny then!" said Jim. "What'll your father say?"

"Rory doesn't need to tell him," said Harriet, who was sorry for the boy. "Nobody will tell on him."

"Harriet, of course I must tell my father," said Rory with surprise. "You don't suppose I'd deceive him or tell him lies, do you?"

"I should jolly well think not," said Benjy. "Rory isn't afraid of owning up to anything. Never has been."

"There's Daddy's car now!" said Penny. She ran to the window and looked out, her face still black. "Hallo, Daddy! Hallo, Mother!"

"Penny! Whatever's the matter with your face?" cried her mother. "What *have* you been doing?"

The little girl's father and mother came to the window and looked in. They were silent with astonishment when they saw the surprising company there, all eating together, and all with black faces and scorched clothes.

Rory stood up. "I'll tell you, Daddy," he said, and he went out of the kitchen, and met his father at the hall door. They went together into the little study.

"I fired the top field," said Rory. "I—I thought it would be all right."

"Why did you do that?" asked his father.

"Well—I thought it looked all right for firing," said Rory. "I know I shouldn't have done it without your permission. I—I—think I got too big for my boots, as Penny says."

"Yes—I think you did," said his father. "But you

332

seem to have gone back to your right size again, my boy. I suppose the field took fire and the sheds went up in smoke too?"

"They nearly did," said Rory honestly. "But the rain came just in time and saved them, Dad. There's not much damage done, except that one hedge is burnt."

"That's lucky then," said his father. "We might have had a serious loss. You must never start a grass-fire unless you've got a whole lot of helpers round to beat it out when necessary, Rory. It runs like magic."

"I know," said Rory. "It was dreadful. I was awfully scared. All the others came to help, and that's why we're so black and scorched. I do blame myself terribly."

"Quite right too," said his father. "You were very much to blame. But I was to blame too! I've forgotten you were only a lad of fourteen, and I've made you think yourself a man. Well—you're not. You're just a lad yet—and a very good one too! But you've behaved like a man tonight in coming to me like this and telling me everything. Now go and wash your face."

Rory went off, feeling his father's hand clapping him affectionately on the shoulder. "Dad's splendid!" he thought. "I shan't behave like that again—getting too big for my boots, and thinking I know everything!"

Everyone went to clean themselves and to put on fresh clothes, for they smelt of smoke. As Penny was just putting on a clean jersey, she gave a scream that made Sheila jump.

"Oh! Oh! What's happened to Dopey, do you think? Did he get burnt? I've not seen him for ages!"

Nobody had seen Dopey. Penny dragged on her jersey, shouting out that she must go and find him, she must, she must!

She tore out into the farmyard, and there she saw True barking frantically at a peculiar little object in the middle of the yard. It was quite black and very miserable. Penny stood and stared at it. Then she gave a yell, ran to it, and hugged it.

"*Dopey!* You're all black, just like I was! Darling Dopey, you're not burnt, are you?"

Dopey wasn't. Silly as he was, he wasn't quite so silly as that! He snuggled against Penny contentedly.

"Penny!" said Mother, appearing at the door. "Penny! What *is* the sense of putting on perfectly clean things and then hugging a black and sooty goat? I think you must be just as mad as Dopey!"

Chapter Twenty-One

Ups and Downs

The first year that the family had been at Willow Farm had been so successful that everyone had rather got into the way of thinking that farming was really quite easy. But the second year showed them that a farm had its "downs" as well as its "ups", as Penny put it.

"We had all 'ups' last year," she said. "This year we've had some 'downs'—like when Daddy bought that mad bull and lost half the price he paid for it—and when Rory fired the field and we nearly lost the sheds."

"And when Mark left the gate open and we hunted for hours for the lost horses, and Daddy had to do without them for a while," said Sheila. "And this year the hay isn't so good."

"But the corn is even better," said Rory. "So that's an 'up', isn't it? And, Sheila, your hens and ducks have done marvellously again this year, you know."

"Except that I lost a whole brood of darling little ducklings to the rats," said Sheila sorrowfully. That had been a great blow to her and Fanny. Twelve little yellow and black ducklings had disappeared in two nights.

Jim had said that it was rats, and he had set traps for them. But the rats were too cunning for the traps, and not one had been caught.

Then Bill had brought along a white ferret, a clever little creature that slipped like lightning down a rat-hole to chase the rats. The men had been waiting at other holes, watching for the scared rats to come out. They had killed a good many and were well satisfied.

"Ah, rats are no good at all," said Bill. "Most creatures are some good—but rats are just the worst creatures ever made. They aren't even kind to their own sort. And they're too clever for anything."

Sheila had been glad to know that the rats around the duck-pond had been killed. She loved all her baby birds and had cried bitterly when she knew so many had been eaten by the hungry rats. But in spite of the damage done to her little flock of birds, she had done extremely well with her eggs and chicks and ducklings. Mother said she was an excellent little business woman already.

All the children on the farm loved the animals, both wild and tame, that lived on and around it—with the exception of the rats, of course. But the farmer used to get cross when he heard Penny or Benjy talking with delight about the rabbits on the hillside!

"Rabbits!" he would say in disgust. "Stop raving about them, do! They've done more damage to my farm this year than anything else. I'd like to shoot the lot."

"Oh *no*, Daddy!" Penny cried every time. "Oh no! You can't shoot those dear little long-eared creatures with their funny little white bobtails."

"Well, if they eat any more of my seedlings in Long Meadow, I'll shoot the whole bunch!" threatened her father.

Penny went solemnly to the hillside to warn the rabbits. Rory heard her talking to them. He was mending a gap in the hedge near by, and Penny didn't see him.

"Rabbits," said Penny, in her clear voice, "you'll be shot and killed if you don't leave my Daddy's fields

336

alone. Now, you've got plenty of grass to eat up here, and I'll bring you lettuce leaves for a treat when I can. So do leave Daddy's seedlings alone—*especially* the vetch that is growing in Long Meadow. It's going to feed the cattle, and it's very important."

Rory laughed quietly to himself. Penny was so funny. He watched his little sister skip down the hillside as lightly as a lamb. He hoped that the rabbits would take notice of what she said, for he knew she would be very upset if they were shot.

But alas! The rabbits took no notice at all. In fact, it seemed as if they made up their minds to do as much damage as possible, as soon as they could. The very next morning the farmer came in to breakfast looking as black as thunder. Rory looked at him in surprise.

"What's up, Dad?" he asked.

"The rabbits have eaten nearly every scrap of that big field of vetch seedlings," said his father. "That's a serious loss. I doubt if we can plant any more seed. It's too late in the year. I'll have to get a few guns together and do some shooting."

Penny didn't say anything, nor did Benjy. But they both looked sad. After breakfast they went to have a look at the field. Their father was right. The vetch was almost completely spoilt, for the rabbits had eaten it right down to the ground.

"Well—you can't expect Daddy to put up with *that*," said Benjy. "I wonder when the rabbits will be shot."

When the next Saturday came Daddy announced that he and three others were going to shoot the rabbits all over the farm. Penny burst into tears.

"Take Penny to see Tammylan today," said Mother

quickly to Benjy. So she and Benjy went over the hill to visit the wild man. They told him about the rabbits. Even as they told him there came the first crack of a distant gun.

"One poor little rabbit dead, never to run down the hillside any more," said Penny with a sob.

"Penny, dear, don't take things so much to heart," said Tammylan. "Your father is a farmer and has to grow food for you and for his farm friends. He would be foolish to allow all his work to be wasted because he wouldn't fight his enemies: the rats, the rabbits, and many kinds of insects. What would you say if he said to you, 'Penny, I'm sorry I've no food for you, because the rabbits and rats came and took it and I hadn't the heart to stop them'?"

"I'd think he was silly," said Penny, drying her eyes, and Benjy nodded too.

"Yes, you would," said Tammylan. "But he isn't silly, so he is taking the quickest and kindest way of fighting his enemies. Now cheer up, and come and see my latest friend—a water-vole who will eat out of my hand!"

Penny said no more about rabbits to her father after that. She even ate rabbit-pie at dinner the next day. After all, you had to be sensible, as well as kind-hearted.

Another time the farmer complained that a whole field of potatoes had been spoilt by the pheasants that came walking among them, devouring them by the hundred, Benjy pricked his ears at this.

"Rory, I've got an idea," he said. "Couldn't we train True to run round Daddy's fields and scare away the pheasants when they fly down? I'm sure we could. Do let me try to teach him."

Rory thought it *was* a good idea—but he didn't want Benjy to do the teaching. He said he would do it himself.

"I dare say you could teach him more quickly," he said, "because you really are a wizard with animals—but he's my dog, and I'd rather do it, thank you, Benjy."

So Rory began to teach True to scare off the pheasants and other birds that flew down to his father's fields. The dog, who now understood almost every word that Rory said to him, soon knew what he wanted. In a week or two, not a pheasant dared to fly down on to a field if True was anywhere about! The farmer was surprised and pleased.

"We'll buy you a new collar," he said to True. "You're as good as any of the children."

"True is one of your 'ups', isn't he?" said Rory proudly. True wagged his tail. He didn't know what an "up" was, but he felt sure it was something good.

"And Dopey is one of our 'downs'," said Sheila. Penny protested at once.

"He isn't, he isn't. Why do you say that?"

"Only because he went and butted one of my coops over, let out the hen and her chicks, and then chased the poor hen into the pond," said Sheila.

"And yesterday he got hold of one of the piglets by its curly tail and wouldn't let go," said Benjy. "The pig squealed the place down. I do think it's time Dopey had a smacking again, Penny. Scamper never does anything like that. He's always perfectly good."

"Well—I don't like creatures that are always perfectly good," said Penny. "I prefer Dopey. Anyway, he'll soon be a proper goat, and then Jim says he'll have to go and live in the field with the cows. I *shall* miss him."

"He'll be a jolly good miss, that's all I can say," said Rory. "How I shall look forward to missing him!"

Chapter Twenty-Two

Happy Days

Mark came to spend part of his summer holidays at Willow Farm. Since the adventure of the lost horses he had been much more careful, and was now almost as responsible as the farm children. He always adored staying at the farm and loved all the animals as much as they did.

"You know, even when there's nothing at all happening, it's lovely to be on a farm," he told Rory. "It's exciting, of course, when you buy a new bull, or make the hay, or harvest the corn—but even an ordinary peaceful day is lovely, I think."

It was. The bees hummed loudly as they went to and from the hive. The children liked to think of the golden honey being stored there. Benjy had become extremely good at handling the bees, and his father had made him responsible for them. They did not sting him at all. Rory had been stung once, and Mark twice, but nobody else.

The humming of the bees, the baaing of the sheep, the cluck of the hens, and the quack of the ducks sounded all day long at the farm. Everyone was used to the noise and hardly noticed it except when they left the farm to go to the town—and then they missed all the familiar sounds very much.

Then there were the shouts of the men at work, coming suddenly on the air—an unexpected whinny from a waiting horse, and a stamp of hoofs—a mooing

from a cow and a squeal from a pig. Sometimes there was the clatter of a pail or the sound of children's running feet coming home from school. It was a happy farm, with everyone doing his work well and everyone helping the other.

Mother used to laugh at the way the animals and birds came to the house. This always astonished visitors too. The hens came regularly to the kitchen door and were as regularly shooed away by Harriet. Mr. By-Himself sometimes did a bit of shooing when he felt like it, but the hens did not really fear him. If there was no one in the kitchen they would walk right in and peck about.

Sometimes they would go into the house by the open French windows of the sitting-room, clucking important-ly. If mother had visitors, the visitors would say "How sweet!" But Mother didn't think so, and out would go the hens at top speed.

Once one of the ducks brought all her little yellow ducklings into the house, much to Penny's delight.

"Mother, the duck-pond is almost dried up, and I expect the duck wants to find the bath for her ducks to swim on," said Penny. "Oh, Mother, do let me run the bath full for them, *please!*"

But to Penny's great disappointment she was not allowed to, and the duck had to take her string of youngsters to the stream, where they all bobbed and swam to their heart's content.

The big cart-horses often came into the farmyard and stood there whilst Jim or Bill went to have a word with Harriet. If they thought Penny was anywhere about they would wander to the house, and put their heads in at the door or the window. It always gave the children a real thrill to look up and see the big brown head looking in, the large eyes asking silently for a lump of sugar.

"Oh! Darling! Wait a minute, wait a minute! I'll just get you some sugar!" Penny would say, dropping her knitting or her book at once. And the patient horse would stand there, blinking long-lashed eyes, her head almost filling the window. Once Captain even went into the hall, and knocked over the umbrella stand with such a crash that he backed out hastily, stepping on the foot-scraper and smashing it to bits.

"Don't be cross with him, Mother!" begged Benjy when he heard about it. Benjy had been in bed with a cold at the time. "Mother, I'm sure Captain came to look for me. He must have wondered why I didn't groom him. I'll pay for a new foot-scraper."

"Oh, I think I can manage that!" said Mother, with a laugh. "So long as you hurry up and get better, Benjy. I don't want cows and horses and sheep tramping up the stairs all day long to ask how you are!"

The sheep never came over to the house, except Hoppitty and Jumpity, who had been brought up by hand. They ran in and out continually, though Mother always chased them away. She did her best, to make the children keep the doors shut, but except for Mark, who always shut gates and doors behind him wherever he was, the farm children left the house-doors open. Penny secretly loved the animals coming into the house and one of her happiest memories was going into the sitting-room one day and finding Hoppitty, Jumpity, and Dopey lying asleep on the old rug in front of the fire! The little girl had lain down beside them and gone to sleep too.

"Well, what a heap of tired creatures!" Harriet had said, when she came in to lay the tea. "I'm surprised you don't give them a place in your bed, that I am, Penny!"

Penny had thought that was a splendid idea, but Mother had said "no" so decidedly that Penny hadn't even bothered to ask twice.

"Willow Farm is such a friendly place," Mark said, dozens of times. "Whenever I come I feel as if the hens cluck 'Good morning!' to me, and the ducks say 'Hallo!' The horses say 'What, you again!' and the pigs squeal out, 'Here's Mark! Here's Mark!' And the . . ."

"The children say, 'Oh, what a bore—here's that tiresome boy again!'" said Rory with a grin.

Even Paul Pry, the new bullock, took to being friendly enough to pay a call at the house. He usually went to the kitchen, because for some reason or other, he had taken a great fancy to Harriet. He would arrive there and stand at the door, his big head lowered, looking anxiously into the kitchen, waiting for Harriet to appear. He only once attempted to go right into the kitchen, much to the astonishment and fright of Mr. By-Himself who was fast asleep on a chair. He awoke to find Paul Pry standing over him, breathing hard.

Mr. By-Himself leapt straight into the air, and spat so loudly that the bullock was scared. He backed hastily and knocked over the kitchen table. It was full of saucepans that Fanny was to clean. They went over with a crash that brought Fanny and Harriet and Mother out of the dairy at a run.

"Paul Pry!" exclaimed Harriet in wrath. "Who told *you* to come into the kitchen then? Knocking over my table like that! Out you go, and don't you dare to come and see me again!"

And out went the poor bullock as meekly as a lamb, sad that Harriet was cross with him. But he was back again two days later, staring in at the door for his beloved Harriet.

"Well, there's one thing," said the farmer, with a laugh, "if ever Paul Pry goes mad like Stamper, we shall know who can deal with him. Harriet would put him right with a thwack from her broom. To see her chase the bullock away is the funniest sight in the world. And yet I think she is very fond of him."

That was the nice part of Willow Farm. Men, women, children, and animals were all fond of one another. The creatures trusted their masters and mistresses and never expected or got anything but kindness and understanding. Nobody slacked, nobody shirked his work, everyone

344

did his bit.

And so Willow Farm, in spite of more "downs" than "ups" that second year, prospered and did well. New cow-sheds were built—beautiful places, airy and clean. New machinery was bought and admired, put to use and then cleaned and stored until next time. New animals were born, named, and loved. New fields were cleaned, ploughed, and sown.

"It's a family farm," said Rory happily. "We've all got our jobs and we try to do them well. Daddy, aren't you glad you gave up your London work and came here, to Willow Farm?"

"Very glad," said his father. "I've seen you all grow healthy and strong. I've seen you doing work that matters. I've watched you learning good lessons as you handle the animals and help to till the soil. You've had to use your muscles and you've had to use your brains. You've grown up complete and whole, with no nonsense in you. I'm proud of you all."

"I hope we'll never have to leave," said Benjy. "I couldn't bear to have to live in town now, Daddy. I hope Willow Farm never fails."

"There's no reason why it should," said the farmer. "After all, ours is a mixed farm, and there is no waste anywhere."

"That's true," said Rory. "We grow corn and it feeds the hens we want to keep. We grow fodder and it feeds the cows whose milk we need. They give us cream and butter and cheese and the skim milk goes to the pigs and the calves. The hens in turn give us eggs."

"It's a pity we can't grow our own clothes," said Penny. "Then we could almost live in the farm without buying a single thing."

"Well, the second year is over," said the farmer. "We've made a lot of mistakes, and sometimes had misfortune and bad luck—but here we all are, happy and healthy, with the farm growing bigger than ever. Good luck to Willow Farm!"

And that is what we all say too—good luck to Willow Farm. We will peep in at the window before we say goodbye and see them all sitting round the fire, one wintry Sunday afternoon.

There is Rory, big and strong, with Sheila beside him, adding up her egg-book. And there is Benjy, nursing Scamper as usual. And there, on the rug, is little Penny, who has been allowed to have Dopey in for a treat. He is trying to bite True's ears, but the dog will not let him.

Outside there is the tread of feet coming to the door. The sound makes Penny jump up and go to the window. "It's Mark—and Tammylan! They've come to tea. Hallo, Mark! Hallo, Tammylan! Wait a minute till I open the door!"

She flies to open it, and it would be nice if we could slip in too. But the door is closed and we are left outside alone.

Not quite alone! A hen pecks at our legs, and a horse whinnies softly from the stables. Davey's sheep baa in their folds and Rascal barks in the distance. The first star shines out in the sky and we must go.

Goodbye, Willow Farm! May you always be the same friendly place that we know and love so well.